Tattooed Love

Simone Elise

Chapter 1

There were very few moments in my life when I could definitely say that I had hit rock bottom. Right now, in this moment, I could definitely say I had hit rock bottom. I was stoned, drunk, and high on emotion, gripping a half-drunk beer; sitting in a gutter outside some pub. I had no one to call, and no one would be wondering where I was, so there was nothing stopping me from throwing back the remaining alcohol in the bottle.

I suppose that is the benefit of hitting rock bottom... you can't fall any lower.

I was wiping my mouth when someone tapped on my shoulder.

"Leave me alone." I grunted. I was at the point where I just didn't care anymore. I didn't care about the looks I was getting, or that I was interrupting the flow of the taxi rank.

"This goes against my better judgment, but you look like a rape case waiting to happen. Would you like a lift?"

It was his husky voice that made me turn my head around to look up at him. Tall, dark, handsome and screaming dangerous; yet he looked familiar.

"Do I know you?" I asked, frowning at him as he lowered himself to kneel in front of me.

"The name is Jackson." He spoke slowly and immediately seemed to realize that I hadn't made a connection, so he added "We go to the same high school."

I nodded, but still couldn't make a connection; hell, at this point of the night, I was lucky to be recalling my own name, which was…

"Amber, you alright?" Jackson placed a hand on my shoulder and my eyes snapped back open, stopping me from slipping into unconsciousness.

"Yeah, I'm fine. Just had a few too many." I took the hand he now lowered to offer me; when did he stand up?

I pulled myself up on to my bare feet; I had managed to lose my heels at some point during the night. "Thanks." I smiled. Even in my drunken haze, I could tell that Jackson was dangerously good looking.

"Do you want me to take you home?" He spoke slowly again, as if I wouldn't be able to understand him otherwise.

"Nope." I waved my hand dismissing the idea. "I'm fine, and I will have you know I'm not as drunk as I might look."

"Really?" He cocked his head to one side. From the expression on his face, he clearly didn't believe me. "Because the smell from you makes me think you drank the bar dry."

My expression changed as soon as I heard the judgment in his tone. "I had a bad day," I snapped. He didn't know. He couldn't understand. I pressed a finger into his chest. "Don't judge me handsome."

"Handsome?" He chuckled at that. "Didn't think you were capable of compliments, Amber."

I suppose he had a point, but it wasn't one I was going to confirm. "Go away, John."

"It's Jackson."

"Then go away Jackson," I corrected with a dry smile.

"You have a bad attitude."

"And you're not the first person to point that out." He was far from it. People seemed to make it their personal mission to remind me of my bad attitude; it wasn't my fault the world sucked. My attitude was simply a side effect of this miserable thing called life.

I waved down a taxi, but Jackson wrapped his hand around my wrist, stopping me from walking towards it.

"I'll take you home." His tone was soft, gentle… and was that slight concern I was sensing?

"Why?"

"Don't trust me?"

"I don't trust anyone."

"Wise thing to do." He tilted his head to the side again, looking down at me. "I'm not going to hurt you Amber, and if I did I'm sure you could handle me."

"You seem to know more about me than I do you."

"That's because I'm not self-absorbed."

I took a step towards him, staring up into those dark eyes of his. "No one ever got hurt being self-absorbed."

"Whatever you say Miss Shields."

He knew my name, and my last name. Where did he say he knew me from again? Oh right… school or hell on earth as I liked to call it.

"Fine then handsome, you can take me home."

"I've got a question first." His eyes flickered to my lip. "Should I be hunting down the man that gave you that cut on your lip, or should I be asking what the other chick looks like?"

My lips curved into a smile. I honestly couldn't remember the last time I smiled. "I always think no question is a good question."

I caught something flash across his face, but before I could read him, he gave a quick nod of the head, and I knew that was the end of the subject.

I would never tell a soul that it was Blake who had done this to me. I knew he regretted it as much as I was trying to forget about it. Our fights were always nasty, but this one had, by far, been the worst.

"Come on then, I'm parked around the back."

I followed him, walking towards the darkly lit car park, as warning signs flashed through my mind. I should've been terrified.

I should've run in the other direction, but I continued to follow him.

"So, where to?" he asked, opening the car door for me.

I couldn't go home; I couldn't risk my dad seeing me this way. I had no other choice. I had to go back to Blake. I silently prayed he had cooled off.

So, I gave Jackson the address, unsure of whether this would be my first or second mistake of the night; the first being getting in the car with him to begin with.

***

I got out of the car rather gracefully, or so I thought. As I wiped the dirt from my mouth after falling face forward on my second step, I began to rethink how graceful my exit actually was.

"You alright?" Jackson dropped beside me, placing an arm around my waist and bringing me back to my feet.

"Two left feet" I muttered, not meeting his eye. I hoped right then that I would never see this person again.

"You live here?" Jackson asked as he looked over at the house he was helping me walk up to.

"Yep." No I didn't. I just crashed here with my somewhat boyfriend, but I wasn't about to tell this person that.

The front of the house was packed with cars, motorbikes and motors. It looked like an automobile junkyard, but it was this very look that kept people away, shielding the 'family' from prying eyes.

We reached the porch, and I grabbed the door knob. Letting go of Jackson, I leaned all my weight against the door. "Thanks for bringing me home." I looked at him for the first time since I had embarrassed myself.

"You sure you're safe here?" He gave the property a once over before looking back at me, visibly torn. "You know if you need somewhere to crash for the night, I can put up the cash for a hotel or something."

I smiled for the second time that night. "What did I ever do to you to deserve such consideration?" I wanted to know. While I may not have known him, he seemed to know me, and I wasn't a nice person. So, why was he bothering?

He exhaled slowly, and then met my eye with an expression I couldn't quite read… "You're the kind of woman who needs a man to protect her from herself, and clearly you haven't found one yet, so I'm just giving you a helping hand."

"You don't seem like you'd be big on community service," I bit back. He certainly didn't look the part. The tattoos and that 'pissed off' expression would scare anyone with half a brain away. My judgment at this point was questionable though, so it was no wonder I hadn't slammed the door in his face yet.

"Maybe I'm a sucker for a good looking woman." The corner of his lips twitched in a half smile. "You know Amber, you're bearable drunk."

I chuckled and pushed his shoulder playfully "You know Jackson, maybe you do know me."

For a split moment we shared a smile, an amused chuckle, and then silence fell between us, but it wasn't an awkward silence. It was the kind of silence that usually compelled me to step into a man's arms; this was sexual tension, and fuck me if I knew how it had come to this so suddenly.

"Night Amber." Jackson took a step back, his eyes darting around one more time, before he turned his back to me and began to walk down the porch steps.

"Oi Jackson?"

He looked back at me over his shoulder. "Yeah?"

"On Monday if I don't remember this, and I'm a bitch, I want to apologize now." I inhaled sharply and exhaled quickly. "You seem like a nice guy. Perhaps you should try and befriend me when there's an actual chance of me remembering you."

He smirked, nodded his head and walked away.

I wouldn't remember it, but that was the first time Jackson Johnston had saved me from myself, and that was the night our love was born.

High school.

It was the dwelling of the stupid, the fake, and the occasional friend. It wasn't like I didn't like school; it was school that didn't like me.

I locked my car, and slowly began to make my way towards the hell on earth.

Once again, I was starting a Monday with a headache, a cut lip, and a massive bruise on my arm. I wasn't the normal teenager who spent her weekends shopping or playing some stupid sport. I spent my weekends doing what I loved - drinking and stealing.

I was more than happy to openly admit I was a young offender.

Now, closer to the school stairs, I untangled my black sunglasses from my long wavy black hair and pulled them down to my face.

I didn't have to push through the crowd; people always made way for me, mainly because they were scared that if they didn't back off, I would make them. I didn't rush up the staircase; I was in no hurry to attend class.

I was a valued member of a group (some may call it a 'gang' but, personally. the mere word 'gang' to me, screamed pathetic. I referred to us as a family). We didn't care about graduating from high school.

But then a memory of Blake and me fighting last week flashed through my mind, and I began to doubt just how long I'd remain a welcome member of this 'family.'

I pushed a stationary middle school student out of my way in frustration. I heard him fall to the ground, but I didn't acknowledge it.

Should have moved himself, I reasoned in my mind.

I got to the front yard and did a quick scan of my surroundings.

Happy, immature teens spanned the yard.

I could safely say I disliked pretty much the entire population that attended this pitiful place. Then my eyes landed on Jackson Johnston.

He was sitting on top of one of the picnic tables, arms crossed, hoodie pulled down over his head, and sunglasses on. His minions surrounded him; little morons. I could feel his stare through his sunglasses, but I didn't pay attention to him, one because I had never spoken to the loser and two because he glared at people more than I did.

Jackson. Jax, his friends call him.

He always had this look about him; like he'd been fighting all night, or had just come out of a fist fight.

I got distracted when I spotted Rachel, leaning against one of the pillars near the entrance, smoking. She caught my eye, flicked her long red hair to the side, and started walking towards me.

Rachel was the only person I spoke to in this place called public high school.

Even though my father was super rich, I didn't let that factor into my choice of high school. I didn't give a toss whether I attended a public or private high school. I was going to fail regardless, because I wasn't into academic stuff, so I saved my father the trouble and the tuition of private school, and didn't publicly air exactly what kind of wealth I came from.

"Amber." Rachel spoke as she sucked lightly on the cigarette.

I nodded my head in acknowledgment, and she handed the cigarette over to me.

I sucked on it lightly, letting my eyes return to Jax's picnic table, as we began to walk slowly towards the school building.

I could never fully understand why he even bothered attending. Everyone knew he had a lot of money, and, from the looks of it, he didn't want to be here either.

"Losers," Rachel muttered under her breath, clearly noticing my line of sight.

"Yep," I replied, and, as we passed Jax's table, I casually flicked my cigarette at one of the cheerleader's heads.

I heard a high pitch shriek, followed by a moan, as we kept walking.

"Can't you put out a cigarette right?" The angry little bimbo barked at me.

I just flipped the bird over my shoulder and kept pace with Rachel.

"So... any memories of the weekend?" Rachel asked knowingly.

"Nope, but I am sporting this highly fashionable cut lip," I teased back, pushing the front door open with more force than it needed.

Students in the hall were caught off guard as the door slammed into the wall.

"Smooth." Rachel mocked.

I shrugged my shoulders and we began to make our way up the corridor as the bell rang.

Everyone scattered and scurried to get to class, but Rachel and I maintained our languid pace.

And so, another day of high school had begun.

Jax

Pointing the gun at Ryan's temple, I waited for him to beg for his life, but he remained silent. I couldn't count how many lives I had ended. Only eighteen and I already had a record of a hardened criminal. Still, it didn't bother me.

I was loyal to my club and my club brothers.

If that meant I had to get my hands dirty to stay loyal to them - I would, and I did.

I cocked my head to the side and ran my hand across the side of my face, which was swollen as a result of him trying to escape.

"Finish it Jax!" Cole snapped from beside me.

I met Ryan's eyes one last time. His eyes were consumed with anger and hate towards me. The gun jerked back in my hand as I pulled the trigger.

Ryan's blood splattered back onto the clear plastic, and his body dropped to the floor, lifeless.

"Clean this up," I said to the prospect and walked away. My job here was done. Another loose end finished with. I was waiting for the day I would regret my life decisions, waiting for the day when the guilt of all the lives I'd taken overcomes me.

So far, it hadn't.

"The accommodation has been organized," Cole informed me, matching my pace as we walked out of the empty shed.

The Shield brothers. Troy Shield. You wouldn't want to cross him. He made a great President. Almost as ruthless as I was; but he didn't nearly come close to the number of lives I had ended.

Cole Shield. He was always the first one to pull his gun; he didn't believe in second chances. He liked two things - his ability to aim straight, and women. Out of all the Shield brothers, he had the worst temper.

Tyler Shield. Loyal and trustworthy. If there was one thing you could always count on when it came to any of the Shield brothers, it was loyalty and trust. Tyler was a ladies man, and when he wasn't charming a woman, he was backing up one of his brothers in a fist fight.

Adam Shield. The one I never could describe properly. He was quiet compared to the rest. Still loved the club as much as his brothers, but he didn't like blood. He didn't get a thrill out of ending a man's life, and, when he could, he avoids confrontation.

"Did Troy pull strings?" I asked as Cole kicked the shed door open. I couldn't stay at one of my houses because I had to be with an upstanding citizen.

"Yeah, kinda. You're staying with our father and little sister," Cole informed me, as he straddled his bike.

"You guys have a sister?" I questioned as I saddled my own motor bike.

"Yep."

"She won't get in the way, will she?" I asked with an eyebrow raised. The last thing I needed was to put up with a brat of a little girl.

Cole let out a grunt.

"She's never home according to dad. Does dance or something. She shouldn't be a problem."

I nodded my head and kick-started my motor bike.

"Have fun at school," he yelled with cockiness to his voice, as I took off.

Time to drag my arse through another day of school.

Bloody parole board.

***

I pulled my sunnies down, seated on top of a picnic table, trying my best to stay awake. It had been a long and bloody weekend.

"I can't believe you tapped her!" Ian exclaimed to Joey next to me.

"She was really good too," Joey said proudly.

I didn't bother joining in; I didn't have the energy. I watched as a small middle schooler was pushed forcefully to the ground. I then saw Amber Shields shoot the kid a dirty glare as she walked away.

She didn't seem to notice the kid cursing at her as she looked around the yard.

Man, that chick had an attitude problem. I recalled the other night when I'd saved her from herself. I doubted she would remember as she was on another planet when I'd helped her out.

I still can't believe she lived in that place. What she wore, what she drove, all pointed to money, but, that trashy place I dropped her off to, said anything but money.

"Man, that chick is hot," Joey muttered with lust in his voice.

Following his gaze, I noticed he was eyeing Amber.

"Yeah, I heard she was linked to some big time gangster," Ian joined in. These two lived for women; when they weren't bragging about their latest score, they were lining a girl up.

"Maybe that's why she's got that cut lip," Joey commented.

I looked a bit closer, and noticed that Amber's lip was broken and swollen. Looks like she copped a good one to the face. Nearly as good as the one I got this morning.

Though I doubted she was with a gangster, because if she was with a big time one, I would have seen her around.

She was talking to Rachel as she approached us; she looked uninterested and tired as she casually smoked a cigarette.

When she walked past us, she flipped the butt into Linda's hair, which merited Linda's shrill yell. It went right through me; I really didn't need to hear that.

Standing up, I put my foot on the butt and squashed it with my foot.

"Your hair isn't on fire, Linda," I spoke as she was running her fingers through it, checking to see if it was.

"Thanks," she mumbled softly and sent me a small smile.

I nodded my head, and walked towards the front doors of the school, cursing the bloody parole board once again for making it a condition of my bail to attend this damn place.

The boys walked in behind me, and I already knew that I was about to waste another six hours of my life here.

***

Amber

What was the point of history?

It was a pointless subject. In fact, I found nearly all subjects at school pointless, but history was the one I found most pointless. I knew I would never use it. I was either going to end up in a juvenile center before I turned eighteen, or, if I got it my way, I was going be on the known criminal list.

Regardless of what happened, I knew this subject 'history' would not play a part in my life.

So I was staring out the window, watching intently as the school gardener tried to mow over the rocks.

"Amber." I heard my teacher's voice and whipped my head to the front of the class.

Our teacher, Mr Woods, had his back to us and was writing on the whiteboard. I looked closely, and I noticed he was pairing students together, writing our names down next to each other.

I skimmed the list and stopped at my name, waiting for Mr Woods to finish writing my partner's name. He finished and moved aside.

Jackson.

Just bloody great.

I glanced around the room, and spotted the pinhead in the middle, talking to one of his mates.

"Ok class, listen up" Mr Woods spoke loudly trying to get our attention. "So, as you can see, I have paired each of you up with a classmate. Your partner will be your partner for the following assignment. Some of you already know what you have to do – put together a written report on World War II, and then research one soldier from the war, which you will present in an oral report at the end of the month."

I groaned inwardly.

"Go on then," he continued. "Pair up, and complete the question sheet on my desk."

All of a sudden, I was filled with more unreasonable hatred towards him. I hated Mr Woods.

He had just forced me into a whole month of one-on-one time with Jackson bloody Johnston.

What was he thinking pairing me up with that pinhead!

I angrily looked out the window, trying to remember what car Mr Woods drove so I could key some friendly advice into his paint work.

The sound of a chair scraping against the floor brought my attention back to the classroom.

Jackson sat in front of me, a bored expression on his face.

I could honestly see why so many girls found him attractive, even with his cut lip and bruised jaw.

He had black hair that spiked up in every direction, and a defined jaw with a six o'clock shadow, though it was safe to state that his most attractive feature was his piercing dark eyes. I had only been able to look at them closely a few times; Jackson usually kept them hidden behind sunglasses, but the few times I had made eye contact, my breath had caught in my throat; those eyes were hauntingly dark.

Pity he was such a pinhead.

"Jackson." His husky voice introduced himself.

I let out a slow sigh.

"Seriously? You're introducing yourself?" I questioned.

He shrugged his shoulders.

"You know me, and I know you," I stated, pushing my sunglasses up to the top of my head.

"Think rather highly of ourselves, don't we, Miss Amber Shields," he said cockily.

I rolled my eyes. "Point proven," I replied, and I leaned back into my chair.

A small smirk appeared on the corner of his lips, and then quickly disappeared.

"Just get the assignment done, and hand me what I need to read on D day. I don't have time to deal with teachers breathing down my neck about stupid assignments so just make sure it gets done," he ordered, pulling out his phone as it vibrated.

He just ordered me. I was gobsmacked for a moment. I watched as he frowned at whatever he was reading.

I let out a soft chuckle.

"Something amusing you?" he asked, not taking his eyes off his phone.

"Depends on what you classify as funny I guess," I replied softly.

He didn't respond.

I tapped my finger on the table, while his attention was on his phone.

Taking my eyes off the pinhead, I scanned the classroom; all partners in the room were immersed in discussions with each other.

I watched Linda, one of the cheerleaders, laugh and talk to one of her girlfriends. It looked like she had moved on from the episode this morning, when I had used her hair for an ashtray.

I leaned over to a neighboring desk and took a handful of pencils. No one even noticed, so engrossed were they in their discussion.

I lined the pencil up, aiming at Linda's head, and flicked it.

It fell short.

Damn.

I lined another one up.

"And what do you find so amusing?" Jackson suddenly quipped.

"Huh?" I replied, bringing my attention back to him. He was still staring at his phone when I shot him a quick glance. My mind snapped back to our previous conversation. "Nothing really," I replied, closing one eye while I lined up my next hit.

I flicked the pencil and it fell short again.

"Darn." I muttered.

Jackson pulled up his chair alongside mine and picked up a pencil. "Explain," he prompted, rolling a pencil in between his fingers.

"I won't be doing the assignments," I announced nonchalantly, closing one eye again while taking aim."You will."

"Nope. I won't be. I don't give a toss whether we pass or fail," I pointed out, and flicked the pencil. This time it went too far.

Bloody hell, what was wrong with me today?

"Don't have a very good aim, do you?" Jax teased.

14

I gave him a pointed look, and flicked the pencils one after the other, willing for one to hit her. As luck would have it, I missed her every time. Pencils littered the floor around her, but she was too slow to even notice.

"Watch and learn little girl," Jax said, and I watched as the pencil glided through the air and hit Linda square in the back of the head.

"OUCH! What the hell?" she yelled, turning around to glare at me.

A soft chuckle left my lips. "Nice," I complimented him. Jax smirked and stood up. "I did you a favor, now do the assignments". In that moment, the bell rang, and he began to make his way out of the classroom.

He didn't even give me a chance to reply and push the point home. Oh well. I would not be doing the history assignment.

***

I lived with my father. Not because I wanted to, but because I had no other choice. Dad was a typical businessman, driven by money and status. He loved two things – money, and the things money bought.

He loved me, I knew that for sure, but he loved me in a particular way. His way of showing me how much he loved me was making sure my account never dried up; I wanted for nothing, and that I had an endless supply of high end cars.

I let out a slow sigh as I drove up to the mansion that housed just my father and I, and well, our endless staff.

I had lived here my entire life, and I still felt like it was more of a display house than a home.

I dragged my feet up the staircase to the entrance of the house. Another downside to this house was all the darn stairs.

The sound of the closing front door echoed throughout the house behind me. I threw my backpack in the direction of a side table and it missed, hitting a vase instead, and sending it crashing to the floor.

Great. I am not cleaning that up.

What was with my aim today?

I usually prided myself on my aim; my ability to aim my gun and not miss a target, but today was just not my day. I couldn't even manage to flick a pencil across the room. If Blake had witnessed that, he might have reconsidered my role in the gang.

"Amber?"

I knew that voice all too well. As luck would have it, dad was home early.

I rolled my eyes and let my head fall back very dramatically. Why did he have to be home so early? I stomped into the living room and slumped into the armchair across from him.

Like always, dad was sitting in his favorite armchair, drink in hand.

"What?" I asked, sounding tired and uninterested.

Dad looked up from his paperwork; his small glasses perched on his nose, still in his business suit. "We are having a guest move in with us for a while."

My eyes snapped wide open. He hadn't let anyone stay here since my brothers had left.

It had just been him and I.

"Why?"

What could possibly have compelled him to let someone move in, or even come and stay for a short while?

"A favor to your brothers," he replied, sipping on his southern comfort.

"A favor to my brothers?" I repeated. That didn't make sense. Why would my brothers want anyone to stay with us?

"He will be here soon," I realized from his tone that the conversation had ended.

I stood up and left the room, walking towards the staircase. I noticed flashing lights and looked out the window to see a car approaching. I quickly took the stairs, two at a time, and ran to my bedroom.

As I closed my door softly, I heard our doorbell ring.

I was in no mood to meet and make conversation with whoever was moving in. My opinion of my brothers was very low, and any friend of theirs wasn't one of mine - it was that simple.

**

It was a beautiful morning, and I skipped down the stairs two at a time. The chefs would have already planned breakfast. I was in the mood for some bacon, and, as I pushed the swinging doors to the kitchen open, the aroma of bacon and eggs filled the air.

My mouth watered at the aroma, until, in a split second, my world came crashing down around me.

No, it couldn't be…

Standing there in just his shorts, no shirt was none other than… Jackson Johnston.

What was he…?

How could this…?

From what I could tell, he was just as shocked to see me as I was to see him. Seconds passed, minutes passed, and we just both stood there, staring at each other. Like maybe, just maybe, this couldn't be happening!

What was he doing in my house, topless? Who the hell invited him here? How the hell did he get in? From the expression on his face, he was asking himself the same question.

How the hell was this happening right now?

Surely, he couldn't be my brothers' friend.

Could he?

"They said they had a sister. I was expecting a ten year old," Jackson said under his breath as he just stared at me, gobsmacked. "I never put your last name with theirs," he said out loud.

"So, you're the friend of my brothers'?" I finally said something, after clearing my throat.

"Yeah, I guess I am."

17

My expression hardened immediately hearing that. "Well then, you are no friend of mine."

And suddenly, I had lost my appetite.

Chapter 2

I didn't know who was going to speak next, but I had a strong need to run; like go back in time and not be hungry, and never come in here and see him!

How the hell did he know my brothers? My brothers were... there weren't words to describe them. I loathed them. Because they left me here, with dad. They're liars, and not even very good ones.

Jax opened his mouth and I'm sure he was about to say something smart, when my father walked into the kitchen.

"Oh good, you've met Jackson," he said casually.

I stood there, frozen.

Shock.

Fear.

Anger.

Shock again.

The flurry of emotions was hard to handle.

"Amber, close your mouth. It's rude," Dad pointed out, walking towards the table and picking up a piece of toast.

I snapped my mouth shut; I hadn't even realized it had been open. I somehow moved my legs and walked towards the kitchen island, slumping on a stool. My beautiful morning, turned into a nightmare as soon as my eyes landed on Jackson.

I couldn't have people at school know I lived in a mansion and that I had more money in my bank account than their parents would make in a year. I couldn't have that. I had a reputation! Sure, it wasn't a very good one when it came to school, but I still had one.

I glanced at Jax. He was rubbing the back of his neck, and his eyes were fixed on me. He seemed pretty shocked himself.

I stared at the toast. I was anything but hungry.

Only the appearance of Jackson Johnston could ruin my unhealthy need for bacon in the morning.

After having seen Jax with his top off, I doubt I would ever be able to eat in this room again.

He had scarred me.

Dad took the stool next to me.

"I received a phone call from the local police today, Amber" Dad said, striking up a conversation I immediately wanted to end. Me and the police never go well.

Great.

"Your license has been suspended again." The disapproval in his voice was clear. I don't know how many times he had been dragged in by the police because of me. Surprisingly, he always spoke on my behalf and usually got me out of it.

He had power, connections, and money. All things in my favor, but it seemed like he wasn't using them this time.

"I told them you would stay off the roads this time. Three months," he added with a tone to say I had to do what I was told.

I slammed my fists down on the island counter.

"Do not start Amber" he warned, giving me a pointed look.

Jax walked towards us, and took a stool at one corner of the island. Looks like he had discovered he could walk again; maybe the shock of seeing me was wearing off? I glared at him, seeing red. If he was a friend of my brothers', he was certainly nothing but a scum bastard.

"Jax and you attend the same school. Perhaps you could ride together?" Dad asked, looking over at Jackson.

I rolled my eyes dramatically.

"I'd be happy to give you a ride," Jax said politely, looking at me.

My mouth dropped open! What a Kiss Ass! I could count on one hand, actually on one finger, how many times Jax had spoken to me, and now he was offering to take me to school? Well, he could go and get fucked.

"That's very nice of you Jax, you are a good man!" Dad praised.

Dad shot me a disapproving look when I didn't immediately start saying thank you. One glance at me, and he could see something was wrong.

"Something wrong Amber?" he questioned.

Not at all dad, seriously, everything is just peachy. I am over the moon with this morning's events. Of course, I never said any of this out loud.

I felt my control on my temper slipping.

"Nothing." I muttered.

"Good, I will see you tonight then." He stood up, nodded at Jackson, and walked out of the kitchen, coffee still in hand.

I glanced at the pinhead named Jackson Johnson.

Why was he smiling? What was funny about all of this? I glared at him. The rage I felt towards him wasn't reasonable.

His smirk still stayed put.

'What?!" I demanded. Why the hell was he still looking at me!

I jumped off my stool and left the kitchen, seething. As I walked up the stairs, his smirk played on my mind.

It was bad enough I had to deal with him at school, and sit next to him in history, and now... now he was in my house!

I quickly changed, not paying attention to my look, and headed back downstairs.

Jax was now standing at the front door, fully dressed.

Thank God. I'm sure there would be women all around the world who wanted to gawk at his every toned muscle - but I wasn't one of them. So, the fact that he was now fully dressed, well, I saw that as a bonus.

There was something about him that drew women in. Maybe the edge to his personality. Maybe the fact that he always looked like he had just got out of a caged fight, and was more than capable of coming out the winner of any fight.

I don't know what it is, but women just love him.

I was not one of those women. Sure, I had wondered why he bothered attending school and sure, I had wondered how he kept his body in such great shape.

But, never once had I asked either question.

Nor would I ever.

Because, when it came to him, I wanted nothing to do with him. He knowing my brothers only made me want to stay away from him more.

I walked down the stairs quickly, passed him, and walked through the open front doors.

"Wait up!' he yelled behind me.

Did he honestly expect me to ride with him?

Was he that stupid?

Surely not.

"You coming with me or not?" he snapped.

Yep, he was that stupid.

I turned to glare at him. Why I felt so much rage towards him I didn't know.

"I would rather ride the bus with the junkies, than get in a car with you," I continued to walk up the drive way.

"Whatever, don't complain to me if you catch something," he yelled after me.

"Complain to you? Fuck, I don't even want to talk to you," I snapped over my shoulder.

I heard his car door slam, and, then, within a few seconds, I could hear him approaching me.

He drove through a puddle close to me, deliberately I'm sure, and splashed water up my legs.

I glared at the back of his Hummer.

I picked up a rock from the ground and threw it in the direction of his car, missing it by centimeters.

I groaned to myself as I walked up our long drive way.

Why me?

And what the hell was with my aim? I really needed to go for some target practice. If Blake even thought for a second my aim was off, well, he would be pulling me from jobs.

He expected me to always be in control. He expected me to always have his back, which meant I had to be able to shoot straight, and right now I couldn't even throw something straight.

I groaned. Not only did I have to get a bus, but I was more than positive I would have to spend more time at the shooting range.

***

I glanced up at the clock. I was about 45 minutes late for class.

Stupid bus. Never runs on time.

On the up side though, I had missed forty five minutes of Mr Wood's class, which meant less time with that pinhead, Jackson Johnston.

I smiled to myself. Suddenly, the day was looking up.

I finally made it to school, and walked up to my locker to dump my school bag in it. I hated school and really saw it as pointless. I wasn't career minded, although I realized that would be a problem later in life.

I began to head up the corridor towards Mr Wood's class, dragging my feet as I got closer.

I could just not go in, I thought to myself.

But knowing it wasn't really an option, I knocked on the classroom door.

It opened slightly and Mr Woods was surprised to see me.

"Nice of you to join us Miss Shields,' he said in an official voice, laced with sarcasm.

"Couldn't prolong my tardiness any longer," I muttered to him.

I wasn't sure if he'd heard me, but he opened the door wider, and I slipped in, walking towards my desk.

I glanced around and noticed that everyone was sitting in pairs.

My eyes landed on my empty seat, and I didn't bother looking at the thing sitting in the next seat; I knew who it was.

Bloody Jax.

I sighed loudly and took my seat.

"Class continue," Mr Woods directed.

The class slowly began to start talking again.

Jax was more in the middle of the desk, then on his side.

"Move," I muttered.

He ignored me.

"Move," I said louder.

"Make me," he challenged.

Well, he asked for it. "Sure," I snarled. I flung my elbow up in the air and brought it down hard onto his thigh. I might have lost my ability to throw things straight, but I hadn't lost my strength.

He groaned in pain.

"Miss Shields! Violence is unacceptable!" Mr Woods screamed in my direction.

"My arm slipped"

"Bullshit," Jax muttered, under his breath.

"Take it like a man," I whispered coldly in his direction.

I heard him grunt.

"Principal's office. NOW Miss Shields," Mr Woods commanded.

I sighed.

"Whatever," I added, gathering my books. I didn't want to be here in the first place.

I heard Jax chuckle.

"Don't worry babe, I will get your homework for you," he said smoothly.

I rolled my eyes. He wanted to talk dirty? Perhaps no one told him that if he played with fire, he was going to get burnt.

"I think you should be more concerned about where your balls are," I said loudly.

There were a few soft chuckles from the class.

"Now, Amber!" Mr Woods yelled.

"Yeah, yeah. I know. Principal's office," I muttered as I walked towards the door.

I was sure Principal Pike wouldn't be happy to see me. I think he leaves me sitting in the hallway on purpose. Apparently, my smart Alec remarks give him a 'headache.' Personally, I think any head that large would give someone a headache by virtue of the sheer weight of it.

I couldn't help but smile a little when the door slammed behind me.

I looked back down at the clock. It had only taken ten minutes to be kicked out. That was a record, even for me.

***

I slammed the front door as hard as I could.

After history class, the day had just gone from bad to worse, with me being put on a behavior watch by the principal. I ended up having to eat lunch by myself, and then afternoon classes totally sucked, and, to top it all off, I had to walk home because I missed the bus. It was fair to state that I was in a shitty mood.

"Amber!" My dad hollered from the dining room.

I was so late because I walked home, that I hadn't even noticed the fact that it was tea time.

I stormed into the dining room.

"What?" I said in a bored tone. There better be a bloody good reason for him to have called me in here.

I noticed Jax sitting, eating at the table.

How lovely. Jax gets a nice hot tea and a snack, and I get blisters on my feet. Fuck, I hate karma.

Oh, how I would love to take that fork and attack his…

"Are you going to join us for tea?" Dad interrupted my, well… evil plans.

"Hello. No." I answered quickly.

Dad frowned.

What? I didn't feel like eating in front of THAT.

"Fine, bed then," he ordered.

I rolled my eyes and walked out of the dining room.

There was close to no chance that I would be going to bed right now. Dad should've known by now I didn't listen. I had listened this morning about not driving, but I think that was about to change.

What was the worst that could happen? I'd get pulled over, and again, lose my license.

I didn't need an early night.

I needed drinks and conversation.

I unlocked my phone and scrolled down to Blake's number.

My off again, on again, boyfriend, Blake and I, had seen more drama than most couples on daytime television.

I hadn't talked to him in over a week; since he'd hit me, and I had got so wasted, I had ended up at some bar - I still don't know how I'd got home that night, but I'd woken up in bed next to Blake who went on and on about how sorry he was for hitting me.

I'd left after that, and hadn't spoken to him.

I think he took my silence as me breaking it off with him.

I knew I shouldn't even be thinking about calling him, but he was once sweet and charming, and I loved him. Love can make you do crazy things, like it was making me do now.

Now, I wasn't sure how I felt about him, but I knew he was one of the few people who could cheer me up right now.

I sat down in the middle of the staircase, and dialed.

I really hoped that it wasn't going to be too weird.

Ringing.

Ringing.

Ringing.

"Hello" said a husky voice.

Aww Blake... how I had missed your voice.

I smiled, just a little. He really did bring out the girl in me.

"Hey Blake, it's ummm Amber,"

"Amber." I could hear his voice brighten. "What you been doing babe? I haven't seen you in a while." Yeah, well I wasn't sure if I wanted to see you again." I spoke the truth. After that fight, I wasn't sure if we could come back from it.

But the gang was family, and you don't walk away from family, unless it's my blood family and, in that case, you run as far as you can to get away from them.

Blake went silent. I'm sorry about..." He started, but I was quick to cut him off.

"Don't say sorry. Anyway, I didn't call to fight." I didn't need to hear him say sorry. I knew he was sorry as soon as his fist had connected with my face.

I heard him sigh.

"So, why did you call?" he sounded disappointed.

"To see if you wanted to do something tonight? Or if you were doing anything?"

"Oh, well I am just at home with the guys. We are pre-gaming and then heading to this party. Wanna come babe?' He sounded almost happy, but we both knew that only a high on drugs and money gave him real happiness.

"Sure, so I'll come to your house then?"

"Sounds good to me. Will I see you soon?" he questioned.

"Yep, you will," I answered, and then hung up.

Finally, something to do. I didn't usually drink on week days, but hell I deserved it.

Having that Jackson Johnston move into your house was more than reason enough to get blinded on a Tuesday night.

I went upstairs and quickly changed into jeans and a long sleeved white top.

I jumped down the staircase, grabbed the keys to my Hummer off the hook and headed towards the garage.

I ignored my dad's warning about my so-called suspension.

If I ran into the cops, I would wing it. What was the worst that could happen? I'd get arrested.

I heard mumbles of conversation coming from the dining room as I passed.

I couldn't believe it! I made it to my car without anyone having seen me.

Life was a whole lot better as I drove towards the front gates.

I smiled. My night was going to improve.

Chapter 3

I slowly slipped into the house; the sun was blinding.

I hadn't woke up till after seven, and, as I glanced at the wall clock, I saw it was nearly eight in the morning.

"Amber?" Dad called from the lounge.

I didn't want to go in there. I was still crying. I hated people seeing me like this; weak and looking like all torn up.

The night before had come flooding back when I had woken up.

Blake and I had got into a fight, although my disheveled appearance didn't have anything to do with him. I looked this way because of my own doing.

I'd run into, and taken on someone I shouldn't have, and, given that it was a three to one fight, I was lucky to have made it out alive.

My face was aching, and, to top it off, I had a massive hangover.

I had tears running down my face.

I tried to slip up the stairs. I couldn't face dad like this. He would think the worst, like always. I'm sure he had questions on why I was always beaten up. Hell, anyone would have questions. A sane person would ask, "Why are you hurt?" I could never, and would never give, someone a straight answer to that question.

Because I lived a life no one would understand. I lived and breathed for a gang that promised me an early grave.

Hell, I was lucky to not be in that grave right now, after last night.

"Amber! I can see you! Get in here!" Dad hollered.

Damn those glass windows! I sighed. Well, I guess I would just have to face him.

I walked slowly into the lounge room, positioning myself staring at the ground. Perhaps he wouldn't mention my face.

"So, Amber I have…" he broke off suddenly, and I glanced up to see his shocked face as he took my appearance in.

I scanned the room and noticed Jax sitting in the armchair, looking calm and collected.

Dad, however, looked super angry.

"DID HE HIT YOU AGAIN?" Dad yelled as his fists curled. Dad knew I had a boyfriend and he just assumed Blake was the one always giving me a beating. This time it wasn't Blake though.

"No, I don't remember what happened," I answered slowly. I could never tell my father the truth.

My dad took a deep breath, and I knew what was coming, as I saw the vein in his neck bugle.

"You're lying to me."

I suppose now wasn't the time to tell him I lied to him every day of my life.

"I'm not," I fired back.

"Then tell me what happened!"

"NO. It's my body, my life."

"I am your father! And, as my daughter, I'm ordering you to stay away from that abusive son of a bitch you call your boyfriend. This time, Amber, is the last time. No daughter of mine will be abused. You are smarter than this! For God's sake, I raised you better! How can you possibly think it is OK to be treated this way? With no respect. Your behavior disgusts me. I have dealt with the drinking, the smoking, the violence, and, not to mention your run-ins with the law, but not anymore. This stops now!" He took a deep breath. "You are getting your act together, whether you like it or not."

My mouth hung open in shock. It wasn't his words that scared me; this wasn't my first lecture or warning. What scared me was his tone, the look in his eyes. This was the real deal; he meant business.

"I'm calling your brothers."

I froze… He couldn't. He wouldn't!

I stared at him frozen, my mind going crazy with possible scenarios, a lot of which involved my brothers killing me; or Blake, if they knew he existed.

Chapter 4

My brothers were dad's secret weapon. I threw a book across my bedroom in frustration. Why I had a book in my bedroom to begin with was a mystery to me.

I slid down my bedroom door, glancing at my reflection in the long mirrors across the room. I was such a mess. I had always told myself that I was a strong, confident woman, but, right now, I looked like a punching bag; an old punching bag.

I ran my hand through my hair. Taking a deep breath, I pulled myself up off the floor and walked towards the bathroom. I scooped up my surround sound controller from the floor and hit play.

A song started playing that summed up mine and Blake's relationship well; I smiled disbelievingly. Of all the random songs lined up, this was the one that played. As I walked towards the bathroom door, I stopped, my eyes landing on a photo of Blake and myself. We looked so happy. So innocent.

The gang had ruined us. My eyes stared at the picture, burning a hole into the happy couple. Tears began to roll down my cheeks, and then my eyes landed on the women in the mirror again.

Bruised, bloody and batted.

I ripped my top off, unbuttoned my jeans, and walked into the bathroom.

I entered the shower and closed my eyes, feeling the water run down my body, but I already knew. The water couldn't wash away my fears, worries or mistakes. It could only wash away the physical evidence of the night before.

"Anywhere But Here" by Sick Puppies filled the room. I placed my head against the cold tiles, as the water washed down my back, and lost myself in the lyrics.

How could life get so complicated, so early?

I put on my bathrobe and walked over to my dresser. My fingers inadvertently reached for the picture of my brothers, tracing their faces. They were in their older teens in the picture, now faded. This is how I remembered them. This is what came to my mind when I thought of them. I didn't think of them as the soulless beasts they had become.

***

I heard them before I saw them. The sound of crushing gravel drifted through my window. They were here, and my fear spiked.

My brothers.

My reasons for fearing them weren't the same as for others. I couldn't exactly claim

I loved them, although I had an independent equation with each of them, but, from the day they'd left, I could safely say there was no love lost.

After all, they'd left me here… with dad.

Not that dad was mean or abusive, but, after they left, he went cold, and, as a result, threw himself into work, and, without supervision, I ended up the train wreck I was today.

I listened closely as the car came to a stop. I wondered if it felt strange for them being back here, after so many years of avoiding the place and the people who lived here. I closed my eyes and took a steady breath; and I listened for the car door.

One car door slammed.

Silence.

I could deal with one brother. I bet it was Troy, he was the eldest.

I then heard the second car door, quickly followed by a third. Before I could let out my breath, I heard the fourth door slam.

I fell back onto my bed. All four were here. ALL FOUR WERE HERE! I shouted louder in my head.

The slamming of the front door brought my attention back to reality. How would my brothers change me? They couldn't, and they wouldn't. I started to give myself a pep talk to calm down the nerves stirring in my stomach.

They wouldn't change me because, for one, I would have to let them, and, two, I would have to listen to them. Neither of these two was going to happen.

Dad must've been out of his mind, thinking my brothers could fix this situation. If anything, they could only make everything worse.

There was only one good thing that would come out of them being here; dad might actually make an effort to be home at a reasonable hour.

"Amber!" My father's voice rang up the stairs.

I stood in the upstairs hallway, trying to put off having to go down and face them, but, just like taxes, I couldn't put it off forever, so I turned the corner and descended the large staircase.

I pulled my eyes from the carpet, and looked up as I entered the dining room.

My eyes were met by ten pairs of eyes.

I instantly directed all my attention to my father, not dropping my gaze or meeting my brothers'.

My father had a smirk on his face, like his master plan was about to unfold. I frowned, because, no matter how I looked at it, the truth was that my father held all the trump cards in this situation.

"Amber…" a dark voice called for my attention.

I finally came to terms with the fact I would have to face my brothers, and, by face them, I meant look them in the eye and try not to let the hatred I was filled with show.

I turned my head sharply, and faced Troy.

He had changed. His long shaggy black hair was gone and, instead, he had a number two haircut. He had become larger; I could see the defined muscles under his black t-shirt. His hand was rubbing his clenched jaw, and I could almost see the wheels in his head churning, planning his next move.

I raised my eyebrow.

A slow sigh left his lips.

His eyes gave me a once over, inspecting me.

I was sick of being treated like a darn science experiment gone wrong. "What?" I insisted.

His jaw clenched again and his hand dropped to the table. "You certainly have grown up," he finally stated.

I gave him a deadpan look, and then rolled my eyes. Was he serious right now? After staring at me for that long, that's what he had to say? Looks like the drugs were finally affecting his mind.

I gave my other three brothers a once over.

Adam. Tyler. Cole.

They all looked older and scarier, if that was even possible.

They all sat at the table, looking at me as if they had just been forced to witness a scene from a horror movie.

They all looked disappointed. Disapproving.

What the hell was the problem? Did they honestly expect to come back to find me still dancing around in my ballet flats? In a pink tutu?

In the silence, you could almost hear the tension brewing in the room.

Minutes passed.

I had to ask myself, why did I even fear them in the first place?

I turned to walk out of the room, not wanting to waste another minute of my life in pointless silence.

I took three steps towards the entrance before another voice stopped me.

"Where are you going?"

I turned my head over my shoulder and stared at Cole.

Maybe they hadn't lost their voices altogether after all.

I raised my eyebrow.

35

"Was there a point to your silence?" I questioned. "Or am I just to stand here all day, to be stared at by a bunch of strangers?"

Cole rolled his eyes

"Well!?" I asked "Are you guys going to start the threats soon? So your obligation is completed?" I asked openly.

A low rumble of laughter filled the room. All four brothers were smirking at each other, as if sharing a secret joke.

"And we thought this was going to be easy," Adam stated to the other three brothers.

"Look, Amber, dad informed us that you've been acting out? I guess that's what you call it?" Adam explained.

"Acting out?" I questioned.

I was sure that 'acting out' was a clear understatement of my behavior.

"Bad grades, a little too much drinking, and fighting with your boyfriend or something," Cole added. With a bored expression on his face, I might add.

I rolled my eyes. Looks like dad underplayed everything. Thank God!

Not to mention he left out the sleeping around, drugs, parties, fighting, stealing and being a member of Blake's gang. Although to be fair, dad didn't know all that.

I smiled.

"Ok, I will try harder with my school grades, and I broke up with my boyfriend," I said innocently. Suddenly, I was seeing a way out and, like a guilty man, I was taking it.

"And the drinking?" Tyler questioned.

"Thing of the past," I quickly added, waving my hand dismissively.

God, this was easy! Pulling the wool over my brothers' eyes is as about as easy as sneaking out of this house!

Fortunately, my brothers couldn't actually believe that their little sister would do anything that wasn't PG rated.

After all, I couldn't be like them.

They really didn't know me.

"Can I go now?" I asked.

A bottle of vodka had my name on it tonight, and I'd had my last drug run tonight, then I had to say goodbye to Blake.

It was going to be hard to walk away from Blake and his gang.

"Don't you want to catch up with us?" Adam asked hurt audible in his tone.

I tried hard not to roll my eyes.

Cole wasn't saying that a few months ago, but that was a different story. A longer one, a darker one and one I wasn't ready to share with anyone but Blake. So, even now, as he looked at me, I couldn't bring myself to telling the story - maybe one day I would, but today wasn't that day.

"Not much to talk about," I said blankly.

Because they couldn't, no, let's rephrase that, they wouldn't tell me the truth about them and what was going on in their lives.

"Do you have somewhere you need to be?" Tyler asked quietly.

Why did he sound disappointed too?

"Yeah, assignments to complete, you know," I brushed off easily.

"Good. We have more important things to deal with anyway," Cole stated and rose from his chair.

"No, you boys said you would stay the night!" My dad piped in.

Annoyance flickered across Cole's face, but Troy quickly interrupted.

"We did, and we are." Troy ended the conversation, giving Cole a pointed look.

Hah, sucks to be him.

"Have a good night studying Amber," Troy softly said to me. A smile appearing on the corners of his lips.

"I knew dad was overdoing it, saying you had gone completely off the rails." Tyler added.

"Yeah, all you needed were some wise words from your brothers," Adam quietly added, with a smile.

Geez, how stupid could they be!

I almost felt bad for lying so bluntly to their faces.

I smiled and quickly turned my back to them, as I curled my nose in disgust!

Wise words from my brothers! Hah.

What a joke.

I took the stairs two at a time.

Now to get changed and go take care of business.

Then, after business was taken care of, I was going to get seriously smashed. I didn't know what was worse, knowing I had lied to them so easily, or that I didn't feel the tiniest bit guilty.

Chapter 5

"NOOOOOOO", I screamed as I stepped out of the black Mustang.

Liam chuckled. "You are! You are seriously hammered," he slurred.

I wasn't going to lie and say this was one of my finest moments. I was drunk, and perhaps high on a fresh break-up. These two factors combined, ended with me wanting a meaningless one-night stand.

I fought another fit of laughter as I stumbled up my front steps.

"You're just jealous! Cause I am awesome!" I screamed at the top of my lungs. I stopped short and wondered whether the front door had always been that big. Jeez, it was huge!

I had seemed to have forgotten that it was the early hours of the morning, and that I wasn't meant to be out of the house in the first place.

"You're a gentleman… taking me home," I slurred, giggling at Liam.

I was hammered; no I was beyond drunk… I had reached a new level altogether - I was on the edge of passing out.

I stumbled to the front door with Liam right behind me.

I didn't have my keys, so I did the next best thing my drunkenness told me to - I picked up the potted plant next to the door, and slammed it through the glass of the front door.

Liam laughed and wrapped an arm around my waist. I reached in and pulled the door handle, and we both fell through the front door.

I laughed loudly. Loud enough to rattle the dead.

Turning around in Liam's arms, I slammed my lips against his.

I could feel his lips turn up into a smirk before they started moving on mine, and hard.

"I'm going to miss you Amber," his lips continued to move with mine.

"Let's make a memory we won't forget then."

"You are so hammered," Liam stated.

I laughed again, finding my own voice amusing.

"AM NOT!" I screamed at him.

And then out of nowhere, the lights came on.

"WHAT IS GOING ON?" A familiar voice screamed from the top of the stairs.

I didn't pull my lips away from Liam's, and his hands began to travel down my body, resting on my lower waist. We were too high to even notice anyone else.

"GET YOUR HANDS OFF MY SISTER!" Another voice growled from the top of the stairs.

Liam pulled away from me, and his eyes widened as they stared behind me.

I spun around, too quickly, lost my balance, and fell to the ground.

I went into another fit of giggles. Ground... that was a funny word.

"Oops!" I slurred as I tried to get a hold of myself.

I felt Liam put a firm hand around my waist and pull me back up.

"Get your hands off her!" a voice snarled.

My eyes landed on two shirtless, toned bodies at the top of the stairs.

Cole and Troy.

Were they staying the night?

Oops.

"Shut the fuck up Shields," Liam snarled back. Then he looked down at me in confusion. I shared his confused look. Why weren't they wearing t-shirts?

"I didn't know you were related to the Shield brothers," he said slowly.

I shrugged my shoulders.

"You don't know I dislike pickles either." I pointed out. Though to be fair, the pickles were a more serious matter then these things that were also known as my brothers.

This made Liam crack up, although I think anything would've caused us to crack up at this point.

Liam's hand was suddenly yanked away from my waist.

I then noticed Troy had him by the collar.

"Let him go," I tried to say firmly, but the words were slurred and ineffective. Now was a great time for cohesion to fail me. Great!

"What the fuck are you doing with my sister Liam?" Troy roared into his face. I could see the red veins in his eyes, as his face twisted in pure raw rage.

Cole was now standing between me and Liam, blocking my view of what was happening.

"OH bloody hell. He was dropping me off!" I stated like it was the most obvious thing in the world.

Troy shot me a glare.

"You were meant to be studying!" he stated, sounding a tad pathetic.

Liam laughed, causing him to glare at me harder.

"I had things to do!" I pointed out. "Now, let him go!" I pointed out to Troy and started flicking my finger at him, for no apparent reason.

Troy pushed Liam away from him.

"Leave," he ordered.

"Wait," I added, and sat down on a step. Liam didn't move an inch.

He smirked. "Are you going to miss me sugar?" he teased.

"Obviously! But…" I began, pushing a hand down my long black boots. I pulled out my gun and laid it on the step, then went back down, pulled out two wads of cash, and tossed them at Liam.

"Tonight's take. Make sure Blake knows."

He nodded.

"Miss you already," he added and winked, then turned around and walked out the door.

I sighed and looked up at my two shirtless brothers.

They were both glaring at me.

I shrugged my shoulders. Heck, what was a girl meant to do in these types of situations?

"Bed time!" I screamed excitingly.

Both flinched at my sudden outburst.

I started to climb up the stairs.

"Aren't you forgetting something?" Cole said, a mixture of hurt and anger in that voice.

Turning my head over my shoulder, I noticed Cole was pointing to my gun.

I giggled.

"Better not forget that!" I smiled.

Reaching down the two stairs, I scooped it up.

Troy eyed me in complete disbelief. His reaction mirrored mine when I had first discovered alcohol, why hadn't I known earlier such a wonderful and numbing agent existed?

I sighed and resumed my long climb up the stairs.

"I hate steps," I stated to no-one in particular.

Before I knew it, I was scooped up by a strong pair of arms, and I was in the air.

It was Cole, jaw clenched, now walking up with me in his arms. Why was he so mad?

Troy was muttering something behind him, but I didn't catch it.

"We weren't to know," Cole snapped over his shoulder.

I glanced up the hall, and saw something that made my blood boil in disgust.

"IT'S HERE!" I yelled at the top of my lungs.

Cole jumped in surprise, but Jax leaned against his bedroom door calmly, eyeing me carefully.

"Another big night Amber?" Jax stated, a certain smugness in his voice.

I flipped him the bird.

"I don't know which room is hers," Troy advised from behind us.

"I don't have a bedroom," I added, joining their conversation.

"It's the door to the left," Jax blurted from his bedroom door.

"LIAR!"

"Amber, lower your voice," Troy warned as he twisted the knob of my bedroom door.

Cole placed me back on my feet.

"Watch where ya step," I advised, before placing my gun on the bedside table.

I then pulled my boots off and flung them in random directions. Without paying attention to my brothers, I ripped off my top and tore off my jeans.

I launched myself into my big, fluffy bed.

I muttered into my pillow. I was going to feel like hell come morning. "You have a tattoo," Jax stated.

I turned to my side, and looked at my two brothers and Jax, all with shock on their faces.

"It's a gang mark actually." These men needed an education. "NOW, PISS OFF!" I said fiercely, but it came out all slurred.

I closed my eyes and drifted off, remembering only my door clicking shut.

43

Chapter 6

I took my clothes off in front of Jax and my brothers!

I took my clothes off in front of Jax and MY BROTHERS!

This thought kept running through my head, as the events of the night before came back to me in waves the next morning.

Another wave of nausea ripped through my body, and I clenched the toilet bowl a little tighter.

What was I thinking? Oh wait... I wasn't!

I shouldn't have drunk so much, but it was so heart-wrenching to have to leave the gang and Blake.

He had hit me though.

But the thing was, before that night, Blake had never laid a finger on me. He protected me, he loved me.

We had the modern day romance; it would have made a great romance novel.

Even the ending was twisted; wasn't that what every reader wanted?

For the characters to be left heartbroken.

Well I was.

And now I had no choice but to walk away, because Blake and I both knew that was the only way to go.

If we really wanted to end it.

Which we had to.

I leaned away from the toilet bowl, and ran my fingers through my hair.

I hoped that I had just imagined that Cole had carried me up to my bedroom.

Maybe they had left already, thinking that it was nothing?

My hand wrapped around the basin for support, and I pulled myself up to my feet.

I suppose I would find out soon enough.

What makes a hangover worse? What doubles the nausea ripping through your stomach? What increases the mind hammering headache?

Knowing that your brothers and wanker of a guest got a strip show when you were wasted, and then to know I now had to go and face them all. Together.

As I twisted the taps and the water started to flow, the bathroom began to steam up.

I hoped and prayed my brothers had left.

***

I stood outside the dining room, leaning against the wall, listening to my brothers' conversation.

"You sure it was the HellBound tattoo?" Tyler asked.

"Yes, it was their tattoo!" Cole exclaimed.

"We would have seen her!" Tyler pressed.

"It was their tattoo Tyler," Troy emphasized.

"How could dad be so fucking blind?" Cole roared.

"She blinded us pretty easily," Adam pointed out.

"I wonder how deep in she is…" Adam wondered out loud.

"Deep enough to carry their mark," Troy said, stating the obvious.

I jumped at the sound of slamming fists on the table.

"Cole, don't take your anger out on us," Troy snapped

I braced myself, took a deep breath and walked into the dining room.

Immediately, everyone's attention was on me.

As I scanned the room, I noticed how everyone was totally focused on me, and I immediately dreaded what was coming next.

"Sit down Amber. Now." Troy ordered.

Like a scared little child, I took the closest seat to the exit. Thank God I now had the comfort of the chair to support me.

"So, Amber. I guess we can say you've been busy," Cole snarled from the head of the table. I should have questioned his reaction. It wasn't like they got on with the HellBound. So, me having their tattoo was going to cause them to hate me a bit more.

Because they would have to hate me, wouldn't they?

Knowing the type of life I lived.

But then it wasn't any better than their lives, and the way they chose to live.

Troy leaned against the wall, his arms crossed, and I could feel the waves of rage coming from him.

Tyler and Adam were seated on either side of Cole, both their chairs arranged sideways to face me.

I cleared my throat and waited for it.

"How long?" Troy asked, his jaw clenched, and eyes glazed over with anger.

"How long have I been drinking? Or how long I have been a member of the HellBound?" I babbled.

Cole huffed.

"I don't believe this," Cole interrupted.

I rolled my eyes.

"Why does it matter?" I demanded, keeping control over my voice. "It's not like you guys really care." I scoffed. "You are just here because of dad and you've done your duty, so you can leave now."

"We are your brothers! Your family. We care more than those gangsters from the HellBound," Tyler growled.

I gave him a deathly glare.

"Please, don't go there," I snapped back.

"When are you guys leaving? When I say leaving, I mean the house; I know you still live in the city." I snarled.

"You're a real piece of work aren't ya," Cole snapped back.

"Here we were, thinking that you needed your brothers," Tyler added. I could hear the hurt in his voice. I had always been the closest to Tyler. For some twisted reason, he most likely thought that was still the case.

"We came here to help you!" Adam continued.

"If I needed help, which I don't by the way, you four wouldn't be the ones I would turn to."

"Well, it's very clear to us now, how immature you really are." Troy growled from where he was standing.

"Because you guys have been a real huge part of my life. Great support," I snapped

"Don't act like you're a mystery to us. You are our sister!" Cole hissed.

"Don't you even get me started Cole," I hissed back, clenching my fists.

He rolled his eyes. "Don't sit there and behave like you are a mystery. Like we don't know you at all."

I rolled my eyes. Fine, he clearly wanted to be embarrassed.

"Am I good enough for you to remember my name then?" I asked

His eyebrows furrowed in confusion.

So I began to explain.

"A while ago, I attended one of your Bike Patch over parties. Not that I even knew I was at my brothers' club party because, silly me thought you guys actually owned a gym and did personal training."

All their faces went blank at this point.

But I continued, ignoring my nagging headache.

"When I saw you four, I was so happy! Stupid me actually missed you fools. It didn't even click for me that you guys were part of a Biker gang. That was until I approached you Cole." I stopped and took a much-needed breath, because I knew the next part was going to take a bit.

"When I screamed your name in excitement, I recall your every word, and I quote, "*Sorry hun, I don't remember your name, but you seem to remember mine. Sounds like I didn't get as much fun out of it as you did.* And then you winked at me!" I was not in the mood to put up a front anymore. Or accept their behavior. "You didn't even realize I was your sister! You JERK! Not to mention how embarrassing it was. You three weren't much better," I said looking at the rest of them at the table. "Not even bothering to pull your lips away from the whores you were with," I continued.

They were all silent at this point. Did they really think I didn't know who they were?

"I haven't seen any of you guys in months and months, and then here you are at a party! And you didn't even know it was me." I shook my head in disbelief.

"In fact, you guys haven't been there for a lot of things," I added calmly, now clearly recalling that night.

I turned my eyes to Cole's, but he just sat there, not even bothering to try to explain himself.

What was there to explain; he didn't know me.

"You guys didn't even know I was part of the HellBound which amazes me, given that we have to give you shares in all our profits," I calmly argued.

"Amber, you weren't meant to get involved with this lifestyle," Troy said quietly.

I huffed and rolled my eyes.

"Like I had a fucking choice," I snarled.

"What do you mean?" Adam questioned.

'One thing led to another," I explained.

"That doesn't really explain much, Amber," Tyler pointed out.

"I don't feel like sharing my reasons with you," I sneered.

"Fine. We don't know you at all. So enlighten us? Why did you join the HellBound?" Adam asked calmly.

I ran my fingers through my hair.

"Because I was in love, and stupid." I snapped back.

Troy raised his eyebrows questioningly, while Cole was still staring at the table, most likely bathing in embarrassment. Out of all my brothers, he had always been the most protective. Maybe now he was realizing he'd failed.

I sighed and began to explain.

"Well, the evening I mentioned before," I started, knowing they would all know what night I was speaking about.

They all nodded their heads slightly.

I glanced at each of them, just to make sure we were all on the same page.

"I was, well… attacked," I confessed. "And that is putting it mildly."

Cole snapped his head up, Tyler's jaw dropped, Adam looked stunned and Troy stiffened.

I put my hands up so they wouldn't interrupt or start asking questions, especially that one stupid question that made my blood boil. *Are you ok?"*

I ran my hands through my hair again, and continued to explain.

"That was the night I met Blake Edwards. You all know him. He is the leader of the HellBound. You guys do a lot of business with him," I paused for a second, not giving them any time to agree or disagree. They all knew Blake, I already knew that. This fact didn't need to be confirmed.

"So, I met Blake the night of the party. He was a real charmer…" I smiled, thinking back to that night.

'Then I ran into you lot".

"You can skip that bit," Cole blurted, before I could progress.

I continued, disregarding his statement.

"Anyway, long story short, I was distraught, and I left. I just took off. I had had a fair bit to drink as well. I don't remember much about the attack. Just that I was grabbed and… I won't get into the details. It's my scar to carry," I disclosed.

Taking a deep breath, I carried on.

"I remember a guy fighting my attacker off me. He was too late, but that didn't stop him from beating the shit out of my attacker." I paused. It was unpleasant to share these memories with them, but it would answer some of their questions.

"I vaguely remember being carried away, as I watched the scum bag writhing on the ground. When I awoke, I was in hospital, with Blake holding my hand. I had barely spoken to him, but there he was with bruised knuckles, holding my hand." I spoke quietly, but continued with my explanation.

"And, yes, dad knew what had happened. I told him that he was, under no circumstances, to tell you guys. That's why he never did," I informed them. "Anyway, I don't feel like sharing every memory with you guys because, like it or not, I don't want to. So that was how I met Blake."

I took a deep breath. I knew I would have to add more for them to understand.

"Needless to say, Blake and I became friendly after that evening, then fell in love, and became stupid, but I joined the HellBound with my head clear; it was what I wanted at the time. Blake didn't encourage the idea, but he would do anything to make me happy, so I pledged. I don't need to tell you guys about what I did as a member of the gang; I think you guys have a fair idea," I reasoned. "But that isn't the point now. I don't want to talk about any of it anymore. To finish my story - Blake and I are over, and I am no longer a HellBound member, unless they call me up which they can do, because I've got the ink."

Sure the story had gaps, but there was little chance I would honestly tell them everything. I had informed them of the main points. Now to wait for the questions.

I leaned back in the chair and sighed.

"So you guys can shoot me questions now," I said. It was already like being lined up in front of a firing squad.

The room fell into silence.

Their expressions were blank.

Bad sign or good?

"Miss Amber?" our butler sang from the entrance of the doorway of the dining room.

"Yes," I responded, taking my eyes off my brothers and directing my attention to him.

"A gentleman is at the door, and wishes to speak with you," he answered, and then turned and left the room.

Sighing, I lifted myself off my chair, and walked towards our bay window and, as I pulled the curtains back, my eyes landed on a black Mustang parked out in our driveway.

I knew who it was.

My heart quickened.

Blake.

I glanced at my brothers; they better not make a scene.

"I will be a minute or so," I softly stated and marched my way out of the dining room, determined to ignore the nagging feeling of wanting to forget everything and run back to him.

I pulled the front door open, and standing there in all his amazing glory was Blake.

He turned around instantly, to face me.

A soft smile spread across my lips.

The corner of his lips lifted slightly.

If you didn't know him, you would call it a small smile.

But I knew him, and when Blake smiled, it mirrored in his eyes.

This smile was a fake, as Blake's eyes were cold.

"Amber," his husky voice murmured.

"Blake," I mimicked.

His hand reached behind his head and began to rub the back of his neck.

"I just wanted to come by and…" he trailed off.

"And see if I was alright?" I finished for him.

This time, a smile appeared on his face for two seconds, and then it was gone.

"Yeah, something like that," he added.

I nodded my head.

"So your run last night… everything went smoothly?" he asked, still not taking a step closer to me.

I don't think we had ever had this much distance between us.

"Yeah, everything went as planned, I gave Liam the taking," I answered.

"Glad they didn't give you any trouble."

"Well, it wasn't like there were any of the big guys. Just a few nobodies."

"True," he agreed.

My hand wrapped tightly around the door knob. Why did this have to be so hard?

Oh, he was the love of your life, that's why, I reminded myself.

"I spoke to the chapter this morning. Even after some explaining, they weren't too happy. So, you aren't a member anymore. Your slate is clean." Blake said, and I could hear his disappointment.

I think deep down, he was hoping they wouldn't let me go, and our unhealthy relationship would just go back to the way it was before he used me as a punching bag.

How should I respond to that?

"Oh" was all my brain could come up with.

Why was I feeling like this?

"Clean slate," I whispered to myself softly.

Did I even want one?

I suddenly felt two muscular arms wrap themselves around me. I inhaled that familiar scent.

I pulled my hand away from the door and wrapped my arms around his back.

"Fuck…" he let out softly in my hair.

"I know," I replied softly. I knew exactly what he was thinking.

Holding onto him tightly, I wanted this moment to last forever.

So we didn't have to really say good bye, did we?

He pulled away, taking a step back, putting distance between us.

His hands dropped to his sides and he stood there staring at me.

"You can get the tattoo covered; I know a guy in the city," he finally spoke, deadpan.

My eyes didn't drop from his.

"I am not getting it removed," I replied. "I know what it means, s but it means something different to me."

Our eyes were still locked.

"It's a mark of the HellBound, Amber," he cautioned.

"But, to me, it's a symbol of our love. What we were." I straightened my shoulders up and said with more determination. "It's a symbol of our memories. I won't and can't remove it. It's… us." It was an easy decision, really.

I broke eye contact, closing my eyes to take a deep breath.

Opening my eyes, I watched as Blake nodded his head.

His right cheek caught my eye, and I looked at it closely. It was swollen.

'What happened to your cheek?" I asked.

"Disagreement," he answered, pulling his shoulders back and standing taller, defensively. I knew that stance. He did that when he was faced with a threat. That look on his face told me that right now, he was furious, but it wasn't directed at me.

I glanced over my shoulder to see Jax shirtless, standing in the middle of the staircase glaring at me and Blake.

I let out an annoyed groan, and stepped forward onto the porch, slamming the front door shut behind me.

"Sorry, this is the wanker my father has staying with us," I explained to Blake.

But anger consumed his face. His expression told me he didn't believe me.

"Why would I lie?" I pointed out.

His shoulders relaxed a little. "Stay away from him." Blake was warning me like Jackson was trouble. He was nothing more than a friend to my brothers, and I couldn't wait for the day when he moved on.

I nodded my head. I had every intention of staying away from Jackson.

"I'm going to miss you," I said, feeling all confused.

His eyes softened and he took a step towards me, but didn't wrap his arms around me like he would normally have done.

He lowered his head to mine, resting it on my forehead.

"I know," he whispered.

It took all my self-control to not wrap my arms around his neck.

"Love you," he murmured.

I nodded my head against his.

"You better go," I spoke softly.

He pulled away.

'If you need me..." he began to speak, but I cut in.

"Your commitment is to the gang, Blake. Your commitment to me is over," I informed him softly.

He didn't move. He looked at me like I was breaking his heart. The look in his eyes was the same look he always gave me - unconditional love. Even though we were breaking up, if he needed me, I would always be there.

"My commitment to you will never be over." He reached out, tucking my hair behind my ear, as if to get a better last look at me. "You need me, call. No matter what Amber, I am always here."

"Ok" I finally muttered. I knew he meant it. He would always be there for me. That love he felt for me would always be there. That need to be together, well, we were always going to fight it. Him and I – well, we had that twisted romance. Undying, and yet a complete wreck.

"Bye Blake. Look after yourself." Because I wouldn't be looking after him anymore. I just couldn't. Our love had always been unhealthy, at times too intense, other times barely there.

That was the thing about Blake and I - we never got the balance right.

Taking a step backwards, I placed my hand on the door knob.

He let out a deep breath.

Turning his back to me, he looked over his shoulder, not making eye contact with me.

"Love you Amber. You will be ok. I'm sorry."

I twisted the door knob and stepped back into the foyer.

In a romance novel, in a teenage love story or in any fairy-tale, this would've been my cue to run after him, kiss him and tell him that I loved him.

That I couldn't be apart from him.

Tell him I would be nothing without him.

Instead, I closed the door.

Because this is real life, and in real life, you don't run after the gangsta.

You walk away while you still have enough pieces of your heart to thread back together.

So I let him go. I let everything dear to me go. The life I knew. The life I always thought I'd spend by his side. I let that go.

I wouldn't trade our memories or scars. I wouldn't change my decisions, the ones that made me fall in love with him.

I wouldn't change a thing.

So, as my heart was breaking, I had to accept that letting him go was going to hurt, but if didn't hurt, then he wouldn't be the love of my life, would he?

Chapter 7

Turning my back to the door, I leaned against it. Closing my eyes tightly, I heard his car start up. This was happening. This was really happening. I wasn't going to see him again. I listened as the familiar sound of his engine grew fainter.

"He's gone," Cole all but barked at me, forcing me to open my eyes. At least I wasn't crying. The last thing I wanted them to see was weakness.

"Thanks, I hadn't noticed," I snapped.

"In here now,"

Right, the bikies.

Now to deal with them.

I rolled my eyes and pulled myself together as I walked back towards the dining room.

I noticed that Jax was sitting next to Adam, with his arms crossed, glaring at me. Why was he pissed off? He wasn't the one about to get a grilling!

Cole went and sat next to Tyler. Troy had positioned himself at the head of the table, with authority.

I stood at the opposite end of the table with my arms crossed.

"You will no longer ride with any gang. You will no longer associate with any gang members. You will go to school, do your homework and, when you attend parties, they will be high school parties. Do you understand?" Troy demanded, his jaw clenched and his arms tightly crossed.

I keep my face blank, showing no emotion.

I was in no position to disagree, but it was against my nature to simply give in.

"Do you understand?" Cole venomously questioned.

"And that tattoo will be removed," Tyler spoke up.

"And you will be handing over your gun," Adam added.

A smirk spread across my face and I cocked my left eyebrow.

No way in hell was I handing my gun over, nor was I getting my tattoo removed.

"Don't give us that look. You have no choice," Troy informed me firmly.

As soon as that sentence left his mouth, my father opened the double doors leading in from the sitting room. He had a smile on his face, clearly happy to have all his kids in his house.

That was when the solution hit me.

If they wanted to ruin my life, I might as well throw them for a loop as well.

As if right on cue, I burst into tears.

And just like that, my dad rushed to my side.

And I fought hard to not let a smile cross my lips.

"Amber sweetie," my father said, wrapping his arms around me.

I took the tears up to another level and wailed into his arms.

"What the devil has happened?" My father asked openly.

I quickly answered before my brothers or Jax had a chance to ruin my performance.

"They..." I broke off, adding a few more tears before I continued, "are going to leave again dad," I whispered with fake heavy sadness.

I heard dad take in a deep breath and his body stiffen a little.

Now time to put the icing on the cake.

"They are abandoning me again," I choked. "Leaving me with no support."

They wanted to ruin my life and make sure I didn't have one; well they could suffer with me. In fact, they could watch my life turn to shit first hand.

Thinking of coming here, ruining my life, and then leaving to watch from afar. Hah!

I snuck a small glance at their faces from under dad's arm.

They looked stricken. Score!

Jax just sat there with a knowing smirk.

My dad let go of me and turned to face the boys. I didn't have the willpower to control my laughter, so rather than facing them, I stood behind dad like a coward.

"You boys will NOT be leaving," my father commanded the room.

Troy cleared his voice.

"We have commitments," he pointed out.

"We can't stay here and babysit," Cole added with disgust.

"Family comes first!" My dad roared. "I expect each of you boys to have fully moved back into this house by the end of today. And no arguments or mention of prior commitments. Your commitment is to this family."

Even the boys knew how strict dad was on family. He had let them leave, but he wasn't going to let that happen again. Not if he thought I needed them.

Which I didn't. I just wanted them to suffer.

A small smile played on my lips as I stared at the marble tiles.

But, as I noticed my father's feet turn, I completely masked my face with sadness once again.

"Now Amber, you go upstairs and rest sweetie. I promise you they won't be leaving," he said slowly.

He then turned his attention back to my brothers.

As I walked towards the door, I cocked a look at my brothers.

Cole was glaring at me and I sent him a sweet smile, and I watched his hands curl into fists. Satisfied, I walked out the door and then skipped up the staircase.

Let's see how long they'll stick around and follow through on the threats. My guess was, they'd be gone, and for good, sooner than I could even imagine, far away from this house that they hated so much.

Chapter 8

My plan backfired. Badly. It had been weeks and my brothers were still here, making sure my life was nothing but miserable.

I attended school, I ate, and I slept.

What a hell of a life I was leading.

It was Saturday night and, just like the other weekends since their arrival, I was trapped in this hell hole called home. I hadn't drunk anything stronger than a coffee since my brothers took up living here permanently.

Though they still spent a lot of time at the clubhouse, but when they were out, a prospect was left at the gate to guard the house. God forbid I go somewhere.

And, as for that pain in the ass, Jackson Johnston, I hadn't really spoken to him since my brothers were back; he was glued to them anyway.

Which I didn't completely understand.

I had come to the conclusion that he was either in the club, or in a brothering club. Or maybe just a tool my brothers liked. Though what was really interesting to me was that if he was indeed a member of one of these clubs, why didn't he sport a cut? A son of Satan's Son was never seen without his vest.

I was debating raiding dad's whiskey, because that was the only liquor left in the house at this point. The boys had drunk everything else and, if it hadn't already been consumed, it had been hidden; God forbid I got my hands on it!

I was getting up when the noise of squealing tires caught my attention.

I quickly jumped off my stool and walked towards the kitchen door, pushing the door open; the passageway was empty.

I heard the car coming to a halt outside the front of my house, followed by loud voices.

I darted down the passage and ran up the stairs, sprinting into my bedroom. I went straight for my top door and grabbed my gun.

Better to be safe than sorry.

Especially after the drive-by shootings I had seen; I didn't want to take any chances. Not to mention the ones I did. I always had a flare for leaving the targets terrified.

Walking down the stairs cautiously, I noticed the front door was still swinging open from being pushed too hard, and a black van, evidently parked in a hurry, and was at the front step, with the sliding door wide open.

I slowly rounded the corner at the bottom of the stair case, gun raised.

"FOR FUCK SAKE!" a deep loud voice screamed from the kitchen.

I lowered my gun.

That voice wasn't a threat.

I pushed the swinging doors open and walked into the kitchen.

Cole was slumped on a stool, leaning over the kitchen bench, with a pained expression on his face. Tyler was a holding a bloody t-shirt to Cole's shoulder and Jax was sitting on an opposite stool drinking from a vodka bottle. Where had he got that from? I noticed his other hand was holding his side.

The side kitchen door swung open and Troy and Adam walked in; Troy was holding a First Aid kit and Adam had multiple bottles of spirits. Again, where was all this liquor coming from?

As Adam handed Cole a bottle, Tyler removed the bloody t-shirt and blood began to run down Cole's arm; his t-shirt clinging to the wound as more and more blood leaked.

Troy grabbed a bandage from the First Aid kit and stuffed it into the leaking wound.

Cole let out a deep scream of pain and sent a flying kick into Troy's knee.

Troy then let out a string of swear words.

"For fuck sake, Cole. It's going to be a lot more painful when I remove the damn bullet!" Troy roared.

My mind raced, putting all the pieces together.

"Well, you could've waited until I fucking had a stiff drink!" He roared in response.

Troy grunted in response.

"Adam, Tyler, hold him," Troy ordered.

Troy pulled out a pair of tweezers, a pair that looked like ones I used to pluck my eyebrows with, and removed the bandage.

Cole took a long swig from the bottle and slammed it down onto the table.

The boys gripped Cole firmly as Troy began to dig into Cole's wound with the tweezers.

Cole's fists curled and his face screwed up in clear pain.

"Stop," I ordered from the doorway.

All the heads whipped in my direction.

Troy frowned before he spoke.

"Go to bed, Amber."

"Before you spew," Cole added, his eyes screwed shut.

I threw a glance in Jax's direction, but his eyes wouldn't meet mine.

Cole let out another grunt in pain as Troy got to work on his wound again.

I rolled my eyes. They were so stubborn!

I took a few steps towards Troy and ripped the tweezers out of his hand.

Troy's eyes hardened.

"For fuck sake, what are you doing?" Cole screamed.

"GO to bed Amber. NOW," Troy ordered.

"I am not a child," I snapped, reaching for the wound. "And you clearly don't know what you are doing!" I have more experience with this than you do," Troy argued back.

"And this is not your business," Cole snapped in his defense.

"Just go to bed Amber," Adam said softly, eyes pleading.

"And let Troy rip into Cole's shoulder? NO," I argued.

"I don't have time for this," Troy snarled and grabbed my wrist firmly, ripping the tweezers from my fingers. "Leave," he yelled, and brought his attention back to Cole's bleeding shoulder.

I pushed Troy away hard, although he only fell back a step, and planted myself between him and Cole.

"I've removed enough bullets from men's flesh to know what you're doing will only leave scarring and cause more pain. Now, let me take over," I informed them firmly.

Troy had a disbelieving expression.

I could tell not many people stood up to him, or defied him.

I ripped the tweezers from his hand and threw them across the room.

"Now, one of you two," I pointed to Adam and Tyler, "Go upstairs and, under my bed, there is a sliver case. Grab it and bring it down here," I ordered as I opened a drawer and grabbed a pair of scissors.

The room fell silent as Adam walked out the swinging door.

"You better know what you're doing," Cole muttered angrily.

I slowly cut his t-shirt from his body, peeling the pieces away; his wounded shoulder was a little more difficult, but I managed to get it all.

By the time Adam had returned, Cole was bare-chested and all pieces from the t-shirt had been removed.

Adam sat the case on the table and I opened it, grabbing a syringe and a bottle of anesthetic.

I grabbed a pair of gloves and put them on, before taking a needle out of its plastic.

"What are you doing?" Cole asked hesitantly.

"Trust me," I replied softly.

I then inserted the clear needle into the anesthetic bottle.

I wiped an area clean just above the wound and inserted the needle; I did this four more times around the wound.

I then opened a bottle of salt water and began to clean the wound.

Then I ripped open a new pair of long medical tweezers from a plastic pack.

I slowly moved the tweezers into the wound.

"Feel that?" I asked Cole.

He shook his head.

I nodded mine and continued.

It wasn't easy removing a bullet.

One, because the bullet doesn't stay in a solid form; it explodes, leaving pieces everywhere.

It took me a while to get the job done; the room was in complete silence.

I forgot about the others in the room, so I was surprised when Tyler spoke up.

"You've done this before," Tyler stated.

I gave him a quick glance as I continued to now sew Cole's wound closed.

"Yeah." I replied.

"I didn't feel a thing," Cole said in disbelief.

I lightly wiped an alcohol wipe over the now-sealed wound.

"Told you to trust me," I advised and shot him a small smile. I couldn't remember the last time I had smiled at any of my brothers, but, right now, I was finding myself giving Cole a smile, but a small one.

"Thanks," he mumbled.

I placed a bandage on the wound and taped it in place. I then finally wrapped a large white bandage over the wound and around his chest and back, repeating this process until the bandage roll ran out.

"Done," I said and let out a low sigh.

This brought back so many memories of Blake.

I handed Cole a bottle of prescription painkillers.

"These will help with the pain. I will clean the wound in two days." Again, that small smile was on my face. I turned my attention to closing my case back up. "It was deep, so don't do any heavy lifting and try to rest or you will rip the stitches."

"Thanks," he repeated, getting to his feet; Cole was doing something he never did! Smiling, at me, surprisingly.

"So, can we say that the other guy looks worse?" I asked, trying to lighten the tension.

A small smirk appeared on his lips.

"He will sis," he smiled, and then sent me a wink. My eyes darted over his tattoos.

"Who was it anyway?" I asked. "Wait. Don't worry about that. Club Business, right? I actually knew a lot about bikers, and I knew they weren't about to tell me who did that to Cole, but if I really wanted to know who had shot Cole, all I would need to do was to make a phone call.

I was actually just as well connected as they were, and my contacts always did give me information, because, well, they knew what happened when they didn't tell me.

Tyler let out a deep chuckle. "You are so full of surprises little one." I sent him a wink and turned my attention to Jax. I noticed how he was clenching his fist on his side.

"I'm heading to bed. We can deal with this in the morning," Troy stated. I didn't pull my eyes away from Jax; I noticed how he nodded his head slightly in response to Troy.

Within a few minutes, all my brothers had left, leaving Jax and me alone.

"What happened to your side?" I answered quietly.

His head whipped up at the sound of my voice, and his haunting gray eyes met mine.

Clearly, he was surprised I was still here, had he thought I'd left?

"Flesh wound," he mumbled.

I nodded my head slowly, stood up from my chair, and went to stand next to him.

"May I?" I asked as my hands lingered near the bottom of his jumper.

He didn't respond and I took a step back.

Perhaps I had been too bold. Hell, it wasn't like Jax and I were friends.

But then Jax removed his vest and pulled off his jumper and t-shirt, flinching as the fabric touched his injury.

As he sat there on the stool, bare-chested, I wanted to run my fingers over his amazingly toned body.

As my eyes landed on his injury, my jaw tightened.

It wasn't just a flesh wound.

It was a gaping knife cut, one that ran right down his side.

"Some flesh wound," I muttered sarcastically.

How could he have just sat there this whole time?

"Had worse," he responded.

I stood awkwardly next to him.

My legs brushed against his jeans, and I was suddenly very aware of my short shorts and tank top.

I cleared my throat and took a step back, reaching for my case.

"Well, it looks like I get to demonstrate my stitching skills again," I said, clearly with a fake smile because there was no situation that could occur, where I would be giving Jackson a real smile.

Now, all I needed was to manage to keep my fingers steady enough to sew his flesh back together.

***

"Can I ask you a question?" Jax asked, as I wiped an alcohol wipe over his fresh stitches.

"Sure," I responded.

Jax and I had remained in silence the complete time I worked on him.

I wasn't sure if he didn't speak because he just didn't want to speak to me, or because he didn't want to distract me.

"Why are you so good at this?" he asked seriously.

I frowned. "When your boyfriend is a known criminal, he doesn't go to the hospital when he gets shot."

"So you used to bandage Blake up?"

"Pretty much." A dim smile appeared on my lips for a second, remembering the first time I did it. "Practice makes perfect." I added, because I had got better over time.

"So I have him to thank for my perfect stitches then?"

"No, you have me to thank."

"Can I ask you something else?" It sounded like he really wanted to know the answer to this question.

I arched my eyebrow, and nodded my head.

"In the HellBound, were you a target shooter?"

I wiped my face off any expression. "I have no idea what you are talking about."

I watched as a full smile appeared on his face, and he arched his eyebrow.

"It's a skill to lie straight to someone's face," he said, calling me out on my lie.

I gave Jackson something I would never ordinarily give him - a real smile - and stood up from my stool, placing my case on my hip as I turned to leave.

"So, you were then?" He got up.

"Again, I don't know what you are talking about." I could act dumb when I wanted to.

A soft chuckle left his lips as he followed me out of the kitchen.

"How many have you taken out?" he asked from behind me.

I grunted in response.

"Who said I have taken even one out?" I threw over my shoulder.

"The way you handle that gun tells me you know how to use it," he muttered. "But then again, it could all be a show."

"What does that mean?" I asked.

"You're clumsy," he pointed out.

"Am NOT!" I yelled softly.

"Are," he argued back.

I picked up my pace and took the stairs two at a time.

Once at the top, I swung around to give Jax a pointed look, but, before I could, I tripped on my own feet and fell backwards, and the case whacked into my leg as I fell.

I cursed under my breath, lying on my back, staring up at the ceiling.

I think Jax's laughter would have woken anyone up.

I sat up and glared at him.

He clutched his side and had a pained expression on his face as laughter emanated from him.

"You could help me up," I pointed out.

His laughter slowly died and his eyes stared into mine.

Our eye contact broke as he walked past me and up the hall, not showing any signs of helping me up.

Reaching his bedroom door, he turned to face me.

"Not clumsy at all," he teased with a wicked grin, and, with that, he shut his bedroom door.

I pulled myself up from the floor.

"Way to show gratitude," I shouted behind him, and stormed towards my bedroom door, the only one across from his.

I heard soft laughter as I passed his room.

So I did the most mature thing.

I kicked his door with a lot of force, and cowardly darted into my own room, closing my door behind me.

As I stood in my dark room, I couldn't help but think about what Jax has been wearing tonight.

He was wearing his cut.

I now knew for sure that he was indeed a member of Satan's Sons.

Jax and my brothers did, indeed, have a brotherhood with each other.

But it wasn't seeing Jax wearing a Satan's Sons leather vest tonight that left me with questions. It was the fact that he wore the patch of 'President.'

I knew for a fact that Troy also wore that patch, which meant Jax was President of his own chapter of Satan's Sons.

I gulped at the realization. Everything I knew about bikers was hitting me. I knew they left every situation the same – bloody, but the one thing I knew more about Satan's Sons was that they were feared.

And I also knew that you weren't innocent if you were a President.

Chapter 9

I'd love to say I had an eventful Sunday, but I hadn't. I'd spent it in the garage, working on my dirt bikes.

The thing that came with this house was the land it was on. Past the manicured garden were dirt tracks going into the deep forest.

So, whenever I could, I was on one of my dirt bikes.

The boys used to go all the time when they were younger. I would never go with them because when it comes to anything to do with me, my brothers are protective.

So me doing jumps at high speeds always brought out the protectors in them.

So I always went by myself.

And still do.

I was actually finding myself taking more risks lately. Maybe it was my disconnection with the gang.

I frowned for a second, my hand on the door knob to the garage. Why was the door ajar? I was the only one who went into the garage.

Because all my cars were in there, as well as my dirt bikes.

I pushed it open, and saw something that made my eyes widen.

"What are you doing?" I asked Cole as he got up from kneeling beside my dirt bike.

"Finishing your work," he said simply, wiping grease on his pants.

I frowned, "And why would you do that?" He had never encouraged me to ride. In fact, he took it upon himself to slash my tires so I couldn't ride. Now he was here, fixing my bike?

He shrugged his shoulders.

My mouth dropped open, seeing the finished bike, which I had left in pieces. "How long did that take you? That would have taken me all day to put back together!"

He shrugged again.

I swallowed sharply. Just when I wipe my brothers off for good, Cole goes and does this.

"You didn't have to." I said. "I am capable of doing it." Me being incapable was the only reason I could think of him doing it.

"I know you can, and you didn't have to sew up my shoulder, but you did."

So this was his way of saying thank you.

"Thanks." I was actually really thankful because this had saved me a full day. That meant I could hit the tracks today.

"You can wipe that grin off your face; you aren't getting out of school today." Cole flattened my hope that everyone had forgotten it was a Monday.

I groaned. "Can you not remind Troy that it is Monday?"

He smirked, like he knew something I didn't. "He actually sent me to go wake you up an hour ago. You can thank me for the sleep-in."

I had wondered why no one was banging on my door this morning.

I sighed. "I guess I should get dressed for school then." I hated school.

"Yeah, you sound thrilled about that."

"I hate school." It was no secret.

"Yeah we all did. But…"

"But what?"

"But dad never expected us to take over from him, like he is expecting you to."

71

My eyes widened. "Over my dead body will I ever work a nine to five job?"

He grinned. "Dad needs someone to hand the empire he has been building over to."

"Then you can take it." I scoffed and walked out of the garage, because I couldn't go to school in what I was wearing.

"All us boys agreed you are to do it."

"I'm not smart enough for that."

His hand wrapped around my upper arm, and he pulled me to a stop. "You're smart enough to be a calculating shooter." He gave me a look like I couldn't argue with him.

"What have you heard?" I narrowed my eyes at him. Why was I suddenly getting the feeling that my brothers had looked into my past?

Cole let go of me. "You aren't a mystery anymore. Now you better get changed before we both get into trouble."

I nodded my head. Cole was usually yelling or screaming or telling me off. Never was he nice. So I took this as a one off.

***

Sitting on the bottom stair of the staircase, I finished lacing my black combat boots.

"You're wearing that to school?" Tyler asked.

I whipped my head up, watching him run his eyes over my black short shorts, army tank top and combat boots. What was wrong with what I was wearing?

"What's it to ya?" I snipped at him.

Adam rolled his eyes as I followed him out the door. Troy was casually leaning on his big black motorbike, while Cole was already on his and Tyler was straddling his.

It looked like they were all going somewhere. I felt someone shoulder me from behind as they walked past, making me stumble forward.

72

Jax walked up confidently towards the last black motorbike, which had fine white detailing over the petrol tank. I couldn't make out the picture from where I was standing; I shot draggers into the back of his head.

He didn't even acknowledge me; just thought it was acceptable to nearly knock me over!

"You're coming with us," Troy informed me, as he straddled his own bike.

"What? Why?" I argued. I was not being baby sat.

"Cause you can't be trusted to go to school on your own," Adam spoke up.

"You will bail, and we will be forced to spend the afternoon looking for you," Troy added.

"Love the faith in me guys," I grumbled, not moving.

"You will be going to school with Jax, after we take care of a few things," Tyler explained starting up his motor bike.

That means I'm missing morning classes!

YES! I screamed inside my mind.

I wandered over to the back of Troy's bike and was about to straddle it when a hand came to rest on my shoulder, stopping me. Jax quickly pulled his hand back, and his other one shot out, offering me his helmet.

I eyed it for a second in disbelief, not reaching for it; he rolled his eyes, and reached over and placed the helmet on my head. His fingers grazed my neck as he buckled it up; I took a sharp breath inwards at his touch.

He quickly turned around and walked back to his own bike, firing it up on the first kick.

I watched as he slowly took off, not giving me a second look.

I felt my side being nudged, and I snapped out of it to see Troy nodding his head sideways, gesturing for me to get on. Throwing my legs over and straddling his bike.

I couldn't wrap my arms right around, given that he was so large and muscular, so I just settled with leaving my hands on either side of his sides.

73

As he took off, the wind whipped around my body. Troy passed the others and quickly took off, head of the pack.

Jax was half a bike length back to our right, Cole was the same to our left, and then Adam was behind Cole and Tyler behind Jax.

I felt my grip loosening at Troy's side; I couldn't help but notice how cars avoided us, either turning off or pulling over. As for the cars that didn't get out of our way, we passed them with ease.

I didn't bother glancing at the speedometer; I knew we weren't respecting the speed limit.

I relaxed as the wind continued to whip around my face.

I loved this feeling.

I had missed it.

***

We slowed as we reached large iron gates, which had barbed wire across the top. Troy brought us to a stop as the gates were being opened from the inside.

Slowly, we took off into a large open space; motorbikes were lined to the side, cars parked on the other, and, in the middle to the side, was a large garage.

I let my gaze fall as I noticed other men standing around giving me questioning looks.

As Troy pulled up to the front, he slowly backed his bike back at an angle and then killed the engine. I watched as all of the other guys did the same; Jax backing his bike back next to ours.

I let my eyes gaze to the side where I noticed two garage doors open and two cars up in the air. Guys were under them, working on them. I noticed 'Satan's Sons' painted into the back of the iron fence that we had just rode through.

When all the engines of the bikes died, my ears were met with a deafening silence, before slowly picking up on low conversation.

"You getting off Amber?" Troy asked, cocking his head to the side to look at me.

74

Before I could answer, arms shot around my waist, pulling me off the bike.

Jax's arms stayed around my waist for a few short moments, as he brought my feet to the ground. This was the second time this morning he had made contact with me.

I couldn't help but feel my heart race a little at his closeness, and I couldn't pull my eyes up to his, so I shot my gaze over his shoulders were I noticed a few skinny girls shooting me disgusting glares.

"Don't mind the pornstars," Jax spoke before letting his arms drop and walking passed me towards where the others were headed. I nodded my head, although there was no point because he had already left.

Troy casually flung his arm over my shoulder, and began to guide us to where the others had headed, behind a closed door, which had Satan's Sons printed on it in red lettering.

As Troy pushed the door open, we headed down a short hallway before walking into what looked like a bar.

Tables, chairs and a few pool tables were evenly placed in the room, and a large black bar ran across the length of the wall to our right.

The smell of alcohol and cigarettes filled the air; I noticed four men sitting on stools with their backs turned to us, facing the bar.

Jax, Cole, Tyler and Adam were all leaning next to the bar talking to each other.

Troy began to walk us closer towards the others, when the guy on the end stool slowly turned around.

My mouth dropped when I took in the man; he sent me his trademark smirk before fully turning his body around on the stool to face me, a beer in his left hand.

"Miss me Amber?" Blake asked, with an eyebrow raised.

I let the words soak in for a minute, before I shrugged Troy's arm off my shoulders and launched myself into Blake's lap.

Chapter 10

Wrapping my arms around his neck, I asked, "And you're here why?" With a hint of excitement in my voice. I don't know why I felt so excited to see him. Maybe it was because I hadn't seen anyone for so long, or maybe it was because I just flat out missed him.

Blake grinned at me for a moment. My eyes took in his bruised skin; clearly, things weren't going as well as I had hoped.

"I heard you were on house arrest or something. You never told me you were the sister of the Shields." Blake raised an eyebrow as his hands wrapped around my back, while I sat on his lap.

Shrugging my shoulders, "I didn't see how it mattered. It's not like I am close to them or anything." I sent Blake my innocent smile.

A hand wrapped around my forearm.

"Off now," Cole growled, attempting to pull me off Blake.

"Back off Cole," Blake warned. Sighing, I loosened my grip around Blake's neck and slid off his lap.

I suppose I shouldn't have been near him anyway. "So what are you doing here?" I asked Blake, while looking down at his feet. I couldn't help but feel a sharp pain, feeling the love lost between us.

"Club business," Cole growled and shot Blake a look which said 'keep your mouth shut.'

"Fine. Whatever," I said lightly and went to sit on the stool next to Blake, pushing my black hair to the side so I could look at him more.

"How have you been Blake?" I asked, locking my eyes with his as he turned on his stool to face me.

"No time for chit chat. Let's get down to business. Amber stay here," Troy shot over his shoulder while walking in the direction of another room.

"Come on Amber." Blake stood up, grabbing my hand.

"Did you not hear her brother? She stays here," Jax snarled, standing in front of Blake, blocking our path to the room.

"Yeah Blake, it's cool." I smiled up at him, but Blake was tight and I noted the rage burning in his eyes as he narrowed them at Jax. Why was I getting the feeling this wasn't their first run in?

"You want the info, you need Amber, which is why I told you to bring her," Blake said, taking a step towards Jax. "Now move."

Blake's grip on my hand tightened and I gulped because I knew Blake's temper all too well, and Jax right now was just firing him up.

"What do you need me for?" I asked Blake, trying to take his attention away from Jax. Cole and the others had already moved in the same direction as Troy.

"Just leave it Jax. Let her come," Tyler yelled over his shoulder, while moving into the room.

I heard Jax grind his teeth before he turned his back to us and stormed off in the direction of the room. Blake pulled my hand, and we followed in.

The room was small, with a large table in the middle; chairs littered around it. The room seemed to have a permanent smoke ring above it. The boys seemed to have their own seats because they all sat at different places, as if seats had been assigned. Troy sat at the head of the table, Jax sat to his right, Cole to his left and then Adam, and Tyler sat down at the other end of the table.

I took the seat next to Cole and Blake sat next to me. Spike and Travis, two of Blake's boys, sat across from us, next to Jax.

"So to business," Troy said, turning in his seat to face Blake. "You have the information?" Troy lit up a cigarette and leaned back in his chair, waiting for Blake to speak.

"You get this information and we get the business on Whitehorse Road," Blake said with that determination I loved in his voice. He also lit up a cigarette.

"That's the deal," Troy said, letting out a puff of smoke.

Blake nodded his head and placed a hand on my thigh. "Amber, I need you to tell your brothers about Marty's crew."

Looking at Blake, I frowned, "What do they want to know?" Turning my head to look between Cole and Troy. "What is it you guys want to know?" I was still frowning at them.

"That's not part of the deal, Blake," Troy snarled, bringing his fist on the table. "You have to give us the information."

Blake shrugged his shoulders. "You said you get the information, I get the business. You didn't say who you had to get the information off. Anyway, Amber remembers more details than I do."

A smile twitched at the corners of my mouth, as I remembered Blake's memory. "Yeah, Blake does have a habit of forgetting things," I turned my attention back to the boys. "What is it you want to know?"

Troy narrowed his eyes at Blake, "You are saying that our sister has the information that we are paying you to hand over?"

I knew pretty much everything about everyone on the streets. It wasn't because I was in with all of them. I just remembered stuff, and I also had a lot of friends; and a lot of business connections.

"Not my fault you don't know your own sister," Blake said, before taking a drag of his cigarette.

"This is bullshit." Cole muttered under his breath, and took a large gulp from his open beer.

"You know it is still early in the morning right?" I said under my breath to him, eyeing the beer he was downing. Cole shot me a look saying 'who gives a shit.' Shrugging my shoulders, I added "Only thinking of your liver."

"So, Amber, what is it you know about Marty's crew?" Troy asked, stubbing his cigarette and narrowing his eyes at me. Like I couldn't possibly know a thing.

78

"What doesn't she know is more like it." Spike muttered to Travis, as they both shared a dark chuckle with each other.

Rolling my eyes, I started. "Thirty four members, last time I checked. Mainly into drug rings, cooking and selling. Marty works out of three factories and four houses... "

"They only work from houses. We know they don't have any factories," Cole piped in, adding a scoff at the end, as if I knew nothing.

Narrowing my eyes at him and turning in my seat, I continued, "They have three factories, all on Flinders Road. I can give you the addresses if you want, but that isn't their main trade anymore." I shot Cole a look.

"What's their main trade?" Troy asked, ignoring Cole's and my standoff.

Arching both eyebrows at him, I added, "Last time I checked, they were moving into running guns." Picking up the cigarette from Blake's fingers, I sucked on it lightly.

Leaning back in my chair, I continued, "They're aiming at taking the trade from the bikers. Like you guys." Blowing out a mouthful of smoke, I locked my eyes with Troy's. "I think a lot of the gangs are over. Only one bikie gang has control of the streets and the distribution of guns. "You think, or you know?" Jax shot at me from across the table. Dropping my eyes from Troy's and looking Jax dead in the eye, I said, "I know."

I jumped in my seat when Cole brought his fist down on the table. "Bloody snakes in the grass. We take them out now!" He was fuming next to me.

"You need to calm down Cole," I scoffed, and put the cigarette out.

"I want the addresses for the factories and the confirmed addresses for the houses." Troy shot at Blake, "Then the deal's done."

"The addresses weren't part of the deal." Blake was picking at the details; he narrowed his eyes at Troy "I'm not helping you."

Letting out a sharp sigh, I pulled my phone out of my pocket and bringing up Marty's information, I slid the phone to Troy.

"Amber!" Blake growled under his breath at me.

Turning in my seat and facing him directly, I said, "What Blake? You used me so you could get more business on the streets." I rose from my seat, pushing his hand off my thigh in the process, "and, at the end of the day, they're still my brothers."

Pushing the chair back and walking towards the door, I turned around, "Give that back to me when you're done." I pointed at Troy and the phone, while opening the door with my other hand.

"Amber. I—" Blake started, but just like always, I knew what he was going to say, so I cut him off.

"Yeah, I know you're sorry. Bye Blake."

I closed the door behind me and headed towards the bar. Slumping in a stool, I reached over and pulled out a bottle of vodka from behind the bar. I suppose somewhere in the world it was after midday.

Chapter 11

I was tapping my finger on the desk in Mr Woods' class; man, school sucked.

"Would you stop that?" Jax slammed his hand down over my finger. "Only you could make such an annoying noise."

Rolling my eyes, I took a shot at him, "Someone's nervous about the presentation."

"I'm not nervous," Jax removed his hand off my finger.

"I think someone's a little nervous," I taunted, enjoying the way Jax's jaw was clenching. "Public speaking not a strong point?"

"I don't get nervous," Jax exhaled sharply, and sent me an annoyed look.

"I think you do," I stated matter of factly, and began tapping again.

Jax shot my finger an annoyed look and then glared at me. "You can't help yourself, can you?".

Shrugging my shoulders, "Don't take your fear of public speaking out on me."

Jax huffed and I grinned to myself. It was just too easy to stir him up.

"You ready Jackson, Amber?" Mr Woods asked us as he stood to the side with his clipboard.

"Ready as ever," I replied with a grin. "I can start us off if you like Jax?"

Jax grunted, which I assumed was his reply. Clearing my voice and straightening up, I smiled at my dense classmates.

"Good morning everyone." My smile got slightly bigger. "This is mine and Jackson's report." I handed the piece of paper over to him.

Jackson took the paper and gave it a once over "Amber and I analyzed a soldier whose name was Captain John H Miller."

Jackson stopped, flipping the page over in his hand, and then turning to glare at me, lowering his voice. "Where's the rest?"

"That's it." I lowered my voice to match his.

Jackson's eyes narrowed into slits. "What do you mean that's it?" he hissed under his breath.

"I had to use the Internet to get that, be grateful," I shot back under my breath.

"Is there a problem Amber, Jackson?" Mr Woods frowned.

Jackson scoffed.

"Isn't that the name of a character off Saving Private Ryan?" A girl with glasses piped up from the front row.

"Yeah, she's right. Tom Hanks plays the character," a boy next to her affirmed.

I narrowed my eyes at both of them "Well, it's based on a true story."

"No it's not," the boy argued with me. I rolled my eyes; man, I could throttle this kid.

I could hear Jackson grinding his teeth. "You had one job," he hissed under his breath.

"I did more than you did. I researched that," I hissed back, while pointing at the piece of paper he was holding.

"Amber, Jackson, are you going to continue with your report?" Mr Woods asked, sounding annoyed.

"You mean you stole a name from a movie," Jackson scoffed at me. "You really put in effort."

"How was I meant to know it was a fictional character? It had a picture of soldiers next to it!"

"Unbelievable." Jackson tossed the piece of paper back to me.

"Amber, Jackson?" Mr Woods snapped.

"We're finished," I replied coldly, and smoothed out the wrinkles on the paper, which Jackson had crumpled the corners of.

"Are you two seriously telling me that that's your report? Those few sentences? And that the soldier you chose just happens to be the same as one from a hit movie?" Mr Woods snapped. "I cannot believe you two! Seats now. See me after class."

Jackson shot me a glare over his shoulder as I followed him back to our seats. "One job, that was all I gave you. One job," he muttered under his breath.

Rolling my eyes, I slumped down in the chair next to him. "You are over-reacting."

Jackson grunted and crossed his arms, watching as another pair stood at the front of the class, ready to begin their speech. I glared at them, realizing it was the same pair who had done me in earlier...

"It's their fault," I cursed in their direction, "if they had kept their mouths shut..."

"Yeah, because then your one line would have scored us a pass," Jackson grumbled next to me.

"I think they did it on purpose," I said, ignoring his lack of faith in my work. "They wanted us to fail."

Jackson shot me a plain look. "You're kidding me right?"

I shrugged my shoulders. "Let's see how they like it."

Jackson grunted "Can you ever take responsibility for your own actions?"

"Shut up, they're starting," I hissed under my breath, turning all my attention to them. "They enjoyed interrupting us. I want to return the favor."

"They didn't interrupt us, we were finished." Jax let out a short breath. "I really didn't need this."

"Would you shut up? I can't hear." The pair began, and I tapped my foot on the ground in anticipation, and that's when they said it.

"Our soldier's name is James Lee Williams."

"Objection!" I shot up from my seat and pointed a finger at them.

"Amber, would you sit back down. This isn't a debate," Mr Woods snapped at me "You're already in trouble as it is."

"Well they are lying! Am I not allowed to point that out?" I stated, arching an eyebrow.

"We are not!" the girl spat in my direction "We did our assignment, unlike some people we know." She placed a hand on her hip.

"Well, why is your soldier's name the same as the one from the very popular Xbox game?" I said firmly, planting both hands on the desk.

"What Xbox game?" the boy next to her shot in my direction. Bummer, I should have said a movie's name. This guy looked like the type who spent an unhealthy amount of time in front of a TV screen.

"Halo." That was a game right? Damn, why did I say an Xbox game!

The boy narrowed his eyes at me and got this weird freaky smile on his face. "There isn't a character in Halo with that name."

"I beg to differ." I saw the annoyance flicker across his face as I continued.

"I would know," he scoffed and stood proudly. "I own the game." The girl next to him shot him a proud smile.

"Why doesn't that surprise me?" I shot back at him, wiping that proud look from his face. Jackson let out a small grunt beside me.

"Enough Amber, sit back down," Mr Woods ordered me.

"Mr Woods, I think we should really Google this. I think they have cheated."

"The game is based on aliens," the boy snorted. "Do you know nothing?"

"Did you just snort?" I suppressed the laughter in my chest. "Here I was thinking only pigs did that."

"Amber, SIT DOWN!" Mr Woods roared.

I pointed an innocent finger at myself. "I haven't done anything!" I then pointed my finger in the boy's direction "He did, the one re-enacting animal noises!"

"SIT DOWN NOW!"

Grumbling, I slumped back down in my seat. Well that was unfair. Shooting the boy a dirty look, I brought my elbows up to the table and leaned my chin in my hands.

"That was a show. Feel stupid now?" Jackson hissed in my direction.

I shrugged my shoulders. "Did you see the kid's face? Priceless," I said. As I turned my head slightly, I saw Jackson's lips twitch ever so slightly.

"God this is boring," I mumbled, glancing at the clock "I'm not sitting here for another hour and a half, listening to drool."

The boy and girl began their speech again, and to me, now was as good a time as any to get kicked out.

"Mr Woods?" I rudely screamed across the classroom. I saw the vein in his temple throb.

"Amber, remain quiet."

"I can't."

Mr Woods slammed the clipboard down on the desk and turned his full attention to me "Why?"

"Because what I am hearing is completely and utterly boring."

"That's it. Get out and go to the Principal's office now!"

Smiling, I got up from my seat, noticing Jackson's smug look. "Jackson dared me to say it," I fired in Mr Woods's direction. If I was going down, he was coming with me.

Mr Wood turned his attention to Jax.

"Don't bring me into this!" Jackson shot up at me.

"Well Jackson, you can join Amber. Get out, both of you, now."

Smiling, I walked to the front of the class, with Jax grumbling behind me. Walking past the couple, I brought my hand back and slapped it down on the pieces of paper the boy was holding.

I smiled proudly as I watched the papers float down to the ground, scattering everywhere. "Oops, clumsy old me," I smiled innocently.

I continued walking, ignoring their empty threats.

"You're a real brat, you know that?" Jackson scoffed as we walked out into the empty corridor, slamming the door closed behind him.

"I got you out of class, didn't I?" I said as I shot him a grin over my shoulder. "You should be thanking me."

"Yeah, now we get to wait out the rest of the period in the café," he shot back at me.

I rolled me eyes. "Screw that, let's go."

"I can't."

"Why?" I turned to face him, frowning. "You want to go to the rest of your classes?"

Jackson gave me a blank look, like I was beyond stupid. "It's part of my parole," he informed me.

I couldn't help the grin that was beginning to spread across my face. "Did you do something naughty?"

"Shut up."

He began to storm away from me with his hands in his pockets.

"So you are like, on school arrest?" I asked, pushing for more information.

He didn't answer.

"Ok well, I have an idea," I said lightly, trying to keep pace with him. "I am sick, and you have to take me home."

Jackson scoffed, "Did you have to think about that one?"

Crossing my arms, I replied, "It's better than your ideas, like always."

Jax pushed the main door open, and as I skipped down the stairs behind him, fresh air slapped me in the face, immediately lifting my spirits. "Where we going?" I asked.

Jax ignored me as he continued to walk in the direction of the school car park. "We're using my idea, aren't we?" I grinned, and skipped up to his side. "Told you it was gold."

Jax rolled his eyes as he stopped at his bike. "Do you ever shut up?"

"Not when I know I'm annoying you."

Jax straddled his bike and handed me his helmet. He kick started the bike. Placing my hand on his shoulder, I swung my leg over his bike and sat down behind him. I gulped; man, he had a good body. I never saw him work out though; did he go to a gym?

As we began to pull away, I wrapped my arms around him. I attempted to suppress the feelings rising inside of me from clinging to his toned body. Why did Jax have to be so damn attractive? Did he know he had this pull on women? Because it couldn't just be me, right? Other women would have to admire his sharp features and toned body. In fact, I'm sure they did, remembering how his cheerleader friends acted around him.

Well, it didn't matter how attractive he was, I wasn't going there. Ever.

***

"So, I heard you got kicked out of class again huh Amber?" Troy asked me from across our dining table as we ate tea.

I turned sharply and gave Jax a dirty look. "Traitor."

Jax shrugged his shoulders and continued to eat. He had been acting weird since we'd got home. We had spent the whole day together - we did lunch, then I dragged him to the mall. Come to think of it, he'd begun to get weird after I dragged him into the changing rooms, because I didn't like the looks the retail assistant was sending me; man, that guy was a creep, I shuddered as I remembered.

Had I made him uncomfortable? I mean, he'd turned his back to me while I'd changed.

Then it occurred to me; how could I have been so stupid! The mirrors!

"Amber?"

I turned my attention back to Troy "What?" I was suddenly in a state of terror.

"Do you want to explain?" he took a sip of his beer.

"Do I have to?" I narrowed my eyes, "Can we not just drop it?"

"Will it happen again?"

"No dad, it won't," I mocked.

"Amber."

Letting out a small sigh, I loved getting kicked out of class, so I couldn't promise it wouldn't happen again. But I could lie; I was good at that. "It won't happen again, ok?" I stabbed the piece of steak on my plate. "Geez, get off my case."

Troy seemed to have dropped the subject, and he began to focus on his meal. I stole a glance in Jax's direction. He was eating with his eyes glued to his plate. Man, had he seen everything? It was my own fault, dragging him in there.

I remember my bra getting caught in the top I'd tried on, and I'd had to take it off. As the image came back to me, I began to choke on the piece of steak in my mouth.

A hard hand slammed across my back, and I spat the piece of steak into my plate.

"Can't you chew your food properly?" Cole pulled his hand from my back and returned to his own meal.

Blushing, I pushed the plate away from me. I was no longer hungry; I couldn't get over what I'd done!

"You finished?" Tyler asked, frowning at my close-to-full plate.

"Yeah, I'm not hungry. Big lunch," I lied and got up from my seat. I wasn't brave enough to look in Jax's direction. I just hoped he'd keep his mouth shut.

"What are you doing tonight? It's Friday night. No weekend plans?" Adam asked, attempting to make conversation with me.

"No plans," I replied quickly, too quickly in fact; which is why everyone's eyes snapped in my direction, apart from Jax's.

"Ok… what have you done now?" Troy asked, putting his fork down.

"What? I haven't done anything!"

"You're lying," Cole said, looking me up and down "Your voice is doing that thing, where it goes higher and borders on shrill."

"My voice doesn't get shrill," I snapped at him, "And I haven't done anything. I just want to go to bed."

The boys all exchanged glances with each other. They seemed to believe me because Cole turned back around in his seat and started eating again.

Exhaling sharply, I turned to leave the room.

"Oh, just a heads up Amber."

Coming to a halt in the door way, I turned my attention back to Troy. "Yeah?"

"We are having a party here tomorrow night. It may be a bit… large."

Excitement began to bubble up inside me. "Am I attending this party? Or am I to be locked up in my room?"

Troy shrugged. "You can if you want," he stated.

"Can I drink?" A real Saturday night was within my reach! I couldn't believe it. I longed to have a conversation with someone other the stupid students from that hell hole called school.

The boys exchanged another look amongst each other, as if they were sharing a conversation through their eyes.

"Don't see why not, we will all be here," Troy said slowly.

I couldn't stop my excitement. I fist pumped the air. "YES!"

Cole scoffed. "Child."

Rolling my eyes, I walked out of the room, but truth be told, I was so excited I had something to look forward to.

***

I threw another shot down my throat. Man, had I missed this! Shaking my hips and waving my hands in the air. This was what I called a good Saturday night.

The music was pounding through the speakers; its thick beat rumbled through the whole house.

And I had somehow ended up with a guy. One minute I was throwing shots, the next I had hands on my hips.

We danced. We grinded. And his hands hadn't stopped exploring my body. The only reason I hadn't pushed him away was because he was devilishly handsome and reminded me of someone, but I couldn't put my finger on whom.

Pulling away for air, I leaned my head on his shoulder. Why hadn't I seen this guy before? My back arched and I pressed my chest into him as he kissed down my neck.

"Want to find a room?" he whispered hotly into my ear, while nibbling my earlobe.

Pulling my hands away from his neck, I found his hand and began to drag him through the crowd of people.

I was being a whore right now, wasn't I? But hey, I hadn't been with anyone since Blake, and it was time to move on; maybe a fling was just what I needed.

Walking up the stairs with him in tow, I was glad I hadn't crossed paths with my brothers in a while. As for Jax, he was going out of his way to avoid me. Last I'd seen him; he was locking lips with a blonde.

"What's your name, cutie?"

I turned my head over my shoulder. This guy couldn't keep from running his eyes up and down my body. Looks like not hitting the gym off late hadn't done too much damage.

"Amber," I sang back, turning on my heels and placing a hand on his shoulder, at the top of the stairs. "Yours?"

"Jason," he answered, with a cocky grin on his face.

Raising an eyebrow at his sudden smile, I turned back and dragged him in the direction of my room.

As I placed a hand on my door knob, Jason spun me around, kissing me with force against the door. I gave up trying to open the door and, smiling at his bold move, I wrapped my arms around his neck.

He moved a hand down my back and, when it rested on my lower back, me pinned to his chest, he expertly flung the door behind me open.

Flipping me around, he kicked the door closed with his foot, not breaking our kiss. I heard the dull slam of my bedroom door. Grinning against my lips, he gripped both my thighs and brought me up in the air, wrapping my legs around him. Pulling his lips from mine, the cheeky grin on his face made me smile.

"Now babe, don't forget my name. Jason. You can scream it all night."

Laughing with him, I shook my head lightly and then pressed my lips back against his. I didn't care about tomorrow, or how bad I may feel.

I let myself get lost in the feel of his touch.

***

My eyes fluttered open and a small groan escaped my lips as I brought my hand up to comfort my head. I hated the morning after an amazing night.

Turning to my side, my head fell comfortably on a hard chest. Jason's. His arm was lightly wrapped around my waist, as he slept on his back.

A small smile crept on my lips. He was one of the funniest guys I had ever met, and he really had kept me up most of the night.

My bedroom door flung open and I screamed; a toe curling scream. Jason bolted up, pulling his arm from under me. My jaw snapped shut, sending my teeth into my tongue. I rolled onto my back, pain shooting through my mouth.

I saw Jason do a sweep of the room, looking for a threat. Finally, his body seemed to relax as he took in the person in the doorframe.

"Shit, Jax. Mate, what you doing?" Jason ran a hand thought his shaggy blond hair and let out a relief coated sigh. I couldn't help but stare at his tanned, well-built body.

Cocking my head to the side, I looked around Jason's bare back. Sure enough, Jax stood in my room, grinding his teeth, his eyes narrowed.

"Why are you in my room?" I raised my eyebrow.

"Why are you naked?" he shot back.

Gulping, I glanced down at myself and cursed as I reached for my sheets.

Jason, however, had thought about this a second before me, because he'd already flung my sheet over my body.

"I will only be a sec mate," Jason replied in Jax's direction as he pulled the covers off himself and searched for his clothes.

Wait. They knew each other?

Jason pulled his jeans up and then turned to frown at me "Wait. Did you say this was your room?"

"Are you dense?" I asked seriously. "Whose room did you think it was?

Jason chuckled lightly to himself as he pulled his t-shirt over his head. "I thought we just crashed it."

I narrowed my eyes and looked around Jason, at Jax. "You didn't answer my question. Why are you in my room? You know it is rude to just burst into someone's room."

Jax rolled his eyes and crossed his arms over his chest. "We didn't know where you were."

"Well, good thing you started your search in my room," I replied sarcastically.

"Oh you found her. I was…"

Tyler poked his head into my room, giving Jason a once over before grinning in my direction. "Did you get lucky last night, Amber?"

Groaning, I fall back into my pillows, keeping the sheets tightly wrapped around me. "Could you all piss off?"

Tyler's laugh ripped through my ears and I shot a glare in his direction. "Some of us are hungover you know."

Jason leaned across and planted a kiss on my forehead. I blushed slightly; that was incredibly sweet. "Thanks for last night cutie." He sent me a charming grin.

"Amber just got the kiss of death," Jax grunted.

Jason rolled his eyes and sent me a wink as he pulled away from the bed. "Oh cutie, do you want my number?"

I suppressed my smile "I don't do phone numbers. Sorry."

"Burnt." Tyler laughed. I saw the smirk on Jax's face, which fueled my next move.

"But, in your case, why not?" I smiled at Jason.

Jason sent me a wicked grin, as if he knew why I was doing this.

"You can get my number off Jackson. I was forced to give it to him a while ago." I smiled sweetly after seeing the annoyed look that crossed Jax's face.

"You call him Jackson?" Jason asked with an eyebrow raised. "The parents don't even call you that."

Jax gritted his teeth and turned his back to walk away. Jason grinned as he followed him out. "See you Amber, nice to have met you," he shot over his shoulder before walking out of the room.

Tyler however, had other ideas, as he strolled into my room, planting his butt on the edge of my bed.

"And you would be in here, why?" I asked him, holding the sheets up to my chest. "You know I'm not dressed right?"

Tyler shrugged his shoulders and shot me a smirk "You and Cole are more alike than I thought."

I narrowed my eyes at him. "You can go now," I said, pointing a finger in the direction of the door.

"You both woke up with last night's mistakes in your beds;" Tyler chuckled lightly "Didn't peg you as the type Amber."

Holding the sheet to my chest with one arm, I threw a pillow at his head.

"ADAM!" Tyler screamed with amusement as he dodged my attack. I was horrified to watch my other brother walk through my door.

"GET OUT!" I screamed.

"Amber woke up with Jason."

Adam scoffed "You didn't?" he took in my face for a moment then scanned the messed up bed. "Of all the guys… " he said, shaking his head.

"Would both of you get out of my room? I AM NAKED!"

"Who's naked?" Troy strolled into my room, like he owned the joint.

"GET OUT!"

Troy gave me an annoyed glance. "I am guessing you're the nude one."

Letting out a sharp sigh, I screeched. "Everyone get the hell out of my room! NOW!"

"She slept with Jason," Tyler piped in, humor in his voice.

"Why does it matter who I slept with?" I frowned "Why do you keep telling people that?"

"You know who he is right?" Tyler asked, raising an eyebrow.

"No. I know his name. Jason."

Tyler, Adam and Troy all shot glances at each other, before bursting out laughing; I felt like it was at my expense.

"What is so funny?" I snapped crossing my arms over my chest. "Clearly I am missing something."

I glared at my brothers; they looked so childish. If you only looked at them when they laughed and disregarded the tattoos and scars, they were awfully cute and endearing.

Troy seemed to pull himself together, as he said, "This is just too good."

Rolling my eyes and huffing, I added, "Fine, don't tell me."

"I'll give you a hint Amber." Tyler's laughter slowly dried, but the grin still wide on his face. "His last name is Johnston."

I frowned. What did that have to do with anything? But then it hit me, like a cold slap across my face. My eyes went wide. "He's Jackson's brother?!"

Chapter 12

This wasn't going to be awkward; I told myself as I walked out the front door, closing it gently behind me. I was prepared to face Jax.

I hadn't seen Jax or any of my brothers for the rest of the weekend. I couldn't believe my luck when I heard their bikes kick off, and they didn't return all weekend.

"Sup Sis?" Tyler smiled, and I was pulled from my thoughts.

"Morning Tyler." My eyes glanced over the other four empty bikes. Where were the rest of them? "Where are the others?"

Tyler straddled his black motorbike "Sleeping. We didn't get in until late."

"Then why aren't you sleeping?" Now taking in his slightly bloodshot eyes and pale face. It was clear he hadn't slept much.

"Got the shortest straw." Tyler grinned. "Come on; let's get your butt to school."

He didn't look like he was up to riding that thing. "Go to bed Tyler. I can take myself to school."

"Nope, no way. Troy will kill me, right after Cole bashes me."

"Tyler, I think my life is more in danger if I get behind you on that death trap. Go to bed. I can get myself to school."

"Not happening."

"Tyler, GO TO BED! Have you even slept at all?" Now that I thought about it, I didn't hear the bikes come back last night which meant they must have got in early this morning. "Wait, you don't have to tell anyone. Just go back in and go to bed."

I opened my handbag and began looking for the car keys.

Tyler frowned but I could see he was caving. "The guys will kill me."

"Tyler, I managed to get myself to school before you, believe me, I can do it now."

I turned my back on him and began to walk up the porch in the direction of the garage, still looking through my bag.

"Um, Amber?"

Turning around I saw Tyler leaning his bike back down. "Yeah Ty?"

I saw his lips twitch slightly; I couldn't believe I had just called him that. I used to when I was little, and it just slipped out now.

"Cole. He had a run in with someone last night. Nothing too serious, but when you get home, could you have a look at him? I know he's too proud to ask you himself."

"Sure, when I get home." I smiled slightly and turned back on my heel. Today I would go to school and I would stay there, not because I wanted to. Hell no. But I didn't want to get Tyler into trouble and I couldn't believe that I was willing to stay at school all day, just for him.

I was going soft.

***

I had to park my Hummer four blocks away from school. So, not only did I go to school, but I also walked to get there.

I shook my head at my own softness; I was getting pathetic. I was on my way home, heading down the highway, perhaps a little over the speed limit. Today only reminded me of how much I really hated school. The teachers were smelly and the students were ruled with hormones and were full of useless information.

Like today, when I was sitting behind Amy in math, she was telling her friend all about how Josh, one of Jax's little school friends, had taken her to the movies, and then they even did dinner! Oh the excitement!

Glancing in the reverse mirror, I noticed how the same gray sedan was on my tail. The mirrors were tinted a deep black, making it impossible to make out the driver. That was what caused me to put my foot down harder on the accelerator. That tint wasn't legal; which gave me a bit of insight into the driver. This was no soccer mom tailing me.

The car automatically matched my speed, keeping pace with me. I didn't recognize the car. The highway was close to dead, and we ended up flying down the road.

I was still a while from home, and I knew I couldn't go home now, not with a tail on me. I glanced at the fuel gauge; three quarters of a tank.

The car suddenly swung around, and slammed on the brakes, sending me off the road and into the dirt on the side. I was grateful our highway had endless dirt on each side and the trees were a few distance away; or this might have been the end of me.

I slammed my foot down on the accelerator first chance I got, and shot off in the direction of the city. I looked behind me, and noticed that my tail had also spun around to chase me.

I pushed the pedal to the metal, and was grateful for the magnificent machine I'd been handed to drive.

I saw a reflection against my mirror. Shit. I saw the large silver gun now being pushed out a side window. My reflexes kicked in; my back arched and my ears rung as a bullet shattered my back window.

I flung open my glove box. No gun. Shit, I was unprotected.

Swinging my car down the first street as we turned off the highway, my tires squealed and the Hummer had a slight body roll. I attempted to keep it under control, although I lost all control when the bullet flew through my back window.

I was in trouble; I reached over and tipped out my handbag, desperately looking for my phone and I was doing all of this while speeding down a residential street, with parked cars lining each side.

Unlocking the phone, I scrolled down the list until I reached Cole's number. Cole would answer; he always did. The others I wasn't too sure; Troy was a heavy sleeper.

I swung the car sideways as another bullet shot into the car. Any minute now, the guys would target the tires, and that's when the shit would hit the fan for me.

"Hello?" His voice was husky and full of sleep.

"Cole, I'm being shot at."

Another bullet sailed through a side window, shattering it.

"Amber, what the hell was that?" Cole now sounded awake as he screamed in alarm.

"I just said someone was shooting at ME!"

As soon as I said that, the car jerked as the back tire caught a bullet. "SHIT! They just got my back tire."

"Where are you?"

I frantically looked for a street sign; I was going to be rolling to a stop anytime now. "Grant Street, half way up. Cole, they just got my other back tire."

I heard the dull stomping of his feet as he ran down the stairs "How many are their?"

"Can't see, the car is heavily tinted." The Hummer was slowing down.

"What color?"

"Gray. They're shooting Shotguns spa 12's, from what I can tell."

"How much speed have you lost?" I heard the dull throwing of something from his end.

"I will be coming to a halt in a few seconds." I glanced at the gray car; they were happy crawling alongside. I spoke seriously into the phone. "Cole, I have a feeling I'm not going to be here long once I stop."

I gulped slightly, not liking the idea of facing off with whoever it was, with no gun or back up. I was still a girl after all; it's not like I could overpower a guy. Sure, I could give him a few good punches, but that was about it.

99

"We're coming."

"What, how did you get the others up?"

Cole ignored my question "As soon as the car stops, run."

I knew that was what I'd have to do; I wasn't going to sit here and wait for them to come and get me out of the car. But I wasn't exactly in top shape at the moment; I mean my body was great but my fitness level, not so much.

"Cole!" I exclaimed.

I heard the roar of a motorbike. "We're coming Amber." His voice was stern and I heard how pissed off he was. I didn't envy these guys when my brothers found them. They would be ticked off enough just for being dragged out of bed.

The phone died, and nerves began to bubble in my stomach. I exhaled sharply; it was time to focus. The boys would still be a bit off, even with their crazy riding.

The Hummer was squealing as there was no rubber left on the tire. Time to run like there was no tomorrow. I forced the steering wheel to turn as I went in the direction of a footpath, a park just behind it. The Hummer was barely rolling as I pushed open my door and launched myself out of it.

I heard the Hummer crash into a tree that lined the footpath, but I didn't look back as my feet hit the pavement, jumping over a bench and darting into the park. I was already out of breath.

Cole

The motorbikes roared as we sped down the highway. Our usual formation lost as I took lead next to Troy. Our formation, rules and politics of riding forgotten, we all fled down the highway.

The street was now in view. My grip tightened around the bars; Amber was in deep shit.

Jax took off in front of us, and he turned sharply down Grant Street. We swung around everything in our way, as we all ripped up Grant Street.

Our fatigue now forgotten, our bodies clicked into overdrive; we had rage fueling us.

Spotting Amber's Hummer, we slowed down. Slammed into a tree, the motor was still running when we pulled up to it.

"Where is she?" Adam yelled over the roar of the bikes. The driver's door was hanging open and the car was riddled with bullets.

A gray car was parked behind it, all four doors hanging open. Four doors, four people, which meant four blokes, were chasing Amber.

Grinding my teeth, I stated matter of factly, "We need to find her."

Troy's eyes were narrow as he looked the car over. "You know whose this is?" he snapped in our direction, half in rage, half disgust.

My lips tightened in a firm line; of course I knew who was responsible.

Jax ripped up the curb with his bike and took off through the park, not waiting for us to confirm a plan of action. We all knew that Amber was in deep trouble and it was our fault; we were responsible for this.

Revving my bike, I took off after him, and I heard the boys follow. Amber would have to be close. Tearing through the park, I came to a stop next to Jax as we reached the corner. He nodded his head in the direction of an alley, and we tore off down the narrow path but the bikes were too bulky, so Jax screeched his to a sudden halt, yanked the key, and shot off down the path on foot.

I ran after Jax, pulling the gun out of the back of my jeans.

Jax was a good few feet ahead of me. Our feet echoed through the alley, and I could hear Jax curse out loud.

He came to a sudden halt, and I practically ran into his back. I looked around and my stomach dropped. There Amber was, on the ground, leaning against the wall, her head in her hands.

She was breathing heavily. Jax kneeled down beside her; I had never seen him so gentle towards a girl before. It's not like he was violent or anything; he usually just didn't care enough.

The rest of the boys came up shortly behind me. I moved back slightly so they could look around me.

"Amber," Jax said, trying to get her to look up, but part of me didn't want to see the damage they had done to her.

Slowly, she pulled her head up, and I was relieved when I saw her face clear of blood. Only tears streaked her cheeks.

Though the pain was clear in her eyes; what had they done?

I found myself grinding my teeth again; we should have been here sooner. I knelt down to face her, and pushed Jax slightly to the side. I ignored the daggers he shot me.

Amber was my sister.

"Can you walk?" I lowered my voice to her as I attempted to hide my rage. When we found these guys, they would be dead; and that wasn't a figure of speech.

"Yes," she muttered through broken tears. I had never seen Amber cry. Sure, we had seen her fake tears, but these tears were real. My blood boiled because I knew they were tears of pain. And it was our entire fault.

I pushed my gun into the band of my jeans and pulled my t-shirt over it. I wrapped an arm around her back and pulled her body up with mine.

She stumbled into my chest and a dull wave of sobs emanated from her. Her legs were weak under her, and I held her body up against mine.

I exchanged a look with Troy; what had happened here? Amber slowly pulled away from me. Looking down at her pale face, I saw it wince in pain.

My t-shirt clung to my body, slightly damp from her tears. I broke eye contact with her long enough to look down at my shirt, and I saw it covered in deep, crimson stains. Blood stains.

Worried, I glanced at Amber. Her black t-shirt didn't show any signs of blood, but it did look damp up close.

Amber's knees buckled, and she stumbled backwards, but, before I could reach her, Jax swept her up in his arms, lifting her off the floor.

"We should get her a hospital," he said firmly, and I saw the desperation in his eyes. He was just as angry as me, and he truly cared for her.

"Has she been shot?" Tyler asked worried, staring at the blood that soaked my top.

"I don't know," I frowned, voice filled with concern.

"I can't go to the hospital," she whimpered. I had never heard pain in my sister's voice and it took a knife through my heart. The bastards would be dead when we found them, and I knew the boys were thinking the same as me.

"You need to go to the hospital," Jax snapped back, the anger clear in his voice. "You don't have a choice."

"Take me home, you guys will have to deal with this." Her voice was wavering as she fought to stay awake. "The police will get involved, when they see all this. You... we can't go..." her eyelids were fluttering closed.

"See what?" Adam frowned. "She's about to pass out."

But Adam was wrong. She had already passed out; her body limp in Jax's arms.

"What should we do?" Tyler asked. "She looks bad."

"We don't even know what they have done. What if they rap...?"

"Don't say it," Jax snapped with venom in his voice.

"We take her home," I spoke up, cutting into the conversation. "It's what she asked us to do."

Troy nodded his head, keeping his jaw clenched. "Fine. Tyler, go figure out a car. We can't take her back on the bikes. Adam, you go with Tyler, and keep pressure on her stomach. We will work out the rest when we are home. I'll call the club, get some of the guys to ride the other bikes home and clean up the Hummer."

We all nodded our heads.

"I will stay with Amber. Adam you can ride back," Jax said, Amber's limp body in his arms.

Nobody questioned his wanting to stay with Amber; right now we had to get her home. I would bring it up with him later. I didn't like the unhealthy attraction he seemed to have to my sister because, when it came down to it, Jax was more dangerous than all of us put together.

Chapter 13

Cole

"Where should we put her?" Tyler snapped, holding the front door open for Jax. Clearly, their ride in together had not gone well.

"Kitchen?" Adam frowned. "We don't even know what the problem is yet, or how bad it is."

Jax didn't wait for our discussion to continue; instead, he walked clean past us with Amber in his arms, and headed in the direction of the kitchen.

Jax was acting like she was his. I had never seen him protective of a female, but, right now, he was protective of Amber.

Biting my tongue, I followed him. Jax put his back to the door and gently swung it open. Using more force than needed, I slammed my fist against the other door to open. This only caused a shooting pain up my arm; my injuries from yesterday, still taking a toll on my body.

Adam spread out a few clean towels across the stainless steel bench and then Jax lowered Amber's body onto them. It really bugged me, the way he was being so gentle with her; he never looked at a woman the way he kept looking at Amber.

Grabbing a pair of scissors from the counter, I shouldered Jax out of the way. I ignored his tight posture and his glare. Reaching for the hem of Amber's top, I waited for Jax to remove the jumper he was holding to her stomach. "Move it," I snapped at him.

Troy and Tyler stormed in; Tyler holding the case Amber had used a few weeks ago on me. When Tyler placed the case on the bench next to me, Jax finally decided to pull the jumper away. As soon as he did, blood began to spurt from her wound and stain the white towel underneath her.

Slowly, I cut the fabric up the middle and then along the base of her bra; leaving the fabric covering her chest. Dropping the scissors to my side, I slowly peeled the fabric from her body, which was now stuck to her stomach because of the blood. I peeled away the other side as well, frowning until her entire midriff was exposed. I let out a gruff of rage, and my brothers joined me.

"They're dead!" Troy spat, bringing a fist down on the bench. "They're FU-"

"ENOUGH!" I yelled at him. Amber was bleeding out right now; we could deal with the threats and killing later. "Get me the threads and needles."

My eyes drifted to the large wound on Amber's stomach. Two lines ran from each hip bone and then met in the middle of her abdomen, to make an arrow, pointing up. To most people, this wound wouldn't have been symbolic, but to us, it immediately spelt 'enemy'.

The mark of a warring bikie group, it was the biggest form of insult, to mark someone with this; especially when their blood and loyalty lay elsewhere. Exhaling sharply, I realized this was going to scar, and for the rest of Amber's life, she would be marked with their sign.

"Move," Jax hissed at me, "I'll do it." He reached for the needle in my hand. I turned to glare at him and narrowed my eyes.

"Don't tell me what to do."

"Cole, give me the needle. You can't sew for shit. I'm covered with scars to prove it." He snapped at me.

Curling my free hand into a fist, I retorted, "You never sew."

"Yeah, because I don't give a shit if you guys are covered in scars."

"But you care if Amber is?" I arched an eyebrow to make my point.

"Cole, just give him the needle." Troy snapped. "If Jax can do a better job, then let him. We don't want to make Amber's scar any worse than it needs to be."

Grumbling, I handed him the needle and stepped back. I never said I was the master of sewing; it's just that I was usually the one who got stuck with the job.

I watched as Jax took in Amber's cold, limp body, before he exhaled sharply and began to thread the needle through her skin. Adam was on the opposite side of the bench, holding a towel on the wound and moving it down as Jax sewed.

Crossing my arms, I watched how delicately he was threading the needle through her. Jackson Johnston, the leader of Satan's Sons, the Head MC, had a crush on my sister.

I had to suppress the growl growing inside me and clenched my fists, stopping myself from charging at him and slamming him across the kitchen, away from her. If he thought we were going to let him be with her, he had another thing coming.

We were here to get her back on track, not to hook her up with our bikies' leader MC. I scoffed, inviting glares from Troy and Tyler. The other two were too focused on Amber to care about anything else.

I took Amber in. Sleeping with his brother was one thing, but Amber was never getting close to Jax, and he definitely was not getting in her pants, I decided. Jax is a good guy sure, and one of my closest friends. That's why I wouldn't stop or think twice before cutting his penis off to keep him away from my sister.

Because I knew him, and knew what he was capable of.

***

"Is he still in there?" Tyler whispered to me, as I rolled my eyes.

"Go in if you are interested," I shot back, lighting up a cigarette outside Amber's door. I didn't give a toss about what dad thought about smoking in the house right now.

"You will set the alarms off again," Adam said, frowning at my cigarette. I gave him a 'shut the hell up' look.

I pulled my phone out. It was nearly three in the morning! It took Jax over an hour to sew her up. When he was done, he had carried her up to her bedroom, which had been hours ago.

I glanced at the closed door. He had another thing coming if he believed we would just leave him in there with her.

I had watched him take his time sew her up. I had seen the protection in his eyes, as well as something else - something I had never seen in his eyes.

And I had known Jax for a long time. So it was fair to say I knew most of his expressions. But the expression on his face as he sewed Amber up – well, it was new.

Turning around, I pushed the door open. The room was in darkness, and then my eyes adjusted. Jax was sitting in a chair he had pulled up to Amber's bed side. Sitting there with his arms crossed, his eyes were narrowed as I strolled into the room.

Adam and Tyler were on my tail, like scared puppies or something. Walking to Amber's balcony door, I cracked it open, tossed the cigarette to the ground, and then stomped on it. Closing the door behind me, I walked back to Amber's bed. Her face was pale, and if it wasn't for the slow rising and falling of her chest, she could pass for a corpse.

Tyler kneeled at the opposite side of the bed from Jax, and took Amber's hand in his.

"What are we going to do?" He whispered, stroking the back of Amber's hand.

"We do nothing," Jax grunted. "I'll take care of it. It's my fault."

"Your fault?" I arched an eyebrow.

Jax didn't look at me; he just kept his eyes on Amber. "They saw me with her at the mall. Clearly, they made a connection between the two of us, and after what we did the other night, Amber got serviced with my payback."

"That was a club vote," I pointed out. "We all made that choice."

108

"And we will all be dealing with this," Adam huffed. "She's our sister Jax. Our flesh and blood has taken the hit. This is personal."

Running my hand through my short hair, I took a deep breath. "He's right. We all deal with this together. As a club."

"Amber has been scarred because of us. She is probably going to wear that mark for the rest of her life," Troy piped in from the door. I hadn't even noticed him come in. I watched him step out of the shadows. "She has been marked; we all know what that means for her."

My lips tightened as I attempted to suppress the rage within. "So what do we do?" I spoke up to the room.

"We take a club vote, pull the boys in." Troy said firmly "Then decide on payback."

"There won't be payback."

I snapped my head around to look at Jax, and stared in disbelief. He was kidding right? Us Shields wouldn't just sit back and take this; not when one of our family had been hurt.

"We show a united front. Call all MC's and pull in our alliances. I'm declaring a war." Jax's voice echoed around the room.

War. A full bloody bikie war? Over this?

"Over this?" I choked out, not meaning to speak out loud. "Why?"

"It's been coming for a while. I had chosen to ignore the threat but The Pythons have been invading our runs, stealing business from us. It's time they were dealt with."

Jax was high up enough to declare a war, and all brothering clubs would have to follow his orders.

Everything Jax had just said was the truth, but we wanted to call this what it really was. Jax was ticked off because someone he cared about had got hurt because, for the first time, Jax actually had someone to care about, and, as luck would have it, it was our sister.

Chapter 14

Cole

"This doesn't make sense," I hissed at Troy as he closed his bedroom door and we were finally alone. "You and I both know what this means for the club."

"We can't challenge Jax," Troy said, as he ran a hand through his hair. He pulled out a cigarette. "He's got a thing for Amber."

"You're telling me," I scoffed, crossing my arms. "We need to send her away or something. Get her away from him."

"Like Amber will do anything we say," Troy shot at me, giving me a pointed look as he lit his cigarette. "We will just have to monitor this. Hook him up with someone else, in front of Amber. Show her he's bad news."

"Bad news! Is that what you call him?" I arched an eyebrow. "He's the most powerful man in bikie history, because of his family, and he's only bloody 18! He's only going to get more powerful as he gets older."

"Jax is never faithful to women; it's not in his blood," He responded, blowing smoke out the side of his mouth. "We don't have to worry about it too much; he will stuff it up on his own."

I settled into an armchair. "Amber's going to be sick when she wakes up. That scar is going to ruin her life."

"I have never seen one cut in before; usually they just tattoo it." Troy frowned. "But they obviously didn't have time for that."

"She has the scar of The Pythons on her stomach and the tattoo of the HellBound on her shoulder. It's fair to say she's a marked woman," I scoffed, running both hands over my head. "We stuffed up, Troy. We shouldn't have left her here."

"How were we meant to know, Cole?" Troy put his cigarette out on his bedside table. "We didn't know she would get involved with a gang member. When I checked in with dad, he said she was fine."

"I didn't even recognize her," I muttered, recalling back to the night I had actually forgotten what my sister looked like. "If I'd recognized her back then, all this could have been avoided." That one night, where Amber approached me and I didn't even fucking realize it was her. If I could turn back time and I hadn't lost contract with my sister, I would have known then - that she was getting into a lifestyle I wanted her to never have a part of.

"Well, we will stop it from getting any worse. We're here now. We can't change the past."

"We go on about family," I looked Troy square in the eye. "We respect the brotherhood, we are loyal members. We pledge that family means everything but we turned our backs on our own sister to build our own charter. Now we are one of the strongest charters. Hell, we've got bloody Jackson Johnston riding with us. But, at what cost? Amber lays scarred and we failed to protect her."

"What do you want me to say, Cole," Troy huffed. "Business came before her? We know that was how it was. We chose the charter. We can't change that."

Staring each other in the eye, we both remained silent.

"If an all-out war is declared, we won't be able to keep an eye on Amber," I thought out loud.

"I know," Troy shot back at me. "But it is blood in, blood out. We can't turn our back on our brothers, or on the brotherhood. We ride, we die. You know that."

"So Amber fends for herself?"

"Not while Jax has this thing for her," Troy pointed out, "And we will just have to keep a close eye on her; the four of us. We can work it out."

111

"One day at a time then," I muttered, rubbing my eyes with the back of my palms. I was beginning to feel my lack of sleep catching up with me, especially now.

"Get some sleep," Troy said as he pulled his boots off. "While you can."

Nodding my head, I pulled myself up from the chair. Sleep sounded good. I could return to worrying in the morning.

***

Amber

Every breath I took hurt. As my lungs opened for air, my stomach clenched in pain. My eyes fluttered open; it was the dead of the night. I noticed the empty arm chair next to my side of the bed.

One of my brothers must be skipping watch. My teeth slammed together as I twisted to my side. I heard my door open, and I quickly closed my eyes. I wasn't up to speaking to anyone. I would just break down in tears.

The armchair creaked as a body slumped into it. I felt guilty; whoever it was should go get some sleep. I heard him exhale softly; he was clearly tired. I heard the muffled vibration of a phone, and he cursed under his breath before I heard him pull it out of his pocket. I kept my breathing shallow, knowing if I inhaled too deeply, I would end up screaming in pain.

"What?" he half whispered, half barked into the phone.

I had to keep myself from snapping my eyes open in shock. Why was Jax in my room? And why was he willingly sitting here watching over me? Had my brothers blackmailed him into this?

"This isn't a good time," he hissed into the phone. "Call back in the morning." He paused.

"Fine, "he continued, "it better be bloody important if it can't wait."

I couldn't believe he was actually keeping his voice low. Was he doing that so he wouldn't wake me?

"I told you dad, I didn't have a choice," he barked into his phone. "Like I said before, it is in the best interest of the club."

He fell silent for a moment, and I felt his eyes on me. Inhaling quickly, I twisted my shoulder without thinking, and a deep frown appeared on my face. It took all my self-control to not wince in pain. How could such little movement cause so much agony?

"Hold on a minute," Jax shot into the phone. I heard him place his phone on the bedside table.

Suddenly, the blankets on me disappeared, and goosebumps ran up my legs as the cold air suddenly hit me.

Jax placed a hand under my shoulder, half in the air, and then threaded his other hand under my side. His breathing was thick as he softly twisted me back over.

I couldn't believe how gentle he was being! Now more comfortable, I lay on my back. I actually could take a breath in without cringing in pain. His hands left my body quickly and he covered me back up with the blankets.

I felt him lift the mattress as he tucked the blankets in. What on earth had got into him?

"You still there?" his voice shot into the phone. "You don't need to remind me where you are," he spat, bitterness in his tone.

The room fell silent and all I could hear was his sharp breathing.

"I know. Blood in, blood out," Jax said coolly into the phone. "I won't forget."

He barked a bye into the phone and hung up. If I was the person who had just called him, I wouldn't be calling back. Was Jax always that rude to people?

A stray piece of hair flew across my eye, and it annoyed me immediately. I was considering just giving in and letting Jax know I was awake, but then I felt his fingers gently brush the stray strand away, and I still couldn't believe this was the same Jax!

"I'm really sorry Amber," I heard him mutter, sitting by my side.

He was sorry? For what? Was the attack linked back to them? Who was I kidding; I knew it was. So that was why Jax had stayed at my side. Guilt really was capable of changing a man.

Jax

I watched a frown appear on her face again as she took a staggered breath in. Breathing was hurting her. I could tell from the frown on her face every time she took a breath in.

I sat back, feeling completely like shit.

I never let anyone get close for this reason. I don't have connections. I just have the brotherhood, and they could all look after themselves when it came to it.

They weren't a weakness.

I should have known The Pythons were watching me. They'd seen me with her at the mall. I was never seen with a girl. Maybe at the clubhouse, but that was it.

Never let anyone get close. That was the one thing dad had taught me before he went to prison and got a life sentence, and I became The King.

The Pythons have been wanting blood for years now. First, they invaded our street; started dealing where we were dealing. Little things that we could argue over.

Sure I got threatened. Every man with bikie blood knew I was the King, and being the King meant everyone, even Troy, answered to me.

Every charter. Every member. Answered to me.

Thanks to dad.

Sometimes, I don't know whether being born into this was a blessing or a curse. Look at Jason; he'd shrugged off the lifestyle, but dad picked me. Groomed me. Wanted me to take over from him.

So I did as soon as he went down for a crime he actually committed when he was young. His first kill ended up getting him arrested, thanks to new evidence.

I lit up another cigarette, my eyes on Amber.

I couldn't even look her in the eye after the mall, but I knew as soon as I saw her naked body, I wanted her.

Even in her underwear, she sent my fantasies into overdrive, and then she went and took off her bra, giving me a sight I will never forget.

I doubted she realized there had been a mirror.

And I watched her change. I couldn't take my eyes off her, even though it would have been the right thing to do. Still, I didn't do it.

And then when she was dressed again, I couldn't get the image of her naked breasts out of my head. The image was on repeat in my head. So much so, I couldn't look her in the eye.

At the house party, I'd attempted to get my need for her, and my frustration, out on another woman, but that didn't work.

Then I went into panic mood when the boys said she was missing. I blamed myself again, because I should have kept an eye on her during the night. Her brothers stopped watching her as soon as the girls showed up.

Then when I did find her, I find her in bed with my brother. I scoffed out loud and then regretted it when I saw her frown. Shit. I didn't want to wake her up.

How did Jason manage to score the one woman I couldn't lock down?

As much as I wanted Amber, there was a reason I kept her at a distance. The reason I didn't make a move. The reason I kept my hands and thoughts to myself.

I inhaled on my cigarette. It was all pointless in the end, because she'd ended up getting hurt because of me.

And I wasn't there to protect her. Fuck, I had pushed her away! I didn't speak to her. Didn't even acknowledge her.

And when my enemy makes a move, and hits my weakness, I'm not there to protect my weakness.

How screwed up is that?

I watched her frown again.

115

It was worse knowing she was in pain and there was nothing I could do about it. Her case was out of morphine and painkillers. I'm guessing thanks to Cole; she had given them all to him.

I watched her body tremble in pain again and that frown that kept appearing on her face was back.

God, what do I do?

What can I do?

I gritted my teeth. There was nothing I could do but fucking watch.

I didn't even realize I was doing it, but I reached out and took her hand.

If I couldn't ease her pain, the least I could do was hold her hand while she went through it. I think what was worse was that she had no idea how I felt about her. Not at all.

She didn't know it was basically killing me to keep her at a distance. Seeing her relaxed around her brothers and also seeing men I knew my whole life turn into mush when they are with her.

Did she know the power she held?

To make Cole feel any emotion should be an achievement. And that's all you saw on his face when he looked at her; emotion.

All of them, they would kill for her and I knew right now it was me holding them back from going after The Pythons tonight, seeking revenge.

The sad part is, I would kill for her too and she wasn't my blood.

I knew she had been targeted because of me.

It had nothing to do with her brothers.

It had to do with me taking out their clubhouse. Sure it was a club vote, but it had been my idea.

Troy still couldn't understand why I sat back and let him take charge of the club, when really I was meant to be in charge.

I sighed. Everyone looked at me for answers, and I was starting to get tired of the questions and expectations.

Just once, I would like to do something without thinking of the backlash.

Like, for instance, how I would really like to kiss Amber; without worrying how her brothers would react, or the heat that might follow her from being connected to me.

When it came down to it, I could handle the heat that came from being with her. Fuck. I'd do everything in my power to make sure she was safe.

So if I could think that now, why couldn't I have thought that yesterday? Why didn't I protect her when she'd needed it?

I should have been with her, going to school. Instead, I was sleeping off a sleepless weekend because I had given orders to shoot up The Pythons' clubhouse.

I needed her to wake up now. I looked at her more intently, my eyes glancing to her stomach. She wore a mark I should hate. Hell, it was instilled in me to hate it and anyone that wore it.

But I didn't hate her. I don't think I was even capable of hating her. Not when she was annoying. Not when she was being stubborn, and not when she was defying what she was being told.

It slowly started to hit me, sinking in slowly; I've never hated her. If anything, I used to admire her.

And now, that admiration was mixing with lust and my need to be with her.

I was fucked because if there was one thing I knew about Amber, it was that she didn't do emotion and I doubted she had any need to be with me.

***

Amber

My eyes fluttered open and I stared at my ceiling. Sighing and grunting in slight pain, I began to pull myself up, and I hissed in pain right away.

"DON'T MOVE!"

117

My eyes snapped to Jax, and he reached over and wrapped an arm around my back, helping me sit up in bed.

"Why are you here?" I frowned. I couldn't believe he was still here!

He didn't answer, but instead reached over and put another pillow behind my head and helped me lower myself back into the wall of pillows behind me; I was now sitting up straight in bed.

My face twisted as another wave of pain coursed through my body.

"How's the pain?" he asked, returning to his armchair.

"How do you think?" I shot back. I knew I should have been nicer, but the pain was getting in the way of my judgment.

"Cole's gone to get you something for it," Jax said.

"So he's gone to knock off a pharmacy?" I attempted to joke, but it hurt just to breathe and speak.

His lips twitched slightly before they returned to a firm line. "Something like that," he replied.

"You can go if you want Jax. You don't have to stay here," I said, slowly and gingerly.

"Your wound has to be cleaned. It's about time you woke up."

I pulled back the blankets slightly, and immediately noticed the light blood stains coming through my t-shirt. "How bad is it?" I asked.

When Jax didn't answer, I looked up at him and he was looking down at his feet with a serious expression.

"I know they cut me, or stabbed me. I just want to know how bad it is," I said, keeping my voice calm.

He tried to make eye contact with me, and then decided against it. Frowning, I looked down at my arms. They were covered in spots of blood and dirt. I was a mess.

"I really need a shower," I groaned. "I smell and look awful."

"You can't shower by yourself. You will just have to wait for one of your brothers to come home," Jax said; like I would actually let that happen.

"Like hell I am having them help me in a shower!" I spat back. "I will be fine."

"You can't even pull yourself up," he pointed out, before crossing his arms. "So how do you plan on bathing?"

I narrowed my eyes. "I am sure I'll manage."

"Fine, whatever," Jax said as he rose from the armchair in resignation. "But at least have a bath or something. Make it easier on yourself."

I reached out to pull the blankets back, but my face contorted in pain at the movement. I heard Jax grunt as he pulled the blankets back for me.

"Don't say anything," I hissed under my breath, as I pulled my legs around and lowered them to the floor.

I looked up at Jax, who stood a few feet away from me with his arms crossed.

"Could you run it for me? The spa?" I lowered my voice to a whisper. I hated asking him for anything but, at the same time, I didn't think I would be able to turn the taps.

"Don't move while I'm gone," he grunted, before walking into my ensuite.

I heard the water gush into the spa. For the first time, I was actually grateful I had a spa in my ensuite.

Standing on my feet, I gripped the bedside table to find my balance. Wobbly, I began to walk in the direction of the ensuite. I wasn't one to sit back and let a male be all controlling.

I had too much pride for that.

I gripped the doorframe for support as I made it into the ensuite. Jax was kneeling on the tiled floor, with his hand under the tap as he adjusted the temperature of the water.

I smiled at his back; this Jax I could get used to.

"I told you not to move," he huffed, getting to his feet. "Would it kill you to listen for once?"

"Perhaps." I smiled at him, "Um thanks." I felt awkward even saying that word.

"Bet that tasted like acid," he smirked, and I took in his tired eyes.

"Yeah a bit," I admitted. I let go of the doorframe and walked in. I noticed how Jax braced himself, like he was ready to reach out and catch me at any moment.

"You can go," I said slowly, lowering myself to the edge of the spa and sitting down. "Really, you look tired."

"I'm not leaving you in here," Jax crossed his arms.

"Why?" I frowned at him. "Scared I am going to drown myself?"

His expression was blank and his jaw was tightly clenched. "You have two options."

"And they would be?" I asked, raising my eyebrows.

"You can either get naked in front of me, or keep your underwear on."

"You're kidding, right?"

"Do I look like I am joking?" He reached for the hem of his t-shirt and yanked it over his head. "Amber, you can't wash yourself, so stop being stubborn. I don't have the energy to fight with you."

"So you are getting in with me?" I questioned, while trying to keep my eyes focused on his face and not let them drift all over his toned body.

"No. Now which option?" He kept his eyes on me, and I just stared blankly back at him. He let out a disgruntled sigh and ran a hand threw his hair. "Do you have to make this so hard?"

"I don't like being weak," I said as I stared at the tiled floor, "And I don't like being helpless. You're making me feel like a weak little female."

"We both know you are anything but a weak female," he said, but I knew what I'd sounded like. As if he knew what I was thinking, he opened his mouth... "Fine. If it makes you feel better, when I got beaten up a few months ago, Cole had to take care of me."

My head snapped up to look him in the eye. "You're kidding."

"No. Now drop it. I only told you that so you would stop looking all sad and sorry for yourself." He moved towards me and kneeled down in front of me. "So there, you have something on me now."

"You didn't have to do that," I smirked, but visibly softening.

"Drop it. Now underwear or no underwear. Personally, I don't mind either." He winked at me.

"Underwear," I spat out quickly, and it only caused him to smirk at me.

"What a surprise," he mocked me, reaching for the waist line of the shorts I was wearing. "Now, this can be as awkward as you let it be."

"As I let it be? I think you taking my clothes off is just plain awkward, nothing else." I hated this. I hated having to let someone help me. "Hey, how did I get these clothes on in the first place?" I frowned down at them. I was not wearing this baggy t-shirt yesterday and I sure as hell wasn't wearing these shorts.

"Tyler changed you after I... after um... yeah, you got sewn up," he stuttered, slowly pulling my shorts down my thighs.

"Oh great, another moment of glory for me," I muttered dryly. "My life just gets better and better."

"Hands up," Jax ordered. My face twisted in pain as I stretched my arms up and he pulled the t-shirt from me.

The room was steamy, and I was grateful for it; at least I wasn't cold. Getting to his feet, Jax wrapped an arm around my back to help me up. A very large white bandage was wrapped around my stomach. Spots of blood covered it.

"Should we take it off?" I frowned down at it.

"Um yeah," Jax said. "But I will take it off in the bath. Wrap your arm around my neck."

Slowly, I wrapped both arms around his neck and he swooped me up from the ground. Walking to the bath edge, he slowly lowered me into the water.

His muscles flexed as he carried my whole weight. He didn't look me in the eye and I also noticed how his eyes weren't raking my body either. Instead, he glued his eyes to the water he was lowering me into.

My body sunk into the spa bath and, once I rested in it, I pulled my arms away from around his neck, and he pulled away from me, kneeling beside the bath.

I was grateful he had done that; I wasn't sure how I would have managed to bend and lower myself. It would have taken me a while.

Pain was still running through my body, but the hot water numbed it slightly.

Jax cleared his throat. "So, how was school yesterday?"

He leaned into the water and focused on the bandage, as he plucked the tape from the sides.

"Yeah, ok I guess." I muttered while lowering my head back and looking up at the ceiling. "Did you sleep well last night?"

"I did not." He pulled the tape off and I flinched as I felt water gush over my wound. I couldn't bring myself to look down at it, so I just stared up at the ceiling. I glanced out of the corner of my eye at Jax and he was glaring at my stomach.

"So, um. What are you doing today?" My voice fluttered as I spoke, and I wanted to slap myself across my cheek – seriously, that was the best chit chat I could come up with? *Great job Amber.*

"Well, after I bathe you, I'm heading into town. Got some stuff I need to sort out." He lifted my arm out of the water and began to rub the blood and dirt away with a face washer. "You are on bed rest, in case you didn't know."

He was washing my body. Jax, the guy I used to think so little of, was washing my body with a face washer, while I sat back in my underwear.

I turned my head to the side to watch him, "Really? I had no idea."

"Well, at least you don't have to go to school," he said, leaning closer to me and washing the top of my shoulder.

"Um yeah, true." I shot him a small smile "So this 'stuff' to take care of... I am guessing it is club business so we can't really talk about it."

He nodded his head and reached out for my other arm, turning it over and washing it. "Can I ask you something?"

I couldn't pull my eyes away from his upper muscles as he leaned over me. "Um sure, Jax, shoot."

"You dated Blake for a while, yeah?"

"Um, yeah."

"Why did I not see you around?"

My heart was hammering through my chest as he bent into the water and began to wash my high thigh. Focus! I couldn't' lose my train of thought. "Um, what do you mean?"

Jax glanced across at me before turning his attention back to my body. "I never saw you around. Their gang reports to us; we take a share in their profits. So why didn't I see you? You were dating the gang leader. It's not like you were with some nobody."

"I kept a low profile. I didn't want to see my brothers." I bit my lower lip. "Blake didn't even seem to notice," I added.

I saw Jax's expression turn serious. "Why did you break up with him?"

"Because."

"Because you didn't want to date an outlaw anymore?" Jax glanced up the bath at me and arched an eyebrow. "Over the lies? The dirty money? Sick of bailing him out of jail? What?"

Why was he saying that as if those were the reasons keeping a girl from him.

Frowning at him "No, it wasn't any of that."

He grunted. "Come on Amber. You don't break up with a guy you've been with for ages out of the blue. Something must've driven you to do it."

"Ever heard of that saying, "You can put a broken mirror back together, but you can always see the cracks?"

Jax nodded his head.

"Well mine and Blake's relationship had gotten to that point."

"So what made it crack?"

A shot of pain ran across my stomach as I moved slightly in the water.

"He hit me," I muttered. "But do not tell my brothers."

"He what?" Jax spat and dropped my leg in the water, which made me flinch and another wave of pain flooded my body.

"Sorry!" He reached back into the water and floated my leg back to the surface.

"Blake and I just needed to go our separate ways. That's it."

Jax glared into the water as he ran the face washer down my leg. "So, the whole gang and outlaw thing wasn't a problem?"

"What are you trying to ask me, Jax?"

"Nothing." He shook his head and got up "I'm done. Do you want to get out or…"

"Out sounds good," I piped up, and placed a hand on the edge ready to pull myself up but Jax leaned down and wrapped his arms around me, pulling me from the water.

Slipping a hand around his neck, I kept my eyes locked on the side of his face as he lowered my feet to the ground. I felt like I was missing something, like he was asking me something but I wasn't quite catching on.

Frowning, I slowly pulled my arms from around his neck, now standing on my feet. "Jax?"

His eyes snapped down to me; he was thinking something and I really wanted to know what it was. He nodded for me to continue.

"If Blake hadn't hit me, if things were or could have been different, I wouldn't have ended it."

"You really didn't care he was a criminal?" His eyebrows frowned as he spoke.

"I loved him for him, what he did couldn't influence my love for him."

"He was a lucky guy," Jax muttered. "A lot of girls wouldn't think the same way."

My eyes drifted down from his eyes and, for the first time, I glanced down at my wound and frowned. It wasn't a stab mark like I'd expected. Slowly, I walked away from Jax and towards the mirror. I rubbed the steam away from the mirror with the back of my hand; wincing as I did.

My eyes widened as I took in the mark on my body. I reached out and touched the mirror, before glancing back down at it, and then went back to looking at it in the mirror.

"No!" I choked, and tears began to fill my eyes. "No!"

Jax stood behind me and placed both his hands on my hips. I didn't look him in the eye; my eyes were glued to my stomach.

I was marked as the property of The Pythons. II wore their mark. Tears of disgust rolled down my cheeks.

"Amber," Jax's voice was calm, but right now he was the last person I wanted to see have seen this.

"Get out," I choked. "Just get out."

"Amber…"

"GET OUT!"

"Just let me dry you first and I will leave."

I turned around sharply to face him, "I said GET OUT!"

Taking a step away from me, his arms dropped to his side. His eyes flashed with hurt for a moment before he turned around and walked out of the bathroom.

I wiped the tears from under my eyes. I couldn't look at the mark again; I felt disgusted.

I had been a part of this world long enough to know what that mark meant. I was forever going to wear a mark my brothers loathed and, well Jax… I wiped tears away. I'm sure he loathed The Pythons more than my brothers did.

"Where is she?" I heard Cole bark at Jax.

"Bathroom," Jax answered, now in the bedroom, but I felt his eyes on me.

I turned around and saw Cole standing in the bathroom doorframe with a plastic bag. He looked over me for a moment before turning around.

"What did you do to her!" Cole roared at Jax, and I was surprised by the venom in his tone. He normally always respected Jax.

"I DIDN'T DO ANYTHING!" Jax roared back.

I grabbed a towel from the counter and wrapped it around my body, wincing as I did.

"THEN WHY THE HELL IS SHE CRYING! WHAT THE FU—"

"He didn't do anything," I cut Cole off. I walked slowly through the bathroom and to the door. Cole took a step back so I could enter my bedroom; he kept his eyes locked on Jax.

"Why are you crying?" Cole shot me a sideways glance as I moved towards my bed.

"Why do you think?" I spat back. "I'm sure you've seen it!"

"Oh..." Cole said blankly, and stopped glaring at Jax.

"Get out," I whispered. "Both of you."

Cole looked at me warily. "Your bandage needs changing,"

"I don't care." I lowered myself onto the edge of the bed, with my back to Jax. "Please, just leave me alone."

Cole tossed the plastic bag on my bed and crossed his arms. "I know this is our fault Amber, I know we failed you."

"You think I care about that?" I choked, rubbing the tears away from my eyes. "No, I don't care that clearly someone has taken their revenge out on me. What I care about is..." I broke off and shook my head, not being able to say it.

"What?" Jax's voice piped in from behind me. "Tell us." He said that like he was dying to know the inner workings of my mind right now. He was basically pleading with me.

Cole looked at me with a serious expression and I shook my head.

"Just leave," I muttered.

"Don't make me call the others..." Cole threatened.

"How can you even look at me?" I pulled my head up and stared him in the eye "I wear your enemy's mark! I'm... I'm ruined."

Cole's expression went blank and he just stood there frozen, not knowing what to say. Perhaps it was because I had just stated the obvious. I couldn't take his silence as a good sign, and it didn't help that Jax was also in the room, also silent.

"Get out," I muttered dryly. "GET THE HELL OUT NOW!" I put my head in my hands; the pain was getting worse as I yelled.

"Amber, it's our fault you carry that mark. Our opinion of you can never change." Cole's voice was firm as he knelt down in front of me. "This is our fault."

It was comforting to hear that he thought that but, at the same time, the others wouldn't be as thoughtful. I was very aware of my own attitude towards people who wore this scar or tattoo because normally, if it was a tattoo, only a lifetime member would have it cut into their skin.

"Your opinion may not change, but others' will. Just leave me alone."

Cole stayed put in front of me. "Someone has to change your bandage. You can't be left alone."

"I will call someone. Just leave," I muttered.

"And who will you be calling? We are your family." His voice trembled in anger as he spoke. Cole could never control his temper when it came to it, so I knew right now he was doing his best to stay calm.

"No offense Cole, but you guys are the last people I want looking at and treating this mark. Not when I know you guys kill people for simply showing it."

"You didn't get this by choice."

"No, but I still have it." I shook my head "Please, I cannot take any more humiliation."

"Fine." He stood up "Who do you want me to call?"

I thought about it for a few moments, and that was when I realized something. There was only one person who wouldn't judge me for this mark; there was only person I trusted to care for me, knowing that I had it.

"I will call him. Just go."

"Him?" Jax piped up. "Who is it?" His own anger now laced his words as he spoke.

"I don't have to answer you, either of you. Now go."

Grunting and shaking his head, Cole placed my phone on the bed and walked away. I heard him and Jax leave and I didn't know why, but I just felt complete and utter disgust at myself.

I wanted to throw up. I wanted to cut the wound out of my body completely. It was like having an awful word tattooed into my skin.

Unlocking my phone, I dialed the one number that I had promised to never dial again, and it didn't help that I knew that number by heart.

***

"Is this all you want?" Blake asked, as he carried the bag he had helped me pack.

Nodding my head, I thanked him. "I feel so stupid for making you do this for me."

"Amber, you are always my number one. No matter what. Come on, let's get you out of here." He smiled at me warmly as he wrapped an arm around my shoulder. "You want me to carry you?"

"No, I can walk. Just not fast."

"Do your brothers know you are leaving with me?" he asked, holding the door open for me.

"No." I walked slowly out of the room and down the hall. "What did they say when they saw you?"

"Nothing. I think they expected me." His face turned sour. "I get why they're disgusted with themselves. I looked after you for years and nothing happened."

"Perhaps don't mention that to them," I said under my breath. I came to a halt at the long staircase; God, this was going to be painful.

"Come on Amber, just let me carry you down. I promise when we get to the bottom you can hit me or something so you don't feel like a weakling."

I glanced at Blake; he knew me too well. I nodded my head and just let him carry me down the stairs. When he placed me at the bottom, I shot him a small smile.

He winked at me and opened the front door. My expression went blank as I noticed all my brothers and Jax, leaning against his car.

"Why are you out of bed?" Adam asked, and then his face went tight as he saw the bag over Blake's shoulder.

"As much as I enjoy seeing you guys draping yourselves over my car, can you get off it?" Blake said coolly and took a step in front of me. "I have somewhere I need to be."

"Then you can leave," Jax snarled at him, and glanced briefly at me, adding, "Without her."

"Like I am leaving her in your hands," Blake scoffed. "You guys couldn't protect her if your life depended on it. But wait... you already proved that."

All of the boys took a step towards him, each with an expression twisted in hate.

"Don't Blake," I hissed from behind him. "Just drop it."

"Fine," he grumbled, "But I just wanted to point out that Amber was my other half for years and she never copped my payback, or got hurt. Just proves what sort of brothers you really are to her, although I guess you guys were never around when she needed you."

Blake dodged Cole's fist and I moved to stand in front of him, holding my ground and not letting them fight; though Blake was baiting them.

"Amber, get back in the house," Cole spat at me. "NOW!"

129

"NO!" I stood my ground. "I'm leaving with Blake and you guys are going to let me."

All of them scoffed and Cole shook his head. "Like hell we are."

"You are because I am asking you guys to." I stopped for a moment, pain shooting through me. I fought to steady my breathing. "You guys are going to let me go, because I cannot live in the same house as you while I cope with this."

"I already told you the mark means nothing to us," Cole hissed, and I noticed his firm fists.

"But it means something to me. Just let me come to terms with it then I will be able to look at you guys without feeling disgusted."

"Get out of our way," Blake snarled from behind me; he never liked people standing in our way, but I suppose nobody does.

I glanced at Jax and he was just glaring into the house behind us, not looking at me. How could I expect him to, after what was on my body.

"Then why go with him?" Tyler spoke up, clearly hurt with my decision. "Why leave and take off with the HellBound?"

"Because she knows I can protect her," Blake snapped from behind me. I couldn't turn around to give him a dirty look; I knew it would hurt too much.

I felt guilty for what I was about to say, but I knew it was the truth. "Because I wear his mark and I know his eyes can never look at me with disgust," I muttered, looking to the ground.

The boys stepped out of our way. Blake looked smug as he shouldered Cole, opening the door for me. He tossed the bag into the back and waited for me to take a seat.

Glancing at the boys, I noticed how hurt they each looked. "I'm sorry," I muttered. "Just give me time."

Blake helped me into the car and closed the door. I knew he had a smug look on his face as he walked around the car. Then, suddenly, I heard his body slam into the side of the car, and I noticed Jax had him by the collar. I had never seen Jax furious, but right now, even I was scared of the look on his face...

130

"If you touch her, I'll kill you," I heard Jax hiss at Blake, before pushing him away.

Blake opened the door, a pissed off look on his face. He slammed it shut, hard, and then turned the key, bringing the engine to life.

He glanced over at me ."You hungry? I think we should get food before heading home." He didn't mention Jax's threat.

I nodded my head in agreement, as I looked into the side view. My brothers were shooting daggers at the car, and that was the last thing I saw as we pulled away.

Chapter 15

Amber

I pulled the t-shirt up and ran my fingers along the two lines. Two simple lines that connect at the top. The stitches now gone, the healing skin was red.

"Amber, you coming out?"

I turned to look in the direction of the doorway. Blake had his arms crossed, his eyes glued to my stomach as I inspected it in front of the mirror. I dropped the t-shirt back down.

"Um yeah," I said as I moved across the room, picking up my phone. "We're going now, then?"

Blake nodded his head, letting his arms drop to his side. "Are you sure you want to?"

"Yeah, I don't mind." I smiled at him. "Come on."

Blake put his hand out for me to take, and I took it without thinking twice about it. Old habits die hard. My phone lit up in my hand and I wasn't surprised when I glanced at the caller I.D.

I hadn't seen my brothers in over three weeks. Three weeks I had avoided their calls, and their eyes. I had even avoided school, but school couldn't challenge a Doctor's certificate, even if it was fake; they didn't know that bit though.

Jax's number flashed as the phone vibrated again.

"They're harassing you tonight," Blake said, as he closed the front door and watched me block the call once again. "Maybe something's up?"

"I couldn't do anything, even if something was," I pointed out, walking to his car as the phone continued to flash. "We're going anyway, right?"

I slid into the car. Blake had so been secretive about where we were going but I was just thankful to get out of the house.

Blake started the car up and I closed my door, keeping an eyebrow raised as he pulled out of the driveway.

"Not going to answer?" I pressed, while pulling my seatbelt on.

"Amber, the last three weeks... You... being back in the house... us being, well, you know..."

"Us being what?"

"We've been sleeping in the same bed." He shot me a sideways glance, "It just feels like we are back in a relationship."

"Yeah, I suppose it has been a bit like that. Apart from you not drinking." I looked out the window. I still couldn't believe Blake hadn't touched a drink for the last three weeks. He said he couldn't protect me if he was wasted. Blake was a good fighter, even when wasted, so I knew he wasn't drinking because he didn't want anything to happen between us.

"Amber? Are we back in a relationship?"

I looked at him gingerly; he looked slightly uneasy.

Blake was never uneasy.

"No. I don't know." I frowned. "I don't know, Blake. The reasons we decided to break up still exist."

"I've shown you! I won't hurt you." He shot me a sideways glance again, keeping an eye on the road. "I won't ever touch you again."

"Blake, we didn't just break up for that reason." I sighed, and ran both hands through my hair. "We both knew what we had was over. Is over. We can't be that couple anymore."

"I don't want to be that couple." Blake slowed down at a traffic light. "I want us to be this. Easy, second nature. Being with you, Amber, is like breathing."

"Last I remember. I was the one suffocating you."

"Amber, I…"

Our bodies were catapulted forward as someone slammed into us from behind. My head snapped forward, and whacked the dashboard with force.

Blake let out a string of curse words as he unbuckled his seatbelt and jumped out of the car. I saw his hand reach under his t-shirt. My head was spinning as I rested it back on the headrest. What was with cars lately?

Groaning, I undid my seat belt, and cracked the door open. I heard Blake yelling, but I felt my stomach twist. Leaning against the side of the car, steadying my breathing, I closed the door.

"Amber, you alright?" Blake lifted my head; his eyes ran over my face with worry. "Shit!" He let out a breath as he ripped his t-shirt off and pressed it to the top of my head. I winched as the fabric came into contact with my head.

"It looks like a surface wound," Blake muttered, and then shot a dirty look over his shoulder. "Bloody P platers."

I glanced at the young kids, who had clearly run into us.

"For some reason, I thought it was someone trying to kill us," I muttered under my breath. Blake's lips twitched up slightly and nodding his head. "And they are the same age as me."

I was beginning to second guess my involvement with criminals. Was it normal to always assume the worst?

"How bad's the car?" I asked, as Blake pulled the t-shirt from my head; I'd only bled a little bit.

"Not too bad. I don't think the kid has a license though," Blake said, shooting me a small smile. We both glanced at them; they looked like they were freaking out.

"Probably lost it for bad driving," I replied to Blake. He nodded his head.

"Let's get out of here before the cops come," Blake said coolly, and reached behind me to open my door.

I got in, and Blake walked around the back of the car, ripping the half hanging bumper off and tossing it in the direction of the sidewalk. I closed my door as Blake got in.

Blake looked both ways, before he took off into the intersection, ignoring the red light. I was sure the teenagers would be back there puzzled, not sure what was going on.

Blake didn't do insurance and he didn't do cops, so, of course, we wouldn't be hanging around to exchange details.

"Amber?"

"Yeah Blake?"

"I love you."

I snapped my head to him; his eyes were glued to the road. Had I heard him correctly? His words rang pretty clear, and through my mind once more.

I opened my mouth and then shut it again. What could I say to that? Blake was my first love, first crush, and well my first serious boyfriend. He would protect me with his life, if needed, but he was also a hard-core gangster; a criminal.

And often, I needed protection from him.

So why did I immediately lean over and kiss the side of his cheek?

Because I am an idiot.

Chapter 16

"Are you sure?"

I looked across at Blake and handed him his t-shirt.

"Yeah, Blake, I am sure." I gave him a small smile as I pushed open the car door. I walked around to his side and leaned into his window. "Thanks, for everything."

He let out a low sigh and kept his eyes locked with mine. "If they hassle you, or you want to come back to me, call ok?"

I nodded my head, while buttoning up the last button on my jeans. "I will. I promise."

Blake shot me a weak smile and I could see the debate in his eyes as he thought about leaving me here. His hands hovered over the key, not turning it; just fiddling.

"Go, Blake. I'm fine." I stepped away from his side of the car, and he twisted the key in the ignition, bringing the engine back to life.

I loved Blake, but we could never be what we were. We both knew that, but it didn't stop us from going out with a bang, if you get my drift.

I took another step away from his car, and he slowly began to crawl away from me. I would always love him, and it was easy to fall into old habits. Being with Blake was easy, but we both knew that easy wasn't a good thing.

I watched his tail lights slowly disappear up the driveway, and I slowly turned around to face my house. The mansion was in darkness; it was only after ten at night, so it surprised me that no one was up.

Slowly, I walked up the porch steps. I didn't know how my brothers were going to react to my sudden return. I paused with my hand on the door knob, and then went ahead and twisted it. They didn't seem to be home. Good. I had more time to pull myself together before I faced them.

If I'd had my way, I wouldn't have returned tonight, but, I knew if I went back to Blake's, I wouldn't have been leaving anytime soon.

I cracked the door open slowly, and crept through the hallway. The house was in darkness, like I had expected. In the night light, the house looked almost haunted. The moonlight flickered across the photo frames that hung in the foyer.

Sighing softly, I walked through the foyer and into the lounge room. I didn't bother to flick the light on; I went in and sat down on the couch.

Laying back down and hanging my feet over the end of the couch, I stared up at the ceiling.

My fingers went under my t-shirt and I ran one finger lightly over my scar. Where did I go from here? What was I meant to do with my life?

The dull rumble of motor bikes broke me out of my thoughts. My heartbeat sped up, and suddenly I felt nervous. I knew my brothers would always love me, but still it was hard to face them.

I listened closely as all the engines died, and I heard the crunching of gravel. I froze as I heard the door swing open. For some reason, I shut my eyes tightly.

"So, are they coming around here then?" Tyler's voice sounded slightly drained as he spoke.

"Yeah, when they knock off or something," Jax replied.

The front door closed and I remained still on the couch, my feet no longer swinging over the edge.

"Well, I am going to bed, you guys have fun with that," Tyler yawned, and I heard his feet pounding up the stairs.

The foyer lights flicked on and the overcast spread lightly through the lounge room, bringing only dull light into the room.

"I heard El was coming to pay you a special visit Jax," Adam said, sounding smug.

"Whatever," Jax grunted. "Women are only good for one thing. I'm going to shower."

Another dull set of footsteps stomped up the stairs and I thought over Jax's words. Women were only good for one thing.

"Did you give Amber another call?" Troy's voice was huff.

"She blocked it again," Cole scoffed. "I think we should just storm the guy's house."

"We all agreed we would give her space," Adam quickly snapped. "We owe her that."

"Yeah, it's been a while," Cole grunted. "She could be dead for all we know."

I flung my legs back from over the couch and stood up, walking from the couch.

"We would know if she were dead," Adam said, sounding annoyed.

"I am alive," I announced, leaning against the doorframe, crossing my arms, bringing myself out of the shadows of the lounge room. Troy and Cole were sitting on the bottom step, and Adam was standing with his hands in his pockets.

All their mouths dropped open, as they saw me standing casually against the doorframe, keeping my nerves in check.

"You're back," Adam finally managed to croak.

I nodded my head and kept my arms crossed. "That I am."

Cole got up abruptly. "So… sick of playing happy family with Blake the gangster then?" He crossed his arms and narrowed his eyes at me.

Inhaling sharply, I pushed myself away from the doorframe and shouldered my way past him, walking up the stairs.

"I'm going to bed," I shot over my shoulder, not looking back. Cole could say what he wanted about Blake, but he was the only person I knew who wouldn't judge me.

"Wait Amber, we haven't seen you in weeks!" Adam took the stairs two at a time, and wrapped an arm around my upper arm. "Are you alright?"

"I'm fine." I glanced at his hand and then back up at him. "I'm going to go to bed," I announced again.

"So, that's it then. No small talk with us?" Cole shot up at me from the bottom of the stairs.

"What would you like me to say, Cole?" I looked around Adam to look down at him, eyebrow arched sarcastically.

"Are you back with Blake?" He yelled up behind me as I kept walking. I stopped to respond, but the doorbell rang, and Cole let out an annoyed grunt as he spun around to open it.

The door flung open, and about six or so females stood at the door. I didn't know them, but given the way they were dressed, it wasn't hard to guess what they were all about. Pornstars.

"Pornstars?" I said out loud, slightly amused, and looked at my brothers pointedly. "I thought you guys had taste."

The girls slowly walked in, and closed the door softly behind them. The boys, however, wouldn't meet my eyes.

"I thought you were going to bed, Amber," Troy shot at me, but still wouldn't meet my eye. I guess your sister meeting your one night stand wasn't particularly a high point, but they were bikies and, of course, girls like them always clung to the tough bad boys.

"Right, night!" I turned around and Adam let go of my arm. Walking silently up the corridor, I heard the conversation starting up as I walked to my room.

Coming to a stop at my bedroom door, I paused and shot a glance at Jax's closed door. I bit my bottom lip; I couldn't believe he had said what he had earlier, but then, what did I expect? He was a bikie; a tough lady's man bikie. I knew all too well now, when it came to love, it didn't rank very high on a criminal's list of priorities.

They wanted sex, they didn't want love. I twisted my door knob and walked into my room. It was cold and dark, and I flicked my bedside light on and closed the door.

Love was over-rated anyway, I thought, as I walked to my bed. Criminals and bad boys were nothing but work so I ignored the feeling that burned in my stomach; that made me want to hurl something across the room. All when I thought about Jax with other women.

Chapter 17

I looked into the mirror and took in my reflection. Lightly, I traced my scar with two fingers. I couldn't wear this. I glanced back at my wardrobe, knowing I didn't have a one piece. Groaning and throwing my hair up in a loose ponytail in frustration, I stormed over to my bed and threw myself backwards into it.

I wanted to swim in our heated pool, but I didn't want to flaunt my scar in my brothers' faces, but when it came down to it, it was their fault I had it so they couldn't hate me for it, could they?

Sitting up quickly, before I lost my confidence, I swooped up an oversized t-shirt and pulled it over my head; it stopped mid-thigh. I flung open my bedroom door and swooped up my phone.

I froze when I saw Jax standing in his doorframe, about to walk out. His eyes snapped to mine, and widened with shock. I froze in my doorway.

It was Jax, Amber. JAX. Pull it together.

We both opened our mouths at the same time, but, before either of us could say anything, his bedroom door widened, and a tall, skinny, beautiful brunette stood in the frame.

Jax didn't look at her, his eyes fixed on me. Was he watching or waiting for my reaction?

"Amber!" Ella smiled at me, before she crossed her arms. "It's been a while."

"That it has El, how are you?" I replied, ripping my eyes from Jax and looking Ella in the eye.

"Good, good." She nodded her head and although her smile was friendly, her body language was anything but. "I heard you and Blake are back together?"

Ella, or El as she was more often known as, was a pornstar; or at least she used to be. She was now a high class model for porn commercials. She was also one of many in the long string of ex-girlfriends Blake had; a list I was now a part of. Although her and I were friendly, we both knew she hated me. Basically, Blake had broken up with her, well… he didn't even really break up with her because he didn't ever really call her his girlfriend, but, when it came down to it, he 'broke' up with her to date me.

"No, we're not actually." I plastered a fake smile and glanced at Jax and then back at her "So you got a new man, El? Good for you."

El glanced at Jax and then back at me nervously. "I don't do relationships anymore." She stood up slightly taller, adding, "Not when I have an endless list of men."

I nodded my head. "Fair enough."

"So what, you were just staying with Blake then? You guys weren't actually back together?" Her eyebrows frowned together as she waited for my response.

What could I say? Pornstars have the looks, just evidently not very good hearing.

"Yep. He was helping me out, like I said before." I reached behind me and pulled my door closed "Well, I better be going."

"Wait Am!"

I turned my eyes back to El; of course she had more questions. "Yep?"

She nodded her head in the direction of my bedroom door. "So, whose room is that?" She smiled, kind of evil, at me.

I frowned for a moment, and then realized she didn't know I lived here. I hid my smirk. If she knew I lived across from the room of the guy she had lined up as her next man, she would be here every night.

"Wouldn't you like to know?" I smirked slightly, and then walked away from them, quickly.

Jax didn't say anything, nor did he make an attempt to speak to me as I darted away from them. Looks like I was really missed, I scoffed to myself. Who was I kidding?

Jax was a player. A cold hearted one at that.

***

I dangled my feet in the heated pool, and my phone buzzed beside me. I reached for it and opened the message. Seeing Blake's number on the screen, I sighed lowly before I read it.

'This song reminds me of you. Just thought I would let you know.'

Frowning, I pulled my feet out from the pool and walked to the side, plugging the aux cable into my phone and clicking on the link to the file that was in the message. I pushed play and slowly the surround sound system came to life.

"You were my everything" by Aviation began to echo through the enclosed pool area. I pulled the t-shirt off and flung it to the side. Walking down the stairs into the pool, I smiled as I heard the lyrics.

The water swallowed my body until I slowly got on my back and floated across the water. Listening to every word pulled at my heartstrings. Should I go back to him?

The only part of the song that didn't fit was the new man line. I didn't have a new man, and perhaps that was a good thing.

We were over, but I knew he would always love me just like I would always love him.

"What the hell is this soft crap?"

I got on my feet and looked at the side of the pool at Cole, who reached for my phone and unplugged it.

"Are you going soft on us, Amber?" Cole gave me a cocky grin before he reached for his phone and plugged it in.

"What are you doing in here?" I tried to mask my irritation.

"You mean what are we doing here?" Tyler corrected me, strolling towards the pool. "And to answer your question... swimming with you."

"NO you are not," I grunted, and then glared at the two of them. "Don't you have something better to do?"

"I thought they were lying to me when they told me this morning that you were back," Tyler shot me his easy going grin and pulled his t-shirt off, putting his toned muscles and tattoos on display.

"Great. You have seen, you have been, and now you can piss off," I shot in his direction, and then looked back at Cole as he played with my phone. "Stop touching that," I barked at him.

He rolled his eyes as he chose a song and "Escape the Fate, Issues," boomed from the speakers. I gasped as water sprayed across my face, as Tyler launched himself into the pool. I turned around to glare at him, but, before I could, two arms wrapped around my waist and pulled me under.

The music hit my ears with a boom as I re-surfaced, splashing a load of water at Tyler in rebellion.

"God, you are a tool," I groaned in his direction. I noticed Cole running towards me, and I yelled out. "Don't..."

But I was too late. My mouth filled with water as he landed with a thud in the water, and I reached to wipe the water from my eyes.

"I forgot how hot this pool can get," Tyler said causally, as he floated on his back. Cole reached out and pulled a big ring from the side, and pulled himself into it, floating.

"So, what made you come back?" Cole said as he kicked off from the side, and floated into the middle of the water. As he spun around, I saw my name tattooed on the top of his back shoulder blade. I remembered the first time he had showed it to me; it was before they had all left.

I softened my tone, feeling nostalgic at the sight of the tattoo.

"It was time," I announced, pushing the wet hair from my face. "I said I would be back."

"No you didn't. You just left," Tyler grunted, leaning on the side of the pool opposite me. "You didn't tell us anything."

"Yeah, well I'm back now so it doesn't matter." I leaned my head back and stared up at the ceiling. "So, what has been going on around here?"

"You know... a bit of this, a bit of that. Dad's gone to some conference; he has been gone all week... comes back next week I think," Tyler said lightly.

I wasn't surprised dad wasn't here; he was a busy man. "So, that would explain why he didn't surface last night, when you guys had your little..." I pulled my head forward and looked between the two. "What would you call that? A group booty call?"

Cole rolled his eyes at me, while Tyler chuckled.

"Yeah, yeah well we weren't expecting you back," Cole pointed out, before kicking off from the side again. "Seeing as you're back now, you can go back to school as of Monday."

"Oh joy," I grunted. "What did I ever do to be so lucky."

"I think Jax has been missing you there," Tyler said, as he slowly began to creep in Cole's direction.

"What do you mean?" I arched an eyebrow at him, as he slowly crept up to Cole who had his back to him, still floating on his giant ring.

Anyone could see what was going to happen next.

One.

Two.

Three.

Cole let out a surprised scream as he went flying into the water and Tyler claimed his giant ring, quickly pushing himself off in the other direction of the pool.

The pool sliding door slid open, and I quickly looked in another direction as Jax walked in, followed by Adam with his hand entangled with a pretty blondes.

Looks like someone hadn't gotten rid of last night's flame. Wait a sec, make that two someones; I noticed El out of the corner of my eye.

"Geez, this room is massive," a light voice said, and I glared at Tyler and Cole as they wrestled for the giant ring. It was their fault that we now had more visitors. I wanted to whack them both over their stupid heads.

"Is the water warm?"

I turned my head to the Blonde as she went to dangle a toe in the water. They couldn't possibly be thinking about swimming in here, right?

I saw the annoyance in Jax's eyes as El slid out of her dress. I wanted to yell that a bra and undies were not a bathing suit, but what was the point?

The blonde followed in Ella's footsteps, and pulled her dress off.

"What song is this?" The blonde asked, as "Changed the Way You Kissed Me" by Example played. Adam told her what it was.

"So, Amber, which one is yours?" El winked at me, and then glanced between Cole and Tyler.

I began to choke on nothing, as I visualized what she was saying to me.

Cole and Tyler looked in complete horror as they waited for me to correct her.

"They're her brothers," Jax answered for me, and I nodded my head. El seemed slightly surprised by this little bit of information and then looked at me.

"I didn't know you had brothers."

"You know what Amber, I am starting to think you are ashamed of us," Adam winked at me, helping the blonde down the stairs.

"Denial is one step closer to acceptance, I suppose," I shot at him, and then cocked my head to look at Jax. He snapped his eyes away from me as soon as I looked at him.

"So Amber, tell me what is new with you?" El said, being friendly, as she began to walk in the water towards me.

God shoot me, or at least give me duct tape, so I can tape that mouth of hers shut. I was not in the mood to make conversation.

"You know… nothing much. You?"

I swung my legs out in front of me as I gripped the edge of the pool.

"This, that and everything in-between," she finally replied, and leaned against the pool wall next to me; of course.

"Exciting," I replied and then looked at Adam and the blonde who were mucking around with each other. "Who's she?" I nodded my head in their direction.

"That's Gab. She's an underwear model," El answered, and then flipped her head back to look up at Jax, who was yet to grace us with his presence in the water.

"You coming in?" she asked him sweetly.

"Yeah Jax, get your gear off, and get in here with your girlfriend," I spun around and said up to him. I was over this silent thing that we had going on at the moment.

"I'm not his girlfriend. I don't do boyfriends remember," El informed me as she blushed.

"That's not what I heard Jax say last night." I smiled up at him innocently, while he narrowed his eyes at me.

El looked up at me and frowned slightly. "What do you mean?" she asked.

"Hey, it's not my place to tell you the one thing Jax loves about you."

Yeah Jax, why don't you tell her that she is only good for one thing. I wanted to slap him across his face for his views on women.

"What is she on about?" El looked up at Jax, while he crossed his arms, keeping his eyes on me.

I knew he knew what I was on about. I wondered if he was shocked that I had heard his confession; well, it had been more of a statement.

"Who knows," Jax said coolly. "You still high on your boyfriend's drug fumes, Amber?"

"I don't have a boyfriend, so the answer to that question would be no." I cocked my head to the side. "You really can't remember

Jax? Well, you said it just before you went to bed last night. Come on, you know what I am referring to."

Jax shrugged his shoulders innocently, and added, "El already knows I care about her. I don't think that would surprise her."

"You do?" Ella's eyes widened in surprise.

"Doesn't look like it," I sang, floating away from them.

Jax shot me a dirty look before looking at El. I wonder how he was going to get out of this. "I don't do girlfriends El, you know that, but, if I did, you would be the one."

I wanted to scoff. What a cop out.

"El and I have heard that line before," I said, looking Jax in the eye. "From a better player than you."

Blake had had many girlfriends, but he would never refer to them as his girlfriends. Well, with me it was different; he would openly say I was his girlfriend, but for all the others, they were all classed as girlfriends, but he never really looked at them like that.

"Yeah, but you actually turned him around," El said in my direction. "But she is right Jax."

Jax groaned and then ripped his t-shirt off; my eyes scanned his tattoos. Man, he had a good body.

Jax was already wearing black branded board shorts. Slowly, he lowered himself into the water next to El.

"Fine, let's do it," he said to her.

My mouth dropped open. Hell no! Don't do it. I had expected him to push her off or set her straight.

"You mean, be your girlfriend?" She looked as surprised as I was. No-one else in the pool seemed to be taking in the scene in front of me.

"Yeah, why not," Jax said, taking her hands from under the water and pulling her slightly closer to him. "You're the hottest chick I know. Plus, you're the only chick I would not want to screw and hurl aside."

Well, I had never heard better reasons to go into a relationship. I gritted my teeth, was he doing this to piss me off?

"I..." El blushed, "For real?" she asked?

Jax lowered his head down to hers. "Yeah."

"I LOVE THIS SONG!" Tyler screamed and startled everyone.

"Where the Wild Things Are" by Bliss n Eso boomed through the speakers.

Tyler rapped the lyrics and I found it really amusing. I glanced back at Jax, but felt disgusted; as he had his lips locked with Ella's.

Oh, that was foul.

I caught my phone flashing behind them, and it immediately spiked my curiosity. Swimming to the side, next to them, I pulled myself up and out of the water, not thinking about the large scar on my stomach for the first time in weeks.

Water dripped from me as I picked up my phone. The number was restricted. I put it to my ear.

"Amber?"

"Um, yeah?" I responded, bringing my other hand to my other ear to block the music out.

"It's Ashley."

I frowned. Ashley... I didn't know an Ashley. Well, not a guy Ashley anyway.

"Ashley who?"

"Ashley Greenhood? Blake's right hand."

"Oh." And now the memories came flooding back to me. "What's up?"

"It's Blake. He's been arrested. The cops have raided the house and, from what I overheard, they are coming for you next."

My eyes widened. "You mean to my house?" I panicked into the phone.

"Yeah. Look, I got to go, we have houses to clean before they hit them. Just giving you a heads up," Ashley said in a hurry, and then the phone went dead.

Blake arrested.

Houses raided.

I was next.

I processed all this information in my mind quickly, and then cursed loudly.

I went running down the length of the pool, the boys sensing my urgency and throwing questions at me.

"Cops are going to raid us!" I yelled over my shoulder as I slid the glass door open quickly.

I heard the frantic splashing as the boys hurried out of the pool, but I didn't stop to get their advice, or listen to their thoughts on the matter.

I had my own evidence to destroy.

***

"What the hell have you got that they would want?" Cole yelled at me as I flung clothes in every direction. Where the hell did I leave it?

"Don't you guys have your own stuff to hide or destroy?," I shot at him.

"Unlike you little sister, we don't bring business home." He grunted in annoyance, and I pushed past him and went to my bedside table.

"So, you are telling me those guns you carry are licensed?" I barked as I emptied the contents of my night stand on my bed.

Cole cursed under his breath and quickly left the room, only to be replaced by Troy.

"Amber, what have you got that the cops want?" He crossed his arms and watched me sift through the junk on my bed.

"Nothing," I shot at him. Well, if I couldn't find it, maybe they wouldn't be able to either.

I heard the pounding on the front door and my eyes went wide. I scrambled to the closet and pulled a t-shirt over my wet bikini top, and then quickly pulled on a pair of shorts.

The boys hadn't even mentioned my scar, or looked at it. Though their minds were elsewhere, they weren't taking in my scar, they were too busy wondering what the hell had me going through my room like a mad woman.

My head suddenly snapped up and relief washed over me. "It's not here." I said out loud. I'd just remembered hurling it over the bridge, into the river.

"What isn't here?" Troy frowned at me, and I shook my head.

"Doesn't matter now." I walked past him and down the corridor, although he turned quickly to follow me.

We both reached the top of the stairs as the cops broke through the door, screaming their usual shit.

I put both hands in the air and Troy did the same.

***

We all sat in the lounge. The boys sat across from me and the girls sat with them. I was on my own in the armchair as the detective with his bullet vest studied me.

"So Amber, been a while," he stated smugly.

"Sorry, have we met before?" I arched an eyebrow and crossed a leg over my knee. "I don't have the best memory."

I knew that they weren't allowed to ask questions when searching the house, but cops were pigs so they didn't really follow the rules; the rules that they created.

Tyler grunted in amusement, and the detective narrowed his eyes at me.

"Did your boyfriend give you a warning? From the looks of your room, you were looking for something," the detective stated as he closed the file in his hand and crossed his arms in front of me. "Why don't you just help us out Amber, and, in return, you'd be doing yourself a favor."

"Do you always use that line?" I leaned back in the chair, keeping my eyes squarely locked with his. "And my boyfriend did nothing of the sort, because I don't have a boyfriend."

"Was the breakup messy?" he asked, lowering his head to stare me down. "Perhaps some payback is in order?"

"I would, if there was anything to tell," I said lightly, and glanced at Cole as he cursed at a cop who was searching him. "Is there a reason you are taking this out on my brothers? I thought you were here to question me?"

"Satan's Sons are always a point of interest," he informed me. The detective took a step closer to me. "Where is it Amber?"

"Where is what?"

"Where is the murder weapon that was used on Ryan Raymond? The gun your boyfriend pointed to his head and shot him with."

Ryan who? We never shot at any Ryan.

"You must have your wires twisted," I replied, honestly confused. "I don't know a Ryan and I don't know anything about a murder weapon."

Well, that was half right anyway. I did know of a murder weapon, but it didn't have anything to do with the murder of Ryan... whatever his last name was.

"Really? Because you and Blake also took care of his brother, Jake Markus."

That murder I did know of, and that murder weapon was floating somewhere in the ocean by now.

"Jake had a brother? Never knew that," I said, crossing my arms. "Although Jake never really talked much."

"Well, he doesn't talk at all now," the detective spat at me. "Give them up Amber. We have solid information that you have them."

Jake was a low life piece of scum, and if anyone deserved to greet death, it was him.

"I don't know what you are on about." I keep my eyes forward and continued, "And I suggest you stop saying I do."

"Trust is an important thing to you, isn't it," the detective's lips curled evilly. "Trust, loyalty."

I nodded my head, not fully understanding where he was going with this.

"To be betrayed by someone you trusted… that would cut deep, wouldn't it?" The cop placed a hand on the armchair, putting his face dangerously close to mine. "To be betrayed by someone you cared about. Someone you trusted."

"What are you implying?" I said hotly, my fingers curling into fists.

"I think you know what I am saying. Blake is going to be deeply cut when he realizes…" The cop stood back up to his full height abruptly and turned around to face another officer who had just walked in. "Search complete?"

The officer nodded his head and I knew they had nothing on me. The detective I think knew this as well, as he turned to face me.

"Pity. Blake wasn't as lucky as you've been today," he shot at me, before walking out the room. The cops followed him.

"What do you mean?" I said with anger as I got up from the chair and walked quickly in the direction of the foyer as they began to file out. Finally, the raid was over.

"You will find out soon enough," the detective shot at me, narrowing his eyes. "I promise you Amber. You will be going down for both of their murders. Oh, and a bit of advice. If I were you, I would get that scar tattooed over because everyone knows a marked woman is a dead woman walking."

He walked out the front door and my eyes widened; only my family and the handful of people staying at Blake's knew about that scar. This means he had someone on the inside, an undercover cop or someone who was working with them.

His reference to trust now slapped me in the face. Someone was betraying us and Blake was now paying the price.

Chapter 18

Jax

"What the heck is this?"

I swiped the DVD from Cole's hands and hurled it back into the plastic bag, where he got it from.

"Nothing." I snapped at him before stuffing the bag under the passenger seat and continuing working on the CD player in my car.

"You into chick flicks, Jax?" Cole said smugly, while leaning on the open door, watching me.

"Piss off Cole." I pulled on the CD player, ripping it out; stupid wiring. Why had I decided to fix this bloody thing tonight?

"Or is it one of those secret movies you keep giving my sister?"

My head snapped up, my face now serious. "Does it matter?" I arched an eyebrow and my grip on the player tightened.

"Guess not." Cole slammed the door closed. "See you at home."

I watched him walk out of the shed. He didn't even pretend to hide his dislike about me being near Amber, but he seemed to be a bit softer about the issue now that I was dating Ella. I hurled the spanner to the floor.

Bloody El was making my life hell. Messaging me, calling me and showing up at the clubhouse. Damn woman couldn't take a hint.

I had asked her out to piss Amber off, which didn't really work as she seemed thrilled by the idea; even encouraged it.

Sighing, I leaned back into the car seat, one word and my mind went nuts; Amber.

Groaning, I ran a hand through my hair and messed it up. I didn't know how to show a female that I cared about her; not that I cared about Amber, I just... Fuck it, I don't know!

I was just protective of her, and jealous when she was with other men... yeah, I cared about her.

I slammed a fist against the steering wheel. I don't do girls, and I don't do feelings for them.

Easy lay, that's what they were to me.

But Amber was different; she stirred something different inside me. I was angry when she left to stay with Blake; I was hurt that she turned to him instead of us, well, mainly me. And now, I found myself bringing her food, watching movies with her, sitting with her at school. Fuck, I was even leaving her chocolate.

I glanced down at the plastic bag that was half sticking out from under the seat. I can't believe I had actually signed up for a Blockbuster card. I gritted my teeth; I was getting whipped.

Groaning, I started the car up, leaving the CD player half hanging out. A smile twitched at my lips; I was actually starting to look forward to spending Friday nights with her.

Her sitting there complaining and huffing about nothing, while gulping down the food I would get her. I would sit there, pretend to be bored. Then, when she fell asleep, I would carry her to her bed.

Flying out the garage, I realized I was definitely looking forward to being with her. Even though she didn't see me the same way... but it wasn't like she'd told me that. She was semi-nice to me and, every day, she was a little bit better towards me.

That is when she didn't slip into her depression and self-pity.

***

155

I pulled a plate from the Shield's cupboard and began to place the contents from the plastic boxes onto the plate, cursing under my breath as I burnt myself on the hot chicken.

I think Amber actually thought her family left her a meal every night. When, really, every night I would go out and get her tea and put it on a plate; this was an example of me being whipped.

"That smells good." Tyler walked into the kitchen and I didn't look up. "Why does Amber get good meals?"

"If you want one, go buy one," I huffed and then went to the fridge, pulling out a beer for her. "Though that involves doing something, so you won't."

Tyler rolled his eyes and I stuffed my school notebook into the plastic bags and threaded it on my arm.

"So, what is with you two?" Tyler asked. I balanced the beer in one hand and the plate on the other.

"Nothing."

"I thought you were with El?"

"I am."

Tyler arched an eyebrow at me, but I didn't say anything else as I walked past him. It wasn't his business; well, it was, to a degree.

Walking up the stairs, I began to question my own actions. I was entering the boys into a bloody war because of Amber. Sure they were entering our land, stealing from us, dealing on our turf, but it was their attack on Amber that sent me off the wires.

Coming to a stop at her door, I reminded myself that this was why Presidents didn't get in relationships because the female gets power over them, and their decisions can get blinded or influenced. Like mine was when it came to opening up the war.

They had hurt her; it was simple… I wanted revenge on them. I wanted to take the life of the man that had cut that scar into her stomach. The money and business they were taking from us didn't matter. It was them hurting someone I cared about, that was what turned my mind to wanting their blood.

I twisted her bedroom door knob and found her room empty. I worried about her not leaving the house. I think she only came to school because I dragged her out of bed and forced her on the back of my bike.

I placed her tea on her bedside table and pulled my notebook from the bag, sitting it next to the food, along with the DVDs, and then I added her favorite chocolates. Was it too much? I frowned. Where was she anyway?

I heard the tap turn off in the bathroom. Well, one guesses where she is then.

If she was back into her self-pity, I would slap her out of it. I didn't get why she was so upset about it, unless she cared for him more than she was letting on.

I froze as I thought that over. Maybe she was planning on getting back together with him. She was just not saying it. Maybe she loved him, even after everything he had done. My hand was still locked on the door knob.

I closed my eyes and exhaled slowly. No way. I was stronger than this. Amber might pretend to be a cold hearted bitch, but I knew she thought a bit of me. Well that was what I hoped; maybe she cared for me, even a little.

Thinking the best, I flung the door open. I would pull her out of this, and just keep my feelings suppressed about her until I understood them.

Amber

The water hit me in the face, and I reached for my towel.

This wasn't how it was meant to happen. We don't get caught.

Placing the towel on the basin, I looked up at myself in the mirror.

My eyes showed they were bloodshot from a lack of sleep, and the stress was taking a toll on my skin. Turning around, I slid down the basin and sat on the cold tiled floor.

This wasn't how it was meant to happen; not now, not ever. The bathroom door flung open and my head snapped up. What a surprise.

"What do you want, Jackson?" I pushed my hair out of my face. "Here to annoy me again?" I quipped.

"Get up Amber." He reached down and clamped a hand around my upper arm, pulling me forcefully to my feet.

"What the heck! Don't touch me!"

"Oh shut your mouth, alright," he snapped at me as he pulled me out of the room. "I'm sick of you moping around since he got busted."

"He didn't deserve to get caught!" I flung a closed fist into Jax's back as he pulled me into my room.

"Do the crime, do the time," he stated. Jax let go of my arm abruptly and I stumbled backwards onto my bed.

"What are you doing in here?" I glared from the bed, pulling myself up on my elbows. "I'm not your problem. You can stop babysitting me."

"I am sick of watching you mope around over a drug dealer. He got caught. Get over it."

"Stop watching me then! It's not like I'm your problem."

"Were you in love with him?"

"Yes."

Jax looked taken back at my response, and his jaw tightened as he glared at me.

"He was one of my closest friends. Of course I loved him." Did I love Blake? Yes. Was I in love with him? No. There is a difference. "You already knew that," I added.

"If you are going to react like this every time someone you care about gets locked up, you shouldn't be friends with criminals."

"Is that what you came here to say?" I arched an eyebrow, "That we shouldn't be friends?"

"What? No!" Jax crossed his arms. "Don't put words in my mouth Amber!"

158

"Whatever. Leave now if you're done with your speech."

"Cause you have better things to do?" Jax shifted his weight, still looking at me. He looked uncomfortable. I narrowed my eyes at him. What did he want?

"Yeah, I do. Avoiding you for starters. So… off you go then." I waved my hand for him to get the point, but yet he remained where he was. "We don't have to watch movies tonight."

"Do you hate me or something?" Jax spat out. "You have been shorter with me than usual. You know I had nothing to do with Blake getting arrested."

"I never said you did!" I pulled myself up on the edge of the bed. "And I haven't been," I added.

"You have been snapping at everyone since your boyfriend got locked up." He raised both eyebrows, "Although I seem to be at the receiving end of most of your bad moods."

"I'm not in a bad mood, and Blake wasn't my boyfriend!" I screeched.

"So, stop acting as if he was then!"

"Why don't you go annoy your girlfriend instead of lecturing me?"

Frustrated, Jax threw both arms in the air. "Fine, go screw yourself."

"I was thinking you should do the same thing."

Jax grunted as he stormed across the room. One hand on the door knob, he was about to pull it open when he turned around to face me.

"I know you aren't taking this well and I am…"

"I don't need you to do anything," I pointed out. "Nor do I need you to understand why I am acting this way. Personally, I don't want you thinking about me," I bit back.

"What the fuck did I do to you?" His eyes were narrow. "Why the fuck did you turn into this self-centered bitch? I've been bloody doing everything I can think of to cheer you up to get you to like…"

"Maybe I was always like this! Just took you awhile to catch on. You aren't the sharpest tool in the shed," I barked.

He stood there for a few moments, looking at me with narrowed eyes, shaking his head with a disgusted expression on his face.

"Fuck you Amber." He slammed the door behind him and I flinched at the force.

Well, that went well. I scoffed and threw myself back against the bed. Had he deserved that? Not really, but at the same time, I didn't care if I'd hurt his feelings. Well, that was a lie. Why was he even bothering with me anyway?

Ever since Blake got locked up, Jax has been making an extra effort with me and it was starting to have an effect on me. He was extending himself, like bringing me tea or pushing a new chick flick under my bedroom door now and then. A few times, he'd even stayed home with me and watched movies, but every time he did something sweet, it only made me start to have feelings for him. Feelings I shouldn't be having for him.

One, he had a girlfriend, which may I say made me question why he was giving me so much time in the first place and two, he was a criminal.

I couldn't fall for yet another man that I would have to take the back seat for. The crime always came before the wife. Not that I would be a wife, but still, a girlfriend always came second as well.

I glanced at my bedside table and saw the steaming plate of food. Jax must have placed it there before he pulled me up from the bathroom floor.

I groaned to myself; God, I was mean. My guilt only worsened when I noticed the rented movies to the side of the plate, and resting on them were his notes from school, along with my favorite chocolates. Looks like he had had our Friday night planned.

I deserved his wrath. He was really making an effort with me, trying to be, well, he was trying to be some sort of friend. Why, I had no idea, but he was trying.

I had to admit it. Having someone to watch TV with at night wasn't half bad. Nor was it that bad having someone leave chocolates and movies in your room. I bit my lip. It was actually really nice having someone to study with; especially considering we had exams coming up and, when it came to school, it was really nice of him to ditch his mates and sit with me.

Nearly as nice as when he brought me lunch from the canteen every day, so I didn't have to line up.

I groaned again. Who was I kidding? I liked him which was the main reason I was just a complete bitch to him. I was trying to lie to myself.

Trying to stop him from being nice to me, so maybe, just maybe, these feelings would go away but my lust was only replaced by guilt and guilt was a lot harder to sleep with at night.

***

I cracked my bedroom door open and, for the first time since Blake's arrest, there were no chocolates or movies waiting for me outside.

Damn, I really had hurt him last night. I crept silently to his door and gulped before I brought a closed fist to it, tapping lightly. Maybe he hadn't left yet; it was still early.

Why hadn't I just gotten up in the middle of the night to face him? I shook my head, thinking of my sleepless night. Guilt really didn't sit well with me. I tapped on his door again, but still, no answer.

Slowly, I cracked it open and stuck my head in.

"Jax?"

I pushed the door open a little wider; it was empty. He must have already left. The room was dark, so I ran my hand down the side wall, finding the light and flicking it on.

On his bedside table sat three empty bottles of vodka, next to an ashtray that was full of cigarette butts. Looked like his night wasn't that bad after all, but as I took in bed that hadn't been slept in, I reconsidered.

He hadn't slept last night. The side of his bed was a mess but the blankets weren't turned back, which either meant he didn't sleep, or that he had been drinking until he passed out.

"What are you doing in here?"

I spun around, guilt on my face, to face Tyler. He was standing in the door frame, looking rather smug, like he'd just caught me doing something I shouldn't have been doing.

"Looking for Jax."

"He isn't here. Did the empty room not tip you off?" He grinned evilly "Searching his room, were we?"

"No," I crossed my arms. "Where has he gone?"

"Clubhouse. And lying doesn't suit you." He pushed the door fully open and leaned against the frame.

"Are you going there?" I flipped my hair to the side.

"Yep. Why?"

"Can I get a ride?"

"Why?"

"Why do you think?" I arched an eyebrow. "I need to speak to Jax."

Tyler nodded his head and pushed away from the frame as I walked past him. Time to go eat some humble pie, the only sort of pie I didn't like.

***

"Tyler, where the FUCK have you been?"

I was standing slightly hidden behind Tyler as Cole barked at him.

"I'm here now," Tyler snapped back, before stepping away from me.

"Why are you here?" Cole narrowed his eyes at me, finally noticing me. "We have club business to take care of. Don't have time to babysit you."

"Oh shut it Cole," I barked as I swiped his half-drunk beer. "I just need to talk to Jax for a minute."

"Why did you bring her here?" Cole quickly shot over at Tyler, with two tight fists. "We already spoke about this!"

"Look, I didn't know she wanted to speak to Jax," Tyler said, meeting Cole's glare, and I kept looking between the two of them. Tyler had just lied; he knew I wanted to see Jax.

"And I didn't want to say no to her," he added, "considering she hasn't left the house in weeks, apart from school."

Cole grunted and said something under his breath before pointing to an open door behind me. "He's in there, make it quick."

Spinning around on my heel, I darted off in the direction of the open door. It was the same room that Blake and them had had their meeting in a while back.

Jax was sitting at the end of the table, studying a piece of paper, a lit cigarette in one hand.

"Jax?"

His head snapped up, and after the shock of seeing me wore off, he glared. "What do you want?" he barked at me.

"Um, just to... well... see you for a sec... like only if you have time... you know..." I trailed off.

"I don't." He butted out the cigarette. "Leave."

Ok, that was blunt. I had at least expected him to give me a minute of his time. He just returned his attention to the piece of paper in his hand.

"Look, I just wanted to say sorr..."

"Accepted, now fuck off." His voice was low and cold. He didn't pull his eyes from the paper to even shoot a glare in my direction when he spoke. "Now."

"Jax look, about last night, I really am..."

"I said fuck off Amber." He glanced up at me briefly, with anger and disgust, before looking back down at his paper.

"No," I crossed my arms. "Not until you hear me out."

Jax didn't look up and he didn't reply. Instead, he just sat there with a disgusted look on his face, directed at the piece of paper, but I knew that it was really meant for me.

"I… "

"Why are you here?" Troy walked in behind me, pulling a chair up at the opposite end of the table. "I thought you didn't leave the house now?"

"I'm here to see Jax. And I do when I want to," I snapped, letting out an annoyed sigh.

This was going to be harder now that Troy was in the room. "Could you leave?" I asked.

"No, we have shit to take care of. So, like I said Amber, leave," Jax piped in, leaning back in the chair. My eyes met his cold murderous look, and a shiver ran down my spine.

"Jax is right. This isn't the best time. Talk to him tonight when we come home." Troy pulled himself up the table and reached for an ashtray.

"Are you coming home tonight?" I glanced back at Jax.

"Not your concern." His voice was cold and my shoulders slumped; I had really hurt him last night.

"Jax, I'm sorry about last night. I was a bitch to you and you didn't deserve it." I uncrossed my arms and let them hang loosely by my side. "I don't say sorry much, so when I do, I mean it. So I'm sorry."

"Whatever, piss off."

God he could be a jerk when he wanted to be.

"Fine. Bye." I turned on my heel and slammed into Cole as he was walking in.

"How are you planning on getting home?" Cole asked as he steadied me. "Tyler has to stay."

"I have legs. I can walk," I grunted. "I'm not lazy."

"No, you're just a bitch," Jax said behind me, and I didn't turn around to address him. I was surprised the boys hadn't come to my defense though but I guess I had been a bit; well, quite bitchy to them as well lately.

"You can't go wandering the streets by yourself," Troy piped in. "We will get a prospect to take you home."

"I'm not going home," I snapped, "and your prospects' names are Matt, Luke and Owen. It wouldn't kill you to learn them."

Troy and Cole grunted at the same time, and I shouldered past Cole as I attempted to leave, but he stopped me. What a surprise. Everyone seemed to stop me before I did anything.

"What?" I arched an eyebrow.

"Where are you going? It's Saturday, you don't have friends."

"I have friends," I said as I pulled my arm from his grasp. "But I'm not going to see them."

"Just let her go," Jax snapped. "The sooner she pisses off, the better. She is wasting our time like always."

"Is that what I am to you Jax, a waste of time?" I turned around to wait for his reaction but he didn't look up; he just stared down at the table.

"Yes."

Well, that was all I needed. I stormed away. What a prick! I may have been a bitch to him, but I'd said sorry. It's not my fault he was too proud to listen! But as angry as I was with him, I couldn't help but wonder. Did he really mean what he'd said?

Chapter 19

Amber

Oh the joys of high school. Modified school skirts, painted makeup, hair styles stiff with products and my favorite, the cheap fumes of knock-off designer perfumes.

I groaned as I walked into the canteen. I hate people. I shouldered a few middle schoolers who didn't get out of my way; sure they hadn't seen me coming, but that was no excuse.

I glanced at the table that Jax and I had been sitting at for a week or so. What a surprise; he wasn't there. He hadn't come home last night either. Shocker. I think he was avoiding me. I'd already apologized. What did the boy want?

I dragged my feet to the canteen line. Oh, how I hated this. For the first time in a while, I actually had to get my own lunch; Jax wasn't around to get it for me. I wondered if he was just running late. Would he sit with me today? Should I get him something?

Standing in line, I glanced over the busy canteen area. My eyes paused when I noticed his toned back to me, a black t-shirt hiding his well-developed muscles. So, he was here. Looks like my theory was right; he was avoiding me. What a tool.

I stepped forward as the line moved. One little outburst and he cuts me off. Slumping my shoulders, I stepped forward again. I untangled my sunglasses from my hair and pulled them down, covering my eyes, hoping it made me invisible.

"Amber?"

Snapping my head over my shoulder, I narrowed my eyes at Andy, one of Jax's minions.

"What?"

He flinched slightly from my tone, shaking his head, "Um, I was just um… you know… ummm…."

I gestured for him to hurry up and get to the point. "Spit it out Andy."

"You know my name?" he gawked. "You know my name!"

"You just repeated yourself," I said as I cocked my head to the side. "You knew my name. I didn't make a big deal out of it."

"Well, I… you..." He rubbed the back of his neck. "That's different, "he said finally.

"Oook." I arched an eyebrow at him, before turning back around.

See, this just proves my point. High school students are stupid. Well, apart from me and Jax.

A finger tapped me on my shoulder and I snapped my head around again.

"What?" I barked, my voice a deadly hiss. Could he not see I was unfriendly? Again, stupid.

"I wanted to ask you something?" Andy grinned at me like I wasn't giving him daggers under my sunnies. "What are you doing tonight?"

"Anything, everything and something in between," I replied.

"Well, what time will that finish, because there is a party tonight, you know, celebrating the win."

"What win?"

"Our win! We beat the Sebastopol team last night and because the game was on a Thursday, we couldn't party, so we're partying tonight. You keen?" He grinned again and flicked his brown hair from his eyes.

"Keen for a party?" I questioned.

"Yeah." His eyes lit up with hope.

"I don't drink with infants." I turned my back to him and took a few steps, catching back up with the line.

"Don't bother Andy, Amber is a bitch like that," Jax said behind my back, and I whipped around to face him.

"Excuse me?"

Jax crossed his arms, standing next to a disappointed Andy. I wished he would wipe that disappointment off his face. It was bugging me. It made me feel... guilty.

"I said you're a bitch," Jax said with ease, looking at me with a bored expression.

"I think we both know you're the bitch in this relationship," I scoffed, and then panicked as the words left my mouth.

Jax smirked at me like he had just caught me in love with him or something.

"I didn't mean it like that," I snarled, and then flung back around, gritting my teeth.

"Sure you didn't," he muttered under his breath behind me.

"Hey Jax, are you sitting with us today?" Linda's voice was soft and sweet; everything she wasn't.

I kept my eyes glued to the smelly person in front of me. Couldn't they all just piss off? I was cringing in embarrassment here. Who did Linda think she was anyway? It wasn't like she was pretty or anything.

I shot a look over my shoulder and saw her link her arm through his crossed arms. So he had a thing for high school students or something? Don't do it Amber. I could feel my mind ticking evilly but, like always, I didn't, no, I couldn't stop myself.

"So, this party Andy, what time is it?" I faked sweetly.

"Um, nine it starts?" he looked confused. Dude, if I was him, I would be too. "Why?"

"I will join you after all. I don't have any plans," I replied as I shrugged my shoulders.

"Do you want me to pick you up?" he grinned like a happy little child.

"Aren't you planning on drinking tonight?" I arched an eyebrow and he nodded his head. "Well, that doesn't make much sense, does it? How about I just meet you at your house and we can catch a taxi together?"

"You? At my house?" he spoke so slowly, I was beginning to re-think this. Wait Amber, stay focused.

"Um yeah. That cool?" I turned to face him. "If not, I can, you know, meet you there, but I don't know where it is."

"NO NO!" he exclaimed, throwing his hands up. "That works fine."

I nodded my head and then glanced at Jax, who was glaring across the canteen at who knows what, but Linda's arm was still linked through his.

"You going tonight Jax?" I smiled. I had this innocence thing down to a fine art. He stopped glaring into the distance and looked at me.

"Perhaps," he muttered and locked his eyes with mine, clearly wondering what I was playing at. Poor boy couldn't keep up with me, even if he wanted to.

"Babe, you said you would go!" Linda tugged on his arm, my theory now proven correct. He had lined her up for a quickie. Scum much?

"Yeah, you should go," I said as I cocked my head to the side. "In fact, you should bring El, she would love it."

Linda frowned at me and asked, "Who is El?"

"His girlfriend," I said nonchalantly, brushing it off like I was talking about the weather. "A really good friend of mine." I looked Linda in the eye, "Like a sister, I would do anything for her. You know…" I trailed off.

Fear flickered in her eyes, and she unclamped herself from Jax. Looks like my reputation hadn't softened. Did I care about him cheating on El? Hell no. But Linda having her paws all over him bothered me. So sue me, I did it for myself, and to ruin the quickie he had lined up.

Jax shook his head at me and his glare could've shattered glass, but I shrugged it off and turned my back to him. He wanted to be a jerk; I was just paying him back.

"Actually, I was thinking of inviting the boys, you know, Cole and the gang," Jax said behind me, his statement sounding awfully a lot like a threat.

"Oh yeah, they would enjoy it," I replied coolly, taking him up on his bluff. The boys wouldn't care if I went to a high school party; they knew it was like childcare anyway.

People spewing their cheap alcohol they had stolen from mummy and daddy's cupboard, then grinding drunkenly into each other. And then there was always that girl, crying when she found her player of a boyfriend cheating on her.

"So come to my house tonight... early if you want," Andy whispered in my ear, before winking and walking off.

Dude, if he thought he was getting lucky, he had another thing coming. I wouldn't be getting *that* drunk. Well, I hoped not.

"My brother wanted me to give you this," Jax said as pulled on my shoulder, spinning me to face him, and then stuffing a piece of paper in my hand. "Seeing you have no standards, I thought I would pass it on."

His eyes screamed hate, but his posture screamed jealousy. I took a step up to him and he froze, as my chest touched his, leaning into his ear. "Accept my apology," I purred, my voice a seductive swirl.

After his insult, he would have been expecting me to punch him, scream at him, all the things I would normally do but he was jealous and I knew it, so I had the upper hand.

I felt his body tense as I leaned against his chest. We ignored Linda's scoff of disgust, and the fact that I'd just lost my place in the queue. He placed a hand on my lower back and leaned into my own ear.

"Mean it, and I will."

I pulled back and cocked my head, to look him in the eye. "I did," I whispered.

"You don't mean anything. You only think of one person. Yourself." He arched an eyebrow as if willing me to challenge him.

That wasn't true! How dare he stand here and call me a cold hearted bitch!

"You know what Jax?" I pulled myself away from him, his hand falling off my back, "I must have standards, because the last time I checked, I hadn't screwed you."

I didn't wait for his reaction; instead I stormed off, leaving the uptight, screw-anything-that-walks, self-centered, pathetic bikie behind.

As I slammed the canteen doors open, it hit me how hungry I was. Stupid man had cost me my meal. Now I hated him even more.

Chapter 20

"It's a bit short Am."

I stopped twirling and I rolled my eyes at Tyler, clipping the back of my earring closed.

"Don't like it Ty?" I arched an eyebrow?

"Are you guys going tonight?" I asked, changing the subject.

"Cole is," he smirked. "I wonder why."

"He's pathetic," I muttered darkly, and pulled the hem of the black dress down slightly. Yeah, it was tight and it showed off my assets, but what was the point in going out looking a rag doll? Everyone went out to impress, whether they liked to admit it or not. "Bloody Jax." I added.

"Yeah, he has a way of being a jerk when he wants to," Tyler said, seated on the edge of my bed.

"I didn't actually expect him to tell you guys about the party," I said as I grabbed my short leather jacket. "Come on, it's a high school party. Talk about lame."

"Will you be drinking?" he crossed his arms, and I nodded my head. "Then one of us has to be there," he added.

"Oh, get off it. You guys were never around when I used to drink," I pointed out.

Tyler remained silent, and I knew that him leaving me behind was a touchy subject but it was the history; facts. And you can't avoid facts.

"Hey Tyler?"

"Hmm?" He was staring at the carpet, clearly in thought.

"Do you think I am selfish?" I asked before putting my hands on my hips. "Like cold hearted bitch selfish?

"I... ummm what?" Tyler began to scratch the back of his arm; he was nervous, and that was his tell. Groaning, I sat down next to him.

"I am, aren't I?"

"Just a little," Tyler's voice was low. "But not in like a massive way. A little selfish, not cold hearted." Tyler rubbed my back.

"Well I am going to do something unselfish tonight," I said, standing up, my confidence better. "I am sure there will be an opportunity for me to be kind tonight."

"Well you are going to drink with toddlers."

"I call them infants," I said as I grinned at him. My brother and I were on the same wavelength; that's why we were related. I pulled my leather jacket on, and Tyler reached for his back pocket, getting the car keys out.

So, tonight I would do an act of kindness. I just hoped I did it before I got wasted.

***

"You look hot!" Andy screamed into my ear over the music. "Like smoking hot."

I nodded my head as he kept grinding against me. I was pulled tight to his chest. The music was pumping through the air at a deafening level, and vibrating through the floor; and even through our blood.

"Thanks!" I shouted into his ear. I gripped his neck tighter, our bodies grinding together. I was looking over Andy's shoulder, still looking for my moment to show 'kindness.' We had been here for hours; I was actually keeping count because I wasn't drinking.

Most of the people around me were heavily intoxicated, including Andy. Why wasn't I drinking? I don't know the answer to that one; when I got there, I just wasn't feeling it.

I think I was holding Andy up more than we were dancing. "Andy!" I screamed into his head and he drunkenly nodded. "I'm going to get a drink."

He sent me a drunken smile before letting go, saying something I didn't quite understand, but I smiled and nodded; I'm assuming he meant come back soon.

I pushed through the 'teenagers'; who knew so many people actually attended our school? Dodging a few people, I walked up the staircase. I didn't need a drink, but I did need a toilet.

I stepped over a guy passed out on the stairs, and then walked past a few couples making out against walls. Seeing the first door, I cracked it open and closed it quickly behind me.

Toilet. Toilet. Toilet. Toilet.

"OH MY GOD!" I screamed at the top of my lungs, and then slapped a hand over my eyes. "OH MY GOD!"

"Shit AMBER! Get OUT!" Cole screamed at me, and I fell backwards, looking for the door handle.

"I'm blind!" I cried. Cole having sex with a girl was permanently burnt in my brain.

"AMBER GET THE HELL OUT!" Cole grunted. OH.MY.GOD. Had he even stopped?

I found the door handle and stumbled out, and slammed it shut. My hand was still covering my eyes. Well it was official; I was ruined.

Pulling the hand from my face, I wondered if I would ever get over this. Didn't think so. I crossed my legs, thinking it was possible I was about to pee myself. I hesitantly placed a hand on another door knob; please, no naked brothers.

I opened the door with closed eyes, waiting for any shouting but there was nothing; cracking one eye open, I noticed the room was empty.

Sighing with relief, I slammed the door behind me, making a beeline for the ensuite. Thank God whoever owned this house had a bedroom with ensuite.

Drying my hands, I pulled the hem of my dress down again. Why did I wear such a short dress again? Oh right, to look drop dead hot.

What was the point again?

Sighing, I walked out of the ensuite and closed the door behind me. My eyes squinted as I struggled to see into the darkness.

"You look amazing tonight."

I froze in the middle of the room and slowly turned around to see Jax sitting against the wall across the room, bottles of beers to his side, and one in his hand.

"But I bet you know that," he added, his voice low.

Why hadn't I noticed him when I entered the room? Oh right, I was completely in need of a toilet break.

"Thanks," I said as I moved to sit on the edge of the bed, but then realized I couldn't sit down without giving him a view. "I think?"

Jax took a long slip on his beer, his eyes studying me through the darkness. I shifted uncomfortably and crossed my arms.

"You can go. I am sure your date is waiting." He shook his head darkly before chuckling darkly and taking a sip of his beer. "Amber and a high schooler. Funny."

Narrowing my eyes at him, I knew something was off. Good deed Amber, time for that good deed. Slowly I walked across the room and slid down the wall next to him. Letting my legs lay out in front of me, the dress rising rather high for my liking. Jax looked at me sideways for a moment before drinking again.

"You alright?" I arched an eyebrow and looked at Jax's profile and he continued to down the contents of the bottle.

"Does it matter?" he placed the empty bottle to his side, along with the others, and picked up a full one from the other side. "You can go."

"Don't be hormonal," I muttered dryly.

Jax sat there with a blank expression. Fine, we could sit in silence, I didn't care. This could be classed as a good deed, I reckoned.

"You like Andy?" Jax said as he lowered the bottle from his lips, still looking forward. "He's a crap man. Can't hold his liquor. Sleeps with anything that walks."

I raised an eyebrow. "I don't like Andy," I said, my voice low. "You don't have to try and make me think less of him."

"Then, why did you come?" he said as he glanced at me sideways, "If you didn't want to sleep with him?"

"I don't know." I shrugged my shoulders "Mainly to piss you off, I guess."

Jax and I looked at each other, our eyes level. A grin broke across his face and we both started laughing. I don't know why I found it funny, but hearing him laugh made me want to laugh.

"I came to keep an eye on you," Jax said, shaking his head. "In case you needed me. Like you would need me," he scoffed and rolled his eyes before bringing the bottle to his lips.

I bit my bottom lip. He came for me, I came for him. Funny how things worked out like that.

"I walked in on Cole… with Linda," I said as I shook my head. "My vision is now stained."

Jax's chuckle went deep and his chest rumbled heavily. "That's just disgusting."

"I know." I laughed and shook my head. Jax slightly drunk was softer, it was like his defenses were down.

"So how much have you had to drink?" I glanced at all the bottles to his side; the empty ones. "A lot I am guessing?"

"Yeah, a few too many," Jax said grinning, and shrugged his shoulders. "But it's a party."

"Then why are you up here?"

"Because I couldn't take seeing that jerk with his hands all over you," Jax's voice switched to bitter. "When I thought about snapping his neck, I thought it was best to get out of there."

176

"Why did you tell me that?" I asked, my stomach flipping over at his confession. "You could have lied."

"Didn't want the truth?"

"Just wasn't expecting it." I pulled at the hem of my dress, as I noticed Jax's eyes drift over it. "Not like you to tell me what you were actually thinking," I added.

We sat in silence for a few moments. Jax continued to drink, and I just sat there, stealing glances at him every so often.

"I think you have had enough," I declared. I reached out and took the bottle from his hand, as it hovered around his lips. Leaning over him slightly, my eyes locked with his.

My heart fluttered as our bodies brushed against each others. I placed the bottle to his side, but my body still hovered dangerously close to his.

I should pull myself away from him, I thought.

"How did you get here?" I finally muttered, my voice coming out in a low stutter.

"I don't remember," his throat audibly dry, and he swallowed quickly. "Why?"

"I'll call a cab. We still have time to watch that movie you got me last week. If you're keen?"

"I'm a bit drunk," he smirked at me, and then placed his hand on mine, which was gripping the floor. "But yeah why not," he added.

He pulled his hand away from me and slowly got to his feet. I got up easy, but he was a little slower. Groaning, he placed a hand on the wall.

"Great," He grunted.

"What?"

"Late fees." He looked me in the eye. "You still have that movie, which means I will have late fees to deal with," he explained.

Laughing, I reached out and took his hand. Even the hardest men have a soft side and the more time I spent with Jax, the more I saw it... and the more I fell for him.

Chapter 21

Oh baggy clothes, the pure comfort of them. The baggy t-shirt hung loosely around my waist, and my favorite sweat pants felt like heaven after that dress.

I walked into our cinema room. The lights were off and Jax was sitting on a middle recliner holding his head.

"You better still be drinking that," I coaxed as I smiled at him, noticing the untouched bottle of water on the side table. "I put Aspirin in it."

"Why would you put Aspirin in a full bottle of water?" he looked up at me. "You know I usually only have it in an inch of water, right?"

"Yeah but this way you drink a full bottle of water."

I sat down in the recliner next to him. "Drink up sunshine."

Jax sighed and picked up the bottle, flipping the cap off. "I think you are enjoying this," he said, glancing at me sideways. "Why didn't you drink tonight?"

"Don't know," I shrugged my shoulders. "Not in the mood I guess."

Jax nodded his head before drinking the water. Silence settled in the air and it was peaceful. Closing my eyes, I leaned back into the chair. Sometimes I enjoyed just staying home and relaxing. Sure I liked partying, but sometimes it was good to come home after it all and just bum around.

Although usually, I was always too drunk to really enjoy coming back.

"Come here."

Snapping my eyes open, I looked across at Jax. "What?" I frowned at him, wondering why he had his arms out.

"Come here!" He smirked, and gestured his head for me to move across to his recliner.

"You mean sit with you?" I looked at him strangely. I was sure he had sobered up a bit by now.

He reached out and pulled on my arm, and I slid over the recliner and moved to sit in the nook of his. He wrapped an arm around me, and I leaned into his side, my legs draping over the other side of the recliner. This felt surprisingly nice.

Oh Amber, you are going weak, I thought to myself.

Jax trailed his fingers up and down my arm and sighed softly. "Next time, we should stay in. Unless you're going as my date."

"Jax, seriously, what has got into you?" I couldn't look up to look him in the eye though. Instead, my gaze was glued to his lap and my head leaned on his shoulder. My heartbeat increased when he touched me; my body so close to his for the first time had me in a fit of nerves.

"Nothing." Jax's voice was low and his hand paused on my arm. "Why?

Do you want me to stop?"

What the heck JAX! Who in their right mind would want you to stop touching them? I swallowed nervously. "Ummm no. I guess not."

Of course I was attracted to him; who wouldn't be? But he was dangerous; he could hurt me. So we shouldn't be doing this.

But that didn't stop me from reaching out and taking his other hand in mine. Jax forced me to ignore my gut. For a smart girl, I became stupid when it came to him.

"Are you going to see Blake?"

Jax's voice was below a whisper as we sat in dead silence in the cinema room. We both hadn't even bothered to turn the movie on.

"I don't know," I sighed, dragging my finger up and down his arm. "He wouldn't want me to."

Jax nodded his head knowingly. Guys didn't like there girls visiting. Why? Well I wasn't a guy, so I couldn't answer that question. Though I wasn't Blake's girl, but still, he would view me so.

I turned my face to the side to stare at his defined profile. Even though the room was dark, I could make out every feature. His smooth jawline; flawless soft skin that just made me want to reach out and run my finger across it. His hair was a mess, but it was a sexy mess. Not the 'you-don't-do-your-hair-and-it-shows' mess.

Finally, my eyes drifted up to his face and locked with my favorite part… his eyes. I was slightly taken back when I saw them looking back smugly at me.

"Checking me out, Am?" He smirked and I felt myself boil from embarrassment.

"I well… no… just umm… yeah." I snapped my eyes away from his and glared across the room.

"Don't tell me, you have a little crush?" His lips brushed across my earlobe as he spoke, his voice husky and thick.

My eyes locked back with his as I turned my head back. Our lips were inches apart; our faces so close. Slowly, I trailed my hand up his arm and placed it on the back of his neck. I caught his eyes flicker down to my lips, just briefly, and it twisted my stomach in knots.

We were waiting for the each other to give in. I shifted slightly on his lap and I heard the muffled groan that left his lips. Like always, the girl had the upper hand, although my confidence disappeared when I noticed his eyes emanate pure and utter passion.

His tight grip on my waist was only confirming my thoughts. Any minute now, I would feel what it was like to kiss Jax. My heart melted and it took all my self-control to not drive my own lips forward and claim his lips.

"Jax?"

I jumped from Jax's lap as if it were on fire and stumbled to the floor. Jax looked startled, not understanding why I had just fled from his embrace but when he heard Cole's call again, he understood.

I scrambled to my feet, climbing over the two rows of seats and flinging myself to the ground in front. The smell of stale popcorn invaded my nose as I lay on the ground. Thank the Lord Jax and I were sitting at the back of the cinema. The doors opened and I froze.

I knew Cole wouldn't be able to see me from where he was, but I didn't want to think of what would happen if he caught me laying down; hiding.

"What are you doing in here?" Cole's voice was rough full with suspicion. "I thought you would be passed out somewhere?"

"Then why were you looking for me?" Jax said, sounding annoyed. I couldn't stop the smirk that spread across my lips. I think I knew why he was annoyed and it made me excited to think about it.

"Amber must have taken off with some guy," Cole grunted, and I heard a recliner move as he threw himself down it in. "I thought you might have seen who, before you left."

"Does it matter?"

"I was meant to keep an eye on her," Cole said slowly, as if Jax couldn't understand words.

"I'm sure she is fine," Jax replied, his recliner moving; he must have shifted his weight in it. "It's Amber after all."

"Yeah I guess you're right," Cole grunted. "Still, I feel bad."

"No you don't."

"She's my sister!" Cole's voice was low. "Of course I feel bad for losing her."

"You're pissed cause she interrupted your root," Jax scoffed, "And when you were done, you couldn't find her."

"How did you know that?" Cole exclaimed, sounding surprised.

"I can actually put things before a root." Jax's didn't seem nervous that he'd just nearly got us caught. "Last time I saw her, she was passed out upstairs."

Great Jax! How the hell was I meant to get upstairs before Cole did to check on me! They were silent for a few moments and I knew my brother, he would be sizing Jax up right about now.

"Right." Cole grunted, "I'm glad you're over your crush. El is a good chick."

Jax remained silent. What did Cole mean by crush?

"Yeah, she's alright."

"She's more than alright mate. If you're going to step up and call a chick your missus, she's worth it."

HIS WHAT! ELLA WAS HIS MISSUS! Since when? I knew that she was his girlfriend, but I didn't think he had taken it to the next step and actually claimed her as his, amongst his friends. If Ella was now viewed as Jax's 'missus,' she was off the market. His.

I was grinding my teeth. He was dead.

"What? Gone cold on her?" Cole grunted.

"I'm dumping her when I see her next," Jax said shortly; no explanations offered.

"Why?" Cole's voice was coated with suspicion, and I knew if I could see him, his eyes would be narrow and his jaw clenched.

"Cause I want to, got a problem with that Cole?" Jax said defensively.

"Stay away from my sister," Cole growled.

"Did I say anything about hurting her?" Jax snapped.

"Sleep with her and I will cut your balls off, got it?" Cole's threat even sent shivers down my spine.

"Remember who you are talking to," Jax said with a low hiss.

"I know who you are, which is why I am telling you. Stay away from her." Cole's threat was still a deep growl, and even if he wasn't scaring Jax, he sure as hell was scaring me!

"I'll stay away."

182

HE WOULD WHAT!

I gripped the carpet in my fingers, stopping me from jumping to my feet and charging at Cole. Who did he think he was? Threatning men away from me? If I hadn't been there, I wouldn't even have known.

"Settled then." The recliner creaked as Cole got up. "Night, mate."

I couldn't believe Cole had the ability to just turn of his threatning tone like that. The voice he just used sounded so light and carefree.

"Night." Jax's voice wasn't as forgiving.

Would he keep his word? I knew Jax wasn't an angel, but for my brother to even think he was too dangerous for me had me thinking. I bit my bottom lip. Was Jax really that bad?

I heard the door close, and slowly returned to my feet. Jax was glaring at the ground, his arms crossed tightly, his face murderous. How had Cole threatened that face, when it had the ability to look like that?

"Jax?"

Slowly, his eyes drifted up to mine. The only emotion I could get from him was anger - everything else was masked.

"It's late," he muttered, and then got up from his chair. "Night, Amber."

He started moving through the recliners, but I was quick enough to block his exit, standing cross-armed in front of the door. He wasn't avoiding me; I wouldn't let him.

"What? Gone cold Jax?"

"Move, Amber."

"Make me."

"It's late," he grunted. "Stop being childish."

"You weren't ready for bed a few minutes ago. What? Did Cole scare you off?" I scoffed and shook my head.

"What do you want?" he narrowed his eyes. "Because right now, I am half hungover and don't have time to deal with your shit."

My glare dropped; in fact I think my whole face dropped. My 'shit'; that was what he had called it. His voice was hard and snappy, and I felt my confidence fall a few notches.

"Fine. Night." I flung around, pushed the door open, and stormed up the hallway. One minute he's sweet, the next seductive, and then BANG, Mr Jerkface was back.

"Amber, wait!" He hissed behind me in a low voice. "I didn't mean it like that."

Oh yeah Jax, because what you just said could be taken so many other ways, I scoffed to myself. I felt him reach out for me, but I was too quick for him; I fled up the stairs. His footsteps were not as light as mine, and when I made it to the top, I darted off in the direction of my room.

Bloody Jax. He'd give anyone a headache.

Closing my door softly, I was finally in the clear. He wouldn't have the guts to come in here; not after Cole had threatened him.

I turned away, but was forced to whip my head back around when the door burst open and he stormed in with an annoyed expression on his face. He closed the door.

"Really? You thought a door would keep me out?" he grunted before walking to my bed, and taking his top off.

"Is there a reason you are taking your top off?" I flicked my hair out of my eyes, trying not to let my voice quiver with desire. "Last time I checked, this wasn't your room, plus, didn't my brother mention something about ripping your balls off if you slept with me?"

"It was cutting my balls off," Jax corrected, hurling his jeans to the floor. He casually lay back in my bed in his boxers. "Do I look like I am scared of your brother?"

"You should be," I said, crossing my arms. "Is that why you are in here? To prove that you aren't scared of him?"

Jax's smirk stumped me; in fact, it startled me! His eyes glinted with mischief as he placed his hands behind his head. Wasn't he dying of a hangover earlier?

It was an act. Big surprise.

184

"No. I'm here to prove I'm better than my brother," he stated matter of factly.

I opened my mouth and then closed it. My mouth formed an O when I understood what he meant, and I couldn't help the blush that crept across my cheeks.

I was only more embarrassed when Jax chuckled at my shock. His pendulum-like behavior was taking a toll on me; it was like he wasn't sure what he wanted, and it showed when it came to me.

"So, Amber. You ready to be handled by a real man?"

His voice was seductive, dangerous and inviting, all at once. Just like the drug you know might kill you. His eyes were locked with mine, drawing me to him.

So I wasn't surprised when my mind turned off, lust took over, and I found myself moving across the room.

Chapter 22

"So, how was the high school skirt?" Tyler snickered.

"Shut it Ty," Cole grunted. "I didn't get any."

There were a few different grunts of disbelief.

"WHAT?" Cole snapped. "I went to it to keep an eye on Amber."

"Sure you did," Troy's voice joined the conversation. "So, did you bring her home?"

Cole remained silent and the room broke out in laughter; I heard Cole snapping at them to shut up.

Putting my hand on the door knob, I closed my eyes tightly. "He won't be there, he won't be there..." I chanted to myself as I opened the door, and my chanting immediately stopped.

"Morning," I muttered, walking across the dining room and slumping down in a chair next to Adam. I shot a quick glance at Jax. He looked normal although his opinion of me would definitely have been different, considering the way I had high tailed out of my room.

Yep. I had frozen about three steps before getting into bed with him. I had realized what I was doing, and sprinted from my own bedroom.

"What's up sis?" Adam shouldered me lightly. I frowned slightly and took in his appearance.

"You got a haircut?" I raised an eyebrow questioningly. His hair was now extremely short, making him look like a gangster from a movie, and he was sporting a new tattoo that was peeking out from under his tank top. "New ink too?" I asked.

"Yeah. Thought it was about time I got the chest piece finished. How's the head?" He asked, offering me some toast. I declined.

"Umm not too bad." I replied with a smile. Sure, I had a headache, but it wasn't from drinking. It was because of that laidback bikie at the other end of the table.

He wasn't looking at me; good or bad sign?

The boys went back to talking casually between themselves, and I just sat cross-legged on the chair, cupping a glass of orange juice and not looking up from it. I knew if I did, my eyes would travel down to Jax, and I already looked like a child to him.

Who runs away?

"Amber?"

My head snapped down the table to Jax, who was looking at me, relaxed.

"Um yeah?" I asked. He was talking to me?

"Got any plans today?"

Shaking my head, I noticed how all the boys had gone quiet.

"Wanna go for a ride?"

I choked on the mouthful of orange juice, and he smirked at me while Adam patted me on the back; I had gone bright red.

He raised an eyebrow, looking rather smug. "It's meant to be a nice day. Thought you would be keen." He shrugged his shoulders. "Don't have to if you don't want to though."

"Well, I have no plans, so why not," I said, wiping my bottom lip. So he wasn't angry at me about last night.

Cole threw his fork down to his plate and made some grunting noise before getting up and leaving the table, making a scene. Jax, however, didn't look at him. His eyes were glued to mine. He was cool, collected and didn't seem fazed by Cole's reaction.

Maybe Jax didn't just want me for a quick lay. Perhaps he actually wanted me for more. Well, a whole day on the back of his bike... I would soon find out.

187

"So, about last night..." I started.

"Don't worry about it." Jax cut me off, handing me a helmet. "I put you on the spot."

"Yeah, but I acted like a child. Who runs away?"

Jax didn't respond. Instead, he got on his bike, straddling it and waiting for me. Placing a hand on his shoulder, I threw my leg over the bike and gripped him from behind, wrapping my arms around his waist, the leather of his patch cold on my arms.

"Amber?" Jax said as he cocked his head slightly over his shoulder. "I broke up with El."

With that, he started the bike up, it roaring loudly, without giving me a chance to respond. He broke up with El, which meant he... didn't care for her?

What does that say about me? Why did I get this feeling that the reason we were going out today was because he wanted to talk to me?

My stomach flipped over. I was falling hard for a bikie.

Chapter 23

"People keep crossing the road," I hissed up at Jax, as we walked hand in hand down the footpath.

He was standing tall, his patch on display for everyone to see. His sunglasses blocked his eyes from view, but I think everyone near us knew that his eyes were deadly. I attempted to pull my hand from his grip again, as I saw yet another family cross the street to get away from us.

"Stop doing that," Jax snapped down at me, and purposely pulled me closer to his side "I'll think you're ashamed to be with me."

Rolling my eyes, I attempted to not be pissed off by his confidence. "When you said let's go for a ride, I thought we would be going for a ride. Not a ride into town," I stated.

"Don't worry Amber, you can cling to me for the whole afternoon." He smirked sideways down at me, "I've just got to take care of something first."

We came to a stop out the front of a pub; men were leaning over the rail, bottles of beer and cigarettes in their hands. These guys didn't even care it was barely midday; actually it looked like they had been at it for a while.

"You can wait here or come in," Jax said as he eyed the few guys who were glaring drunkenly at us.

"I'm not waiting out here," I scoffed, and holding his hand, I walked into the pub, although he was quick to step in front of me.

Guys and protection, I thought to myself. God forbid a woman walked in front of them. I shot daggers into the back of his head as he guided us to the bar.

"Stay here," he said, and gently pushed me onto a stool. "I'll be back."

"So I either get to be ditched outside of the dirty pub, or inside it," I scoffed. "Great."

Jax put his sunnies to the top of his head and I saw his slight eye roll at me. "I won't be long." He glanced behind me. "Stay here. Got it?"

"Yep, crystal clear," I muttered dryly, and spun around on the seat to face the bar front on. I shivered as I felt his hand brush across my lower back as he walked from behind me, leaving me there.

"Want anything?" an old bartender huffed at me, dragging a dirty towel around the edge of a beer mug.

"I'll pass." I stated. I purposely turned back around and leaned on the bar behind me. If I didn't face him, maybe I wouldn't have to chat with him.

This place smelled like a bad mix of alcohol, cigarettes and stale food. I glanced at the closed door; Jax must have gone in. How long was he going to be?

I sighed. I wanted to ask why he and El had broken up but it wasn't like I could just come out with that, was it? I bit my bottom lip. He broke up with her... that was a good thing right?

"Get your fucking eyes off her chest!" Jax roared. I snapped my head at him, as he glared murderously across the room at a table full of men. "Fix your top," he snapped in my direction, before slamming the door behind him.

I didn't know those guys were even staring at me! I glanced at them briefly, each of them now staring into their beers.

Blushing, I pulled the hem of my top up; it wasn't like I'd pulled it down on purpose. Annoyed, I got up from the bar stool and walked out, casually brushing Jax's hand away as he went to hold my hand behind me.

"Amber," Jax growled behind me, as I took long strides away from the pub and him.

I was flinging my arms at my side as I walked, determined and embarrassed. Geez, Jax. He really knew how to talk to a woman. I gritted my teeth.

Jax caught my hand and pulled me up short, twisting me around to face him.

"Don't walk away from me."

"Don't talk me like that then!" I narrowed my eyes. "Seriously Jax, what do you want? What was the point of this 'ride' you wanted me to come on with you today?"

"I thought you might want to get out of the house," he said calmly, shrugging his shoulders. "It's not a big deal."

"I ran away from you last night, remember that?" I arched both eyebrows.

"I'm not making you be with me," he barked, his jaw clenched tightly and his lips pressed into a firm line.

"I didn't mean it like that."

His expression still remained the same, and I had the feeling I had already done the damage. Sighing, I let my head drop slightly and I glared at his feet. "I didn't mean it like that, you know that." I gritted my teeth, I hated being seen as weak or needy.

"Come on," Jax said, letting go of my hand. I glanced at him as he walked towards his bike.

Had I stuffed this up? What was I even thinking; there wasn't an 'us.' Running a hand through my hair, I took the helmet he handed me. Without looking at me, he straddled his bike and shielded his eyes with those sunnies I was beginning to hate.

I placed a hand on his shoulder and threw my leg over, pushing myself back a bit so my chest wasn't pressed into his back, and I wasn't clinging to him like a Koala.

I placed both hands on his side, lightly. The engine roared to life, and I noticed the way people wouldn't look in our direction.

Jax placed a foot on each side of the bike, and took his hands off the hand bars. I frowned for a second, before he placed his hands on mine and pulled them around his waist, pulling me into his back at the same time.

He seemed pleased by this, and he placed his hand back on the handlebar and revved the bike, pulling us away from the curb. I couldn't stop smiling; he'd kept one hand covering mine, on his waist.

We were slowly going up the middle of the road, not caring that we were getting dirty looks from each side. At least the street was wide.

Jax pulled his hand away from mine and placed it back on the handlebar, gripping the brakes. Seeing the light green ahead, Jax revved the bike to the max, and we fled up the street.

I squealed slightly at the surprise increase in pace, and I heard him chuckle. I tightened my grip around him. I caught his expression in the side mirror and stared at his smug expression.

Laughing, I leaned my head back and enjoyed the air whipping around me. I did notice the 60km sign as we passed it, doing close to 100.

I should've been scared, but I wasn't.

Because I trusted Jax.

***

"Not again," Jax groaned. "Seriously Amber, why?"

"Because I know you hate it," I smirked, placing the DVD in the player.

Jax gave me a mock hurt look. "This is the treatment I get after riding around with you all afternoon?"

"You loved having me on the back; don't make it sound like a chore," I teased, scooping up the remote and flying into the couch next to him. Sitting on my knees, I watched him cross his arms grumpily and glare across at the TV.

"Come on Jax, don't be grumpy," I teased, and poked his arm. "We all know you love Grease."

Jax shot me a blank expression, but I saw something flash in eyes, before he turned around on the couch and, reaching out for the remote, stole it from me.

"Oi!"

"I'll give it back in a minute," he grunted, and placed it behind him.

"Why take it if you are going to give it back?"

"Because the opening scenes of Grease will make me not want to do this." He flung his arms around me as he spoke, and pulled me across to him.

I gulped, slightly scared. No not scared; nervous.

"Amber," Jax's eyes were level with mine, and I felt his chest rising heavily as I was pressed against him. I straddled my other leg over his; now I was a little more comfortable.

"Jax," I said, mimicking his tone.

"Do you like me?"

I opened my mouth, both eyebrows arched in shock from his blunt question. I think I may have made some incomprehensible noises, while I just sat here looking like a shocked puppet.

"I... umm. Well, you know... umm... define... umm like."

I wanted to slap myself when I heard that come out of my mouth. God, I wanted Jax to slap me for babbling like that.

"You know what sort of like I mean,"

Jax smirked. Oh his amused look was not needed right now!

"Well, no. I like you as a friend, but you know, nothing else," I found the words, and they just so happened to be a lie.

Jax's face went blank, taking that smirk with it. His hands suddenly disappeared from my lower back and his expression went hard.

"Right, I get it." He slowly lifted me off him and placed me next to him. Putting the remote in my lap, he added, "You can press play now."

"Right," I muttered, and then pointed the remote at the TV, while keeping my eyes on Jax's clenched jaw and narrowed eyes.

"So Jax, do you like me?" I asked softly, watching for his reaction, but he just gripped his arms tighter as he crossed them. He was angry, and I had made him angry but I had a feeling he was more angry at himself in this moment, than me.

"No."

"Pity," I said slowly, and let out a loud sigh. "Because I lied."

Jax's head snapped over at me, so quick that I was sure he had whiplash from it. "What?"

"I said I lied," I repeated, saying each word slowly and then smirking at the end. "I like you," I finished.

"Like me," he repeated, his expression suspicious.

I nodded my head and fiddled with the remote in my hand. "Yep, I like you."

"What are you doing tomorrow night?" Jax spat out, and I giggled at the rush of his words.

"Nothing. Why?"

"Go on a date with me?"

"A date? Have you even done a date before?" I cocked my head to the side and watched as he thought that over. Clearly from his frown, he hadn't.

"No."

"So why don't we just skip that step."

I smiled and then slowly wrapped my legs around him again, straddling him. "Why don't you just ask me what you want to ask," I whispered in his ear.

Three words Jax, I know you can say it. Enough with the games, enough with the time wasting. Let's just dive in head first. I bit my lip; he would ask, wouldn't he?

"Amber," he pulled my head forward, our faces an inch away. "Your brothers will kill you," he finished.

"No, they will kill you," I corrected him, hiding my fear of what could come. "Look Jax, I won't be just another one of your girls. It's all or nothing."

"I don't do girlfriends."

"You did with Ella."

"That was different, I did that to piss you off." He scoffed. "I didn't care about her."

"And me?" I arched an eyebrow, and leaned closer into his lips. "All or nothing Jax," I repeated.

"I can't have people close to me," Jax softened, as he brushed the hair from the side of my face, his eyes begging me to understand. "Having you as a girlfriend makes you a target, something that can be used against me."

"I'm not a flower Jax. I can take care of myself."

He went silent at that, his hand still on my cheek. "I can't..."

I pulled my face away and brushed his hand from my cheek. "So, when you asked me if I liked you, you just wanted me to say yes, and then what? You would sleep with me?"

"No."

"Then what?"

"I want you as mine, I just..."

"Don't want to make it official?"

"You don't get it Amber, I'm not a normal guy!"

"You think I don't know that?" I leaned back and glared at him. "Do you think I don't know that every time you guys go out, there is a chance you won't be coming back?"

I got up from his lap and slapped his hand away as he attempted to pull me back.

"I think you forget Jax, that you're not the first guy I have fallen in love with that is a criminal."

His expression went blank as his hand fell to his lap. "Fallen in love with?" he whispered.

I slapped a hand over my mouth. Shit, had I said that out loud? I quickly changed the subject. "Don't ask me to be your girlfriend, fine, but that means we are just friends, nothing more."

Jax's face turned in disgust. "So what, we don't do anything but watch gay movies together?"

"We can do lots of other things Jax, just nothing sexual because I will be doing that with my boyfriend." I crossed my arms, "Because I don't do friends with benefits."

"You had no problem sleeping with my brother!" he spat, and got up from the couch. "Is he a friend of yours too?"

"That was a one night stand," I spat back. "I didn't care about him, but now that I know that there is no future for us, apart from friendship, maybe I will give him a call."

"Don't threaten me," he snarled.

"It wasn't a threat."

"Fine!" Jax roared. "Will you be my girlfriend?"

"No," I scoffed and glared at him. "Go screw your whores Jax!"

"I can't win with you!" he snapped and shook his head. "You are impossible."

"I wanted you to ask me because you wanted me to be your girlfriend, not because you felt like I made you."

"Women," he huffed. "All they do is mind fuck you. This is why I don't do relationships!"

"You're not in a relationship," I pointed out, and glanced at the closed door. I was surprised not one of the guys had come in, given all the yelling. "So you're safe Jax. You don't have to have your mind consumed with relationship problems."

"You know what, fine!" Jax stormed away from me. "I've got an endless line up of women who won't whine at me to be my girlfriend," he screamed over his shoulder.

"Don't worry Jax, I won't be asking you again," I spat at his back as he opened the door. "We aren't friends either."

Jax growled at me before slamming the door behind him, hard.

"FUCKING WOMEN!" he roared outside the closed door, and I heard something being thrown before his heavy footsteps disappeared.

I hated men. No, I hated Jackson.

That was a lie. The whole reason I was this worked up and angry was because... I cared for him. Stupid, selfish bikie he was.

Chapter 24

Jax

I wasn't known for having great control on my temper; when things were getting to me, I would just let it out but when it came to Amber, I couldn't.

So I was permanently in a bad mood.

The boys were over my answers, sick of my bad attitude. I knew that, but it still wasn't stopping me from taking my frustration out on anyone that got in my way.

Amber wanted strings. I didn't do strings. I didn't do relationships and I sure as fuck didn't do girlfriends.

So, how could she ask the two things of me I was incapable of giving? To top that off, she was flat out ignoring me.

Didn't help I was ignoring her too though.

I ignored the fact that she made me go crazy. I tried to ignore her the other day when she was in the garage working on one of her dirt bikes, wearing only a bikini top and shorts. Why she was only wearing that was beyond me; I guess it had something to do with the weather.

Then I did my very best to ignore her at school, even when she wore clothes that showed off every inch of her body.

I don't think she realized she did it. Showing off her figure like that.

She basically had boys drooling over her.

But her reputation kept them all at bay.

Then when she wasn't torturing me at school, or at the place I am forced to now call home, she was at the clubhouse because one of her idiot brothers brought her.

She had taken a shine to the prospects. Maybe because she knew their names and didn't just bark orders at them.

I caught her confronting Luke when one of the club girls ended up going after Cole instead. I didn't know Amber did feelings, or cared about anyone but herself, but she proved me wrong yet again.

Just like she proved me wrong when I thought her and I were on the same page about where we were heading.

I didn't do girlfriends. Surely she should have known that?

Did my reputation say nothing to her?

I glared down at Adam as he worked on the motor.

Then I caught sight of her out of the corner of my eye. I wanted to groan. In fact, I think I did, softly. Could she look any more attractive?

I didn't know why she was dressed up but I had a strong feeling the boys were going to get it out of her.

Amber

"And where are you going?" Cole snapped at me as I closed the garage door. Motorbikes half together and different parts littered the garage floor but I didn't pay attention to the boys as they worked on the bikes; not even Jax, who was glaring at the motor him and Adam were pulling out.

"On a date," I said over my shoulder and stepped over Troy legs, as he worked under a car.

"With whom?" Tyler spoke up.

"No one you know," I said lightly, and pressed the button to unlock my car. I was thankful we had such a large garage, so that the boys weren't making their mess in front of my cars.

"Try me," Cole challenged, placing an oil-stained hand on my door, blocking me from opening it.

198

"He's a guy from school. Now move!" I pushed him, but then decided it was best not to touch the grease monkey.

"Is he a criminal?" Troy now entered the conversation, having pulled himself out from under the car.

"No," I sighed. "Now move, I'm going to be late."

"What sort of guy makes you go pick him up?" Cole scoffed.

"He isn't picking me up because I said I would meet him there," I huffed. "MOVE!"

"Where's there?"

"We're going to…" I stopped short and pointed a finger at him. "Nice try Cole. I'm not telling you."

"Fine, we will tail you," Cole shrugged his shoulders, and I noticed he began to wipe his hands on a towel.

I glanced briefly at the other boys and they seemed to be packing up too.

"You have to be kidding me!" I snapped "For God sake! Let me have a life!"

"No," Troy said bluntly, and closed the lid of a tool box.

"Ok fine!" I crossed my arms tightly. "It's not like you guys will get in anyway." I grinned and leaned back against my car.

All the boys now took in my knee length, deep blue dress, and my curled hair.

"Why are you so dressed up?" Cole frowned.

"I said I was going on a date," I sighed.

"Where to?" Tyler scoffed "You're dressed like you're going to one of dad's events."

I arched an eyebrow at him and then all the boys let out a noise of disgust.

"You're kidding me! You're going to dad's business thing tonight?" Cole looked at me, like I was an alien.

"Is that so hard to believe?" I snapped "He asked me, and I didn't want to say no. I'm not rude, unlike some people."

"So you said yes." Troy crossed his arms, "And you taking a date? Does dad know?"

"Of course he knows!" I sighed and tapped my foot. "He's already met Mark before."

"Mark?" Jax growled. "Your date is Mark Phillps?"

"Yep." I shot him a bored glance. "Got a problem with that Jax?"

Jax grunted, but didn't reply.

"I think he might actually have the guts to ask me to be his girlfriend tonight," I added with a smug expression, and faked a dreamy sigh at the end.

"LIKE HELL!" Cole roared. "If we haven't met the bloke, there is no chance of this boyfriend talk."

"Fine, come then, and meet him. Oh wait, you guys don't wear suits. Bugger, out of luck then," I chirped as I placed a hand on my hip. "Now move Cole."

"Why would you willingly go to something of dad's," Tyler asked, looking at me suspiciously. "Unless you are getting something out of it." He narrowed his eyes, looking at me closely for a few moments. "Ok, spill it Amber, what has he promised you?"

"NOTHING!" I threw my hands up in the air. "And Cole, stop putting marks on my car!" I slapped his arm, which was leaning on my car.

My phone buzzed in my purse and I shot the guys a dirty look, and they all suddenly went quiet. Did they know what personal space was?

"Hello?" I sighed into the phone, frustrated.

"Amber, you're running late," My dad said.

"It's not my fault, the boys won't let me leave." I shot them a smug look.

"Tell them you'd better be here in five minutes, or they will all know what it is like to ride a push bike," dad said in a lowered voice, most likely preventing people around him from hearing his threat.

"I'll pass the message on dad," I said as I smiled out at the boys, who all rolled their eyes.

"Five minutes," he stressed.

I hung up. "Dad said..."

"Don't bother threatening us," Cole snapped, and then pushed away from my car completely. "Fine. Have a nice night."

"I will," I said, opening the door and ignoring the death stares from my brothers. "I'll tell Mark you guys want to meet him."

I closed the door smugly, blocking out their low threats.

Turning the key and bringing the car to life, I smiled slyly as I pulled out of the garage.

Mission one complete - making sure Jax knew there was competition. Now, just to make him man up to his feelings; I hoped a bit of jealousy would push this along.

I glanced in the rear view mirror and noticed Jax throw a spanner across the room.

Success.

***

"Thanks for yesterday Mark!" I smiled at him as we walked up the school corridor. "Really, you made the night not boring."

"Us secret millionaires need to stick together," he said, winking at me.

When dad had introduced me to his business partner's son, you could imagine Mark and my shock when we realized we'd been connected this whole time. Mark's dad placed him in this hell called public school because Mark hadn't made an effort at any of the private schools.

Mark and I had that in common.

"So, you going to come watch the game tonight?" Mark asked.

"Nah, I don't do school events." I smiled. A locker slam jolted us from our conversation, and we both glanced in the direction. Jax didn't even give me a second look as he stormed away from his locker.

"Well, I'll see you at lunch," Mark said politely, and I noticed his eyes trail off in the direction of Linda as she walked past us.

"Right," I smirked. "Bye Mark."

I turned the corner and looked over bobbing heads, looking for Jax. Why was he taking so long to man up? I thought he would've said something last night when I got home, but he didn't.

Troy had taken me to school that morning; Jax had already left.

And what annoyed me more was the pleasant smile on Cole's face when he noticed Jax giving me the cold shoulder.

Jogging down the stairs, I entered the canteen and spotted Jax sitting on a bench with his friends; they could be known as his sheep.

I just wanted to go up to him and slap him across his face and tell him to grow a pair.

"Amber?"

I spun around and smiled politely at Rachel. Well, look who it was; my somewhat friend.

"Rachel, how have you been?" I asked as we fell in step with each other.

"Yeah, normal. Hey, I was wondering if you are keen on some drinks at the beach tonight?"

I hadn't talked to her in weeks, maybe longer, and she was inviting me out?

"I can't, sorry. Got plans."

"Right." Rachel rolled her eyes. "Sure you do."

"I do," I snapped, annoyed. "Look I got to go. Bye." I brushed her off and quickly turned around, now walking in the opposite direction. I didn't want to hang out with her.

I glanced at Jax, who looked at me, bored. Maybe that was what I did for him now; maybe I was just a bore.

I groaned and pushed the canteen door open; all I wanted was to have him admit he wanted me! Why was that so hard for him to do?

***

I ran my fingers under my t-shirt, outlining the scar on my stomach. This had become a habit of mine. I dropped my head to the side and looked out the bay window, watching the storm roll through. The rain was heavy on the roof, and the cracks of thunder kept making the lights flicker.

I knew any minute now the lights would go out, and I would be stuck in darkness. I watched another streak of lighting across the sky. I turned my head back and stared up at the ceiling, lying on my back in the sitting room.

The room was like another lounge room, apart from the fact that it overlooked the gardens. The lights flickered again and, this time, they went out. The room fell into darkness and the only light that entered the room now, was from the lighting.

Home alone in a storm; well tonight was just looking great, wasn't it? I pulled my t-shirt up a little higher and kept running a finger down each line.

It was late and everyone had better things to do than be home tonight. Well, everyone but me. I didn't want to beg Tyler to stay home but when I saw the storm warnings on TV, I knew I should have.

"AMBER?"

I sat up straight "JAX?"

I narrowed my eyes, trying to make out the figure that had just pushed the door open.

"Are you ok?" Jax's voice was laced with panic.

"Yeah, I'm fine." I crossed my legs, watching Jax's chest rise heavily. He pushed the wet hair from his forehead.

"You didn't answer your phone," he said, his breathing settling slightly.

"I lost signal." I rubbed the back of my neck. "Sorry."

"It's not your fault," Jax muttered, and then pulled his patch off, and peeled the wet jumper under it off. "Fuck, it's awful out there."

203

"Did you ride in this?" I frowned. "Are you crazy?"

Jax shrugged his shoulders and pulled the wet t-shirt off, now standing there bare-chested. He unclipped the gun holster from around him and placed it on his wet clothes. Walking across the room, the dark blue light that flashed across the room highlighted his scars and chest tattoos.

I inhaled slowly as he lowered himself to his knees in front of me, his eyes solid as they locked with mine. He placed a hand on my waist; I saw the way he waited for my reaction.

"You could get sick," I stuttered, and ran a finger down his icy cold chest. "You shouldn't have ridden in this weather."

Another loud crack of thunder roared overhead.

"Amber, I would ride through worse to make sure you were OK." He gripped my hand, which was on his chest. "I can't take this anymore."

My head leaned back, just slightly, as I saw the lust in his eyes.

"Do you know how hard it was for me to let you go out last night, looking as hot as you did?" he said, smirking, and I shamelessly blushed.

"Be my girlfriend," he whispered down at me, while bringing his face closer to mine. "Please?"

I placed my other hand on the base of his neck. I felt his chest rising heavily under my other hand, pinned to his chest.

"Yes," I whispered.

I didn't need to think of my answer, so when the word flowed from my lips, I wasn't surprised.

His head dove down and he claimed my lips. He kissed me hungrily and I caved. His hand dropped mine and went around and gripped my waist, pulling me tighter into his cold chest.

Finally he'd stepped up, I thought to myself, as my lips broke into a soft smirk through the kiss.

Chapter 25

Jax's hand ran down my back, and I curled more into his chest. The rain drummed down on the roof, deafening in the room. Jax's hot lips slowly worked a pattern down my neck, his fingers softly running under my t-shirt up my back, causing my skin to shiver with desire.

His hands ran further up my back, his cold hand pulling me closer into him. "Don't tease," I stuttered, as he sucked the base of my neck. I ran my fingers up his bare chest, and then slung both my hands around his neck.

Lightning flashed through the room, and another rumble of thunder roared overhead. "Do you want to take this upstairs?" His words were broken as he continued to kiss up my neck. He pulled his head away and the smirk on his face made my pulse race with passion.

Tracing a finger down his tight jaw, I asked, "Are the guys coming home?" As I spoke, I felt my chest rise against his.

He shook his head slightly, and I felt his hands grip the hem of my t-shirt. My hands slowly crept down his strong tight chest, pausing on his defined abs. My head tilted up, our lips dangerously close.

I smirked slightly, as I let my hand drop from his abs and brush across his crotch. A low growl escaped his lips, and his hands quickly yanked my t-shirt off over my head. Threading my arms out of it, as soon as the t-shirt landed on the ground, Jax wrapped his arms around me and clenched me to his chest.

"Upstairs, downstairs?" he asked, his voice thick.

"Impatient?" I smirked.

His lips drove forward and claimed mine. His tongue flicked mine and I gripped each of his shoulders. My lace bra brushed across his chest, and I was thankful his eyes were locked with mine. I gripped his shoulders and kept his lips against mine; when he attempted to pull away, I tightened my grip and kept his lips pressed to mine.

His hand brushed across my stomach, and I quickly planted my hand on his and guided it back to my hip. His lips broke from mine quickly, and I didn't have a chance to try and keep them there.

"What's wrong?" his voice was thick, and my eyes floated to his tan chest; I just couldn't keep my eyes level with his.

"Nothing, I'm fine." I placed my hand on his belt. Jax grabbed both of my wrists and holding them, pulled my hands away.

"Look at me," he instructed.

Sighing, I looked up into his eyes and my head tilted to the side slightly. "I'm fine," I stressed.

He wasn't buying it. He let go of one of my wrists. Slowly, he placed a hand on my side, his eyes watching my reaction. Gently, his hands crept further towards my stomach. Gulping, I put my hand down to push his away, but he pulled his hand away quickly.

Placing a hand on my back, he pushed me back gently into the carpet, holding both of my hands up above my head; his thick hand trapped both of my wrists up.

"What are you doing?" I frowned, as he leaned on his side beside me. "Jax, look at me."

But he didn't. His eyes were raking my stomach. I watched as his eyes trailed up and down the scar, the scar that I was embarrassed to show anyone, but here I lay on display, for him.

"You're ashamed of it," he mumbled and his finger reached out to trace it. I wiggled under his grasp, trying to stop him. "Stop that," he said, and slapped my stomach lightly.

"Then stop touching it," I snapped. "You don't have to."

He lowered his head to my stomach, threw a leg over my waist and straddled me. Slowly, he lowered his mouth to the base of one

206

of my scar lines. He kissed it, before he slowly traced his tongue up the line and then did the same on the other side.

"I'm sorry," I sighed. I wanted to touch him, but my wrists were still held under his hand. "I know seeing that mark isn't exactly a turn on."

"This scar…" Jax pulled up and kneeled, his hand brushed across a faded thick scar line on his hip. "Your brother gave me this, and Cole doesn't let me forget it." He grunted. "This one," he turned slightly and I saw the long line down his side. "Pub fight," he added, "And the ones on my back, well it comes with the club I guess."

"Yours are scars, not marks."

"You wear the scars, Amber, don't let the scars wear you." He lowered his head back to my flat stomach and placed a soft kiss in the middle. "Don't shy away from me again."

"But…"

"But nothing!" He arched an eyebrow at me. "Now shut up… girlfriend."

I chuckled and couldn't stop grinning. "I think I like the sound of that."

Letting go of my wrists, his hands went to work on my body. He slowly kissed along the waist band of my shorts, and I felt his fingers slowly undo the bow.

Slowly, he pulled my shorts down. The smirk on his defined jawline only made me want to drive my lips back to his red, moist mouth.

He dragged my black panties down my thighs, his eyes full of admiration. I reached forward, undid his belt, and pushed his jeans down his hips.

"Impatient babe?" Jax smirked, while he unclipped my bra, and slowly pulled the straps down my arms. He hurled it to the side.

And then he looked down at me with an expression I had never seen on a man's face before. Blake didn't even look at me the way Jax was looking at me right now.

I frowned "What's with the look?" I couldn't stop myself from asking.

"You're beautiful Amber." The words just spilled out of his mouth.

My frown hardened. "No I'm not." I knew I didn't even come close to the women he was used too. He was used to models and pornstars. And I was, well, just me - a scarred and tattooed wreck.

His expression tightened. "You are." And he lowered his lips to mine. "And now, completely mine."

Just as he said that, he thrust into me, making a gasp escape my lips. As if he was proving to the world that I was his now, and his alone.

Jax never claimed any woman, but, right now, as he took me, I had a strong feeling he was making a point to me; that I was his.

"God, you're tight," he groaned in my ear as he pulled back and then thrust again.

"What's that meant to mean?" I gasped, my nails accidentally digging into his back tattoos, as he thrust deeper into me.

"Nothing," he muttered in my ear, and his hands gripped my lower waist and threaded my legs around his waist. He pulled me from the ground; he moved inside me, causing me to bite my tongue. "Don't hold it back babe," he chuckled in my ear, and I pulled back slightly to see his smirk.

"Where are we going?" I gritted my teeth as he pushed up inside me; he began to walk up the stair case.

Jax nibbled the base of my earlobe. "Don't worry babe, I'll take care of you soon."

"You could be taking care of me now."

"What if your dad comes home suddenly," Jax grinned at me. "You really want him to see you like this?"

"Then why didn't you wait to take my clothes off? Or, for that matter, to start the job?" I arched an eyebrow and gripped him slightly tighter as he balanced me with one hand and opened the door with the other.

"I didn't think of it before."

Jax kissed my neck as he kicked the door closed behind him. I gasped again as he flexed inside me again. "God, you're tight," he muttered.

"Again! What is that meant to mean?" I kissed his shoulder, and slowly he lowered me to the bed.

"Later."

Jax moved me back into the middle of his unmade bed.

He looked at me again with that expression I didn't understand, and then he smirked.

"What?" I said.

He shrugged, "This is how I've wanted you for a long time now." He kissed the mark on my neck and pulled back. "Naked, and in my bed."

I arched an eyebrow at him. "Well, it took you long enough to make a move." My hands ran over his toned shoulders. I sighed. "Seriously, what took you so long?"

He was still inside me; I could feel him and I knew if he thrust into me, my question would remain unanswered.

His eyes locked with mine and, like always, when I stared into his eyes, I found myself losing my breath.

"Reasons and opinions of others," he said calmly, and his eyes ran down my naked body. "None of which matter anymore."

"Why? Because you finally got what you wanted?"

"Amber, if you think one night with you is all I want, then you're wrong." He thrust into me, causing me to gasp again. "I've never had a girlfriend before, but I want you to know now, sex is an every night thing."

I laughed. "Seriously? What about my brothers? "

"We live in the same house and our rooms are directly across from each other. I think we will manage the late nights."

"Sneaking around, hey?" I went up on my elbows, smiling like an idiot. "What other expectations do you have of a girlfriend?" I was interested now. A part of me dying to know, while the other half was scared I wouldn't measure up.

His lips went to the top of my breast and he kissed me. "Whenever we are alone, I want you on me, sitting in my lap." He pulled out and thrust into me again, this time causing me to fall down to the bed, my elbows buckling. "I want you always ready for me at night, expecting me."

A moan left my lips as he took my nipple in his mouth. God, I'd told him not to tease me! I was so turned on right now, that what he was saying wasn't really hitting me.

He pulled out and thrust into me with more power. "I want you willing to get naked in a second for me. And I want to shower with you. You, naked and soapy, has been one of my fantasies. In fact, no showering without me."

I was already smiling, "Is this showering thing going to be an everyday type of thing, like sex?"

He ran his tongue down my jaw. "Sex in the shower is fine with me."

Suddenly, I was looking forward to showers. Actually, I was going to look forward to when night came. Sneaking around wasn't something I would normally do. I was blunt and direct but if it meant I had a relationship with Jax, then I would do it gladly.

"I'm going to make you come every night and moan my name, and I'm never going to get sick of hearing it and when the next night comes, I want the same - you coming and moaning my name. You understand Amber?"

He thrust into me hard when I didn't answer.

My hands went to his chest and I nodded my head.

He smirked. "Good. Let's start that tonight."

Wait a sec, weren't we already having sex? Then I realized this was just him outlining the rules, and the sex was still to come.

"You ready babe?" He whispered in my ear, like he was about to fuck me so hard, I wouldn't just be moaning, I'd be screaming his name.

He was slightly out of me and before he could thrust into me, I moved my hips and engulfed him, giving him my answer.

He started at a steady speed, and it already had me clamping my mouth shut.

He kissed my lips for a second before pulling back, "Come on sweetheart, and don't hold back on me."

I kept my lips clamped shut.

He picked up the speed; just when I thought that wasn't possible. A moan left my lips and my back arched.

"Come on sweetheart, I want to hear you." He thrust deeper into me, causing my lips to part.

I had never felt this overwhelming, intense feeling before. Sure I had had sex, but this… this was something else.

"You moaning my name and coming is part of the deal." He took my nipple in his mouth and I didn't automatically let the moan escape my mouth; I was dying to at this point, as he killed me with pleasure. "Every night sweetheart, starting tonight." His mouth moved from my breast and kissed my lips.

Again, he was fucking me so hard and intensely, it was causing my whole body to tremble.

Just when I thought it couldn't get any better, he started fucking me harder, causing the moan to escape my lips.

He smirked, satisfied, like that was what he had been waiting for. His kept the insane pace and lowered his head to mine, his arms taking his full weight.

"I want to hear you and feel you come. Don't hold back." He kissed my forehead.

Another moan left my lips as he kept pleasuring me, and, just as he wanted, I didn't hold back on him.

Chapter 26

I skipped down the stairs, my hair bouncing as I jumped the last few stairs and landed in the foyer.

"Why are you so happy?" Cole asked with an eyebrow raised, as he walked through the lounge room door frame.

"The sun is shining; is there a reason not to be?" I grinned. "Why are you here?"

"I live here." His eyebrows furrowed together as he studied me. "TROY!" he roared behind him. "AMBER'S DOING THAT SMILING THING AGAIN!"

"Real mature Cole." I rolled my eyes and then darted to the front door, opening it quickly and slamming it behind me. I heard the dull rumble of Troy's voice as I walked down the porch steps.

I, Amber Shield, am Jax's girlfriend.

I bit my lip, suppressing my grin. God, he was mind blowing. I glanced across at the lined up bikes, his missing.

Sighing, I dug my hand in my handbag and searched for my car keys. Jax had left early; what a surprise. Unlocking the Hummer, I frowned slightly before getting in. Maybe he was over me? He got the goods last night, more than once then when I woke up this morning, he was gone.

Suddenly, my happy mood was fading as I thought this over again. Closing my door, I thought, why the heck was I now willingly going to school?

I jumped, startled by the knocking on my window. Frowning at Tyler, I pressed the button and the window went down.

"What?" I asked.

"Can you give us a ride to the clubhouse?" Tyler shifted a large bag on his shoulder. I glanced behind him and noticed my other brothers walking towards us, all carrying big black bags.

"Why?"

"Cause."

"I have school."

"Aren't you guys on holiday?" Tyler gave me a blank expression, "OR did you forget that?"

"How the heck did I forget that!" I cursed, and shook my head. "Well then, doesn't look I have an excuse not to take you guys."

Tyler was already opening the back door, not really listening to me. I glanced sideways at Troy, as he sat down in the front seat next to me. The other three loaded into the back, all with big black bags on their laps.

"So, where's Jax?" I asked causally, and placed the car in drive. "Or was he not lucky enough to get a black bag?" I smirked, while glancing in the rear view mirror. All the guys seemed to miss my dig and looked out the windows, bored. Cole grunted a reply - 'clubhouse' and then the car fell silent.

"Didn't sleep well last night?" I asked openly. Each one of them seemed pissed off to the max. I didn't know when they came home last night, because what my brothers were doing or where they were was the last thing on my mind at the time.

I sighed internally as I remembered Jax's hands roaming my body, and his ability to multi-task.

"No," Tyler grunted and leaned his head against the window. "God, I would do anything to be asleep right now."

"Yeah," Adam yawned.

"Dad's gone again," Troy huffed. "Don't ask me where he went, I wasn't listening that closely."

"I think he made us stay, just so someone was home for Amber," Cole scoffed and then muttered 'babysitters' under his breath.

"Well, don't you guys function well with no sleep," I muttered matter of factly, lowering my foot on the accelerator.

I went to turn the radio on, and Troy quickly slapped my hand away, giving me daggers too.

"Fine, we will remain in silence," I huffed, and glared out the front window.

Boys with no sleep were more hormonal than females. Tapping my finger on the steering wheel, I thought, why did I get the feeling today was going to be a long day?

***

"FUCKING MANIAC!" Cole slammed the car door and continued to curse about my driving skills as he walked away. Adam and Tyler both still looked terrified, while Troy was exhaling slowly.

"Oh come on! I was nowhere near it!" I defended my driving again.

Troy looked across at me, his face twisted in disbelief. Leaning over quickly, he swiped the keys from my hand and got out of the car, ignoring my protests.

So I may have overtaken a car, and may have just not seen a truck coming towards us but really, they were overdoing it. I had managed to get us off the road in time. Sure, we may have spun out onto the gravel road, but we made it here!

I glared into Troy's head as I followed slowly behind them. Entering the clubhouse, the smell of cigarettes and alcohol consumed my nose once more.

"Finally, you guys show up," a deep voice greeted my brothers, as we walked in. I noticed Cole was already at the bar, reaching for a bottle of spirits.

Troy was talking and shaking an old guy's hand and, when he pulled away, I saw Jax. Sitting causally on a couch, he had a beer grasped in one hand, and the other arm wrapped around a female.

214

Gritting my teeth, I inhaled very slowly. Do.Not.Kill.Her. I continued to chant this, as the female moved closer into Jax's side.

"Hey Jax," I chipped, and then crossed my arms. His expression dropped, and I saw the horror in his eyes. He was totally caught out.

I was more annoyed than angry. I knew he couldn't avoid females altogether, that would clue my brothers in.

So I guess I had to get used to him... screw it, I was not convincing myself that this was acceptable. I wasn't the type of girl to hide in the corner.

"Oh hi Amber," someone quipped. I turned around, and Jason walked around from outside the bar. "Jason, didn't see you there!" I grinned, and I noticed Jax's eyes narrow slightly.

Oh can't life be a bitch, Jax? I sniggered to myself as I grinned freely at Jason. What a perfect time for him to show up.

"Amber, get that look off your face," Cole snapped at me. "You can go now."

Jason chuckled, while smirking at me. I ignored Cole altogether. "So Jason, what are you doing here?" I asked.

"To see me," Jax huffed, but I didn't look at him. Instead, I bit my lower lip slightly, my eyes glued on Jason.

"What are you doing now?" I asked Jason, while pushing the hair from the side of my face.

Jason opened his mouth to speak, but Jax's loud voice stopped him.

"Amber, a word, first." Jax got up from the couch, and my brothers didn't seem to care as I followed Jax. Jason sent me a pitiful smile.

Sighing and crossing my arms, I walked into the room Jax held the door open to. Closing it, his cool blank expression turned deadly as soon as the thud from the door echoed in the small room.

"Don't play with me," he threatened, pushing me slightly back against the wall, his eyes narrowed and deadly. "You're mine now."

"Yeah, I am yours, so tell me, are you mine?" I arched an eyebrow, not caving into his possessive posture.

"That chick was nothing and you know it."

"My conversation with Jason was nothing."

"I might be soft on you Amber, but don't make me show you another side," he growled. "You're my girlfriend. I will be the one to protect you. I will be the one to kill any bastard that touches you so don't make me kill my own flesh and blood."

His voice was so thick and threatening; I had never seen Jax this defensive before.

"I'm not going to lose you," he added, and leaned his head slightly closer to mine. "I have never been faithful to a woman before, so when Katie sat next to me, I didn't even think about pushing her away. I'm sorry. I'm new to this," he said softly.

"Don't tease me, and I won' tease you," I said calmly. "And for the record, touching another female like that does cross a line for me."

Jax slowly wrapped a hand around my waist and pulled me closer to his chest. "Then I won't let it happen again." His lips were slowly getting closer to mine. "Although, it might be noticed by your brothers."

I threaded my arms around his neck and held his head closer to mine. "Good thing, I'm dating a hardcore biker then who is fearless."

Amusement flashed in his eyes.

"Yeah, it is," he muttered, before he drove his lips against mine. I had a feeling that this relationship was going to be hard work but the passion that was firing through my body as he kissed me told me it was worth fighting for.

Chapter 27

"God, I wish we could just go home," I grumbled, pulling away from Jax's lips just slightly so I could speak. My hands were firmly planted on his back, and his arms were pinning me to the table I was now sitting on, my feet dangling over the edge.

"If we stay any longer, they will come looking for us," Jax said quickly, before he claimed my lips again with a quick kiss, sealing our fate as he pulled away. "Come on."

Groaning, I let my hands drop back to my side and Jax helped me down, pressing me to his chest; slowly, I slipped down his body. My feet softly met the ground; man, that was a turn on. "Come home soon tonight?" I pleaded with my eyes. I wanted to finish what we had just started.

"I won't be coming home tonight." His lips formed a firm straight line. "We're leaving on a run tonight, we won't be back for a week."

"WHAT!"

"Babe, keep your voice down."

"You're leaving, for a week?"

"We all are," Jax said as his hand snuck under the back of my t-shirt, and his cool skin was sending shivers down through my skin.

"Why now?" I groaned. I couldn't keep my hands to myself, so I placed a hand on each of his shoulders.

"We had to wait for school to close so I could go," Jax said, looking disgusted. "You will be alright babe." He kissed my forehead lightly. "I can get someone to watch the house, while we are gone."

"It's not that, it's just..." I bit my lip for a moment; I didn't want to be that needy girlfriend. Sighing, I wiped my expression and hid my true thoughts and disappointment from him. "It's nothing, don't worry about it. We should get back." I pulled my hands away from him.

Jax continued to frown down at me, but nodded his head slightly and pulled his hand away. "Call me if you need me." He stuffed his hands in his pockets and I smiled, nodding my head at him.

"Try and keep it in your pants while you're gone," I teased, and he shot me an annoyed expression before he turned around and opened the door.

I swallowed the disappointment, knowing that I wouldn't be touching him again until he got back and we had privacy; away from everyone else.

"What the fuck were you two talking about for so long?" Cole snapped from behind the bar.

"Blake." I closed the door behind me and shrugged my shoulders innocently, with a bored expression. "Jax needed some details."

Jax didn't look back at me. Instead, he walked back to where he was sitting before. I wanted to grin so wide when I noticed he decided to stand instead of sitting back next to the skank.

"Ok, I'm off." I said, swiping the car keys from Troy's back pocket. "See you guys when I see you."

"It won't be for a week," Troy spun around quickly. "We're going away for a bit. You will be alright, right?"

"Yep, fine." I began to tap my foot nervously; I just had to keep my cool for a few more moments. "Have a safe trip." I sent a smile at each of my brothers before I looked back at Troy.

"Ok..." Troy dragged the word out, while frowning. "Call if you need us."

I nodded my head, walking away quickly, and waving over my shoulder. I wouldn't be that weak little girl; I just couldn't be. Not in front of Jax, and not to my brothers.

I pushed the clubhouse door open, and knowing that I would be by myself for a week consumed my thoughts.

I was dreading this.

Chapter 28

Jax

Troy tapped the hammer, and the meeting was officially in session. I glanced at Drake and Swan, both Presidents from leading charters. They both looked slightly stunned that I was letting Troy still be in charge. After all, I was the son of the great, I over-ruled all of them.

"The run, will it be a week, or two?" Drake's voice was a low growl, like it normally was.

"A week," Troy spoke up and lit the cigarette in his mouth. "Perhaps two, if things go longer."

"They shouldn't," I cut in, fearing what two weeks could do to mine and Amber's fresh relationship. "If it does, we will send the job over to the New Castle charter."

Troy shot me a dirty look, clearly not liking me pulling rank but I would be fucked if I spent two weeks away from Amber. I was throbbing at the thought of being away from her for a week.

"Whatever you say," Troy muttered bitterly, before glancing at his brothers, then back at Swan and Drake. "Could you boys clear out for a moment?" Drake and Swan looked offended, but they weren't in a position to deny Troy's direct request.

Grumbling under their breath to each other, they pushed their chairs back with anger and stormed from the room. Clearly, both Presidents didn't like being spoken down to. I looked at Troy; why would he do that?

When the door closed, it was only us five once again. Mike and Dale, our other seated riders at the table, were in Melbourne doing some collecting.

"We have something to discuss," Troy pulled his chair up and placed his cigarette on an ashtray. "It's slightly personal," he directed at me. "But still club business."

Cole leaned back in his chair, Tyler too moved in his chair to give Troy attention, and even Adam put his beer down.

"It's about Amber." Troy's eyes were still on me. "I know that this may come across as personal, but it relates to the club."

I nodded my head for him to continue.

"I don't think we should leave her behind," Troy sighed. "She won't last."

Won't last? What the heck did that mean?

"I was going to bring this subject up," Cole grunted and crossed his arms. "I want her to come."

If I had been drinking, I would have choked, and if I had been smoking, I think I still would have choked.

"Why?" I spoke, and looked at the four of them. Each had an understanding expression, but yet I was in the dark.

"She doesn't like being left alone," Tyler answered me, and turned to look me in the eye. "She might look tough and fearless, but she isn't."

I knew this, and I felt like punching him for telling me about my girlfriend. My expression turned bitter, and I knew they saw it.

"Look Jax, we don't like asking for personal favors. Fuck, it pisses me off having to ask this but I want Amber on the ride; but it is club business so it can go to a vote," Troy said as he crossed his arms.

"She doesn't like being alone isn't a big enough reason for her to join a gun run," I crossed my arms. I wanted to be near Amber, but her coming on this ride would place a greater responsibility on my shoulders. I would have to keep every wanker away from her, without bringing it to her brothers' attention, and, on top of that, I have to lead a successful dangerous run.

But then if she was with me, I would know she was safe.

"She's coming," Cole growled at me, but his statement meant nothing.

"Not if that is the only reason," I snapped back.

"Amber can't be left alone," Adam said calmly at me, knowing that threats wouldn't get any of them far. "She isn't well enough."

"She's sick?" I arched an eyebrow, although I knew she wasn't. She had been anything but sick last night. I wanted to groan; why would I bring those memories to myself at this moment?

"She's on a list," Tyler muttered. "We have been handling it, so it didn't relate to the club."

"What sort of list?"

"A hit list. Blake got her on it," Cole snarled and glared at the table. "After he went to jail, she has been placed as the informer."

Amber was on a hit list? I gritted my teeth; I was pissed off that they had kept this to themselves. "Has anyone approached her?"

"No, not yet," Troy added. "Which is why we want to keep her close."

Now another job had been added to my plate, although this job I would complete with pleasure. Someone was threatening my girlfriend, my only weakness. These poor bastards had no idea who they were messing with. They were dead men walking.

"She comes," I grunted. "My vote is in favor."

The guys looked at me, each expecting to have had to do more to get my vote but they had it now, and I knew they wouldn't question it any further.

"We will deal with the hit list when we get back." I got up, my expression blank. "Next time, don't keep things from me."

"The hit list doesn't affect the club," Tyler said slowly.

"Amber is your sister. It splits my Charter leaders' attention; it affects the club." My voice was firm and harsh. I couldn't have them running around behind my back, leading their own war. "We will leave tonight like planned."

Troy brought the hammer down, and the meeting was closed. It would be impossible to keep mine and Amber's relationship a secret for much longer, especially once we get back and I hunt those bastards down for thinking they can hunt my girlfriend.

"I'll pick Amber up," I said. "It will stop the conversation." I opened the club door and Troy nodded his head at me with a thankful smile.

Bringing your sister on a run wasn't going to look good in the other riders' eyes, but if she was on the back of my bike, not one biker would doubt why she was here. If they did, I would shoot their head off; as, unlike the Shield boys, I could actually kill a member and I would, for only two reasons; betrayal and Amber.

***

"Amber?" I knocked on her door, and pushed it open slowly. "Amber?" Where the heck was she? I heard the running tap and walked across her room quickly.

"Amber?" I said louder. It was late; after ten.

I pushed her ensuite door open, and running water was filling the spa, but she wasn't in it. Alarmed, I took the scene in quickly. I felt myself being pulled to the ground as I took her in, sitting on the floor, her knees to her arms and her head in her hands.

"What the fuck is wrong?" I panicked, and her head snapped up as I placed my hand on her knee. Her eyes were wide, and her cheeks stained with tears.

"What are you doing here?" She choked. Her skin was freezing and I began to wonder how long she had been on the cold floor.

"For you," I said, reaching behind her and turned the tap off. "What's wrong?"

"I... nothing." She inhaled quickly and bit her lower lip.

"Don't lie to me," I kneeled back in front of her, placing a hand on each side of her. "Now I'm going to ask you again. What's wrong?"

223

"It's pathetic," she whimpered. "Don't worry about it... you should go."

"Tell me."

She shook her head stubbornly, and her hair whipped across her face.

"Go," she muttered, and wouldn't look me back in the eye. Each tear that fell down her cheek angered me more. I didn't like watching her cry, and it pissed me off that I didn't know how to stop it.

"Fine, get up."

I wrapped my arms around her waist and supporting all her weight, I pulled her to her feet. She didn't fight me, and I scooped her up easily. I knew Amber hated being seen as weak and I knew right now she would hate herself.

I carried her out and softly placed her on the edge of her bed.

"Where are your bags?" I grunted, before pulling her wardrobe doors open. I groaned as I took in all her stuff.. How the hell was I going to be able to pack her shit, when she had so much stuff to pick from?

"What are you doing Jax?" she wiped the tears from her cheeks.

"You're coming with us." I pulled something from a hanger, and when it turned out not be a jumper, I flung it to the floor. Her walk-in wardrobe was massive, and it was full. Suddenly, I was facing a new nightmare.

"On the run?" Her voice was dry.

"Yes," I snapped. "If I can get your shit into a bag."

I snapped around when I heard her giggling, frowning at her. She held her stomach. Her cheeks were red, and her eyes were bloodshot but she was laughing.

"I've spent the last two hours depressed. You didn't think of calling me and telling me this?" She shook her head. "God, Jax!"

"How the hell was I meant to know you would be crying?" I crossed my arms. "I didn't think you would care that much."

She automatically looked offended and then I watched her face turn to disgust. "Fine. I'm not going."

I sighed; I'd set myself up for that one. "That wasn't what I meant."

"It sounded like you weren't going to miss me, so fuck you, I'm not going to miss you." She crossed her arms, like the headstrong woman she was.

I walked across the room and stood in front of her. Why did I have to fall for this strong-willed woman?

"Babe, I didn't mean it like that." I placed a finger under her chin and pulled her head up. "Next time I will call. Now please, help me pack your crap. The guys are waiting."

Amber's eyes were fierce, even under the red stains. She wouldn't let me see her emotion, and she wasn't letting me off the hook that quickly. Pushing my hand away from her face, she got up and pushed past me.

I couldn't help but smirk as I sat on the edge of the bed, watching her begin to pack. She was one hell of a woman, and she was my woman; I had fallen hard.

Chapter 29

Amber

I stood, arms crossed, casually at the back of the car park, like I had been told. I gritted my teeth watching a black haired woman cling to Jax's side like a leech. Perhaps I would be happier if she had been ugly, or looked like a normal whore who would cling to a biker, but she wasn't. She was beautiful and, when I say beautiful, I mean drop dead stunning, and it only made me want to wring her neck so much more.

"Amber bed, now."

I looked at Cole with a dry expression. For some unknown reason, all my empty headed brothers had made it their mission to boss the life out of me while on this trip. Ever since we pulled out of the club gates last night, and considering I had already put up with it for 24 hours, I was ready to bring my claws out.

"No," I snapped back, and stubbornly pushed back to the wall. Like hell I was going to sleep in a dirty old club room; not while my so-called boyfriend was out here with a woman who looked like she had just stepped out of a magazine.

"Amber," he growled, and stepped in closer; blocking my view of Jax. "We allowed you to come on our conditions, remember?"

I don't know how Jax had got them to agree to me coming, but I wasn't going to ask questions. He told me this trip was important to him, and, after much consideration, we decided it best in both our interests to keep our relationship on the downlow while on the trip but lines were drawn, well one line; if he slept with another woman, or women, we were done.

"Fine," I grunted and shouldered him as I stormed past. I narrowed my eyes at Jax as I strode across the biker club car park, which was packed with members; bonfires sent shadowed light across it.

Pushing their clubhouse door open, I noticed it was surprisingly a lot dirtier than ours; who knew that was even possible.

"Amber?"

"I'm already going to bed," I snapped over my shoulder to Tyler. "Want to tuck me in?"

"Bitchy much?" Tyler scoffed. "And no, just wanted to check on ya, alright."

"Why wouldn't I be?" I spun around and I noticed the surprise in Tyler's eyes as he locked eyes with my murderous ones. I just had to keep a lid on it, because it wouldn't be fair for him to cop the full lash of my anger. "Everyone loves bedtime."

"Third door down the hall, and don't take it off the hinges when you slam it," Tyler said dryly, backing away quickly; most likely the smartest thing he had ever done.

"Who knew the Shield's had a baby sister?" A deep, amused voice spoke after Tyler shut the door. My eyes darted to the lounge chair, taking in the gruff, older man.

"Who knew couches talked?" I snapped back, before taking in his patches on his vest. Looked like the club President of this chapter didn't have the partying fire.

"Snappy aren't we?"

He butted the cigarette out and nodded his head towards the armchair next to him. "Take a seat."

"Prefer not to, got to get to bed." Lame cop-out excuse, but, seeing the mood I was in, I knew I could do damage if I chatted with the President. "Night."

"The Amber I knew didn't listen to anyone, let alone her brothers. Perhaps it is your new boyfriend that has these sudden reins on you."

My mouth opened and then shut. For once, I had no comeback.

"Take a seat Amber," he said, his lips curling in amusement.

"Who... Do I know you?"

"It's been a few years, but surely I haven't changed that much?"

I took in his gruff face again... his solid body... his appearance didn't ring a bell, but, as I took in his tired eyes, it hit me.

"Been a while Grant, although last time I saw you, you weren't wearing club colors," I said. I arched an eyebrow at him, "You also weren't exactly in a fit state. Off the beer, are we now?"

Grant's chest rumbled with laughter and he shook his head at me as I sat down in the chair to him.

"Tell me, how is my nephew?"

The small smile disappeared from my face as I answered, "Prison."

Grant's broad smile went firm into a tight line. "Good leaders often end up locked up for short periods of time." Grant moved forward in his chair, slightly turning his eyes to me. "So, why are you playing with your brothers when the gang needs a leader? Blake only ever really trusted you."

"We broke up a while ago," I muttered. "Things just didn't work out."

"My nephew never realized how important you were. I always knew he would lose you." Grant leaned back in his chair. "Though I already guessed that you had broken up, seeing as you have a new man."

"What are you talking about?" I crossed my arms. "I don't have a new man."

"Went from dangerous, to deadly;" he arched both eyebrows as he spoke, "And I thought you were smart."

"Don't know what you are talking about old man. Since when were you a member of the Deadly Dozen anyway? And, from your vest, it looks like you are President."

"Blake's father and I were prospects together. He left after a few years to form the gangs that Blake proudly runs now, and I... well... I stayed."

"Talk about family tension," I muttered, liking the fact that the subject was now off me. "So that's why you didn't wear your patch at the BBQ when I met you."

Grant nodded his head causally. "Once a year I take it off, for the family."

"Well I'm guessing your family BBQ is off this year."

"Considering Blake won't be attending, I have no need to go." Grant moved forward and leaned across the chair to me. "Now tell me, why you are dating a walking time bomb."

"Excuse me?"

"Jax is deadly man, Amber. He isn't someone you want to get close to."

"Good thing we aren't close then," I snapped at him, while narrowing my eyes. "We aren't dating."

"Seeing that he has had his grips wrapped around my daughter for most of the night, I tend to believe you to some degree."

"The beautiful woman he is with is your daughter?" I asked, shocked.

"Yes, and every time Jax rolls in, she is his pick."

"And you let him?" Surely Grant wasn't that much of a pushover.

"Mai goes to him, and I don't want to pick a fight I can't win." Grant lit another cigarette and the chair crackled as he moved in it.

"Jax isn't that tough," I grunted, as the memory of him picking me up from the bathroom floor flashed across my mind.

Grant's deep rumble of laughter brought me out of my flashback, and his wicked smile had my full attention.

"I suppose he isn't to women he sleeps with."

"I'm not a bed warmer."

"No, you've already been kicked out by the looks of it, by Mai."

"My brothers wouldn't exactly be thrilled to hear we are together. We don't have a choice."

"Your brothers are weak when it comes to Jax, just like I am." Grant looked at me with a knowing, warm, fatherly smile. "So why are you staying in the shadows?"

Grant knew the headstrong Amber; the one that would put a gun to someone's temple and not even blink. He'd heard of the girl that could help Blake take a hit out, and eat and laugh, all in the same night. That girl was unstoppable, but now I realized I was only unstoppable because I'd had Blake. Without him, I was robbed of the little strength I had left and now, well now, I was a shell. One that cries when left at home, and whose boyfriend runs around doing whatever he wants. All because I was scared of my brothers?

"I don't know," I muttered, rising from the chair. "Jax isn't Blake."

Those words settled it. I knew Jax was strong, but maybe his new found love for me wasn't. Blake would've stood up and declared me his, and anyone who got in the way would be shot.

"Not all relationships are crystal clear. Night old man," I said.

"Don't let him make you feel weak Amber."

I stopped in my tracks as I was retreating to the bedroom that I was meant to have been in all this time.

I sighed softly before I began to walk away again. Maybe he was right.

But I still knew I was going to learn the hard way, because I always did.

***

Pulling my arms through the long singlet that stopped mid-thigh, it was clinging to my body from the heat already. I pulled my hair up loosely; I was sick of the heat alright.

The bedroom had turned into an oven and I had the pleasure of staying in here all night. Opening the bedroom door, I allowed the cool air to swish around me, and it felt like taking a dip in a cool pool. Anything would feel cooler compared to the oven I had been baking in.

"Last night's leftovers have woken," a guy chuckled to me darkly from a bar stool as I walked into the main living area. His eyes raked up and down my body as he belittled me.

"Don't speak to her like that," Grant roared from across the room. The room went silent and only now did I realize it was full. Jax and my brothers were also in there. Suddenly, there was an uneasy tension in the room, as everyone's eyes darted between me and Grant, all most likely thinking I was his last night.

"How did you sleep Amber?" Grant broke the silence in the room.

My eyes were locked with Jax's for a moment and then his narrowed with suspicion as Grant spoke directly to me. "Fine, old man," I said. Breaking my eyes from Jax's, I strolled across the room to sit next to Grant. "You?" I asked

Conversation had returned to the room, and I had a feeling that I wouldn't be receiving any more comments from a Deadly Dozen member again. I was thankful Grant had done that; it had saved my brothers from having to come to the rescue.

"Not well enough. Considering you left me in the dark," he said. His lips curled slightly; he was stirring shit on purpose, making a play on words to make me look guilty.

"Whatever," I muttered and glared at the floor. Swallow me ground, swallow me I prayed. I hated attention on me!

"Let's get to business," Jax's voice ordered, and I heard his chair legs drag along the ground. "We have a run to lead this morning, as you are aware…" Jax was speaking directly to Grant, making sure his attention was off me. "Clear the room," he said.

"All people currently in this room are people I trust, so Jax, no need to take this private," Grant said. I felt Grant's eyes dart in my direction, as he continued, "Unless there is someone in here you don't trust, then we can."

I glanced up at Jax and was surprised to meet his angry eyes directed at me. Did he not want me to be here? He looked as if he was having a debate with himself on whether to order me out or not.

"The guns. Where are they?" Jax snapped and crossed his arms, clearly coming to the decision he couldn't ask me to leave.

"At the boatyard. The delivery was smooth. Did you take care of that problem at your end?"

"There wasn't a problem." Jax's voice was firm as he glared at Grant, clearly indicating that Grant just mentioned a subject he shouldn't have.

"The buyer has changed," Grant spoke as if he wasn't receiving a silent death threat from Jax. "The TNS will be buying them. Pick up is still the same place."

"We don't know them!" Jax roared "Why didn't you mention this before? We don't have a dealer with them, how can we make a deal with someone we don't trust!" Jax's voice was booming across the room. I couldn't believe he could look so threatening.

I wasn't sure how Grant was facing him off right now, because even I was slightly scared of Jax's rage at the moment. Slowly, I was beginning to see a different side to the man I cared for.

"They are paying double and mistrust was their main concern also, until they realized there was someone who they trusted dearly within your organization."

If I'd thought I was in trouble before, well now I was sure my death was sealed. My brothers were going to kill me. I silently hoped that Grant would leave me out of this, but I had a feeling I was about to get dragged into this fire.

"Who?" Jax asked. "We don't have any contacts with them, which is why we haven't dealt with them before."

I was glaring into the side of Grant's face as he turned around to face me. His eyes were twirling with humor and cunningness; I was about to be burnt badly.

"Amber."

"Amber isn't to get involved," Cole interrupted, not even asking why he would say my name in the first place.

"You don't have a choice. She does the deal or you keep the guns." Grant looked dryly at Cole "And we all go out of pocket."

"How do you know them?" Jax's voice scared me. He was calm and authoritative.

"I just do," I replied weekly. What could I say? Grant had put me in a hard place on purpose, and I knew why. He was making me face my relationship with Jax, though I would love to know how he'd changed the plans of this deal within such a small timeframe.

"That isn't good enough," Jax spoke calmly, with coolness. He was boiling on the inside and I knew within minutes he wouldn't be as calm because I couldn't answer his question.

"It's personal." My eyes pleaded with him to not question me further; to just leave it be. I could do the deal without everyone knowing my history with the TNS. I hoped Jax had enough trust in me to just let me not answer.

"Fucking do as you're told!" he roared at me, and shivers of fear ran up my spine. "Now, how do you know them?"

For once, I wished my brothers would step in and roar at Jax for speaking to me like that. For humiliating me like that! How dare he order me! I wasn't his to order-around. I felt my rage begin to take over.

I would've done this deal for him, because I cared for him and I knew this deal meant a lot to him, but, if he didn't back off, I knew I would be tempted to tell him I wasn't going to help.

I attempted to get a hold on my rage, and my fear of him had completely disappeared, because I knew, or hoped actually, he wouldn't hurt me but hell, when it came down to it, everyone who had meant to care for me had hurt me in the end.

233

"I'm not a member of your club." My voice was low and threatening. "You don't need to know how I know them. All you need to know is that I'll do the deal."

"If you think I will hand this deal over to a little girl who has a fuck buddy in the TNS organization, you're sadly mistaken. This deal means a shitload of cash for us and I won't let you fuck it up." His voice was cold as steel, and just like a blade, his lack of trust in me cut through me sharply.

I could scream at him. I could tell him of all the deals I had done with the TNS before. I could belittle him in front of everyone.

But telling him of the deals I had done, or my relationship with the TNS, would only answer his question, and give him reassurance, and right now that was the last thing I wanted to give him.

I stood up from the chair, my eyes squarely locked with Jax's. "I hope that you find someone who won't fuck it up for you then," I said. With that, I began to walk away, the bikers stepping out of my way as I made my way to the door.

"Did I say you could leave?" Jax snapped behind me.

"As you pointed out," I turned around slightly to glare at him, "I can't help you."

I quickly made the last few steps to the door, and walked out of it quickly. I knew as I shut the door that their deal would fail, because the TNS would not deal with them; because, unlike Jax, they trusted me.

Chapter 30

I pushed the button and locked my newly acquired SSC Ultimate Aero. It was dark now and I had finally returned to the clubhouse everyone was staying at. I had thought about taking off and heading home, but I didn't really want to. Sure, I didn't like my brothers, but they still were good to have around.

The door creaked as I pushed it open; I was already prepared for the screaming and yelling I would be getting from them; but, to my complete surprise, the club lounge room and bar area were empty.

I had left my phone in the room I slept in last night, so I made a beeline for it. Luckily, I kept my license and cards in my boot; otherwise I wouldn't have been able to buy that car. Well I didn't buy it; I made a call to dad at the car yard and he took care of the financial part.

Slipping into the room and scooping my phone up from the bed, I was sure my eyes had doubled in size when I saw that I had no missed calls or messages.

Not one of them called wondering where I was.

Biting my bottom lip, I realized that maybe I had caused more damage than I had thought. I sat on the edge of the bed. Sure I was angry with Jax, hell I could throttle him, but that didn't mean I wanted him to fail.

It had taken me all day to calm down and to stop planning different ways to inflict a lot of harm.

I unlocked my phone, and slowly scrolled down the numbers. Finally, I settled on Troy's number and pressed dial. I totally wasn't calling Jax; I was way too stubborn for that.

"Amber?" Troy's voice actually sounded shocked; who knew he had it in him.

"Where are you?" I cut right to the chase.

"Out. Now where the heck are you? Do you know how long we have been looking for you?"

"Looking for me eh?" I couldn't stop my voice from sounding amused.

"Where are you?" His voice had now turned into a low growl but I had to admit it was nice to hear that they cared enough to be looking for me.

"At the clubhouse."

"What... ours? Back home?"

"No, the Deadly Dozens. You know... where I am meant to be staying." I rolled my eyes. Did he actually believe I would take off back home? Well, I guess I did think about it but I'm not that much of an attention seeker.

"Oh, well stay there," he ordered, and I heard whispers in the background like a few others were listening in on the conversation.

"I wasn't planning on going anywhere," I announced. I hung up. Falling back into the bed, I smiled slyly. I wondered how far the boys had made it on their way back home, in their effort to find me.

***

It was late when I heard a roar of engines pulling in. I knew that the Deadly Dozen must be out on a ride, considering not one of their bikes could be located and not one member had disturbed me all night; there obviously weren't any members around.

I swung around on the bar stool, waiting for them to make their entrance. I heard the door being forced open abruptly and I gulped the last shot I had lined up, just in time; they all walked through the passageway.

"Glad you are nice and fucking comfortable," Cole snapped at me, with a look of complete anger as he threw himself down in an armchair.

"Where have you guys been?" I smiled cheekily. "I have been waiting for hours."

Not one answered; Adam was already behind the bar pouring himself and Tyler a drink. Troy was taking a seat next to Cole, but not one seemed to want to answer.

"Coolies, well I might as well go to bed now," I said as I slowly got up from the bar stool.

"Don't you bloody well dare!" Cole pointed a finger at me. "Sit."

"Why?" I frowned, sitting back on to the stool but then the door opened again, and within seconds, Jax's figure stood in the door frame. I quickly glanced in the other direction, and attempted to put my business face on.

"Found her," Cole's rough voice spoke to Jax.

"Yeah, Troy called," Jax grunted.

So the room was completely silent, and filled with complete awkwardness. Sighing, I finally lifted my head up and met Jax's dark eyes, which happened to be staring directly at me.

I just had to keep my head strong, and I was relying on the little strength I had within me to keep myself strong.

"Figure your problem out?" My voice was hard.

Jax grunted, but didn't break eye contact.

"The deal is off," Cole spoke up, but I didn't turn to look at him. I was afraid if I broke eye contact now, I wouldn't have the strength to reconnect.

"Wouldn't deal with a stranger?" My voice was still cold and empty towards him.

"I think you know the answer," Jax growled.

"I'll do the deal." I said, swallowing my pride. "For my brothers," I added that fact quickly. I did not want Jax thinking I was doing it for him.

"You would do that?" Troy grunted.

"I'm only doing this because of you guys. If it was just for anyone, I wouldn't even consider it," I snapped, shooting a quick glare at Troy. "Take it or leave it, either way, it doesn't affect me."

"It doesn't matter, the deal's been called, and it's off." Jax moved from the doorframe and to the bar, stealing a shot glass from Tyler and downing it.

"I can call them and change that." I said, meeting Jax's eyes as they wandered back in my direction. "There are a few other considerations, however."

"And they would be?..." Troy cut in.

"One, don't ask questions about my background with them. You have no right; I'm not a member of your club."

"Sounds like a fair deal to me." Tyler said me with complete seriousness. "Considering she could be asking a fee for doing it," he added.

"Yeah, good one idiot, encourage her to ask to get paid," Cole snapped at him. "It comes out of his share, seeing as he's the idiot who brought it up," he added.

"HEY!" Tyler flew back at him.

"The money doesn't matter," I shouted over both their voices. "You guys are family." That silenced all of them.

"So, you're doing it for them and no other reason?" Jax's face was wiped of emotion.

"There is a second condition." I stepped down from the stool and looked Jax solidly in the eye. "I don't have anything to do with you. All my dealings go through Troy and he can pass them on to you."

Jax's eyes narrowed, and he growled, "Fine, like I give a fuck." There were a few grunts from around the room and it seemed like my brothers tended to disagree with what he said.

"If I don't have to deal with a whiney bitch, it works for me!" Jax snapped at them all, acting as if I wasn't in the room.

"This is why I don't want to deal with you Jax, you're so moody." I rolled my eyes. "Really don't cope with rejection well, do you?"

Jax gave me a narrowed look, as if tempting me to keep going. Little did he know I was tired and really didn't have it in me to keep fighting with him.

"So, new car?" Adam spoke up, cutting the dead silence that had coated the air for a few moments.

"Yep, seeing as I am sticking around..." I spun on the bar stool, looking at Adam and having my back to Jax now, "got sick of the bike, well... the rider."

Adam shook his head a little, knowing I was having a go at Jax. "You know you have other bikes you could get on the back of?"

"Or I could just drive my car."

"You're driving with the service vehicles then, at the head of the pack," Cole grunted behind me.

"Like I expected to be in your silly line up Cole," I shot over my shoulder. "Just in case you didn't hear, I brought a car, not a bike."

Boys. All Cole cared about was me ruining his special line up. Who really cares who they ride next to anyway? It is simply an ego thing.

***

No.

Yes.

No.

Yes.

Maybe.

No. Fuck it. NO

This was the continual battle that went around and around in my head, while staring at the door of Jax's room. I sighed, biting my bottom lip. I had to get a grip.

AMBER, GET A FUCKING GRIP, I yelled at myself, and then brought my fist up and knocked softly on his door.

It was the early hours of the morning. We'd only gone to bed a few hours ago, but willing to hit the road early but I couldn't sleep. Jax just kept running through my mind and I had questions that needed answers. For one, what the heck was he doing with Mai?!

I brought my fist back up, ready to knock again, when the door slowly opened. Jax was holding a cigarette in his mouth; clearly, I wasn't the only one not sleeping.

"Can we talk?"

Jax looked me in the eye for a split second before widening the door and letting me in.

"What?" he grunted as he closed the door.

I pushed the few empty beer bottles to the other side of the bed, and took a seat. Jax went back to where he most likely was previously sitting; in an armchair just near the side of the bed.

"What's the go with us? You belittled me in front of everyone this morning and the other night you were all over that Mai chick. And don't you dare say she wasn't anything, because I know she means something to you or you wouldn't sleep with her every time you're in town."

"The old man tell you that?" Jax butted the cigarette out in the ashtray and reached for his beer, carefully studying me as he did.

I arched an eyebrow. Who I got the information off really didn't matter.

"Mai is Mai. You don't really care about her," he said.

"Yeah I do actually. I sorta have a problem with my boyfriend running around with other women."

"Maybe I shouldn't be your boyfriend anymore then."

I froze. Well, that was as blunt and as cold as he could get it.

"You're breaking up with me?"

"I don't have time for petty drama." Jax slipped from his bottle. "Like this right now."

"You're breaking up with me?" I repeated.

"Never took you as the dumb type Amber."

What could I say to that? I cared for him and he was breaking up with me like this!

"Why?" I couldn't believe I was letting myself ask that question, but I needed to know.

"What you did this morning just showed me how immature you are."

I could have fought him, told him my point of view and how I felt. But what was the point? I would be fighting for someone who didn't want to be won. I got up from the bed slowly, mainly because I was still in shock. I couldn't say I had experienced this before. I was usually the one to end things, not the other way around.

"Amber?"

I turned around, the door knob already in my hand, ready to be twisted.

"Keep your shit together while on this ride. Don't be crying or moping around."

Chills overtook my sadness, and I narrowed my eyes at as I replied, "You're not worth a single tear Jackson."

Closing the door behind me, I gritted my teeth, trying to stop myself from going back in there and punching him raw for how he had just treated me.

"Amber?"

I looked down the hall with wide eyes, seeing Tyler standing there, fully clothed.

"Hey!" I kept my voice low, and I knew there was tears filling up my eyes, as much as I fought them.

"What's wrong?" Tyler went to move forward towards me and I raised a hand to stop him.

"Nothing. I just found out that you guys were right. Night Tyler."

I turned away quickly and walked fast to my bedroom. My brothers were right! Jax was a user. Nothing more than a man who sleeps with one and then moves to the next. He wanted me, he got me, and then he dumped me.

As cold as it sounded, why had I ever expected different from him?

***

"Morning." Troy greeted me as I walked outside, pulling my sunglasses down quickly, blocking the sun.

"Morning." I muttered back, heading in the direction of the car. "I made the call, everything is set," I added, before opening the door and slipping into my car. "The deal is set for tomorrow night."

We had a few hours' drive to the town over, and the deal was meant to be tonight, but tomorrow night was as good as any. Troy nodded his head understanding what I meant. The deal was in place; now all we had to do was deliver.

I fiddled with the radio while the boys straddled their bikes. A knocking on my window got my attention.

"Here, the channel is all set." A prospect said, handing me a small hand-held radio. "Jax has the ear piece, and we have the other one."

I nodded my head while placing the hand-held in my console and winding the window back up. I guess it was a smart idea to keep in contact. Finally, the bikes roared to life, and slowly they took out the drive, followed by me and then the prospect van. It was the van's job to mind the scanners and police scanners, making sure we have a safe police-free ride to our destination, and I hoped the ride went smoothly. The sooner I was away from Jax, the better.

***

242

I glanced at the clock on the dash. We had been driving for over an hour. I looked back up at a sight I was already sick of - the line of bikes.

"Jax, cops ahead, slow down," came from the little hand-held, which was sitting on the console. I got nervous as I waited for Jax's rough voice to come over the radio, but it didn't come. The prospect called it again, but still no answer, and I heard the tension in the prospect's voice.

Picking the hand-held up, I held the button down. "How far off are the suits?" I asked over air.

"Not far. Jax's ear piece mightn't be working," the prospect shot back with panic. "We have to get them to slow down."

The highway was dead, and the boys were over the speed limit by a lot; we all were, but the speed wasn't what was concerning me… it was the fact the boys were riding with illegal guns.

"What should we do?" the prospect asked me. He was buckling under the pressure of the situation.

I knew the cops wouldn't be far off; I could see a bunch of trees far ahead, which would be the perfect place to hide. The road was dead ahead, with no oncoming traffic.

Sliding into the right lane, I put my foot to the floor. This was meant to be a fast car and I was about to put that to the test. The car jumped to the challenge, and I flew past the boys, who clearly weren't going as fast as they could be going; most likely due to what they were carrying.

I knew they would be all thinking about what the heck I was doing, but their question would be answered soon. I put enough distance between me and Jax before sliding over and overtaking them. I kept the foot down as I approached the trees. I had just passed the trees when the highway parole car came flying out after me.

Slowing down, I came to a stop on the side of the road. I knew I was about to cop a lot of heat for this, especially with my track record, but my heat would be nothing compared to the trouble the boys would have been in.

I was out of the car and up against the bonnet, with a policeman handcuffing me when the boys finally passed. The cop's hadn't even asked me for my license, arresting me straight off. The boys were looking in my direction as they slowed slightly.

I was pulled back to the cop car and pushed into the back seat. I watched the boys keep moving, and I hoped someone would pay bail to get me out.

Well if they didn't, the deal would be dead in the water. Looks like I would be making a phone call to dad, after all, he was the only man I could rely on.

Chapter 31

Jax

"Fucking jail," I muttered under my breath and hurled a shot glass across the bar, watching it shatter into pieces. The bar was crawling with people when we showed up, but the locals took the hint and pissed off. The bartender had also disappeared and we were just servicing ourselves; but that wasn't my main concern. "FUCKING JAIL!" I roared.

"How high is bail?" Cole yelled at Troy who was on the phone trying to find out where the hell they had taken Amber.

I gritted my teeth and waited for Troy's answer. Anger and guilt roared through my veins; it was my fault Amber had taken the fall.

Troy cursed when he closed the phone. "They won't tell me."

"What?" I snarled at him, "Why won't they tell you where she is?"

"She's locked up. They won't tell me where though."

"Let me guess, your record?" Adam spoke up with a deep roll of disgust in his voice. "Fucking pigs."

I stormed across the room and shouldered the bar door, swinging it open. I lit up a cigarette, getting ready to storm every police station looking for her.

"Whatever you're thinking, I suggest you stop," Cole stood behind me, arms crossed. "We'll fix it."

"Fuck up Cole."

It was taking all my self-control not to throw him out into oncoming traffic.

"Just reminding you of the other night, in case you've forgotten." Cole shrugged his shoulders.

"Threatning me again?"

"Stay away from her."

"We're over."

"And that's the way it will stay." Cole moved forward, his eyes deadly. "Got it?"

"Back down," I ordered. I was taking his shit for Amber, but, if he crossed the line one more time, I would punch him back into his place.

"Amber deserves better than you and I just don't want you forgetting that." Cole's voice was a low hiss and I would kill a bloke for talking to me like this.

"Cole?" Troy stepped outside.

"Just reminding Jax to stay the fuck away from Amber," Cole spat, still having the guts to stare me down.

"You know what pisses me off?" Tyler said, now stepping out too. Clearly, everyone knew what was going on, and that pissed me off.

When no-one answered, Tyler just decided to tell us anyway.

"You're not asking Amber what she wants. She would kill you if she knew you threatened Jax to break it off with her."

Cole grunted and leaned against the brick wall, smoking.

"I'm serious, you should have seen her face last night." Tyler looked carefully in my direction. "She was heartbroken."

"Heartbroken?" Cole looked at his brother, "Grow a pair, would you."

"She looked cut this morning," Troy carried on.

It was cutting me up hearing this shit. I felt gutted hurting Amber like that. Her face when I told her; I grimaced just remembering her hurt face.

"We need to find her." Adam had now stepped out too, swiping the cigarette from Cole. "The deal won't work without her, and plus I'm telling her what you did Cole."

Cole had Adam by the collar and against the wall within a second.

"You can punch me if you want, but Amber doesn't deserve to be lied to." Adam glared at Cole, not even bothering to fight. "It's rubbish making Jax break it off with her." Adam looked over Cole's shoulder, looking me in the eye, adding, "Surprised you fucking let him."

"I didn't really have a choice," I grunted. All the boys looked in my direction apart from Cole, wanting an explanation. "Cole has an old pic of El and me. He was going to show Amber."

"Did you cheat on her?" Tyler crossed his arms, fuming.

"NO!" I spat, and glared into the back of Cole's head. "Amber and I weren't even together when he took that pic but like Amber wouldn't believe me over him."

"You're still no good for her," Troy said calmly to me. "We didn't want her messed up with this crap."

"She was always a part of it," I challenged him. "You were just to blind to see it."

"So, you want her for her connections?" Cole spat over his shoulder at me.

"Mind your own business."

"Get off me!" Adam pushed Cole off him finally. "We have to find Am."

"She's safer in prison," Cole huffed as Adam sent an elbow to his stomach. "Away from him."

That was it.

I pulled my fist back and sent it flying into Cole's face. He cursed continually as his hand went to cradle his jaw. His eyes were fierce when he looked up at me; I wanted him to come at me.

But he didn't. Instead, he straightened up and glared at me.

"Remember who you're fucking talking to," I said as I walked to my bike and straddled it. "Let's go bail your sister out."

"What do you mean she's gone?" I glared at the pig behind the counter, who was glaring right back at me.

"She was released hours ago."

"How?" Troy was standing next to me, mirroring my pure hatred towards the officer in front of us.

"She made bail," he said, examining Troy's patch, his eyes hovering over the 'President.'

"Who bailed her out?" Troy shot at him, and eyed the officer who had now joined the other pig behind the desk.

The officer glanced down at the paper work, but then with a glint of smugness, he looked back up at us. "We can't release that information."

I wasn't taking this fucking crap. I leaned across, swiping the piece of paper from his fingers. A whole lot of yelling and threats came flying at me, but I had already tossed the piece of paper back before the pigs could move.

"Let's leave." I shot at Troy and we both walked to the door. The pigs didn't even bother stopping us, because we all knew they just wanted us to leave. After all, we just cause them more paperwork.

"Where's Amber?" the boys asked as soon as we walked out of the cop shop.

"Been bailed out," Troy answered.

"By?" Tyler frowned.

"Your father." I announced.

I straddled my bike. "Better give him a call, find out where they are."

All the boys cursed under their breath because they knew that they would be in shit for this. Their dad would have had to have flown in for this, although he would most likely do anything for his little girl.

"Dad's gonna be pissed," Tyler grimaced, and just like taking a bullet, he pulled out his phone and called the only other man the Shield boys were actually scared of - their dad.

Chapter 32

Amber

"You boys have some explaining to do!" I heard dad tell whoever was on the other side of the door. "She was in jail. JAIL!"

I jumped slightly in surprise when I heard the hotel door slam shut. The bedroom door was ajar, so I was able to hear all that was going on out in the lounge room and I didn't think that was a good thing. I wonder how the boys had found out that dad picked me up?

Well, it wasn't like I could call anyone else. I knew dad would bail me out, and I knew he would actually come to get me although I was sure flying in in our private jet to bail me out hadn't been on his agenda for that night.

Surprisingly, he wasn't angry with me; he was just concerned about me, making sure I was ok, which I was.

"Is she with you?" Troy's voice broke the silence.

"She's sleeping." Dad's voice was stern, "You boys want to explain why Amber was in jail?"

"We didn't make her speed," Cole's voice was short and snappy. "I need to talk to her, she in there?"

"Don't disturb her!"

"Why? It's Amber, I'm sure she is awake," Cole snapped back at Dad. I had never heard him disrespect dad before.

"I brought you boys here to help Amber. Not drag her deeper in!"

"What are you talking about dad? We aren't dragging her into anything," Troy scoffed, "Amber was in trouble when we got here. We aren't miracle workers."

"I'm not stupid. I know what you boys are, and I know what Amber was involved in," Dad roared. "But you boys were meant to pull her out of it! You boys were meant to pull her from the gangs and maybe give her some small role in your club, but not this. She wasn't meant to get more involved."

The boys went silent. I think we all did believe that dad knew nothing about what we really did and I was sure the boys had no idea dad knew about their club. I was stunned.

"Can I talk to Amber?"

My eyes widened when I heard Jax's voice. Jax was here?

"No. I think it best you all leave. Amber will be coming home with me." Dad's voice was hard and I knew the boys wouldn't argue with him. "Leave now."

"I need to talk to Amber first," Cole stood up to dad, and I didn't know where he was getting the guts right now, especially after knowing that dad knew more than he let on. "It's important, and then we will leave."

The silence in the air was deadly; I could hear dad steaming from here. "Fine, she is in there." Dad's tone sounded as if he was breathing fire.

I quickly lay down in bed and pulled the blankets up, pretending I wasn't listening. Well, we all knew I was, but I didn't need to have my ears glued to the door.

The door cracked open. "Amber?" Cole's voice was slightly softer, and I was surprised to hear the tender tone.

"Cole?" I pulled myself up in bed, and crossed my arms. He flicked the light on, and the room bounced with light.

Cole was standing with his arms crossed. "I thought you would be up." He closed the door behind him and walked further into the room, before sitting on the edge of the bed. "I need to tell you something."

"Must be important then," I arched an eyebrow; let's face it, Cole wasn't much of a talker. "Well spill! What is it?" I pushed.

"I told Jax to dump you. He didn't get a choice in the matter. There. I told you. Now everyone can get off my back." Cole got up from the bed, "Don't rant at me about it, I'm not in the mood," he added.

He seriously thought he could just drop a bomb like that and leave? I knew he would be expecting me to rant, yell, curse and maybe inflict harm on him but if there was one thing I'd learned from them, it was that it didn't work. Silence and disappointment hit them harder, so that was what I was going to do.

"Ok, night."

Cole turned around, startled by my reaction. "Seriously, you aren't going to rant? Or threaten me?

"Good night Cole."

I slid back down into the covers and got comfortable. I wanted to kill Cole but if I'd reacted, Jax would hear about it and, after how he'd treated me, the last thing I wanted was him knowing he'd hurt me. Also, Cole didn't deserve a reaction; my plan would work out better in the long run. No one likes a cold shoulder.

"Right, umm night."

I closed my eyes and waited until I heard the door close. Why would Jax listen to Cole? No, wipe that. Even if he was blackmailed into dumping me, why did he do it the way he did? Not to mention, how could he be so cold towards me.

Jax dumped me because Cole wanted him to? Here I was, thinking Jax was a fearless biker. How wrong was I?

***

"Dad, I can't come home. The boys need me." I said, and looked up from the cereal bowl in front of me. I sat across from my dad, who was reading the morning paper. "They need me to do something."

252

"I know," Dad placed his morning paper down, frowning at me. "You shouldn't be getting involved with them."

"They're my brothers," I pointed out, pushing my bowl away from me. "I don't really have a choice."

"You always have a choice!" Dad gave me a warm smile. "But I know you want to do this. I just hope last night serves as some sort of warning to you Amber."

I nodded my head, knowing that jail was where I would go if I kept doing what I was doing. Jail time would look good for the boys, but for me, it would break me.

"Did they say where they were staying?" I asked dad, getting to my feet.

"They haven't left. Last time I checked, they were across the road at a bar."

"Of course they are." I rolled my eyes. Really, where else should I have expected them to be?

Chapter 33

"Hey." I slipped onto the stool next to Tyler. He was looking at me like he was seeing a ghost. "So, is the deal still on?" I asked.

Tyler gulped his drink, coughing and patting his chest, splattering beer everywhere "You mean to say you are still in?"

"I didn't say I wasn't."

"We assumed you were out." Jackson piped in, pulling a stool up next to me, and the hairs on the back of my neck stood. This was awkward.

"Well I'm not." I stated, and chewed my bottom lip. Did Jax know that I now knew? I wonder if Cole told Jax that he had told me.

"If you're in then, we'd better leave. We're running late," Jax gulped down the liquid in a small shot glass.

"Troy, Cole, Adam, we're leaving," Jax shot over his shoulder, and when he turned back, I finally got a look at him.

Dark shadows were under his eyes, and his face was white. If I knew Jax, he was actually broken up about breaking up with me, or something was playing heavily on his mind, keeping sleep at bay for sure.

"Did you want to ride with me Amber? Your car has been impounded," Jax said as he pulled his leather vest on; he wouldn't meet my eye.

The boys politely walked out of the quiet bar, although Adam shot me a small smile. Troy, however, wouldn't look in my direction; neither would Cole. Most likely they were embarrassed that their little sister had helped them out by taking the fall. That, and they got told off by dad.

Looking back at Jax, I saw he was staring at the ground, pretending like he wasn't waiting for my answer.

"I'll get on with one of my brothers. I don't want to cause you any more trouble."

"Amber, look…" Jax gripped my upper arm, and leaned in.

"We should just focus on this deal Jax, and get it done," I said as I glanced at his hand, and then looked him in the eye. I was strong-willed and I knew I couldn't just go back to him after he dumped me. Not just yet. He had to work for it.

"You're right," he said. He let go of my arm. "Let's go." He walked past me, his arm brushing against mine.

I slowly exhaled, and then turned to follow him out.

I had a feeling this was going to be more difficult than I thought.

Jax

The deal went smoothly; Amber seemed to have everything under control. Watching her take control like that… I had never seen her so mature and switched on. She knew how to handle them. It was perhaps the only deal that I had ever attended that guns weren't drawn and arguments didn't break out.

No. They seemed to have an understanding and respect for Amber, and it worked in our favor. The deal took not even an hour, and we were back on our bikes with bags of cash. I glanced in my side mirror; Amber was still clinging to Troy.

She wouldn't ride with me. I thought that maybe she would ride back home with me, but she wouldn't; stubborn woman that she was.

Slowing down, we rolled through town. There were familiar looks and glances in our direction. The deal was done, and now we had a few good weeks off. Only local businesses, until the next shipment came in.

I signaled the boys to follow me to the clubhouse. We were all running on nothing, and falling into bed was second on the list, after I dished out the cash.

The big iron gates were open; club members were hovering around. Troy backed his bike in next to mine. Amber wouldn't look at me, her head turned to face the other way.

"I need sleep," Troy said as he switched off his bike, and helped Amber off.

"Yeah." I muttered, still looking at Amber. What the heck would I have to do to get her back?

I unzipped my leather jacket, and placed my helmet on the handle bar.

"I'm going to head home," Amber said, her hands stuffed in her jacket, staring at the ground.

"I'll take ya," I chimed in. "Boys, get the bags inside, start splitting the cash."

"No, Troy can take me." Amber's head shot up, and looked at her brother.

"They can't," I said; my voice was firm. I was not letting her get out of this. I grabbed my helmet and held it out for her. I noticed the draggers she shot in Troy's direction but he was not going to help her. Shrugging his shoulders at her, he followed the rest of boys into the clubhouse with the bags.

"So?" I nudged the helmet out to her. Stubbornly, she pressed her lips together firmly, not liking the idea but she didn't have a choice.

She snatched the helmet from my hand and put it on. With a small smirk on my face, I straddled the bike and kicked the engine to life. Amber placed a hand on my shoulder, and slid on the back seat behind me.

She loosely placed her hands around me, trying her best to avoid touching me.

I took off quickly, and braked suddenly, sending Amber sliding firmly into my back forcing her to wrap her arms around me tightly.

"You'd better hold on," I shot over my shoulder to her. I smiled smugly, taking off again. Amber didn't let go of me, or push away from me. She was holding on tightly, just the way I liked it.

***

Amber jumped off the bike as soon as I pulled up to her front door, like it was burning her to be close to me. She quickly walked to the front door, and I nearly dropped the bike trying to get off to catch her in time.

"Amber, wait!" I walked up behind her.

"What Jackson?" She spun around, pursing her lips and crossing her arms. Jackson? Don't tell me we were back to that!

"Did Cole talk to you?"

"Yes." She cocked her head to the side, her eyes glaring holes in my face. "I didn't know you actually were scared of Cole."

"I'm not." I said as I clenched my jaw.

"Whatever, it doesn't matter." Her hands fell to her side, no longer holding them in a tight cross. "We're over. Thanks for the ride."

"Wait," I said as I grabbed her wrist. "I'm sorry," I said. Sorry usually works, doesn't it? That's what I'm meant to be saying in this situation, right? Fuck, women were difficult. This is why I didn't do relationships.

"Thanks?" She didn't sound sure. "But it doesn't make a different Jackson. We just aren't well, you know... right together." She moved uncomfortably.

She was as strong as nails. She thought we weren't right together? I couldn't think of anyone more perfect for me. "We ARE right together," I said. I hated talking about emotions; she was torturing me.

"Don't lie to yourself Jax," she said, her face softening slightly before her head dropped. "You should go. I'll see you later."

"So what? We go back to being friends?" I snapped. Couldn't she just take me back already? She knew I hadn't meant it.

"We were never really friends," she pointed out, and then pushed open her front door, closing it in my face.

Why was she going to make this harder than it needed to be? Lighting up a cigarette, I straddled my bike. She was going to make me work for her. Christ, just another thing I had to do, although Amber was worth it.

***

"GET OUT!" I roared, as some idiot attempted to pull me from my drunken slumber.

"You have to get up!" Troy grunted, "SCHOOL!"

"Piss off," I scoffed into the pillow, and rolled over the crushed beer cans scattered across my bed. The whole weekend I had slept, and drank, and slept. I hadn't left the bedroom, let alone the Shield's house.

"It's Monday. Don't want to break your parole." I heard the smug tone in his voice. Stupid blood parole!

"Bloody hell," I slowly dragged myself out of bed. My head was splitting.

"Amber's already left," Troy said, standing with his annoying smug look. I wanted to kill him. "You're going to be late."

I said a few curse words under my breath as I searched the floor for clean clothes. "How's Amber?" I picked up a black t-shirt and pulled it over my head.

"Don't know. She hasn't been home much."

"What?" I looked up too quickly and the room started spinning. Gripping my forehead, I attempted to calm the hurricane inside. "Where has she been going?"

"Don't know." Troy shrugged his shoulders. "We aren't allowed to follow her."

"Daddy's orders?" I smirked, the smug look on Troy's face disappearing.

"No, Amber's orders," Troy crossed his arms, "And we are respecting them."

"Hah, for how long?"

"Not your concern. You'd better leave."

"Yeah, yeah I know... school." I picked up my packet of cigarettes and Troy moved out of my way as I went to walk past him. "I'll talk to Amber at school, see where she is heading off to."

"That would be helpful," Troy said as he nodded his head. It must've been bugging the hell out of them not knowing where Amber was going, or why she was disappearing.

I pulled my sunnies out of my jacket and blocked the light. Today was going to be a long day.

Chapter 34

Jax

The crowds naturally parted as I walked through the hall. I noticed the chatter had stopped when I was close. People knew to be scared of me. I didn't influence it; rumors and my reputation did it all for me.

I glanced down the hall, her ripped jeans catching my attention. Amber was going through her locker, what do you know, she actually looked like she was getting ready for class. "Amber." I called, and leaned against the locker next to hers.

"Jackson." She acknowledged, and glanced at me briefly. "Nice to see you awake."

She closed the locker door and I walked beside her up the hall, people naturally getting out of our way.

"Yeah." I yawned slightly, adding, "I heard you were up to stuff."

Amber shrugged her shoulders. I don't know whether it was because I was now fully caught up on my sleep, but Amber looked extremely beautiful today. In fact, it was catching me off guard.

"So your umm, brothers were worried about you," I said as I stuffed my hands into my pockets, and our pace had slowed slightly. I was aware of glances from everyone in our direction but I didn't care. If they had a problem with me talking to her, they could take it up with me. It was true Amber was sort of an outcast here, but that was because she made herself one.

"Yeah, they were whining at me too," she said, her free hand brushing mine by accident. "Sorry," she said, quickly making sure there was more space between us.

"So, want to tell me what you are up to?" I asked as I gently wrapped my hand around her small arm and stopped her. "And don't lie."

Her moody eyes stared up into mine. Her skin so pale and flawless; I always knew she was beautiful but this morning it was like she was shining.

"I met someone," her words were a hushed whisper although they registered perfectly.

Fuck.

"Who?" I swallowed the feeling of complete disgust. How the hell had I let this happen? All I did was sleep for a weekend, and she finds herself a new man!

"I can't say," she blushed. AMBER BLUSHED!

I gritted my teeth. "Right, whatever."

"Jackson, are you jealous?" She smirked tauntingly. "You shouldn't be."

"I'm not." I let go of her, adding, "I'll see you at home."

"Jackson, wait," she called.

"It's Jax," I snapped at her. I noticed her smirk had now gone. Well, I had a right to be angry. She'd replaced me within, what, days? Yeah, I meant heaps to her, didn't I.

"You don't have a right to be jealous." She pursed her lips and gripped her textbooks tighter. "You broke up with me."

"To protect you!" I scoffed. "Whatever, it doesn't matter." She could do whatever the heck she wanted. Why should I care? I'd never cared for a woman before, and this was why.

"You're right. It doesn't matter," she said.

The school bell rang and she quickly turned her back to me, storming off. Why had I fallen for a moody one?

But it doesn't matter now. She'd found a replacement. I gritted my teeth and stormed down the hall. It showed now, how much she really cares about me.

I glared into the back of Amber's head. The whole day she had made it her mission to avoid me, but, now as we sat in, well whatever class it was, she was trapped. She sat as far away from me as possible, sitting down in the front of the class by herself.

How had she found a new guy over a weekend? A WEEKEND! I snapped a pencil. The boy next to me flinched. I gave the boy a look over. Who was he? I hadn't seen him before.

"Can you believe her?" I said as I nodded my head in Amber's direction. "She found a new guy." I didn't know the guy next to me, but he was the only one close enough to listen.

"Are you talking about Amber Shield?" The guy pushed his glasses up his nose, and looked closer at Amber, when I nodded my head. "He would have to be brave to date her," the boy added.

"Brave?" I scoffed. "I doubt it." I tapped my foot under the table, feeling irritated.

"I wonder if he likes orange too…" The nerdy guy had a bit of a snigger and looked at me with an amused grin. I gave him a look that wiped that look off his face. Like what the fuck was he on about?!

He quickly snapped his head down, and turned back to his work as I continued to glare at Amber. Who the heck had she met? I knew that I had a thing for her, but the jealousy that was ripping through me made me realize it wasn't just a thing.

Bloody hell, I was in love with Amber.

***

I stabbed the piece of steak, cutting a large piece of it off and stuffing it in my mouth.

"I hate peas," Tyler announced, flicking a pile of peas off his plate and onto the tablecloth. "Why the heck does the cook always put so many on?"

"Would you like to cook instead Tyler?" Mr Shield asked, from the head of the table.

The Shield boys were feared, and here they were sitting at the table having a good old family dinner together.

"There, there Tyler. Stop moaning about the fucking peas!" Cole grunted, with a mouthful of food.

"Language!" Mr Shield snapped at Cole, and that had everyone smirking.

Cole got told off by daddy.

"How was school, Jackson?" He looked at me. Jackson? What was I, ten?

"Fine," I grunted back a reply; would have been rude to ignore him completely, considering I was still staying at his house.

"Where is Amber?" Troy asked, and I was grateful he had asked, because I had been wondering where she was. She didn't come home after school. Maybe she was off with her new boyfriend. I clenched the knife in my hand.

"Here!" Amber announced as she walked into the room. I automatically looked up at her. Why was she looking so pretty lately?

"Amber! You hungry?" Mr Shield asked, and she nodded her head and took a seat next to Troy, even though there was one free next to me.

"So, where you been?" Adam asked her, and then pushed the bread basket across the table at her.

"Nowhere," she replied. She took a piece of bread, beginning to nibble on it.

"She has a new boyfriend," I spoke up, loudly. I knew one thing the Shield boys hated, and that was any other male close to their little sister. I was going to use that to my advantage.

"WHAT!" Cole was the first one roaring at her, demanding more. "Who?"

"Thanks!" Amber shot me a glare.

"Didn't know it was a secret," I said as I shrugged my shoulders.

"No one you know," Amber answered Cole, but she should've known better. The boys wouldn't stop at that. All of a sudden, all the boys were throwing questions at her and the dread across Amber's face was amusing… to me at least.

"ENOUGH!" Mr. Shield shouted from the head of the table, and rose from his chair.

"Thanks dad," Amber smiled, relieved.

"Amber isn't…"

"DAD, YOU PROMISED!" Amber quickly cut him off, slapping her hands on the table. She was fuming with anger.

Mr Shield was actually chuckling. All of us were in silence. Mr Shield looked too serious to be chuckling and, by the shock on the boy's faces, they weren't used to it either.

"Amber's boyfriend's initials are C.S, and that is all I am saying. Now, leave her alone." Mr Shield sat back in his chair with a grin.

"Thanks dad," Amber rolled her eyes, and left the table with a huff. Now all I had to do was find out who C.S was and threaten him until he buggered off.

***

"I don't know anyone named C.S." Adam said. He was laying on the grass, smoking and thinking of who Amber's boyfriend was.

"Neither do I." I said as I lit up my own smoke. Adam and I were out in the backyard, with beers, enjoying the fresh air, and quiet - two things we didn't usually get much of.

"You know Troy was saying that dad was thinking of sending her away," Adam said as he sat up. "Troy was trying to get him to change his mind."

"He wouldn't send, her would he?" I asked and blew out the smoke. Amber couldn't be sent away like a naughty child; she was an adult now, although she rarely acted like one.

"Don't know," Adam shrugged his shoulders, putting the cigarette out. "But he doesn't want Amber to get mixed up with what we do, so he might."

Amber was strong-willed; you couldn't make her do anything she didn't want to do. There was no way she would go anywhere she didn't want to go.

"I'm turning in; night Jax," Adam said as he pushed my shoulder slightly, walking passed.

"Night mate."

I had more important things to think about than Amber. I should be organizing and planning our next run and I should be taking care of business.

But my thoughts were consumed with Amber.

Chapter 35

Jax

Leaning against my bike, I watched Amber move quickly through the school gates; she was jogging to her car. Putting my cigarette out, I quickly mounted my bike and started it.

It had been a week, and Amber was still meeting this secret lover; today I was going to follow her. Every day after school she would take off as soon as the bell rang, and then she wouldn't be back home until late.

Yes, I did have more important things to do than stalk my ex-girlfriend, but all I needed was an address, and then I would be able to get a name.

I slowed the bike down and followed two cars back from Amber. She was frustrating me, not giving me the time of day. I even bought her flowers last night and left them on her bed. The next morning I woke up to find them thrown out in the hall, outside her door.

To think I wasted an hour picking the bastards. I changed lanes, still following her; why was she going so damn slow? She was holding the traffic up! I crept up behind the car in front, and looked up. Shit.

She had spotted me.

I saw the lights ahead changing, and sure enough, she put her foot down, floored it and ran the lights. I gritted my teeth as I came to a stop behind a car. I had lost her; there was no chance I would find her now. She would be taking every back road possible.

Bloody Amber being too smart for her own good. Maybe I should just take a hint and stop stalking her. She clearly wanted nothing to do with me. I needed to get trashed and forget her.

***

"Jax? Where you been?" Troy grunted when I switched the bike off. I got off the bike and placed my helmet on the handlebar.

"Out," I shot back, not in the mood to tell him I had been stalking his sister.

"Did you find out who he is?" Cole walked out the front door, with that normal cocky grin on his face, and guessing correctly where I had been.

"Don't know what you are on about," I grumbled.

"Right," Troy smirked. "You ready to go?"

"Go where?" I only had one thing on my mind; drinking my sorrows away.

God, I sounded depressive. Bloody Amber.

"Club meeting, remember?" Cole huffed, still with a cocky undertone in his voice. Cole really knew how to piss me off. "Or did you forget, having other things on your mind," he added. He was being relentless!

"Shut it Cole," Troy jumped in, before I managed to answer him.

Damn meeting. I would cancel it, but I had set the damn thing in the first place. Grinding my teeth, I nodded my head. "Right, let's go."

"I'll drive," Troy unlocked his sedan.

"Why the fuck aren't we taking our bikes?" Tyler grunted from the back seat, moving uncomfortably between Adam and Cole. "Cole, when the heck did you get so fat?" he grumbled.

I glanced at them in the back; they reminded me of clowns in a tiny car.

"It's muscle, you tosser," Cole snapped, and punched Tyler's thigh.

"Get OFF ME!" Adam yelled and pushed Tyler back to the middle. Tyler had been groaning in pain, rubbing his thigh and leaning into Adam.

"Shut up! All of you!" Troy snapped over his shoulder, taking his eyes off the road. The whole trip into town, all the three did in the back was bitch.

Your leg is on my side, stop leaning on me... the bitching went on.

"CAT FIGHT!" Tyler yelled, loud enough to deafen me. I shot a deadly look in the back at him; he didn't even notice though, he was too focused on what was happening outside of the car.

Troy slowed down, and sure enough, two chicks were going at it, both wearing orange jump suits. Community service workers, or highway trash pickers. The two guards that were meant to be looking after them were just hanging out, watching the fight.

"Ouch, the one with the dark hair is on a roll!" Tyler said, while Cole cursed him for leaning on his knee.

My eyebrows knitted together as I took a closer look at the girls. "Troy, pull up closer would you?"

Troy frowned, but indicated and pulled up to the side of the road. We were barely crawling along anyway.

"Is that...?" Tyler started, then stopped.

"Nah, it couldn't be..." Adam added.

"It bloody is!" I fumed and pushed the car door open roughly. Everything was beginning to make sense now.

"Jax, don't get involved," Troy yelled out the car window.

"Do you want her up for manslaughter?" I yelled back at him, but kept walking towards the fighting girls. "Can't you do your job?" I grunted at the guards when I walked past them.

"Not so lippy now, are you bitch!" Amber snarled at the girl after sending a flying right hook into her face, again.

I wrapped my arms around Amber's small waist, and pulled her off the girl she was beating.

"GET YOUR HANDS OFF ME!" she roared at me, before she went limp. "You have to be kidding me," she groaned, as she glanced at my arms.

I placed Amber on her feet, and she spun around instantly. Her mouth was half hanging open; she was in shock.

"Want to explain?" I arched an eyebrow at her, still holding onto her waist.

"How did you find me?" she frowned, cocking her head to the side. The girl she was bashing up before was cupping a bloody nose behind her. "I thought I'd lost you in traffic."

"Cat fights draw attention," I nodded my head in the car's direction, and when she saw her brothers, she let out a long groan.

"So community service, huh?" I smirked at her, taking my hands from her waist.

"Not all of us can get away with crime, Jax," she threw back at me.

God, it was nice to hear her call me Jax instead of Jackson. "True. So this is your boyfriend then?" I said as relief washed over me. Looks like I wasn't going to have to threaten anyone. Wait no, I had decided to stop stalking.

"Yes. Go on. Rub it in. Get it over with," she said as she crossed her arms and pursed lips. A light pink blush crossed her cheeks. Embarrassment suited her.

"So you don't like roses then?" I didn't care about community service. If she thought I would, then perhaps she was stupid after all.

"Wait, aren't you going to come up with some good lines… aka insults?" Amber looked surprised.

"Your brothers will do that for me."

"Right, of course then will," she said as she flipped the bird in the car's direction; I'm sure they saw it.

"The flowers?" I prompted her, and shifted my weight from foot to foot. I hated this feeling. The nerves.

I should just forget it. Amber didn't give a shit, why should I? She was over me.

"They were from you? I thought dad had put them there because he was sorry for babbling at tea the other night!" Amber uncrossed her arms, and she actually looked sorry. Well, who knew she could be sorry for anything. "I'm sorry. If I'd known they were from you, I…"

"You would what?" I wanted her to finish that sentence; maybe she wasn't fully over me yet. She would give me another go, right? She had to! It wasn't every day that I stood in front of a girl asking if she got my flowers.

"Would've thrown them in your face," she finished.

And there went the little chance I had.

"If you think you can buy me back after what you did, with flowers, you are mistaken," she said as she jabbed a finger in my chest. "You are going to have to do a lot more Mr Jackson Johnston."

I took the finger from my chest, and held her hand. "Like?"

She puffed her lips, rolling her eyes at my corniness. "I don't know…"

Smirking, I leaned into her ear, "Well when you do, let me know."

I wasn't giving up, she still cared. It she hadn't, she would have hit me by now, or at least threatened to.

Watching her face twist, I dreaded her next sentence. I knew that face, and that face only meant trouble.

"I have one thing," she said sweetly, with a very large smirk. What a surprise. She'd thought of something quick though; was that a good thing or a bad thing?

"Of course you do," I said. I prepared myself for her evil plan. Clearly, whatever her thing was, it wasn't going to be pleasant.

"Tell my brothers you are dating me."

That was easy. "Done," I promised.

She'd said dating, which meant we were back together. Gee, this had worked out easy.

"And…"

Of course there was an and.

"And that you love me," she pulled her hand out of my grasp. "Then we can be boyfriend and girlfriend again."

"Not happening," I said. A bikie didn't say the word love, especially when it came to a woman. I would be seen as weak, and them being the Shield brothers would take the piss out of me for life.

"Then we're done." Amber turned her back to me abruptly, but I saw the hurt in her face before she did.

Why would she ask that of me? Couldn't she ask for something easier, like a new car or, I don't know, a house? Or a new gun? I kicked the ground and walked back to the car.

Well, it really was over between us. I wouldn't say those words to her brothers. Nothing would drive me to say them. NOTHING. My reputation depended on it.

"You all right?" Troy gave me a sideways glance when I slammed the car door.

"Just drive," I said.

I looked over at Amber, who was stabbing a piece of trash. She couldn't expect me to say those words. Not to her brothers. I just couldn't.

Chapter 36

Amber

Smoothing the wrinkles out of the skin tight black dress, I was breathing slowly. After days of doing dirty community service work, it was a relief not have to rock the orange jumpsuit. I let my hair freely swing around my face. Applying my last coat of red lipstick, I swooped up my purse and headed out of my bedroom.

I hadn't seen Jax since yesterday, when he flatly refused to say he loved me to my brothers, and to be honest, I'd expected it, but that didn't mean I wasn't disappointed when he confirmed it. Although, when it came down to it, I was just stupid. What bikie would actually admit to loving a woman?

I reached the top of the stairs, chewing my bottom lip before I went down. I was making the right decision, I knew that, but it didn't mean that I didn't feel slightly sad at the thought of leaving Jax behind but it had to be done. I took a stand a long time ago that I wouldn't fall in love with a criminal; that I would leave this life behind, and it was time I finally put that into action.

Walking down the stairs, I wasn't surprised to see Troy, Cole and Jackson lounging on the stairs, shirtless. It was a boiling hot day, and the night was now only beginning to cool down.

"So, dad said you are going out with an office jerk?" Cole sniggered at me, when I finally reached the bottom step.

"You mean dad's business partner's son," I corrected him, ignoring Jax all together. "I think dad would have also told you to leave me the fuck alone." I showed Cole a dry expression before opening the front door.

"You'll look a bit keen if you wait out in the front for him," Cole shouted at me, before I slammed the front door.

I gritted my teeth, when I noticed Tyler cleaning his bike. "What are you doing out here?"

Tyler looked up at me, with his carefree smile. "Someone is a little grumpy tonight," he teased.

"Nervous." I said as I walked towards him. "This guy dad has set me up with, well, he isn't a nobody." Tyler was the most approachable out of all my brothers, followed closely by Adam. Actually, where was Adam?

"Yeah, don't worry, we know... done our homework." Tyler placed his dirty rag on the bike. "You know dad won't care if you don't go out with him," Tyler's voice softened, and instantly my face melted into a smile for him. Although he was covered in tattoos, and his hair was messy, he really didn't suit the bad boy image he had.

"Can you keep a secret?" I lowered my voice and Tyler nodded his head, walking away from his bike, and standing at the bottom of the porch steps, looking up at me interested. "I asked dad to set me up with him."

"What for?" Tyler's eyes were wide, and, by his look, it was clear he thought I was crazy.

"Jackson and I broke up," I muttered, fiddling with my purse. "But that isn't the main reason." I knew the boys knew about my community service, but I was overly thankful that not one of them had brought it up, and I think dad had had some role to play when it came to that. "I broke up with Blake because I wanted to get out of this life, and I guess Jackson made me forget that for a while until..."

"Until?" Tyler prompted.

"Until he reminded me why I made that decision in the first place." I glanced at the car lights coming up the driveway. "I can't keep making the same mistakes," I added.

Tyler sighed, and nodded his head "The past can't be left behind little sis. You need to remember that." He gave me a pat on the shoulder, then he walked up the stairs, past me. "Good luck on your date."

"Thanks," I said to his retreating back, before he closed the front door. Nerves burst inside me, as I looked back to the car, now coming to a halt at the bottom of the porch. Why the heck was I so nervous?

The car door opened, and I catapulted into an unnatural state of panic.

"Amber!" Scott smiled at me, getting out of the car.

"Scott!" I suddenly felt a lot less nervous, seeing his easy attitude. "I've heard a lot about you."

"Well.. let's hope I don't let you down." Scott smiled at me and walked to stand in front of me. "These are for you..." he handed me a bunch of long stemmed roses.

"You brought these for me?" I was astonished. First date, and he'd arrived with flowers.

"Come on. I am sure I'm not the first guy to give you flowers on your first date." Scott smiled freely at me, catching me off guard. What was I meant to say to that? Surely I couldn't tell him that he was actually the first guy I had dated who wasn't a criminal; in fact, this was like the first date I had ever been on.

""So should we get going?" I smiled smoothly at him. He offered me his hand, and I willingly took it. First date with a real guy; I was actually excited about this! Though I knew deep down I wasn't over Jax.

"You didn't want to put the roses in water?" Scott asked as he walked me to his car.

I cringed when I heard the front door open. Scott naturally turned around to see who it was, still holding my hand. I slowly turned around and I met Jax's eyes.

"You must be Scott?" Cole jumped down the porch steps and reached a hand out towards Scott, which Scott shook. "Cole," he introduced himself. "Amber's brother."

"Nice to meet you," Scott said politely, but I noticed the change in his voice; it was more businesslike now, far from soft and carefree.

"We're leaving," I said through gritted teeth to Cole, and shot a deadly look up at Jax and Troy, who were still standing on the porch. Why the heck couldn't they put a top on? There bikie tattoos were on display for the world to see.

"No worries, I won't be a minute," Cole said as he shot a dry smile my direction, before stepping into Scott's personal space. "Just wanted to make sure that Scott here knows a few things."

I crossed my arms. "I think he knows a hell of a lot more than you Cole so we best be going," I announced.

I was surprised to see that Scott was actually not backing down to my brother; instead, he let go of my hand, crossed his arms and spoke up. "As Amber said, we have somewhere to be."

"Do you know who we are?" Cole's voice had dipped into a threatening hiss. "We just want to make sure that you know Amber is very important to us."

"Messaged received." Scott said dryly, and my insides were on fire with hate right now. Who did Cole think he was!

"Cole…" I started, but Cole being the rude person he was, just cut me off.

"Hurt her, and we will find you," Cole said, his lip curving in a nasty manner, "And trust me when I say, you don't want to get on our bad side."

"Cole, get back in the house now!" I shouted and pointed to the mansion behind him. I did notice Jax looking too smug for his own good.

"Actually, Amber…" Scott said, taking a few steps away from Cole, "I think tonight was a mistake."

"What!?" I watched Scott move around to the driver's side of the car.

"I just wanted to take you out for a nice meal, and I was hoping something more would develop in time," Scott said as he smiled at me pitifully. "I just wanted a simple relationship. This…" he glanced at my brothers, "Is not something I'd like to get involved in."

"Please Scott, come on! They won't do anything!" I could not believe I was begging this guy to take me out!

"Sorry Amber, but I just don't have time for drama," he said as he glanced at my brothers once more. He shot me a smile and got into his car.

I stood there gobsmacked, my mouth hanging open as I watched Scott pull away. I turned around to see Cole with a large smirk on his face. "How dare you!" I said, and pushed him hard. "Who the heck do you think you are!"

"I'm doing you a favor!" He grunted at me. "You don't really want to end up that man's trophy wife."

"Oh piss off Cole!" I shoved past him and stormed up the porch steps. "And you!" I pointed at Jax, who was sitting on the window ledge, looking smug. "Wipe that grin off your face!"

"Don't take your hormones out on me," he said calmly as he looked up at me. "Not my fault you got dumped."

I clenched my fists, shaking with rage. Not his fault? He was the one standing on the porch acting like the muscle. "God you are insufferable!"

"Just go inside already Amber," Troy said as he put out his cigarette. "We actually have other things to do tonight."

I shook my head. How dare they! They had things to do, and he was getting annoyed as if I was stopping them from doing them! Well for his information I had plans tonight too, until he helped ruin them!

I stepped up to Troy, straightening up to my full height, challenging him. "Tonight was the last time. Consider your stay here over," I announced. My voice was like a calm threatening storm. "I'm going to make sure that by the end of the week, dad has all of you kicked out, including your mutt."

Jax scoffed at my reference to him, but I didn't turn around to look at him. I was dead serious; I had had enough. I had dealt with them being there, but I was done.

"Get out of my sight," Troy said as he gave me a hard look, which I brushed off easily. He thought he was the one with the most influence over dad. Being club President had gone to his head. He walked around with authority, and, for a while, I let him push me around. But not any longer.

"Gladly," I barked, and opened the front door, slamming it with great force behind me.

Maybe it was time to face facts; I'm not the good girl. I'm the girl who carries a gun in her handbag.

Taking my heels off and bolting up the stairs, I thought - if the boys were fighting dirty, I could too.

Time to get back to business, and the first thing to do was to get dad to kick these good-for-nothing- bikies out of the house so I could return to doing what I did best.

Behave like a criminal.

Chapter 37

I softly cracked open the window, and then slid into the dark study. Carefully, I closed the window behind me, making sure not to make any noise. Dull, soft music floated from under the closed wooden doors, and I positioned myself in the large armchair, and waited.

Pulling the gun out from behind my back and placing it on my lap, I could hear the thudding of footsteps get louder as someone walked towards the room. I was pleased when the door opened up, and the lights were flicked on. Looked like I wouldn't spend the whole night waiting in the dark after all.

Scott walked towards his desk, with a scotch glass in hand.

"Didn't take you as a scotch drinker," I said, breaking the silence with an evil little smile. Scott spun around, dropping his glass. "That will stain," I said as I twisted my head to the side, enjoying the panic on his face. "Don't be scared Scott, I just came to chat," I offered.

I saw his eyes move to the gun in my lap. People always took you more seriously when you were carrying one of these babies.

"What are you doing in my house?" he gulped, looking terrified. It was wrong, how much I was enjoying this. "How did you get in here?" he frowned.

In his defense, he did have a very good security system, but just like so many other people, he relied too much on technology.

I looked at him calmly. Strangely, the calmer one was, the more worried one's victim tended to be. "You do have a very good security system..." I said as I picked up the gun in my lap and turned it in my hand, studying it aimlessly. "But not good enough," I finished.

"What do you want?"

Right now, he was most likely thinking I was here because I was crazy enough to chase him down for bailing on me.

"I have an offer. Consider it a... business proposition." I got up from the chair smoothly, and walked towards him.

"What would that be?" he said, trying to keep his eyes on me, but every few moments, he would glance down at the gun in my hand.

"I think you should take a seat Scott."

I really didn't like drama; I sucked at it to be honest. I hated the class, but most of all, I hated acting. Lucky for me however, my acting skills didn't suck, and they were about to be put to the test.

***

"Amber!" my Dad hollered from the dining room, as if on cue. Readying myself, I took the smile off my face and walked into the dining room with a sour expression.

"Have a seat," Dad said as he nodded to the empty chair to his right, next to Troy.

"I'm not hungry," I said as I glanced at Jax briefly. Why did he have to look so damn good in the morning?

"I didn't ask if you were." Dad's voice was stern and I slowly made my way to the empty chair. I had just sat down when he started. "How could you do that to Scott?" Dad placed his fork down. "Do you know how that makes me look? You canceling on him like that?"

"I'm sorry dad," I said as I chewed on my bottom lip, trying to look nervous. "But I just couldn't go out with him last night; nerves got the better of me." I saw Cole look blankly at me from across the table, in fact, I reckon all my brothers and the mutt were shocked. They probably expected me to give Cole up to our dad.

"Well… I…" Dad frowned at me. Was he expecting me to rant at him? No, I had a better plan than that; much better.

"But it actually worked out better dad," I said as I grinned sheepishly, looking down at my plate. "We have a date tomorrow night, and he understood about last night. He's a really nice guy."

Dad looked pleasantly surprised. "Well, that's excellent," he smiled proudly at me. "He is a good guy."

"I think so too dad," I gushed, and got to my feet. "I'd better get going. I'm doing extra credit work before school."

"Ok darling," dad beamed at me.

I kept my head straight, not acknowledging anyone else at the table as I walked past.

"Amber, wait a second," Dad stopped me. Turning around, I looked at him. Happiness had engulfed his face. "You're really growing up, I'm proud of you. You're showing a new side; a better side," he said.

He was already pleased with how I did my community service work without asking him to bail me out, and well, me dating Scott now was the icing on the cake.

"Thanks dad," I smiled a flawless smile st him. "Who knows, you might actually let the boys go back to their busy lives instead of baby-sitting me. I'll see you after school," I said as I waved goodbye in a carefree manner, not letting anyone see my evil smirk. I really was good at acting.

***

Lighting up a cigarette, I leaned against the back school gate. School was in full swing, and like the good student I was, I was skipping. I had just sent Scott a text making sure he understood the agreement. Well, more like reminding him of the agreement.

Which basically was to do what I said temporarily, or I'd kill him. Had I actually said I would kill him? No, I let his imagination do that for him. All I did was point out how easy it was to sneak into his house without anyone knowing, that and I was holding a gun which I made sure he was aware I knew how to use one.

"Real model student you are," Jax barked from behind me.

"What do you want?" I snapped, looking sideways at him, as he leaned against the fence next to me.

"Just having a smoke."

I didn't reply. Instead, I dropped mine on the ground, put it out, and turned to leave.

"It's not going to work you know," Jax said smoothly, after taking a long drag on his smoke. "Making me jealous with this Scott guy."

"Please! Scott is just a chess piece I am using."

"So you admit you don't care for him?" Jax turned around to look at me. Why did he have to look so damn good all the time!

"I don't care for him." It was the truth; I wasn't using Scott to make Jax jealous.

"Then why are you going out of your way to be with him?" Jax looked at me slightly worried. I gulped slightly, seeing the worried look for my safety in his eyes.

"Like I said, he's just a piece I need to win the game." I brushed off the concern in his eyes. I couldn't let him pull me back in.

"And what game are you trying to win Amber?" he asked as he tossed his cigarette to the ground, stomped on it, and then crossed his arms, watching me carefully. "What has you pretending to date a suit?"

"You." I was completely honest; if he really wanted to know, I would tell him because my acting wasn't meant to fool him; my acting was for my dad. "You don't want me."

"That's not true," Jax interrupted me, but I raised a hand for him to shut up.

"You want me on your conditions, and I can't have a relationship with someone who is…."

"A criminal?"

"Who won't stand up for me." I overlooked his criminal comment. I didn't care about that. I wanted him, but I wouldn't have a semi-relationship with him. "It was all or nothing Jax, and you chose nothing."

"You didn't say that before." He took a step closer to me. "You didn't tell me it was all or nothing."

"I shouldn't have had to!" I was trying to put a wall up to hide my emotions from him. It wasn't working. I knew he could see the sorrow in my eyes.

"So what then?" Jax pursed his lips "We're over? You want nothing to do with me? That's why you're dating the suit?"

"I was pretending to date Scott, so my dad thinks that I have changed, and then he can kick my brothers and your sorry arse out, and I can go back to doing what I always did."

"What? Petty crime?" Jax scoffed "Going to go back to Blake's little gang and run it for him?" The bitterness in his tone was poisonous.

"Something like that." I knew crawling back to Blake's gang was a long shot and cowardly, but what else was I meant to do? I had no other connections.

"Have fun with that," Jax fumed, and turned his back to me. "I was sick of you anyway."

I knew he was saying that because I must have hurt his feelings, but still, his words hurt me.

"I love you Jax. If only you could have been a man and said it back," I muttered to myself as I turned to leave, trying to swallow the sickening feeling in my stomach.

Chapter 38

I bit my bottom lip, trying to ignore the nagging feeling inside of me. I glanced at my bedroom door, listening to the sounds outside it. That high pitch drunken giggle was grating my nerves. Finally, pushing my laptop away from me, I jumped out of bed.

I was sick of listening to that stupid bitch laughing and carrying on with someone I cared about. Yanking the door open, I stormed across the hall and banged on Jax's door. I'd put up with this for hours!

I went to bring my fist back up to bang on the door again, but it opened. The barely dressed giggling machine was grinning at me.

"What do you want?" She giggled at me, half hiding behind the door. Did she do anything but giggle?

I crossed my arms. Why did Jax always go for the model-like ones? "For you to shut the hell up." I barked, looking at her bitterly. "Think you can manage that?"

The smile disappeared from her face, and her expression changed to a challenging look. "Maybe you should get some earplugs," she quipped. arching an eyebrow with a belittling look. "Think you can manage that?" she smirked, and slammed the door in my face.

That stupid, good for nothing, daughter of a mutt. If she thought she could disrespect me in my own house, she was sadly mistaken. I slammed my fist on the door again.

Cockily, she opened it back up, wider this time. "What do you want now?"

"I'll make it quick," I said, stepping one foot into the doorframe. I pulled back a tight fist and, with a smug expression on my face, I slammed her nose in.

Cursing and crying, she cupped her bloody nose. "Next time, don't disrespect me," I shot at her, and looked over at Jax, who was laying on the bed shaking his head at me. Pointing a finger at him, I barked. "Keep your whores out of my house."

I slammed his bedroom door behind me, and being the jealous girl I was, I stubbornly stormed back across to my bedroom. I knew it had been stupid of me to act that way, and yeah, I had no right to go into his bedroom.

Huffing, I threw myself backwards onto my bed and glared up at the ceiling.

Why couldn't I just fall for the easy ones? And why the hell couldn't I just get over him already!

***

"No." I crossed my arms and looked at dad across the desk. "And I won't think about it," I added.

Was he mad? Did he really think I would agree?

"Amber," he put down the file he was holding. "It will be good for you." His lips curved slightly. "I only want what is best for you," he added.

I shook my head quickly. "I said no and I meant it. Thanks anyway, but no." I was not changing my mind, and if he thought he would get me to go willingly, he had another thing coming.

"Amber, I don't think you were listening, I wasn't asking you, I was informing you." Dad gave me a stern look "Like I said, it's best for you."

Narrowing my eyes at him, I felt boiling anger in my stomach, "I'm not moving to England to live with your stupid sister. Anyway, there is no reason for me to move. Everything is going fine here. You said so yourself!"

He didn't really have the power to send me away. Well, I hoped not. Where was this coming from anyway? I thought dad had been buying my act. Heck, please don't tell me that I had been spending unnecessary amounts of time with Scott when I didn't have to!

"Jackson spoke to me," Dad said as he pulled his chair closer to his desk.

"Jackson spoke to you?" I repeated, boiling with anger. Through gritted teeth, I asked, "And what did Jackson say?"

"Just filled in some blanks for me."

Dad pushed a stack of photos across the table to me. "And Scott filled in the rest."

I looked at the pictures of me, in Scott's office, holding a gun. That prick had cameras in there! Scott was a dead man.

"Before you get any bright ideas, Scott has relocated," Dad said. He pointed a finger at me, adding, "You embarrassed me."

"So what then?" My sweet act now aside, and my normal bitter self showing up. "You are going to ship me off?"

"Why would you want to stay here?" Dad looked at me in a way he hadn't before. "Your brothers don't want you here. Your ex-boyfriend is in jail and I am barely here. Tell me Amber, why would you want to stay here?"

I opened my mouth and with nothing to say, I closed it again. I had no answer. I got up from the chair, hurt. "If you didn't want me here dad, that was all you had to say."

"I thought I could help you Amber. Clearly, I can't," he said to my back before I slid out his door and closed it softly behind me.

I had always thought dad's love was unconditional, but it looked like I had crossed a line. Dad was sick of my lies and trouble, and, in all honesty, why wouldn't he be?

I really was a disappointment.

***

285

I cracked open another can of Jack Daniels and crumpled the empty one, throwing it in the direction of the others on the kitchen floor. Drowning my sorrows; how pathetic was I?

I knew I had had a tad too much to drink when I had to grab the third six pack from the fridge. I chugged and swallowed quick, reaching for the lit cigarette sitting on the ashtray.

How the hell had I got to this point? How the hell did I end up being that girl? You know the one that had no-one, and nothing.

A few months ago, I thought I would turn my life around, and now I had no life to turn around. I either moved to England and lived with my batty Aunt to keep my trust fund, or move to the streets and well...I didn't even know what that was like, and I didn't want to know.

Great! What options!

The kitchen lights flickered on, and I immediately yelled, squinting, "TURN IT OFF!" I was so lost in my thoughts, I hadn't even heard them come home - let alone walk into the kitchen.

"Fuck, Amber!" Tyler waved the air in front of him, coughing, "Trying to set the house on fire?"

Ok, so smoking in a closed room for hours wasn't healthy, but neither was drowning myself in alcohol.

"Just piss off," I said, and downed the rest of my can. "And turn the lights back off on your way out."

"What happened to you?" Cole asked, and he actually looked concerned as he pulled a stool up and sat on the other side of the bench; much to my unhappiness.

"You and Scott break up or something?" Tyler opened the fridge door. "Did you drink all my cans?!" he added.

"Piss off!" I yelled.

"Fuck, is Amber cooking?" Jax's voice was laced with amusement as he strode through the door cockily. He crossed his arms smugly and examined me; I saw through the crap and picked up on the concern in his eyes, and it only drove the betrayal deeper.

How could he have gone to dad?

"Fine, I'll leave," I announced, and pulled myself up from the stool, holding the bench for support. I only took one step, stumbling, before Tyler wrapped his arms around me, taking the weight my legs couldn't.

"Why don't you just sit back down," Tyler propped me back on the stool. "And don't fall backwards," he instructed. I felt him leave his hand on my chair, just in case.

"Just leave all of you, I'm fine!"

"If you said that without stuttering, I would have believed you," Jax said, and naturally, he pulled a stool up next to me, and being the know-it-all that he is, he took the remaining cans away from me.

"What has you drinking so hard?" Jax asked in a lowered voice; he spoke softly to me, "Are you ok?"

What's this? Jax actually pretending he cared about me? Hah.

.Turning slowly to look him up and down, I asked, "Why would you care?"

"Ok, what happened?" Cole snapped before Jax could reply. "You never do this."

"Do what?" I bit back. Couldn't they all just leave me alone? Why did they care anyway? It's not like I was nice to them.

"This!" Cole gestured at the cans. "Drinking and looking depressed."

"You're right," I spoke bitterly at Cole, and shook Tyler's hand off my back. "I have no right to be depressed!" I got up abruptly from the stool, thankful my legs didn't cave under me. "It's not like my own dad just told me he wanted nothing more to do with me and is shipping me off to the other side of the world, and that I don't even have one person that would care!" I couldn't hold the tears back any longer, and they began to run slowly down my cheeks. I turned my head slowly to look at Jax. "And the one guy, that for some reason I really cared about, told me flat out he would never love me."

My emotions were exploding everywhere, and I couldn't keep them to myself anymore. I shook my head, consumed with this feeling of worthlessness. "I have nothing to be depressed about," I said slowly. I managed to put one foot in front of the other, swiping a can from the bench as I left.

The boys looked shocked because, for the first time, my emotions were on display. They were raw and ugly. What man wouldn't be stunned after witnessing that? I drunkenly made my way to the foyer. I had a choice to go upstairs and sleep it off, or get behind the wheel.

Choosing neither, I pulled a jumper from the coat rack and stumbled out into the fresh night air. I just wanted to walk it off, and each drunk step I took was one further from my problems.

Well, that was how my drunk mind was reasoning with me.

"AMBER!" The front door slammed, and Jax ran up the driveway after me. The gravel crunched under his heavy boots and he yelled after me, "Amber, wait!"

I had barely made it halfway up the driveway, so Jax caught up with me quickly. Grasping my upper arm softly, he stopped me.

Pure panic covered his face. "I'm sorry," he gulped, looking at me regretfully. "I don't like people knowing who I care about because it puts them in danger. You being with me Amber, could lead… if you were to get hurt because of me…" he shook his head, brimming with tears. "I can't lose you," he added.

I closed my eyes briefly, letting the pent up tears flow down, and then I looked him back in the eye. "But you don't have me to lose. You either risk it or let it go, and you chose to let me go."

"I would rather have you alive than dead," Jax said gently, and cupped my cheek with his other hand, lowering his head to look me in the eye "I'm not going to change Amber. I'm always going to be an outlaw, and I'm only going to get deeper into it."

I stomped my foot shaking my head, coughing back the tears. "I can deal with that; I will always stand by you," I said, as I gripped his shirt. "Please just don't give up on us." I was begging him to not turn away from me.

"I can't expect you to live this life," Jax said as he shook his head and brought me in closer to his chest, trying to comfort me. "I can't let you waste your life waiting for me." He let go of my upper arm and wrapped his arm around my back.

"Jax, we are perfect for each other!" I knew the alcohol was helping me speak my mind as I wasn't holding anything back. My walls had crumbled; I wasn't playing a game. I simply was telling him the truth; how I really felt. "Please don't give up on us before we even had a chance."

Jax looked at me deeply. I could see him fighting his own reason. I just wanted him to forget about what was right and just risk it with me. If I was willing to, why couldn't he?

"Amber..." he sighed, running his thumb down my jaw. "I.."

The roaring of an engine and squealing of tires grabbed our attention. Just like that, everything faded and suddenly time slowed. In slow motion, I registered the gun shots and the black sedan at our gates, firing bullets at us non-stop.

My body hit the gravel as Jax pushed me to the ground, covering my body. I felt Jax reach to his back, pulling his gun out and firing in the direction of the car. The noise stained the air. The car spun around and took off in the direction it came from. Turning my head to the side, I saw my brothers on the porch, guns raised, and swearing.

"Go after them!" Jax roared up at them, but he didn't need to. Cole and Tyler were already straddling their bikes, and they shot up the driveway.

"Amber?" Jax put his gun on the gravel, and got off me. "Come on, you have to get up, you need to get in the house." Jax's eyes drifted to the road following the sound of the motorbikes. I knew he wanted to be chasing them too.

"Jax, I can't get up," I looked at him calmly, and frowning, he looked back at me. For the first time in ages, he scanned my body, and when his eyes widened, I knew.

He ripped off his leathered vest, quickly pulled the hoodie off he had under it, and pressed it to my upper thigh.

I cringed in pain, feeling the pressure.

"It will be ok," Jax attempted to calm me, but his attention was on the bullet wound. The distant sound of an engine flowed up the highway, and Jax scooped me up quickly and jogged to the house.

Wrapping my arms around his neck, I clung to him. Pain was shooting up my leg as he carried me. The front door was already open, and Jax slammed it shut with his foot, behind him.

"We should leave," I gritted my teeth. "Head into town, you need to…"

"I'm not moving you; not while you're bleeding." Jax said and moved to the staircase quickly, his jaw tightening every time I cringed in pain.

"Where's your case?" Jax asked, swinging my bedroom door open.

"Under my bed. Please tell me you have removed a bullet before?"

He placed me on the bed, but didn't answer me. Blood was already staining my white blanket. "I suppose it's a good thing I am wasted," I mumbled, pulling myself up the bed so I could sit up. Jax pulled the large case out from under my bed and flipped it open.

"You're bleeding more because of it," Jax said, and grabbed a pair of tweezers and a small bottle of sterilized water.

"You know what's funny?" I watched Jax rip my jeans up the middle, relieving the wound. I laid my head back and prepared myself for the coming pain.

"This is the first time I've been shot," I said, gripping the metal bars of my headboard behind me, cringing as the water burnt my leg. "I thought it would hurt more."

Jax didn't say anything; he was focused on my leg.

My eyes began to droop, and a wave of fatigue washed over me. "Amber?" Jax's voice heightened in panic. "Amber, open your eyes!"

"Jax, you should call an ambulance," I muttered. My eyes were tiny slits, but I could see the blood pumping out through the small wound, and smell the rancid odor of blood.

It was funny how things could change so quickly. It was true, life could be here one second and gone the next.

Chapter 39

Amber

The dryness in my throat had me struggling to swallow. My eyes opened and I automatically looked for water. Throwing the blankets back, I stumbled to the ground; a sharp pain ran up my right leg, and I hopped to the bathroom. My right leg gave out from under me, and I crashed to the ground. Hissing in pain, I slowly crawled my way into my bathroom, and pulled myself up to the basin.

Turning the cold water on, I gulped it down fast, not getting enough. The water was claiming the desert in my throat. I glanced in the mirror and I noticed his figure behind me.

"What?" I croaked.

Jax's eyes were solid, and I couldn't see one emotion, although his crossed arms and posture were screaming anger towards me.

"Feeling better?"

Pulling my head out from under the tap "No," I said and turned around slowly. "How bad is my leg?" My body was beginning to look like a battlefield.

"It was a flesh wound," he announced, and pushed himself off the doorframe, his leather jacket crackling. "Guessing you passed out from having drunk too much, and not from the wound."

"Oh." Well that was embarrassing, Let's face it - it was cooler to pass out from a gun wound than passing out from alcohol.

"Why were you drinking so hard?" Jax didn't move further into the bathroom. He just stood there, radiating anger.

"Dad spoke to me," I said, the memory now becoming clear and the thought of it made me want to go look for a bottle of vodka. "Well, I guess you could say he gave me a choice."

"It being?'

"You should know." Bitterness entered my voice. "He did say you helped him decide."

"I didn't help him do anything," he snapped at me, getting overly defensive. "Whatever it is, the credit is all his."

I eyed him carefully. Was he telling the truth, or was he lying? Sighing and pulling myself up to sit on the basin, I realized it didn't matter if he had or hadn't.

"It doesn't matter anymore, I guess," I played with my fingers in my lap, "His mind is made up."

"Want to fill me in?" Jax pretended like he didn't care, but I caught the eagerness and emergency in his voice.

"I'm being sent away." I looked up from my hands, "To live with my batty aunt."

Jax scoffed loudly and the corner of his lips twitched upwards. I was expecting him to be angry or something, not happy. "As if you are going to let that happen," he added.

"I don't get a choice."

Hearing that changed his attitude.

"You aren't really going to go?"

"Like I said, I don't get a choice, and dad reminded me of something else. I don't have anything to stay here for." My eyes were locked with Jax's. If you have ever imagined a girl pleading for a man to say he loved her, this would be it. I just needed a reason to stay, couldn't he be it?

"If that's how you feel," he shrugged his shoulders, "I can't change your mind."

My mouth fell slightly open. Was he bloody serious? How thick could he get! Snapping my mouth closed, I began to grind my teeth and glare into the tiled floor. For a smart guy, he sure could act dumb.

"Amber?"

I didn't know when but Jax had made his way to me, his big black buckled boots now blocking my view of the white tiles.

"What?" I didn't look up at him. Stupid dumb male.

"Want to go get some food?"

Was he serious? I snapped my head up and glared at him. "No."

"Fuck, you are hormonal," he ran a hand through his hair, like he didn't know what to do.

"Well, piss off then." If he didn't want to be here, he didn't have to be. The stubbornness that ran thick through my veins was beginning to surface.

Jax was standing still, staring at me while grinding his teeth. What was he thinking?

"Fuck it," he finally said, and then searched his jeans pocket and pulled his phone out.

"What are you doing?" I watched him search his phone for something, with a determined expression on his face.

He didn't answer. Instead, he raised the phone to his ear, dialing someone. I kind of felt bad for whoever was about to receive his phone call.

"Troy?" he snapped into the phone. "Yeah, she is fine," he said, glancing at me briefly. I arched an eyebrow at him; what was he doing?

"Yeah that's fine, whatever." Jax said quickly into the phone, not seeming to really care about whatever Troy had just asked him. "I'm dating your sister."

My mouth dropped. He did not just say that, did he?

I couldn't hear what Troy was yelling at him, but I was sure it would be a long string of threats.

Jax was rubbing the side of his temple, glaring at the ground, while just letting Troy yell at him. I lowered my feet to the ground, and walked towards him; slowly, not wanting my right leg to cave under me again.

I took Jax's fingers from his temple, drawing his eyes to me. Holding his hand, I could hear Troy's muffled yells from the speaker.

293

Jax's eyes were melting with desire. "I fucking love her, so get used to it Troy." He hung up, determination in his eyes. "You are mine now."

"I'm not property," I gulped, running my fingers down the middle of his chest and stepping closer into him, hoping I wasn't making the worse decision of my life.But, I suppose if it was, I could just add it to my long list.

"Is your dad really shipping you off?" his voice was low, and he pulled me in closer to him. My neck bent right back to meet his eyes.

"Going off what he said, yes."

"Are you going to go?"

I saw the concern on his face and I felt him clench me tighter.

"Not if I don't have to."

"I'm not letting you go," Jax's voice confirmed, and he gently pushed the stray hair from the side of my face so he could see my eyes clearly. "Which means we need to find somewhere else for you to live."

"What? The clubhouse?" I asked, raising both my eyebrows. "Really don't see that working."

"It won't be permanent," he reassured me. "Once this parole is done with, I can get access to my money."

"Then what?" I wanted to laugh "We get a white house with a picket fence?'

The corner of his mouth twisted up, and his eyes narrowed playfully. "I'm more of a barb wired fence sort of guy."

Laughing and shaking my head, I realized this didn't really sound like a bad idea.

"Amber, there is one more thing?" Jax's face was still playful, but I noticed a hint of seriousness. "No more games, I don't do well with jealousy."

"Neither do I," I replied

Lightly, he guided his hand up my body and cupped the side of my cheek, "I don't play games."

"Neither do I," I snapped back, pushing up against him harder and moving my head slightly closer to his. "Looks like we both have nothing to worry about."

"Looks that way," he whispered before driving his head forward and locking his lips with mine. An uncontrollable desire fired through my veins at his touch, and I wanted more.

As he stepped out of the bathroom and into my room with me clinging to him, it was easy to come to the conclusion I was most definitely going to get more, and, as he kissed me with such passion, I had to wonder, how the hell did I live without this for so long?

Chapter 40

Jax

"Do you have any idea what you are doing?" Troy yelled in my face. The veins running up his neck were bulging, and his eyes were narrowed, the rage on his face would send any man running scared but I wasn't a man who was easily intimidated.

Cole was glaring at me from the bar, his lips curled with disgust. Adam was the only one who hadn't attacked me with threats when I'd walked into the clubhouse. Tyler, however, couldn't even stand being in the same room, and left out the back when I came in.

"Get out of my face," I growled at Troy, and pushed him back, hard, so he was out of my personal space. "How about you stop questioning me, and start debriefing."

There had been a run that night; it wasn't major, and Troy being President should have handled it easy. Still, he had to tell me how it went.

Cole scoffed loudly from the bar, wanting my attention. "Dating her is only going to bring trouble," he snorted.

"What I do in my personal life is not your business." My voice dropped into a deadly growl, "I think you both better remember your place and who you are talking to."

"Putting Amber in trouble makes it our business," Troy said as he slammed a closed fist down on the bar, finally getting the hint and staying out of my personal space.

"She isn't in trouble," I gritted my teeth; this was why I didn't want to tell them, their protective instincts were sickening. "Anyway, before I came along, she had the ability to bring trouble all by herself without my help."

"You said you loved her." Troy looked disgusted. "Did you say that so she heard you? If you think you are using my sister as a root rag..."

"I'm dating her. Now fucking drop it before I drop you," I roared at both of them. "Now get back to fucking business and remember I'm the one in charge."

I stormed out of the clubhouse; the heat and anger in the room was suffocating. I couldn't let them think they had a right to tell me what to do. The Shield boys had to be brought back in line and it was going to be a challenge.

I let the clubhouse door slam shut. We had more important things to worry about than my dating life, like finding the fuckwit that tried to kill us the other night.

I straddled the black beast and kicked her to life. Nothing like a long ride to clear the mind, although knowing Amber was sleeping, half-naked, made me want to make a detour.

Amber

Ever wanted to just hide from the world? Pull the covers up and pretend that you have disappeared from the world? I don't usually, but today that was exactly what I wanted to do, because I didn't want to have to face today.

Did I think something would happen today? Well, no, not really. I just simply did not want to get up because, right now, everything was how I liked it. One could say it was perfect.

I finally had Jax, and although I would never admit it to a living soul, I really had deep feelings for the guy. It was an overwhelming, gut wrenching, bring me to my knees sort of love.

"Amber, get out of bed alright?" Jax said as he pushed me again, and I clenched the blankets around me tighter.

"NO!" my voice was muffled under the blankets "Just come back to bed."

"Don't make me pull you out!" I heard the snigger in his voice.

"Do it and you're dead."

Jax went silent and I knew that only meant one thing - trouble for me. "Jax?" A few more minutes passed and I tried to listen for movement, but there was nothing.

I squealed when the blankets were suddenly ripped off, my grip not having a chance against his.

"I hate you!" I flipped over onto my back and glared up at him.

"School; leaving in ten minutes." Smirking, his eyes raked my body. "Better put some more clothes on too."

"PERV!" I threw a pillow in his direction. He easily walked out of the room and closed the door behind him.

I groaned loudly. Looks like I would be facing the day after all.

***

I always believed that whatever I did didn't really matter. Like no-one really cared; boy had I been wrong.

"That's it." I slammed my locker shut. "Get away from me."

Jax rolled his eyes at me, and took the books from my hand. "Amber, get over it."

"I'll get over it when people stop staring at us!" I shot a dirty look at the girls across the hall that were eyeballing us. "Seriously, it's not that big of a deal."

"Who said they are staring at you?" Jax smirked at me, "They are just checking me out."

"Yeah, couldn't get a tight enough t-shirt?" I glanced up and down his body again. I swear that black t-shirt was just designed to define each of his rather well-crafted abnormal muscles, and to tease the hell out of me.

Jax moved in closer, his lips just touching my ear lobe. "Don't worry Amber, you can take it off tonight."

I whacked his arm immediately. "Please! As if your body is all I think about."

"So, what were you enjoying last night?"

"Just shut it," I hissed under my breath. "They will hear you, and that won't help anything, will it?"

Jax sniggered. "Come on, give me your hand."

I pulled it quickly behind my back, away from him "No." I was sick of people staring at us. For God's sake, had they never seen a couple before?

Ever since I got off Jax's bike this morning and held his hand, we had become the school's only source of entertainment. Or maybe someone had plastered a 'stare at me sign' on me, and I hadn't seen it.

"Give me your hand!" He went to reach around me, and just missed it. "Amber…"

"No, and while we are at it, hand my books over."

"Why do you care about what others think?" Jax held my books behind his back. "Embarrassed of me?"

My eyes narrowed instantly; I knew what he was playing at. I didn't care what others thought of us, I just didn't like being stared at like a zoo animal. "You know that isn't it."

"Whatever you say," Jax said, handing my books over to me as he shrugged; but his job was done. He had already stirred the demon inside of me.

Grinding my teeth, my eyes flickered to the circle of girls who were hovering across from us, still staring. The anger was boiling inside of, and I felt myself ready to explode. Didn't they know who they were staring at for Heaven's sake? They had once feared me! I shot an annoyed look at Jax.

It was his fault for being so damn popular.

A glance from a passing football player sent me off the edge.

"STOP FUCKING LOOKING AT US!" I roared through the hall. Everyone in the hall stopped and looked at me; each one of the stupid twits had a stunned expression. "Jax and I are together, now get the heck over it! If I see one more person even glance in our direction, I can PROMISE you it will be the last thing you DO!"

The threat in my voice was deadly, and it would scare anyone in their right mind. Let's be honest, any crazy woman screaming in the middle of the hall would scare someone.

"Smooth," Jax muttered behind me, and I looked over my shoulder at him. He was holding his laughter in.

"Someone has to be the man in this relationship," I hissed back at him, before noticing that everyone was still frozen. "What the heck are you waiting for?" I snapped at them. "Move on!"

Students' eyes snapped to the ground as they walked past me, and, slowly, conversation began to rebuild.

"Way to strike fear in the hearts of our peers, Amber." Jax reached out and grabbed my hand. "Come on babe; let me get you to class before you scare anyone else."

Chapter 41

"Stop glaring at her," Jax hissed from beside me. I gave him a dry expression, while rolling my eyes. Did he really expect me to listen to him?

"Tell her we're dating then," I said and leaned into him, and then shot another filthy look in Linda's direction. "Now."

"I'm not standing up in the middle of class to tell her that. Anyway, she would know by now," he reassured me.

"You don't know that."

I tapped my foot under the table, and my eyes traveled back in her direction. I knew it was under me to even care about what she thought, but I will admit the evil side of me wanted to see her face when she realized Jax is mine.

I always thought Linda had a crush on him and this was only proved right when Jax just happened to mention that she liked him. Well that just created a beast inside me, who wanted to rub my new relationship in her face.

"Amber, just drop it." Jax's voice was serious, and he placed his hand under the table on my leg "Please."

I looked into his haunting eyes, which always seemed to draw me into him. Not being able to fight it, I surrendered. So much for not doing what he told me to.

***

"Noticed how people get out of our way?" I hummed happily to Jax as we walked up the corridor; not one person got in our way.

"What do you expect when you are with me?" He smirked at me and naturally I gave him a crabby look.

"Don't go all high and mighty on me."

"Ok babe."

"I'm not a pig," I huffed, and reached into my bag to look for my buzzing phone.

"You should clean that thing out," Jax said as he pointed at my bag. "The crap you have in there..." he shook his head disapproving.

"Please! Everything in here is important," I informed him. I finally found my phone; of course it was at the bottom. "Here," I handed him my textbooks. "Make yourself useful." I sniggered at the slight disgust on his face when he took them. Also, the look in his eyes which told me not to mention this to the boys.

"Hello?" I smiled into the phone, my eyes still on Jax.

"Amber!"

"Blake?" I was shocked to hear his voice; he hadn't contacted me since he'd been arrested; although he was in jail, so he had a pretty good excuse.

"The one and only."

"Why are you calling me?" I didn't beat around the bush; I went straight to the point. I held a hand up to stop Jax from reaching for my phone. Why would he want to talk to Blake anyway?

"I need you to come see me."

"Why?"

"You have a lot of questions," Blake stated, his voice hard, and with an edge to it. I couldn't put my finger on the problem, but there was something up; I just wasn't sure what it was.

"You have a weird request," I bit back. Why would he want to see me? We weren't together and I wasn't in his gang. I was sure he would know I was thick with the bikies now, and close to my brothers.

"Not really," he snapped. "You were an important part of my life for a long time, and I helped you when you needed it."

Oh! He wanted something.

"Do you need something?" I asked.

"You could say that," he said. "Come visit me, and we won't have as many ears listening."

His conversations must be being recorded. Sighing, I was torn at this point. Should I go? But then Blake was there when I needed him; I owed him.

"Ok, I'll come this week."

"Looking forward to it…" Blake hung up abruptly.

"What did he want?" Jax was glaring at my phone. His face was tense and he was crunching my textbook.

"Just wants me to go see him. Want to loosen that grip on my textbook there?" I reached out to take it off him.

"Did you tell him to fuck himself?"

"JAX!"

Jax was deadly serious, and I was seriously getting angry. "What the hell is your problem?"

"You're not going to see him," Jax announced, turning to stomp off, as if that was the final decision. Normally, I wouldn't care what he thought, but he was my boyfriend now, and I had to work this out with him before I went and did whatever I wanted anyway.

"I am, because I said I would. Now, would you stop getting so angry over this? Last time I checked you couldn't have sex in a visiting room, so you have nothing to worry about."

Jax shot a dirty look over his shoulder at me and I had to give myself points for trying to throw a joke in the mix but it was pointless, it didn't lighten things up.

"You aren't going,"

I picked up on the authority in his voice, and it planted seeds of anger within me. "I'm not a part of your club Jax, you can't tell me what to do." I narrowed my eyes at him; looked like a fight wasn't going to be avoidable after all.

"For once Amber, just listen to me," Jax insisted, stopping me in the hallway with crossed arms. "You aren't going. Now drop it."

I clenched my closed fists. You can take the bikie off the bike, but you can't take the stubbornness out of him. Looks like I was going to have to take the gloves off. I could just drop it, but I told Blake I would go, and the bottom line was, I did owe him.

"I'm going to go see him tomorrow. Now just get over it," I snapped at him. Seriously, was he really insane enough to think I would go back to Blake? He didn't have to be jealous.

"You're NOT!" Jax roared at me, and I quickly looked up and down the hallway, embarrassed. Lucky for me, no one was around; had the bell rung already?

"You know what Jax?" I stepped in closer to him, meeting his fierce eyes, "I don't like being told what to do."

Jax's lips formed in a tight line. He knew he had dug his own grave; I wasn't backing down.

"Fine, piss off to him them," he said as he looked down at me angrily. "But you can tell him the answer is no."

Answer to what? I arched an eyebrow at him. "He didn't ask anything of you..."

"He will." Jax stated, and looked at me with anger. "And you can tell him no."

"Whatever." I didn't want to argue over something that wasn't important. If Jax wanted to think the world revolved around him, fine.

"Make sure you carry," he said, before storming off. Well, what other words of advice could he give me.

"You know Jax, you really need to learn that I'm your girlfriend, not a member," I snapped behind him, and stopped him in his tracks.

"You need to learn you aren't bulletproof Amber. You are mixed up with shit that just makes my life harder," he informed me.

"What, you want to bail already?" I sounded confident, but, inside, I was angry at him for even thinking of walking away from me so soon. For Heaven's sake, I had just received a phone call from Blake! He was blowing this out of proportion.

"You know what Jax?" I stomped up to him. "If me getting a phone call from an ex is too much 'shit' for you, then you aren't worth my time."

I shouldered past him, and stormed towards the corridor doors. Looked like today was going to be cut short for me; I knew he wouldn't follow me because he had to stay for his parole board.

Right now I was grateful for that, because I needed some space from him. Everything was going good for a few moments, and then it all turned to shit.

Seeing as I'd just got a free afternoon, Blake might as well see me sooner than he'd expected to.

You know there is always one thing you can count on, and that is that men suck. I kicked my car tire in frustration, and when I got in, I uncontrollably smacked my steering wheel.

I thought as much that Blake had a favor to ask of me. I looked up and glared at the prison, but it wasn't what I'd thought. What made it worse was that Jax had expected it but of course he did, he was the cause of all this to begin with.

Not only had he managed to yell at me for Blake calling me, and wanting to see me, but he was also the reason Blake had called me in the first place!

I leaned my head against the headrest. My hands ached from hitting the steering wheel.

My mind going over what just happened.

Blake had already told me once he had thought it was my fault he was in jail, and I couldn't stop the disgust in my stomach from boiling over when he'd said this. He'd also confessed to having me put on a hit list. I gave the steering wheel another whack.

That explained all the attacks! It also kind of explained why Jax had over-reacted today.

But it was his damn fault I was here. Jax had put a hit on Blake in jail. I know a normal girl would be shocked and scared when hearing this, but for me, it was just another thing in my twisted life.

Blake had taken the hit down weeks ago, [SVD1]when his trial had started and he'd found out who had really put him in jail; it wasn't me but Jax being the man he is, wouldn't take the hit down.

When I saw Blake today, he was a mess and told me he was confined to his cell for protection.

So my ex-boyfriend, who'd wanted me dead, was now being hunted down by Jax's club brothers[SVD2], who all answer to Jax and would jump at any command he gives. Blake was sure he wasn't going to last long.

I knew Jax's heart was in the right place, but I still had a soft spot for Blake. Even though he wanted me dead, I didn't want him dead but after I'd make Jax pull his club brothers off Blake, I wanted nothing else to do with Blake.

I started my car up. Now I had to come up with some really good reasons for Jax to let Blake live.

I had a feeling no reason I'd give would be good enough. I would have to convince him in other ways.

Looked like I would be losing my clothes tonight.

Chapter 42

"Trying to kill my ex-boyfriend is a bit low, even for you." I crossed my arms, standing in our lounge. Troy was sitting across from me, a beer glued to his right hand and a smoke in the other. I gave Troy a hard look. "You know we aren't allowed to smoke inside," I said.

"How was your jail visit?" Troy arched an eyebrow, and didn't make a move to put his smoke out. "Catch up?"

I knew he was trying to distract me. I shot another look at Jax, but he wouldn't look up. He could glare outside all he wanted, but he could only ignore me for so long.

"Jax? Did you hear me?" I snapped at him.

"Blake tell you all about the hit list?" Troy questioned me, while Jax remained mute.

"Yes, he did." I glared at Troy. "Don't you have somewhere to be?" I could try and get rid of him, but I had a feeling he was going to stay anyway just to piss me off.

"Nah, I'm fine here." Troy smugly pushed himself back into the couch. "Don't let me stop you," he added.

Grinding my teeth together, I came to terms with the fact that I was going to have to beg in front of my brother. This night was just getting better and better.

"Jax, can you come with me please?" I huffed.

Jax looked up, a coldness in his eyes. He slowly slipped his beer while studying me. Finally, he placed his empty bottle on the ground, and turned slightly on the couch to face me.

"What do you want Amber?"

"Can you please take that hit off Blake?" It felt like I was throwing up knives when I asked him. I hated asking anyone for anything because it then meant I'd owe them.

"No." Jax's narrowed his eyes. "I told you that before you left."

"No you didn't! You didn't tell me you were trying to have him killed!"

"Oh stop it Amber!" he roared at me, the vein in his neck bulging slightly. "He wanted you dead! What was I supposed to do!"

"Nothing! It wasn't your problem."

"When it concerns you, it concerns me!" he roared, getting up from the couch. "What did you expect me to do? Sit back and watch him get you killed?"

"You should have told me!" I roared.

"Ok, I'm leaving," Troy said as he got up.

"What? You want to leave now?" I snorted, shouldering him slightly when he walked past.

"Drop the hit," I said as I brought my eyes back on Jax "Now." My voice was firm, and I couldn't believe that I was able to stand my ground in front of Jax when he looked so angry.

His knuckles were turning to a shade of white, he was clenching his fists so hard. "Why should I?" he spat "And why do you even care if he lives or dies?"

"Because I owe him," I said as I crossed my arms defensively. I knew what angle Jax was coming from, and it pissed me off.

"More like you care for him." He scoffed, and the jealousy was clear in his eyes. "I'm not a fucking fool!"

"Can you hear yourself! Really Jax, how much have you had to drink?" I narrowed my eyes at him, making sure I didn't back down. If this relationship was to have the slightest chance, I had to be as strong as him or I was going to be walked all over.

"Get out of my sight Amber."

I gulped at the seriousness in his tone, and the look he was giving me was scaring me. This wasn't working. Hating myself for what I was about to do, I decided to give another angle a shot anyway.

I softened my face. "Please Jax, just do this for me," I said tenderly; softly. It was a quick change from my deadly, forceful tone before.

Jax automatically frowned at me. He seemed taken aback and that was what I'd wanted.

"You really want me to?" He looked me straight in the eye.

I nodded my head quickly. I didn't like owing anyone anything. Blake was in my past and I was sick of him influencing my present.

"I just don't want to owe Blake anymore," I told Jax. "That's all."

"He wanted you dead," Jax said, not hiding his disgust. He was really angry about this, and for some sick reason, it actually made my heart flutter; his protective instincts. I really was twisted.

"But it is over now." I went to stand right in front of him, and looked up at him. "Thank you for having my back."

I did have to thank him, because he had been looking after me while madmen were out to get me.

"That must taste bitter," he said, as the corner of his lips twitched slightly up. I rolled my eyes at him, but he was right. I hated saying sorry. It just didn't taste nice coming out.

"Are you hungry?" Jax changed the subject, while reaching out and looping an arm around my back, bringing me closer into his chest.

How had I found someone so perfect for me? We could go from fighting to loving each other so quickly.

"Yeah, it was a long drive in," I admitted. I hadn't had lunch, and my body was craving food.

Jax's eyes twinkled with slight amusement, "You are one hungry beast."

"So... take out?"

The house doorbell rang through the house. Who could that be? It was rather late.

309

"You expecting someone?" I asked Jax.

"No. You?"

"Nope." I let go of him and walked out to the foyer. Whoever it was, they'd better piss off quickly because I was hungry, and seeing how I'd just sucked up to Jax, I deserved food.

I opened the door, and I couldn't believe what I was looking at. Of all the people to be here right now!

"Jax," I turned to the side. Jax was still standing in the lounge, although now he had a confused look on his face. "It's for you."

Chapter 43

Jax

"Mai?" I looked her up and down. She was a mess, her hair was everywhere and her cheeks were stained with tears.

"Jax, I had nowhere else to go." Mai said as she swallowed back tears, and I saw her glance at Amber, who was hiding slightly behind her front door.

I could feel the anger from Amber. The quicker I got rid of Mai the better, or Amber was going to explode.

"What do you need?" I looked back at Mai; she was shaking on the porch.

"I just…" Mai's eyes were blurry as she spilled another wave of tears. "Can I come in?" she asked, with a desperate tone in her voice.

I couldn't turn her away. I stepped out of the door frame and let her inside. Amber was standing behind me now, and her slim fingers were poking me hard in the back.

I gritted my teeth and bared it for a few moments before I reached behind me and grabbed her hand.

"Do you remember Amber?" I pulled her out from behind me, and introduced her to Mai.

Mai looked at Amber and nodded her head. "You came with them on their last ride."

"Yep." Amber crossed her arms. Looks like she was going to go easy with Mai.

"Mai, so what's wrong?" I took over the conversation before Amber started taking shots at her. I didn't need any extra drama.

"Can we talk?" Mai glanced at Amber, then back at me. "Alone?"

And things were about to get messy. I didn't even have a chance to say anything; Amber cut in.

"It's my house," she said as she stepped in front of me. "If you have something to say to my boyfriend, you can say it to me too. We don't keep secrets."

Fuck, women were difficult.

"Boyfriend?" Mai looked confused. "Jax are you actually dating this girl?"

"This girl?" Amber's voice was threatning, and I immediately reached out and gripped her upper arm, pulling her back to me slightly.

Amber had a really bad temper, nearly as bad as mine but it was hot seeing how protective she was over her claim on me. I kept the smile to myself though, knowing Amber would only turn around and rip my head off if she saw it.

"Yeah Mai, I am," I said, keeping my grip on Amber. "Now can we all just calm the fuck down. Mai, what are you doing here?"

Mai looked at me thoughtfully. "Why are you dating her?"

For Christ sake, why did it matter who I was dating! See, this is why I didn't date; everything got harder. Jealous women were deadly.

"What are you doing here, Mai?"

She ran a hand through her messy hair, and my current relationship status seemed to drop from her mind.

"It's dad… he had a heart attack…" Mai broke out in tears, and launched herself into my arms. I had to let go of Amber's arm, so I could hold Mai up. She had collapsed in my arms, a sobbing mess.

"I'll leave you two alone." Amber gave me a dark look before storming up the staircase. I watched her, and I knew she would be jealous or hurt right now because I was holding Mai.

Great. Every time Amber and I are just getting on, shit happens.

Chapter 44

Amber

Damn human hearing. If only I had the ears of a wolf! I would've been able to hear what the heck was going on! I pushed my ear harder up against Jax's room.

"What are you doing?" Cole's voice boomed, and I quickly spun around, waving my arms for him to shut the hell up!

But like the thick head he was, he just arched an eyebrow at me. I watched his face as something clicked, and then he seemed to understand what I was doing.

"Amber, back away from the door," he said as he crossed his arms. "Now." I was grateful he actually hissed it at me, and hoped Jax hadn't heard too much.

Rolling my eyes, I slowly walked up the corridor to Cole, stopping in front of him. "Thanks for blowing my cover." I narrowed my eyes at him. "Really smooth."

"Didn't take you as the jealous type," Cole said. He was enjoying this, I could tell.

"Jealous?" I hissed at him, "You and I both know Mai isn't here just for comfort." I hated her for stepping into my house, and yeah it was sad her dad was sick, but come on, running to my boyfriend for help? The bitch had my rage coming at her.

"No, we don't," Cole said in a firm voice, and he slung his hand under my arm and began to drag me away from the scene. When we were further away from Jax's room, Cole stopped. "Mai and Jax have a special relationship, and you need to accept that."

"What do you mean special?"

"Amber," Cole ran a hand over his bald head. "Just leave it alright."

"Leave what? Leave that bitch to my boyfriend?" I scoffed and crossed my arms tightly. I didn't like sharing, and hell I would take her out if I had to.

Cole's face twisted with anger, and he shook his head, furious at me. "He has a past Amber, and if you are so in love with him, then you have to accept it. He isn't the faithful type. You wanted him, flaws and all. Well, this is what you get when you date a bikie. Now grow up and stop being needy." Cole stormed off and left me stunned.

Suddenly my anger was fading; I hated to say this, but Cole was right. I had no right to expect Jax to change, after all, records can't be wiped, and I knew Jax was a ladies man. I was stupid to think that his past wouldn't come back to bite me.

Cole

I waited for Amber to leave before I rounded the corridor again and stormed up to Jax's door, slamming my fist on it once before just walking in.

Mai was on the edge of Jax's bed, and looked like her normal self; not a tear in sight. Jax was sitting in front of her in an armchair that had been pulled up to the side of the bed. He had that normal, smug look on his face.

I slammed the door behind me. "Mai. Jackson." I used his full name to piss him off. I turned to face Mai. "I see the tears are gone." Amber had hit the nail on the head when she called Mai a bitch. Personally, I thought Mai was the Queen of Evil.

Mai narrowed her beady eyes at me. "Cole, always a pleasure."

"Must be important, for you to have let yourself in." Jax arched an eyebrow at me, his voice coated with annoyance.

I had respect for Jax, but right now he was going down in my eyes. Yeah, I knew he was a player, but, for some stupid reason, I actually expected him to be different with Amber. Mai being here showed me he wasn't going to be.

Amber had to see what she was in for; maybe she would get out before he used her anymore.

"Yeah, just wanted to say Jax," as I walked over to him, glaring down at him, "that you better get your fucking act together, because I don't like my sister feeling threatened." I shot a filthy look at Mai "Especially by a slut like you."

Mai laughed sourly. "Really, standing up for your little sister? Who knew you actually had a heart Cole."

"Whatever this is," I pointed between them, "End it." I looked Jax in the eye and I saw the rage boiling from the way I'd spoken to him. Yeah, I was meant to always show him respect, but when it came to Amber, nothing got in my way from protecting her and I knew my brothers would be on my side. "Before you cross a line Jackson, remember who you are about to cheat on."

Jax was up quickly, kicking the armchair over in his hurry to get to me.

"I suggest you get the fuck out Cole, before I remind you who you are speaking to." He growled at me, barely being able to keep his fists away. I knew he was aching to just pound his anger into me for the way I'd spoken to him.

"Whatever you say, boss." I spat on the floor in front of him. He could throw his title around all he wanted; it meant nothing when it came to Amber. "Make sure the slut is out of the house within an hour," I threw over my shoulder before slamming the door after me.

He might run Satan's Sons, but he didn't run this house.

Amber

"Really mature Amber!" Jackson shouted at me when he walked into the room.

Getting up off the couch, I ran my eyes up and down Jax. Why was he so mad? From what I remember, if anyone had a right to be pissed, it was me, after all, he was the one up in his room doing God knows what with Mai.

"If you're got a problem, talk to me, don't go crying to your brother." The veins running up Jax's neck were bulging, and his face was slightly red. To put it simply, he was furious.

"Don't speak to me like that!" I shouted back. If he wanted a shouting match then fine; I could yell just as loud as him!

"I thought you got it!" Jax paced back and forth, not pulling his eyes from me. "But I was wrong. You're still are just as..."

"As what Jax?" I pushed him to finish his sentence. "Come on, finish what you were going to say." I had never felt so much anger towards him. This whole time I had been sitting down here, telling myself to trust him. Telling myself I had to back off. And this was how I got treated?

"What's the point?" Jax stopped pacing, his eyes squarely on me. "I can't do this."

Suddenly, this argument went from insane to deadly serious. "What?" my mouth dropped slightly. He couldn't be serious?

"You know what..." Jax was still angry; I could see that, but he couldn't mean what I thought he meant.

"You want to break up with me?" I spoke each word slowly, trying to explain it more to myself than to him. Surely this can't be happening. "After everything we have been through, after everything you put me through! All the chasing, and you finally saying you loved me, and now what? You changed your mind!?"

I went from shocked to pissed instantly. He couldn't do this to me!

"I thought I could have both..." Jax's locked his eyes with mine. "But you aren't worth the loss."

"Loss of what?" I hadn't done anything! I certainly hadn't lost him anything; nothing that I was aware of anyway.

"I can't lose this club." He said each word clearly, for some reason speaking to me like I didn't understand basic English.

"And I would never let you lose this club," I said, faking calm, when, on the inside, I was just a bubbling mess of nerves. I knew how important the club was to him; heck, I would do anything to help him. Why would he think I would ever take the club from him?

"I couldn't take that shit in front of Mai. I can't let you think you have control over me." Jax's voice was deadly. I can't believe the man I was willing to risk everything for was threatening me right now!

"I don't want control over you! I just want you! Bloody hell Jax, when are you going to see that I only care for you! I don't want to ruin your life, or take the club from you! I just want to make your life better. I want you to want to share your life with me."

Jax crossed his arms, and just kept looking at me coldly; like I was scum.

"Why would I want to share my life with someone who is so pathetic, she goes crying to their brothers instead of trusting me? I thought you understood that this relationship wouldn't be easy but what happened tonight, it proved to me you can't handle this."

"What are you talking about!?" I yelled at him and moved closer to him. "I haven't done anything!"

"Amber, we're over." Jax meant it. His face, his body language, everything proved it to me. He was done.

"No!" I shook my head. This couldn't be happening. "I said I loved you…" I gulped, feeling myself melting in front of him. "I love you Jax, you can't give up on us."

I went to go to him, but he just stepped away from me; keeping me at arm's length. "I want to make it clear Amber. I want nothing more to do with you," he said coldly.

It was happening. After everything, all the chasing, all the games. He was walking away from us.

"We're perfect for each other," I begged him, and I didn't bother to wipe the tears that were streaming down my cheeks.

"Just drop it Amber." Jax went to turn his back on me, but I quickly walked around him and blocked the doorway.

"No."

"Move."

I placed my arms across the doorway. Seriously, I was blocking the guy who just broke up with me from leaving? I must really be pathetic.

"Just tell me why? What changed?" I begged him. If I knew what'd changed, then maybe I could fix it. Maybe I could explain whatever was worrying him.

"Nothing changed, I just saw clearly for the first time." Jax crossed his arms. "You can't handle this life."

"I have been living this life as long as you have Jax," I snapped at him. "I don't see that as a reason to break up with me. To walk away from us."

"I can't have you crying to your brothers every time there is a problem. I thought you were mature enough to at least take it up with me."

"I didn't go crying to anyone!" I yelled in his face. The anger, shock and just pure hurt coursing through my body began to take control over my actions.

"He doesn't want you. For Heaven's sake, stop begging," Mai said, her voice floating to my ears from behind me.

I didn't have the strength to turn around and answer her, or even bother to punch her. Because right now, Jax was breaking my heart and I couldn't take my eyes off him.

He was what mattered; he was the only thing that mattered in my life.

"What? No comeback Amber?" Mai prompted from behind me.

I kept my eyes on Jax. "We can just work this out Jax, just give me a chance to explain," I begged him again but when his face didn't change, I knew it was pointless. I swallowed the fear inside me, and prepared myself for what was about to come. "If you end us right now, you end us for good." I had to make sure he understood what he was doing, because I couldn't take the games anymore.

If he was done, he was done.

"My, she is clingy," Mai said as she tapped her foot behind me. I was pleased when Jax threw her an annoyed look over my shoulder.

But when his eyes met mine once again, that little bit of pleasure disappeared.

"We're over Amber." Jax didn't say it calmly, or even with any compassion. His voice wasn't soft or caring, and it hurt.

"Ok." I moved from blocking his way, and turned around to see Mai standing at the bottom of the stairs, a smug expression on her face.

"Finally, you're done. Not that seeing you beg Jax wasn't amusing." Mai taunted, her smug expression getting on my nerves.

I didn't bother taking her on, even though I had a few nasty ones I could pull out. I didn't see the point.

I opened my front door, and closed it softly behind me. I didn't even slam it, or scream at Jax for hurting me this way.

I felt like a zombie as I walked down the porch stairs. Silent tears slid down my cheeks. I should never have let myself fall for Jax.

"Amber? What the fuck is wrong?"

I stopped and looked at Troy. I hadn't even seen him cleaning his bike.

"Can I take your bike?" I asked, my voice devoid of emotion but the concern on his face told me he wasn't going to just let me take it.

"What happened?" He placed a hand on each of my shoulders; he towered over me.

Jax had somehow managed to blame my brothers for us breaking up but really, what was wrong with having them concerned about me? At least I knew they would always be there; even when I didn't want them to be.

"Please let me take your bike?" I begged him.

"Are you ok?"

"I just need to get out of here."

Troy reached for his back pocket and pulled the keys out. "Ride safe ok?" he handed them to me, and I quickly made my way around him.

"Amber, promise me you will call me and tell me where you end up?"

I buckled my helmet up, and nodded my head at him. "I promise."

I kicked the huge beast to life, and took off. I just needed to get away from here. If Jax wanted nothing more to do with me, where did this leave me?

I accelerated harder as I thought that. I loved him, and that was what was burning the knife through my heart.

Troy

I slammed my front door, and wasn't half surprised to see Mai and Jax in the foyer.

"What the fuck did you do?" I yelled directly at Jax. There could only be one reason for Amber to be that upset.

Jax. He had done something.

"What a surprise. Another Shield coming to his sister's defense," Jax growled at me. What the heck had gotten into him?

"Excuse me?"

"Amber and I are over. She will get over it." Jax pulled out his beeping phone and announced, "I'm taking Mai back to her dad's, and then tomorrow I want you all at the table."

"Why did you break up with her?" I gave Mai a filthy look. If she had caused this I swear I would give that slut a work over. She needed a face job, and I would cross the line, hitting a chick, if she'd hurt Amber.

"Did you know Amber has a relationship with Mai's dad?" Jax crossed his arms. "He's Blake's uncle."

"I know." Why would that mean anything? Fuck, I knew everything Amber had done with them, nothing that was important now.

"You knew?"

"Get to the point Jackson," I threatened.

"Amber did deals with them behind your back a few months ago, did you know that?" Mai stepped in. "She made a hell of a lot of money for it too."

"Why does that matter?" I glared at her.

Mai went to answer, but Jax cut in.

"It doesn't. What matters is her relationship with you and your brothers," Jax stepped in, a deep glare in his eyes. "I can't deal with her going crying to you every time she has a problem with me. If Cole had spoken to me like he did today any other time, he would have had a bullet between his eyes. It is time you boys were reminded of your position."

"Position?" I growled.

"A bullet between my eyes?" Cole snapped from the top of the stairs. "You couldn't pull the trigger if you wanted to." Cole stomped down the stairs and pointed at Mai. "I told you to get that bitch out hours ago," he growled.

"Things changed." Mai smirked up at him. "Jax can't have a witness to your disrespect. Jax wouldn't want anyone else to know how much of a pushover he is now."

"Mai!" Jax growled at her.

"What Jax? It isn't my fault that you let your boys walk all over you now." She placed a hand on her hip. "Or should I say that you let your missus control you so much."

"What do you mean come crying to us? Fuck, do you not know Amber at all?" Cole snorted, not standing next to me. I had a feeling Cole was just waiting for the right words and then he was going to launch at Jax.

"Back off Cole, it is finished," Jax warned. "I broke it off."

"What? You really broke it off?" I hadn't actually taken him seriously before. Shit. I just gave her the keys to my bike. Fuck.

"I can't date someone who doesn't trust me," Jax snapped "Not that it is any of your business."

Cole chuckled evilly, and even I was arching an eyebrow at him.

"You think Amber didn't trust you? She didn't trust the whore. And Amber didn't come crying to me about it." Cole stepped up and was in Jax's face. "It seems more like you didn't trust her," he snapped.

Jax didn't push Cole away like I was expecting.

"And that deal you think Amber did behind your back. Wasn't what you thought neither. She had only met Blake's Uncle once, and it was at a Christmas party."

"Amber told us to back off, and we did," Cole smirked at him. "But now we have nothing to worry about. Amber won't have anything to do with you now."

"She didn't go to you thinking I was having an affair with Mai?" Jax asked as he took a step back from Cole. "Then why did you break down my door threatning me?"

What a surprise? Cole had something to do with this. His hot head always got us in trouble.

"Just brother love." Cole shrugged his shoulders "Plus, I hate Mai."

Mai made some nasty gagging noise.

"But Mai heard you and Amber talking. When Mai went out to call her dad, she heard Amber crying to you," Jax said, and then all our eyes turned to Mai.

She looked innocent, but we all knew her better than that.

"What?" She rolled her eyes. "So maybe I lied. Jax come on, she was costing you the club. When I heard how controlled you were, I had to come see it for myself."

"You lied?" Jax growled at her through gritted teeth.

"Why would you believe her over Amber anyway?" Cole snapped at him.

"Because of what you did tonight," Jax roared at Cole. "Because of the two of you!" Jax looked between Cole and Mai.

"Jax, I did you a favor tonight. Everyone knows a great leader doesn't have a missus," Mai defended herself. "Please! You saw how protective Cole was of her, and how little respect he had for you. All I did was come up with a reason after that for you to get rid of Amber and take back your position."

Cole was throwing curse words at Mai, but I wasn't interested in their spat. My eyes were on Jax, as he realized what he had done tonight.

"Where did she go?" Jax looked up, finally out of his thoughts. "You saw her. Where did she go?" he looked at me.

Cole and Mai shut up and waited for me to answer. Not that I really had one to give, although if I did, I don't think I would have told him. He had hurt her enough.

"I don't know, she took off on my bike."

"You let her take off on your bike!? Fuck, Troy!" Cole roared at me.

"I didn't know what had happened," I shot at Cole. "Maybe you should have told me about your little argument with Jax."

"How was I meant to know he was going to go off and dump her!" Cole snapped.

"SHUT UP!" Jax yelled at the two of us. "Amber is on a deadly machine. She barely knows how to ride and is fucked up because I broke up with her! Would you two save your argument for later!"

"I taught her how to ride," Cole barked through narrowed eyes, ready for another fight.

"Jax is right, we should go find her," I cut in, and searched my pockets for my phone. "I'll call Tyler and Adam. Cole, go get the car started."

"I'm coming," Jax spoke up and followed Cole out.

I could fight with him, but I didn't want to waste any more time. "Mai, make sure you are gone before we get back," I said as I pressed the dial button and left the front door open for her.

Putting my phone to my ear, I hoped Tyler and Adam were close to town, because I had a feeling Amber would be heading that way.

Chapter 45

Amber

I watched as people rushed past me, all wanting to be somewhere. I swallowed the feeling of loneliness as another happy couple walked past me. When I saw the long black limo pull up to the curb, I was quick to make my way to it.

The window went down, and I actually was pleased to see my dad's face.

"Amber," he reached for something beside him and then handed it out the window to me. I saw dad was torn about what he was doing for me. "Are you still sure you want to leave?" Dad looked at the busy airport behind me.

"You were right, there isn't anything keeping me here," I muttered, stuffing the passport, flight information and ticket in my pocket. "Anyway, this is what you wanted."

"I just want you to get a life you can be proud of Amber." Dad's voice was soft, and he gave me a kind smile. "Did you tell the boys about this?"

"No." I shook my head, knowing that they would try and stop me, but there was no point in my staying. Their lives would be easier with me out of the picture. They could stop having to look after me.

"Would you like me to?" Dad offered, and I shrugged my shoulders.

"If they ask you, then I guess yes. Just don't tell them before my flight has left." I pulled the key from my pocket and a note, and handed it to dad. "Make sure Troy gets this. It is the key to his bike; the note tells him where I've left it for him."

Troy treasured that bike, so I couldn't just leave it at the airport.

"I will." Dad smiled at me. "Call me when you land."

I nodded my head, and added, "I'd better go."

"Have a safe flight Amber."

"Bye dad," I said, and quickly walked away from the limo and into the airport. I wasn't good at goodbyes.

***

I sat in a plastic chair, waiting for my boarding call. I unlocked the phone in my hand once more, debating on whether to call Troy or not. I knew I'd said I would, but I just couldn't build up the courage to tell him I was leaving.

Biting the bullet, I finally just dialed his number. The boarding call was going to get over any minute and the more I thought about him finding out I had left from dad, the more I realized it just didn't sit right with me.

It only rang twice before he answered.

"Amber?"

"Troy."

"Where are you?" his voice was rushed and panicked.

"I'm fine," although the emptiness in my voice was a dead giveaway.

"We've been looking for you for hours! Where are you now? We are coming to pick you up."

When he said we, I knew my other brothers must be with him and that brought a slight smile to my face.

"Troy. I have to tell you something," I sighed. "I'm leaving."

"What do you mean leaving?" Troy's voice was firm, and I could hear the hushed voices in the background, demanding to know what was going on.

"I spoke to dad, and everything has been arranged." I felt the tears building up. "I'm sorry I'm telling you like this."

"Amber, where are you going?" I knew that tone; that tone said that he wasn't going to let me leave.

"Troy, look there is nothing you can do. I've made up my mind. Dad was right. I need a fresh start."

The boarding call went over the speaker. I had to hurry this up now.

"Was that a boarding call?" Troy's voice spiked with concern "Amber, whatever you are thinking about doing, don't."

"I'm sorry Troy. Can you tell the others that? I know now all you guys ever did was try to protect me."

"Amber, don't hang up. Look, about tonight there are a few things you need to know. Just don't get on that plane until you let Jax explain a few things."

What? Was Jax already regretting his words? I smiled bitterly to myself.

"Jax made himself very clear Troy. Look, I have to go." I looked at the people boarding the plane.

"Amber, don't leave. Don't let what happened tonight drive you from your family."

"This isn't about that," I said as I stepped into line in the boarding queue. "I can't keep being the girl I am Troy. My life is going nowhere."

"Jax loves you Amber..., I know we don't say it all the time, but we love you too. Don't just give up on us."

"I'm not giving up on you guys. You boys have done enough for me, and it's time I did something for you all."

"Don't board that plane!" Troy's words were firm.

"Tell Jax to not doubt himself, he made the right decision." It physically hurt me to say that. "He needs someone stronger than me and I'm sure he will find her." The tears began to fall.

"I'll call you soon Troy, I promise."

"Amber, please don't do this!" His voice was raw. He really didn't want me to leave. "Just let us talk and then if you still want to leave, you can get the next flight, or if you won't do that, just tell me where you are going?"

"I love you Troy," I said softly, "I'll call you when I land." I handed my ticket to the lady. "I've got to go."

I hung up my phone quickly, not letting Troy say another word because nothing he, or anyone for that matter, could say, would stop me from boarding this plane.

I swallowed the doubts in my stomach and boarded the plate. Time to start somewhere fresh, with no boyfriend or family to have my back. I was in this alone, and, for some reason, that truly terrified me.

Troy

I closed my phone after listening to the beeping for a few seconds. I couldn't stop her, as much as I attempted to. I was sure she had boarded that plane.

"Well, did you stop her?" Cole said, his eyes darting from the road to me, as he sped in and out of traffic.

"No. Turn around." I threw my phone in the center console.

"What do you mean no!" Jax leaned into the front, his expression torn with guilt. "Did she board the plane?"

"Yes." It killed me to say that one word, because it meant Amber was gone, and most likely was gone for good.

Cole eased off the gas a little and slowed back into normal traffic. We were only a block away from the airport, but we were too late.

"She's gone." Cole's words seemed to echo in the car.

"Did she say where?" Tyler asked from the back seat, his concern for her clear. "Did she sound ok?"

"No, she didn't." I turned around in my seat and looked Jax in the eye. This was all his fault. "She was a fucking wreck and now, thanks to you, we have no idea where she has gone."

Jax sat back in his seat. I could see that he was hurting, but he should be. He had driven my sister from our house, from our city!

Turning back around, I glared out the front window. "From now on Jackson, it is only business." My voice was hard. He had caused this, and, by doing so, he had lost my sister, and all my respect.

Chapter 46

One month later

Jax

I splashed a handful of cold water on my face; I was struggling to wake up. I hadn't been sleeping since Amber had left. Guilt and regret consumed me. I was finding it harder to get through a day without my thoughts drifting to her.

The 'should-haves' began to race through my mind again. I should have stopped her, I should have let her explain. I should have trusted her.

I grabbed my leather vest off the bed. I was craving some action; for anything to happen today that would take my mind off her for a few hours.

The smell of cigarettes was strong in the air when I walked out into the lounge area. Now that parole was over, I could move out of the Shield's and into the clubhouse. I couldn't have left quick enough, because the Shield's didn't want me there. They blamed me for losing Amber, and they had a right to.

It was my fault she was gone.

"They're doing that video chat thing with Amber." Adam yawned from the couch, "Thought I'd let you know."

Surprisingly, Adam hadn't changed much since what had happened. He still treated me the same, and, for some unknown reason, was actually pushing me to speak with Amber.

"Of course you did," I scoffed.

"Yeah, you should go in there," Adam nodded his head towards the table room.

I could hear the other guys in there making a fuss, but I wasn't interested, because hearing her voice just pulled at my heart strings, and brought emotions I didn't want to deal with to the surface.

"I'm going out," I muttered, storming through the room. Like I said, I needed action, something to take my mind off her. The last thing I wanted to do was hang around here and listen to Amber's voice.

Hearing her only reminded me that I would never have her.

Troy

"Cole, stop that!" I slapped his hand as he went to re-adjust the laptop camera again. "Or I will fucking break your hand off."

Cole glared at me and sat back in the chair beside me.

"Look, it is Amber!" Tyler pointed to the computer screen, and I quickly whipped around to see.

Sure enough, Amber was smiling at us through the computer screen. The first thing I noticed was that she had cut her hair.

"You got a haircut!" Cole exclaimed, noticing the same thing.

"Yeah, it was annoying me." Amber's voice echoed through the computer speakers.

"How's England?" I asked her. Since she'd left, I'd been worrying about her more than normal. I could only imagine the trouble she could get up to, all by herself over there.

"Yeah, it's awesome here," she grinned, looking happy. "The only downside is not having a threatening motorbike gang to back me up." Cheekiness flashed across her eyes. "How are you guys?"

"Troy's got a girlfriend," Cole gruffed, and I punched him in the arm as soon as he said it.

I didn't like anyone mentioning April, because I wasn't used to having a girlfriend, and it still stumped me slightly when I heard it out loud.

"You're kidding!" Amber exclaimed. "Who is it?"

"April Reyes," Tyler answered straight away, and he stepped back before I could slug him.

"April Reyes, the chick that works at the video shop?" Amber asked, curiosity in her voice.

"She hasn't worked there for years; it closed down!" I snapped, defending her; for some reason it just came naturally to defend her. Dating someone was new to me, and being lucky enough to have April, well... I wasn't used to it.

"Well, who knew Troy, that you had it in you." Amber smiled at me, and I hated it. "April is really nice, from what I remember."

"Enough about me," I snapped. "It's not interesting."

"It kind of is," Amber giggled at me. "Troy, I can't believe you actually have a girlfriend!"

"Get over it already! I didn't make this big of a deal when you started going out with Ja..." I regretted it as soon as I said it. My temper always got the best of me.

Amber went silent and so did the boys. Really, couldn't they bring something else up already? The silence seemed to last forever and, funnily enough, it was Amber who broke it.

"How is Jax?" Amber didn't have any emotion in her voice. "Is he still with Mai?"

"He was never with Mai," I answered, seeing as it was me who brought this up and the boys had suddenly become mutes.

"Didn't seem that way when I left," Amber muttered, and looked down into her lap.

"Maybe you should call him?" Adam said as he walked into the room, and positioned himself behind me, looking at Amber. "Work things out?"

Amber looked at Adam, and I wanted to smack him. The last thing I wanted was her back with that dipstick, but, on the other hand, if they worked it out, maybe she would come back...

Amber looked away from the computer screen for a few moments. Someone must have entered the room. She covered the microphone so we couldn't hear.

"Look guys, I have to go," Amber said quickly, "I'll um call you guys soon." She gave us a quick smile before disappearing on us and a 'disconnected' signal flash on the computer.

"What was that about?" I frowned.

"That was your fault," Cole huffed, getting up from the chair. Hating the fact his time with Amber was over. Out of all of us, he was missing her the most. He was grumpier than normal.

I glared at his back as he walked out of the room, his normal air of arrogance following him.

"She's up to something," Tyler muttered; he was as curious as I was.

"Yeah, I agree." I looked up at Tyler. "And I don't like it."

I didn't like not being able to keep a track of her; it didn't sit right with me. Amber always had a way of getting herself into trouble; in fact, she had it down to a fine art.

"Nothing we can do from here," Tyler said, annoyed, before leaving the room. He was right. There wasn't anything we could do. I just hoped Amber wasn't getting into anything. Anyway, how much trouble could she get into? It was England after all. It wasn't like she knew anyone there.

Amber

I still don't know how they knew. But they did. As soon as my plane landed, they were at the airport, waiting for me. TNS. Well, not any member of TNS. TNS stood for his name. Tae Neal Smith. An English gangster. He started his empire in the UK and then branched out.

I had met him once at home. He was in the country organizing a new head role. At the time, we got on. Because I'd met him directly, TNS trusted me. At the time, I wasn't scared of him but that changed when I found him waiting for me at the airport.

I closed my laptop abruptly as my Aunt opened my bedroom door. "Tae is here." She smiled. "He said it's important."

My aunt wasn't batty. If I had to describe her in one word, I would say... caring. She cared about me. I didn't understand why; we had only known each other for a month but what really got me, was that she also supported me.

England wasn't huge so she knew Tae and his reputation. She was startled at first when he approached her at the airport, while he was waiting for me. He knew everything there was to know about her; he'd done his research, but who he'd also researched, was me.

"Thanks." I got up and picked up my duffle bag. "I won't be back tonight."

Tae shouldn't be here. If he was, it meant something was wrong and he was counting on me to fix it.

I walked down the hallway and bang, there he was, waiting in the foyer.

"Amber," he greeted me, his normal, non-caring smile on his face. "We have a problem."

"And here I was thinking you just came to say hi." I moved the duffle bag on my shoulder.

"We can talk in the car," he said as he opened the front door.

"Wait a sec; you are coming with me tonight?" I looked at him surprised. Tae didn't get his hands dirty; he left that to the rest of us. Well, that wasn't completely true... he left it to me.

Well, he had for over a month; as soon as I'd got here. He'd made me a proposal and I didn't hate the idea of working for him. He wanted to train me. He wanted me to become the invisible hand back home that controlled his interests.

I still didn't want to head home, and I was going to put it off as long as I could.

I didn't want to see....Jax.

I cringed as I walked down the porch steps. How could just remembering his name hurt?

But it did.

Time. That was what I needed; time to pass, so my wounds would heal. That... and distance. Two things. That's all I needed. I had the distance but the time, well, that was harder. Every day I woke up and hoped that hole in my heart would be healed.

But so far, I still woke up with a hole.

But I think what was worse was the piece of heart that was left... well, it was empty. Empty of emotion. I didn't feel anything. I was literally bulletproof now. Heartless, as Tae had pointed out the other night.

I still didn't know the real reason we broke up. Something to do with my brothers. I sighed as I got in the car. It really didn't matter anymore; we were in different countries. And yet, here I was; even though I was off to threaten and kill someone, he was on my mind.

How the hell was that fair! I was throwing myself into Tae's lifestyle, breathing his ruthlessness. Trying to follow his lead. Yet, I was still hung up on Jax!

Who wasn't even in the country!

I was stupid.

But also when it came down it, I had been blinded.

I loved him. And he simply didn't love me back.

Maybe that was what really hurt me? I'd told him over and over how we were perfect for each other. Yet, when it came down to it, he used my brothers as an excuse.

My brothers. Guilt washed over me. If they knew how deep I was getting in with the TNS, even though I would always be invisible, just pulling strings and taking out hits. Still, if they knew - they would be seeing red.

Then wanting to kill me.

You would think a new country would mean a new me.

It was clear - my past was going to influence my future. I knew that as soon as I saw Tae at the airport. Just because dad wanted to give me a fresh start didn't mean I was going to get one.

Tae had made good points. He knew I wasn't going to be capable of working a nine to five job. Hell, he knew when it came down to it; my skill with a gun was just that - skill. Something to be trained and focused on. Improved on.

Which is what we had been doing - at the shooting range, at his place, on his land, and with his enemies. With each one I took out, I got better. Each one I killed took something from me though. I thought one day I would wake up regretting the lives I had taken.

And I found out that day came, and went just as quickly. Guilt wouldn't stop me.

Nothing could stop me. It was like I didn't have a heart anymore, to care. Jax had taken it, stomped on it and handed it back and I had declined the offer to take what was left of my heart.

The ache I felt for him, waking up every morning still with it – well, that was the only reason I even considered I still had a piece of my heart.

Because when it came to business, I was getting as ruthless as the man grooming me.

"Amber, the address has changed - they are at the shipping yard. Can you calculate for that?"

I unzipped my duffle bag and nodded my head. "I'll do the math and the readings when I get there." I looked down at my sniper. It was the first thing Tae had given me. State of the art. Top of the line. And I knew how to use it.

Which was beginning to strike fear in the underbelly of London.

Jax

I lit up another cigarette. Another party, another reason to get drunk. Yet, here I was at the bar, women everywhere, and I could only think of one.

One with perfect curves that I loved to explore. One with those sharp eyes that stared straight through all the bullshit. One that was always in control. Those lips of hers, how sweet they were, and how she was always up for anything I wanted to do.

I exhaled on my cigarette. I still didn't know if she was a devil or an angel. I couldn't get her out of my mind. Couldn't turn her off. It was killing me knowing she was in another country, living a new life. One far, far away from me.

Katie put a hand on my shoulder and I shrugged it off. I wasn't in the mood. I hadn't even so much as glanced at another woman since Amber had left. There was only one woman I wanted in my bed, and she was in fucking England.

"Can we talk?"

I turned to see Troy. What did he want? It was fair to say when he said things were going to be business and business alone, he wasn't lying. Our years of friendship were gone.

He blamed me for losing his sister.

And it was my fault, so I didn't hold it against him.

I nodded my head and got up, following him to the boardroom. I closed the door after us, blocking out some of the noise of the party.

"What's up?" I said, butting my cigarette out in the ashtray.

"You." His eyes hardened. "What you are doing hasn't gone unnoticed."

"I don't know what you mean."

"You haven't touched another woman. You haven't so much as even argued at one of my points and now, now you are acting like I'm in control."

"What's wrong with that? Didn't you want to be in control?"

"I'm not the king!" He basically yelled. "Your job is to always put the club first! It's in your blood!"

Yeah, I knew I was letting things slide. Yeah, I knew I wasn't living up to my responsibilities, but Troy had everything under control. Wasn't like I had completely turned a blind eye to the club.

"Everything is going fine." I shrugged. "I don't see the problem."

"You need to step back up." Troy was saying that like I wasn't going to. I would one day. Maybe on the same day I had Amber back because, right now, I wasn't functioning without her.

How could I lead a group of men, all expecting me to have their back, when the only woman I loved… well I broke her heart and made her move to another country.

"I didn't want to do this, but I don't see another option." Troy got his phone out and I didn't know what he was doing until my phone buzzed in my pocket.

Pulling it out; it was a message from Troy. My eyes widened when I saw that it was a contact. Amber.

"Call her. Get it out of your system." Troy said. "I know she can take it now. She's stronger and I spoke to my Aunt today. Amber's really settling in there. Rarely is home and is excelling at her studies so I know a phone call from you she can take."

"She excelling in her studies?" I looked at him like he couldn't be serious. Amber never did school. She couldn't care less if she passed or failed.

"Maths apparently."

"She hated maths."

"Well now she is an A grade student in it. She's moved on Jax. Time for you to do the same." He walked past me. "I know you calling is just so you can move on because I'm telling you now, Amber doesn't care anymore. Hell, she even asked how you were the other day, like you were just one of the many."

Was he trying to hurt me? I turned to read his expression. Nope. He was just stating facts. Amber had asked how I was. And she really had acted like I was one of the many. I clenched my phone tighter.

Troy left and I followed him out to the party but I was even less interested in the party now. I took the stairs two at a time. I was going to call. I was going to hear her voice. Not overhear one of those stupid video calls.

Although I wouldn't mind face-timing her to see her face.

I unlocked my door and closed it. The party was a dull roar now.

I unlocked my phone and dialed her number.

I hoped she answered out-of-country calls.

I waited for it to connect and then, when it started to ring, my heart basically slowed. What if she didn't want to hear from me? What if the last thing on earth she wanted was to hear my voice? That grabbed my heart; after how I'd treated her, I shouldn't even be calling. I knew I had made a mistake and went to hang up.

"Hey Tae, look, everything went smoothly but I'm telling you now this is going to backfire on us," Amber spoke into the phone, like she had been too busy to check the caller ID. Didn't even realize it was an out-of-country call. "Tae?"

Who was Tae? What was going to backfire on them? My eyes narrowed. She was up to something. All this time I had thought she had moved on from this life, and suddenly I was getting the feeling she had just moved to another country and got herself involved in something else.

Something I couldn't protect her from.

"Tae, I don't have time for games! It's late! You know very well I don't do mornings. And that advance math class is at eight."

I frowned. Do I say something? So, she really did have a thing for maths.

I cleared my throat. Yep, I was going to do it. I was going to talk to her. "It's not Tae."

Whoever that was.

If I had been with her now, I could bet she was wearing that cute frown on her face.

"Wait a sec…" Amber said into the phone, and I heard muffled noises. "Who is this?"

She didn't even recognize my voice. That hurt. "Um, it's Jax."

Silence. It was deafening.

Was she just going to hang up and block my number? Hell, it wouldn't surprise me after how I'd treated her. I had piled onto her about trust, how I wanted her to trust me, and then me not trusting her in the end.

"How are you?" Her voice was steady; no emotion. Her normal wave of happiness when she spoke to me wasn't there.

I didn't answer because I don't think she would really want to hear the answer.

I was lost without her.

How was I? I was a mess. A failing, epic mess.

"Jax, are you ok?" Her voice was still steady; no emotion.

"No." I blurted out. I was nowhere near ok. I couldn't be described as ok. I was fucking depressed. The only woman I wanted, the only woman that would make me feel better was in fucking England.

"Talk to me, what's wrong?" Amber said, as if putting what I did aside and still having an interest in why my life was going to shit. "Are you having problems with the club?"

For once in my life, I didn't give a fuck about the club. Maybe that's what was wrong with me. When Amber had left, I realized the club didn't even come close to her. I had said I couldn't have her cost me the club but, in the end, she had.

"I don't give a fuck about the club." I blew, and sat down.

"Come on Jax, we both know that isn't true." Her voice was kind, soft, like velvet; so welcoming. "You love the club."

Was it possible that Troy was right? Amber had got her life together. Right now she was proving that to me. She had moved on. She had the ability to have a conversation with me, when I flat out broke her heart and then said every hurtful thing possible, but she was putting that to the side.

The old Amber wouldn't be speaking to me right now.

"I don't anymore," I said, and that was putting what I was feeling mildly.

I had let my pride get in the way of us. I had let the club get in the way us. I didn't realize it at the time, but she was my purpose, and now I was lost without her.

"What has you saying that?" Her voice was gentle. Like she wanted to comfort me.

"You."

"Jax, you ended us," she said bluntly.

"I was wrong, Amber. I was so fucking wrong. Please just come back home. Please! I'll do anything. Just come back."

She went silent.

I took a shaky breath in. "I should have trusted you. I'm sorry. You don't know how sorry I am. If I'd listened to you and not Mai, you wouldn't have left."

I heard her sigh. "Come on Jax, you are better than this."

"What do you mean?" It was all the truth. I wasn't better than anything and I wasn't above begging for her to come back. "Please come back."

God, I needed her back. I needed to see her. I needed to touch her. I needed to see that smile of hers.

"The Jax I knew wouldn't be letting an old relationship get in the way of his club. The Jax I knew would be over this and onto something else. You should be planning your next move, increasing members, banding out your empire," she blew out; I was hooked on every word she said, loving the sound of her voice. "The Jax I knew wouldn't be calling me."

"The Jax you knew was a dickhead," I said bluntly. It was the truth.

She laughed. "Yeah he was, but he was always a good leader."

I smiled, hearing her laugh. I had made her laugh. I never thought that was going to happen again. Hearing her laugh eased all my nerves. Made my permanent frown disappear.

"Come home Amber, please?" I begged. "I need to see you." Need didn't even come close to how I felt. I couldn't function without her. I couldn't keep going without her. "Please, Amber."

She sighed again. "Jax, you don't need me. Do I need to remind you, you broke up with me?"

"I was a dick!" I admitted.

"No Jax, you said facts. You love the club. You can't have anyone get in the way of the club. And now you don't have anyone in the way. The only one stopping you, is you."

She was speaking the truth, but what she was leaving out was that I did have one person stopping me. Her. She was missing. I knew now that she would never cost me the club. She was just going to support me, as she'd said. She only wanted to make my life better and somehow, I'd screwed that up.·

I'd pushed the only woman capable of leading beside me, away - to another country!

"Amber, I can't..." How do I say this?

"You can," she said firmly. "You can lead. You can make the club bigger, better. You can do it."

She had faith in me, pity I didn't have the same faith in me.

"I need to see you," I said. My need to see her was killing me.

"Ok, then facetime me."

Was she serious? She was seriously going to let me see her? After everything I'd done?

"You serious?" I said, not believing her.

"Yes."

"Alright, I'll be one second." I didn't want to hang up on her just in case she didn't answer my call when I called again. Was she just asking me to facetime her so she could get off the phone to me?

"Ok," she said, not sounding like she was blowing me off.

I hung up and facetimed her. My heartrate increased when I read the 'connecting' on the phone.

She actually answered.

Then there was a black screen.

"Give me a sec," she said, and then the lights came on, and my screen lit up. She was frowning, and squinting from the light. "Ok, that's bright," she said, and yawned then looked into the camera, a frown on her face again. "You look tired Jax."

I had given up on sleep. I couldn't sleep. Not without her.

"You look great." I said, matter of factly. She looked fucking perfect. Her black hair fell forward, and I frowned. "You cut your hair."

"Yeah, it was getting too long. And in the way." She moved on the bed, and I noticed a tattoo on her collarbone.

342

"New ink?"

She frowned and then realized I had seen her tattoo on her collarbone. "Oh yeah." She smiled. "Got it when I got here. Thought it was about time I made a mark on my body, and not someone else."

"What is it?" I looked closer, trying to work it out; looked like writing.

"It says exhale the past," she answered me and shrugged. "Sort of was fitting."

Was I the past she was exhaling? The small smile on my face that appeared when I saw her disappeared. She really had moved on.

"So, what have you been doing?" I asked, wanting to have a normal conversation with her. How many times had I wondered what she was doing? How many times had I just wanted to call her, just to know was she ok?

She smiled, and it was a full blown smile. "I'd tell you, but you wouldn't believe me."

I arched my eyebrows. "Your brothers have reason to be worried about you, don't they?" She already had me worrying. But I was starting to think maybe there was more to it now. What was she up to?

"I'll have you know, I can look after myself." She said smugly. "And..." She got up and the camera followed her as she walked through her bedroom and then her face disappeared and I was looking at math notes, "I've just been studying."

"Advance maths, hey?" I said, taking in the figures. "You hate maths." It was a statement, not a question or a maybe; it was a fact. Amber was allergic to homework and anything to do with school.

"That was when I didn't think it was important," she said, and the camera was back on her. "So want to explain the whole club thing?" She arched an eyebrow at me, knowing me too well.

"Don't want to talk about the club." I wanted to talk about her. I wanted answers to all my questions. One that was bugging me from when she picked up the phone. "Who is Tae?"

Her expression dropped and she looked up in shock. "Um well... um." She nervously frowned. "Not important."

"Nah, don't give me that line sweetheart. Who is he?" Was he her boyfriend? Had she not just moved on with her life, but also her love life?

She sighed. "He is someone that is very important in my new life."

I knew immediately she was down-playing it. She had moved on. Not just in life, but in her love life as well. She had someone who was now very important in her new life.

Like her tattoo said, exhale the past. Well, I was that past.

"I'm happy for you." And I was; she deserved to be happy. She deserved this new life. Hell, she deserved a better life than I could ever give her. And now she was getting it.

"I'm not dating him." That cute frown of hers appeared on her face again and she looked down. She was nervous. "After what happened with you, I'm never letting anyone get close to me again," she muttered; I barely heard her.

I sighed. "Just because I screwed up doesn't mean you should wipe men out completely. I was a dick, Amber. Not all men are like that." I didn't want to say it, but she had just said Tae was an important part of her new life. "Maybe this Tae could be the right guy."

One that wouldn't take her for granted. One that would see how important she was before he lost her because that was what happened to me; I didn't know how important she was in my life until I'd lost her.

"He's not." She scoffed. "I'm never giving someone that power over me again. Hell, I still haven't got myself back together after you!"

"Yeah you have sweetheart. You are more than fine without me." I smiled dimly, only stating a fact. She had moved on. She had picked up the life I had trashed by being in it and she had somehow, well, turned her life around.

"No, I'm not. I'm nowhere near fine," she said, like I should've known that, and that 'everything is fine' expression dropped and I saw the hollowness in her eyes. "You nearly killed me Jax."

The guilt I felt was crushing me. The weight of it. The hollowness in her eyes. That was my fault.

"I'm so sorry sweetheart. I really am," I said. She would never know how truly sorry I was, and I was sure she was never going to let me make it up to her. "Just because I treated you like shit, doesn't mean another man will."

"I've learned my lesson when it comes to men. Blake hurt me physically and you, well..." her words dried up. We both knew what I had done

I watched pain split across her face for a second; then it was gone.

"Like I said, you will find a guy that will realize how important you are." I knew it would happen. She was stunning, beautiful and perfect, and I wasn't just talking about her body. Her attitude, her unconditional love for her family, and her faith in the people she loved; all that made her the perfect woman.

And I was an idiot for letting her go. Hell, I'd pushed her away.

She pursed her lips and nodded her head. "Maybe one day I will risk it again, but not now, and not for Tae."

"Why, is he not as good looking as me?" I had to cut the tension somehow and she rolled her eyes, a small smile on her face.

"You know, no one is as good looking as you, but that's not the reason. Tae actually is pretty fit."

"Fit, hey? You sound British."

She laughed. "No, I mean physically, not as in attractive. He pushes me to my limits."

I arched my eyebrows at that. What did she mean her limits? Was she talking about in bed?

"Not like that!" She picked up on my expression. She knew what I was thinking. "He is, well..." She sighed. "You actually know him."

"I don't know anyone called Tae."

"You do."

"No I don't. I don't know anyone in England, well apart from you."

"His name is Tae Neal Smith," she said, like I should know what that means.

I just frowned. "No idea who you are talking about sweetheart."

She rolled her eyes. "Of course you wouldn't know him personally, he keeps a low profile. Well, not here, but back home. I think he has only visited twice, and I met him once."

I frowned still. "So you knew this Tae guy from here?"

"Tae Neal Smith, Jax!" she repeated. "I helped you sell guns to them! Well, his empire at home that is. His one in England is larger."

"You helped with TNS." I said, not making a connection, but recalling how mature she had been when she'd handled that deal, and how they'd trusted her. Then it hit me slowly. Tae Neal Smith - TNS. "YOU'RE WORKING FOR TNS!"

"God, wipe the shock off your face will you!"

"Amber, they are dangerous. How the fuck did you get involved with them?"

She shrugged. "He was waiting for me at the airport."

That pissed me off instantly. "He was waiting for you?" He must have been keeping tabs on her.

"As soon as I got off the plane, he was there, standing with my aunt."

"Did he have a track on you?" I wanted him dead. Keeping track on her. He must have been watching her, to just be waiting for her at the airport.

"He was monitoring me, yes. As soon as I ended it with the HellBound, he was interested in recruiting me. Then he found out I was working for you a lot so he monitored me again. Then he said my passport flashed across his screen when I boarded a plane to England."

I was furious. "So, did he recruit you?" I had not only pushed her away, but I had pushed her into the arms of a man nearly as deadly as me.

She really attracted bad men in her life.

"Yeah, he did."

"AMBER!"

"Calm down Jax. I'm well looked after." She gave me a pointed look. "Tae doesn't put me in harm's way. And I don't do anything I can't sleep with."

"So, have you been doing those hits? They were linked to TNS in the paper!" I was furious. She was meant to be creating a new life! One that didn't involve getting a criminal record!

"You've been reading the headlines? The London news headlines?" She said alarmed, like it wasn't possible.

I was a subscriber to the London times because, well, it was a connection to her. "Yes or no Amber?"

"Yes," she said simply.

"YOU'VE BEEN KILLING PEOPLE!" I was up and she was fucking lucky she was in another country. "WITH A SNIPER!"

"I've been trained, yes."

"Don't sound so cold!" I hated hearing coldness in her voice. Like she was disconnected from the world. Like she was disconnected from her heart.

"What did you expect, Jax? Like I said, you nearly killed me." She wiped an angry tear away. "I have to go."

"No you don't. Don't you dare hang up. Do your brothers know what you've been up to?"

She scoffed. "I think you would know if they knew." She shook her head. "You should get some sleep."

"I'm not tired," I said through gritted teeth. I was more concerned about her, more concerned than I was a minute ago. At least then I thought she had moved on in a good direction.

"You look tired."

"I can't sleep without you. So, unless you are coming back, I won't be sleeping," I snapped. "What does he have you doing? Killing people? What else?"

I needed details because that man kept in the shadows. Lived on the dirty money and his empire but no-one knew his face.

Well, not here anyway.

Her eyes narrowed. "He treats me like I'm an equal. He doesn't see me as a weakness. Like you do. Like my brothers do. He looks at me as a strength."

Well, she had me there. I always thought she was my weakness. And it was true; she still was my weakness.

"I'm sorry." I didn't know what else to say. It was my fault she was trusting Tae, because he was treating her as an equal when all I had done was look at her as my one weakness.

"Don't worry about it." She looked away from the camera. She frowned again. "It's not your fault. What I'm doing… it's not on you. It's all me."

"I made you leave Amber. What is happening is all on me." If she got herself killed, I wouldn't be able to live with myself. "Can you stop it? Just cut him out of your life?"

She smiled. "No." And then added. "I rely on him now, as much as he relies on me."

"What does he give you?"

"Money."

"Don't you have your dad for that?"

"He cut me off."

"What!"

She sighed. "As soon as he found out I wasn't going to school, he cut me off. I'm on Tae's payroll. It's my only source of income."

"I have money. You can have it." My money could be touched now. She could have all of it, if it meant she would leave him and his dirty business and all this shit with TNS behind.

Her lips twitched. "Thanks, but I'm not letting my ex-boyfriend bail me out. I can look after myself."

348

Ex-boyfriend. That hit me hard in the chest, right in the heart; the heart that was beating for her.

"Just take the money Amber."

"No."

I sighed; she was going to be stubborn. "What can I do to get you to change your mind?"

"Nothing. It's actually weird you called tonight." She frowned for a second. "Because Tae is forcing me to take my new role."

"What role is this?"

"His invisible hand. Just handling the cash, taking out hits. You know, keep his empire running but from a distance, not have anyone know I report directly to him."

"Why can't he just do that? He is in England. I'm sure he is capable."

"It's not here, it's back home," she said slowly, looking torn about it.

"Here?" She was coming back?

"Well, I'm not sure if I will be located back home, but I'll be in the country somewhere." She smiled dimly. "Wherever he decides I'm needed the most."

I hated someone else having control over her. She was mine.

"Make him locate you here." I basically demanded it of her. "Make him choose here."

If she was back in the country, back here, I had a chance to get her back. I had a chance to get my girlfriend back. I'd never had a girlfriend before; she was and is the only one I will ever have.

"I'm not really in a position to ask a favor."

"I'll make a call."

"NO!"

"I want you back."

Her eyes widened. "Jax, even if he does locate me back home, that doesn't mean I'm coming back to you."

That hurt, but if she was back home, I could use all my charm to get her back. There was a slim chance she still felt something for me, and I would take full advance of that when she got back.

"I'll make a call." I said, more set on my plan. "I'll make sure you are located here."

She looked at me startled. "Jax, NO!"

"I want you back Amber. I don't care what I have to do to get you back." Anyone that got in the way had a death wish.

"Well, I don't want you." Her eyes were hard. "I told you. I told you that if you broke up with me, that was it. I was done. Well, you broke up with me Jax, and that ended us. So you aren't getting me back."

She was cold, harsh and stated facts. Like I should've known them.

"Amber I fucked up…"

"I don't want to hear it!" She cut me off. "I'm tired and I have advance maths in a few hours. I need to sleep."

She was going to hang up on me. Wait a minute. "You said your dad cut you off because you aren't studying? But you are doing advance maths?"

"I'm doing maths for my sniper abilities. Improving maths is important. To get the right headshot. I'm tutored by one of Tae's men."

She was getting into something deep and the more she got into it, the less chance I had of getting her out of it. I might have pull, but even I couldn't take down TNS.

"I'll make a call," I repeated.

"I don't want to come home."

"I want you home."

"Yeah, well we all don't get what we want," she snapped.

"You're right, because in this case, you aren't getting what you want. I want you home. You are coming home." I had a way of getting her home now and I was going to use it.

"If I come back, that doesn't mean that you and I will ever be anything. I'm not coming back for you. Even if you force me back.

I won't… no… I can't be with you." She looked down at her lap. "I can never trust you again Jax."

I had broken her trust, but I was going to get it back. "I still love you Amber."

Her head sprung up hearing that, and she looked at me with wide eyes. Like I couldn't have possibly said that. I watched her expression; she was thinking she hadn't heard me correctly.

"I love you Amber." I repeated. "I know I hurt you. I know I pushed you away but I fucked up and I will do everything possible…"

"You can't get me back Jax," she said, cutting me off. "But," she sighed. "I will always love you too." My hopes went up and then she looked at me with tears in her eyes. "But I can never experience the pain of losing you again. What you did to me. What you are capable of doing to me. Well, it's not fair." She wiped away a tear that fell. "You've left me a hollow mess and I won't ever give you the power to hurt me again."

I knew then that she was never going to trust me again. I had really hurt her.

I nodded my head. "Doesn't mean I won't do everything possible to try and get you back." Hearing what she'd said didn't change my plans. Hearing she loved me, but would never be with me again… well, it didn't deter me.

"You're wasting your time. You should move on. Let me go."

Wasn't that the whole point of Troy giving me her number? For me to let her go. To move on. To focus back on the club. Well, that wasn't going to happen.

"No."

She rolled her eyes. "You know I'm safe now. You know I'm looking after myself. Now you need to stop moping around, pick yourself up and start breathing and living that club you love."

"Fuck the club."

"Jax! If your dad heard that, he would break out of prison to kill you!"

"I don't care anymore. Don't you get that? I care about you!"

She looked at me in disbelief. "I was always the one telling you we were perfect for each other and you were always the one pushing me away." Her voice was steady; serious. "Now I'm telling you Jax, you were right. We aren't perfect for each other, and every reason you pushed me away, well, you were right."

"I was a dick."

"No, you were thinking with your head and not your heart." I watched her face drop. "Something I was never capable of doing when it came to you." She straightened her shoulders up, sitting up. "But that's different now."

She was saying she no longer thought of me with her heart, but I knew her. If she loved me, even a tiny bit, I had a chance.

"Expect to be on a flight back within days."

She tilted her head. "You really think Tae will locate me back home? All because you make a phone call?"

"Not just a phone call, a business deal, and the TNS doesn't turn down business sweetheart." I had been ignoring my responsibilities at the club. I hadn't arranged new guns deals. I knew we had a huge shipment coming in next week, and we still didn't have a buyer.

I may have been taking a back seat in the club, but I still listened to Troy's concerns. His main worry at the moment was being left with all these guns.

But I'd just got us a buyer.

TNS will jump at this chance to re-stock their guns. They were secretive; didn't deal directly with anyone, but I was going to make sure they dealt with us. Again, they didn't trust me; but, if Amber was in charge, she would be making the decision, who was to be trusted and who not.

She yawned and I saw how tired she looked.

"I'll let you sleep," I said.

"I should be saying that to you. You look exhausted." She'd pointed out the obvious.

How could I tell her I couldn't sleep until she was back? I couldn't sleep worrying about her. Worrying if she was ok.

Worrying that she was moving on. Feeling physically sick, thinking of her making a life without me.

"I'll be seeing you soon." My finger hovered over the hang up button. Still not bringing myself to be able to end the call. "I love you Amber." I found myself needing to say it again. Reminding her I did love her.

"Doesn't change a thing Jax. Even if you somehow pull it off and get me back home, I won't ever be with you, because I can never trust you again."

"But you still love me right?" I asked. She said she loved me and always would, but the way she had said it was like how one speaks about the dead. Like the love would always be there but it was dead.

"I'm not capable of love anymore Jax. You didn't just break my heart, you killed it and now, well I'm, as Tae says, a ruthless yet effective leader." She shrugged. "He said in order for one to succeed, sometimes you can't have a heart. You taught me that too."

Was she saying I was heartless? "I fucked up and I'll prove to you, somehow Amber that I do have a heart and you aren't a weakness. I'll fix your heart that I broke."

"That isn't possible."

"I did the damage. I can fix it."

She smiled dimly. "I wish it was that simple." She looked into the camera. "I need to go, Tae is expecting me in a few hours now."

"I'll see you when I'm holding you[SVD3]."

She rolled her eyes. "You aren't going to give up are you?"

"No." And this time a full smile spread across my lips. "I can't wait to see you and I won't believe you are back until I wrap my arms around you."

She nodded her head. "Night Jax." Looks like she was going to be the one to end the call. She paused, "Try and get some sleep, would you?"

She said that like she knew how little sleep I was getting. I guess it did show on my face. "I can now, knowing you are coming home."

"Well, you won't believe it until you are holding me, right?"

I nodded my head. I wouldn't believe she was back until I could wrap my arms around her.

She yawned and laid down. "Well, knowing you, you will get your way."

"I will. Night, Amber." I was really looking forward to the day I could wrap my arms around her again, when she was back. I was going to make sure it was by the end of next week, because I couldn't last any longer and now it was in my control; I wasn't going to stop until she was back.

Hell, I'd give them the guns if it meant she was back for the deal.

"Night, Jax." She hung up, her face disappearing, and I was looking at my wallpaper, which just happened to be a picture of her and me.

I was getting her back, but in order for my plan to work, I needed sleep because I was going to have to be switched on. I needed to take back control of my club.

As Troy had said, I needed to stand up again.

Well, I was going to. All this time I had been blaming the club for costing me Amber, and now I was going to rely on it for me to get her back.

***

"I don't know how I feel about this," Tyler grumbled. "We don't have any history with them. What is stopping them from turning these guns on us?"

"They don't have a problem with us, and a buyer is a buyer." I said. I had got in contact with them- TNS, offered them a deal of a lifetime. Our shipment was usually split into smaller portions. And sold off.

We never sold the whole thing to one buyer.

We were giving them enough weapons to start a small war.

"Still don't know how you pulled it off," Troy said, his eyes on me. He moved in his seat, leaning forward. "How are we going to pull this deal off without Amber?"

She had been our contact, but now she was in charge of who and who wasn't trusted so I knew she would trust us to make the deal. She had to approve it and, as soon as they realized how serious I was, they said they would be in contact.

I had lined it up to not be a one-off, but a regular transaction. I was also trafficking them our drugs. I was making sure they had a strong business connection with us so it only made sense - if they were going to have someone pulling strings, well they would set them up here.

Which meant Amber. Here.

"Just made sense and the opportunity presented itself," I said simply, ignoring the grunts of disbelief.

Troy thought his plan had worked because, after my phone call with Amber, I was focused on the club. I was focused on this deal. I had pulled every string possible to get in contact with them.

Then I had to throw my name around to even get a phone call.

But it had worked. I got the deal set up and it was for Friday so it only made sense that they would make sure their hand was in the country, supervising. As Amber said, she would be the invisible hand.

I hadn't told her brothers what she was up to because then they would know what I was doing, and this time I wasn't letting them get in the way of Amber and I.

I was getting her back.

And I wasn't going to stop until I had her.

"Well, we will split the money come Friday," Troy said, and closed the meeting.

Everyone got up and started to leave, but, by the look on Troy's face, he wanted to speak to me.

So I waited until everyone left; wasn't even surprised when he spoke as soon as the last member exited.

"What did Amber say to you?" he asked. Trying to find an explanation for me stepping back into my role.

"She just reminded me of a few things."

"Amber got you to man up again. I told you she has changed." Troy stood up. "Now don't bring her back down."

He had thought that one phone call with Amber was all I needed. I needed Amber in my life, for the rest of my life and I wasn't letting him or anyone stop me from getting her.

I never thought I would have a weakness, but I didn't see Amber as a weakness anymore. She had proved to me she could handle herself - multiple times. I was just too blind to realize it.

"Yeah, I won't be hurting her again," I said, getting up and following Troy out. I frowned for a second. "Have you heard from her?"

Usually, they always talked on a Monday, but it was Wednesday and I hadn't had Adam annoying me with new facts about her, or heard them mention her.

"Dad's visiting her," Troy said over his shoulder. "So she's busy."

Would that stop her from coming? I started to panic. "Why would he be wanting to see her?" He wouldn't stop her from coming home, would he? If he gave her money, she wouldn't be relying on Tae for cash and could do what she wanted.

"It's a stop-over, from what she said. Actually," he turned back to look at me, "She didn't even mention speaking to you."

I shrugged my shoulders. I was thankful she hadn't because they would have had me backing out of my plan.

"She's pissed about seeing dad though," Tyler picked up on our conversation at the bar. "She told me last night that he keeps dragging her to dinner parties."

"Surprised she is even putting up with him after he cut her off," Cole said as he threw a shot down.

So they knew she had been cut off. "So how is she living if she doesn't have his money?" I asked them. How did they explain her finances because she told me she relied on Tae and she wasn't lying when she told me. I saw it in her face; she was telling the truth.

"Trust fund. Dad gave it to her," Cole grunted.

"Before he cut her off," Tyler added. "Or at least that is what she has told us." He gave his brothers a pointed look. "We all know she is keeping something from us."

"What has you saying that?" I said. Amber had thought she was pulling off a great show. Hell, even I'd believed she had got her life together and moved on.

"Some bloke she is dating," Adam gave me a heated look, "Whom she wouldn't be dating if you hadn't fucked up."

Dating? She isn't dating anyone.

"Yeah, this Tae guy doesn't seem her type," Tyler added. "Too crystal-clear cut."

"I don't see a problem with her dating a normal guy," Troy shrugged. "She meant it when she said she was done with criminals." Troy threw a look my way.

When she was back, that was exactly what she was going to be doing. Dating me. I was going to be relentless once she was back. I would use my charm, I would use my looks. I would use anything and everything to get her back. Hell, I was relentless now, trying to get her back.

I smiled. Two more days. She would have to be back before the deal.

Chapter 47

Troy

"I'm out of smokes again!" Tyler snapped, looking at us. "I told you lot to stop using my packet!"

I glanced at Jax, who was smoking Tyler's last cigarette.

"I told you to replace my packet," Jax said, taking the cigarette from his mouth, sounding and looking calm. I don't know what had changed. One phone call from Amber and he was back to his normal self.

Hell, I wanted him involved but he was basically taking over from me; finally stepping back up to his position. After over a month of doing his work and mine, I had got over it. If I'd known one phone call from Amber would have got his work off my plate, then I would have made him call her earlier.

Jax and Tyler started to get into an argument, while my phone buzzed in my pocket. I pulled it out.

Amber.

"Would you lot shut up, it's Amber," I shouted at them, and immediately their argument ended.

"Yeah Amber?" I answered.

"Did you know dad's dating?" She basically barked at me.

"So?"

"So I don't want a stepmom!"

"Dad never lets one get close, you know that." I sat back in the chair. I was panicked for minute, she never just called. I thought something was seriously wrong. "Has he left yet?"

"Yes. I was forced to meet this one." Amber made it sound like it physically hurt her to meet someone dad was dating.

I grinned. "Lucky you. Is that why you called? To rub your luck in our face?" I knew Amber hated the thought of dad dating anyone.

"No!" She blew out. "I was actually wondering what you've got planned for tomorrow?"

Weird question. We actually had the gun deal tomorrow. "Nothing of importance, why, need me to do something?"

"Yeah I do."

"Name it."

"Pick me up."

My eyes widened and I stood up. "Wait, are you saying…"

"Yes, I'm coming home." She answered the question I hadn't even managed to get out. I could basically see the smirk that would be on her face as I went speechless for a second.

I grinned. "You're coming home?"

All eyes snapped to me. I didn't believe it. Amber was coming home. Was it dad making her come home? All this time I thought she would never come back on her own.

Tyler started firing questions at me, and Cole started barking them and I waved an arm at them to shut up.

"What time do we have to pick you up?"

"My flight gets in at ten in the morning. I suggest you bring a car."

"I'll make sure there is a car." I was grinning so fucking wide. "When do you leave?"

"I'm boarding now," she answered, and I could now hear the muffled sounds in the background.

"Wait, are you going to stay at the clubhouse, or did you work things out with dad?"

359

She scoffed. "Trust me when I say dad and I are not on good terms. No, I'm staying with a friend."

"And who might this friend be?"

"Tae."

"What, your boyfriend?" She couldn't be serious right now. She was coming back and he was following her? "How serious are you two?" I had to ask. Surely they had to be serious if he was heading back here with her. "You make it sound like he lives here!" I picked up on it. She said staying with a friend, implying he had a house here.

"He has houses across the globe. One just so happens to be in our city. Actually, he is the one paying for my flight. I'm kind of tagging along on one of his business stop-overs."

"What does he do again?" I remembered he was a suit. That was it. I was really kicking myself for not looking closer into him.

"Computer software; he is CEO."

"And he is paying for your flight?" I said slowly. "Again, how serious are you two?" They had to be serious for him to be paying for her flight.

"He is a friend. A really good one Troy, so don't make a bad impression when you meet him. Tell the rest that too," she said sharply. "He has been paying for everything."

"What?! You've been relying on this guy! If you needed money, why didn't you ask? When did dad cut you off?"

"You knew he cut me off."

"Yeah, but you said you had your trust fund."

"No, I implied it because I didn't want you worrying."

Cole was barking questions at me by this point and was a second from taking the phone off me; I pushed him away.

"So, what are you his escort or something?" I didn't hide my disgust. "You never rely on a man. Ever."

"I've relied on Blake. I've relied on dad and now I'm relying on Tae so don't screw things up for me when you meet him, and he wants to meet you." She lowered her voice. "I'm begging you Troy, make a good impression."

She was saying that like my life depended on it.

"Fine, I'll tell everyone to behave," I said, finally seeing it was very important to her. The last thing I wanted was for her to decide not to come back because she was scared we would scare off her boyfriend.

"See you tomorrow." She hung up.

"Amber's coming home?" Tyler looked delighted. "I knew she would change her mind."

"Yeah, she is, but I don't know if she is staying in town for long," I muttered, finding holes in her story. She said she was tagging along on one of his business trips so did that mean when he flew out, so would she?

"What do you mean?" Jax got up and looked way too interested in the answer to that question.

I frowned. Why was he so interested? Did he still love her? I hadn't seen him with another woman since she'd left. He'd even made it a point to push women off him. Did he still love her?

Was he thinking he could get her back? Because I wasn't about to let that happen.

"Answer the question!" Jax snapped at me. Again, sounding too interested in the answer.

"She is coming along with her boyfriend. She said she is tagging along on one of his business trips." I glanced down at my phone. "I don't know if she is staying or flying out with him when he leaves."

"Is it that Tae guy?" Cole asked. Cole had been the one to find out about Tae to begin with. We'd run him through the system; he was clean.

"Yeah, and she told me dad cut her off. She never got a trust fund and he is paying for everything, including her flight back here." I gave my brothers a pointed look. "She wanted to make sure we made a good impression. Like our lives depended on it."

"When I looked him up, it said he was single and a billionaire from designing software. Surely Amber wouldn't settle for that

361

type of guy," Tyler said. "She's never gone after a man for money."

"No." I glanced at Jax. When it came to Amber, she always followed her heart. "She must like him."

"Well, that means we must be nice," Cole said really clearly, causing all our heads to snap in his direction. "What!" He snapped at us. "I want Amber back. If that means she is dating a billionaire, so be it. I don't give a fuck. I just want her back in the same country so if us being nice means she stays, then we will be nice!"

Cole was actually being level-headed and making sense. His normal temper usually goes up at the thought of Amber with any bloke but he had missed her so much he was willing to put that aside and let her date someone we would have no control over.

Hell, when it came to Amber and her boyfriends, we never had control.

"Ok, we play nice," I said, confirming Cole's plan. "We need to buy a house too. I don't want her living in one of his places while he flies around the world screwing whoever he wants."

Adam scoffed. "If Amber can do one thing, it's make sure a guy is faithful to her." Then he glanced at Jax. "Even you were."

"Until you didn't trust her," Cole barked at him. "And we lost her." He pointed a finger at Jax. "You and her are done. Don't even think about breaking up her new relationship."

Jax had been calm all week, but that calm expression he usually had on his face was gone. He was pissed off. Was hearing Amber had moved on hurt him?

"Amber isn't in a relationship. You lot are jumping to conclusions." Jax looked between us. "Seriously, she says a guy is supporting her and you all think her heart is involved."

I scoffed. "Amber follows her heart. And we put up with it. We put up with it when she picked you, and if anyone is her friend, it's you." I took a step closer to him. "Don't even think about crossing a line of friendship."

"Like she is even going to be his friend!" Tyler looked at me like I was stupid. "She moved to another country to get away from him and now is coming back with her 'friend' who just so happens to pay for her lifestyle. She's moved on."

I nodded my head. "Yeah, she has, and we don't screw that up." I looked at Adam. "Organise a house." With that said, we could all go back to doing what we were doing, which was waiting for this gun deal to be settled.

But I wouldn't lie. I was looking really forward to seeing my little sister tomorrow. I just hoped this time she had picked a boyfriend that was worth her time.

Jax

Nerves. Wasn't something I did. Never got nervous. My hand never flinched when I took a life. I never got nervous when it came to club decisions. Never once got nervous over a woman, but all that changed when I met Amber.

She made me nervous.

And right now I was nervous. I had played the chess game, put all the pieces together so she would end up back here. And now, as we waited at the airport for her, I kept clenching my hands into fists so the boys wouldn't see I was that nervous.

They actually all looked pretty nervous themselves. Cole was saying in the car that he was freaking out a little about seeing her, seeing as they didn't leave things on good terms, although he did say he actually made more of an effort to speak to her while she was away.

It was the first conversation Cole and I had had where he wasn't barking at me, or disrespecting me. I had opted to go in the car, because I knew she would be in the car once we picked her up, so I left my bike at the clubhouse, and caught a ride with Cole. I had expected him to bark orders at me to stay away from her, but he politely asked me to be nice to her boyfriend.

Like he knew if he threatened me I would just take it out on Tae.

I kept reminding myself of my conversation with Amber. She said she worked for him. She said she didn't date, but the voice in the back of my head told me there could be something more between the two of them.

The boys didn't know the money Tae was giving her, she actually earned. They thought some billionaire was claiming their little sister.

They weren't thrilled with it, but I think they would pick Tae over me. I was in a sour mood as soon as I realized that.

"Is that her?" Cole said, who was showered, clean and even had a shave.

I followed his eye line and saw the crowd part. And there she was. She didn't look like her normal self. She wasn't wearing jeans, or a dress. She was wearing a business suit; jacket and skirt. She looked like she had just stepped out of an office. Her hair was down though. My eyes were glued to her body as she moved. That suit framed her perfect figure.

People were stepping out of their way. My eyes bounced to the man I had competition with. Tae..

God, the way they were laughing and walking together, they looked like a happily married couple. Not business partners.

I knew then. This guy had feelings for her. Then I watched him take her hand, smiling at something she'd said.

"Looks like we were right about the couple thing," Tyler all but groaned. "Seriously, she is going for someone like dad!"

That was exactly what Tae looked like. An upstanding businessman, with money. His suit, his rings, even his hair screamed it.

"Yeah, well our job is to not give her a reason to fly out when he does," Cole grunted. "Behave, all of you." He looked at me. "Don't upset her."

They all thought I would upset her, being here.

I looked back at her, and then I found her eyes were locked with mine. She had spotted us. Wasn't hard to; people were giving us space.

Well, she hadn't spotted us. She had spotted me and her eyes were glued to mine, and immediately I saw pain. She gulped and

364

ripped her eyes away from me, and smiled when she looked at her brothers.

"Behave." Cole said again just as Amber burst into a sprint, which was impressive in those heels.

"God, she looks older," Adam said what we were all thinking.

Troy pushed Cole out of the way and walked towards Amber; seemed like he wanted to be the first to welcome her home.

I watched her wrap her arms around his neck, a wide smile on her face. We all walked towards them. Her boyfriend had grabbed the handle of the suitcase she had abandoned.

"Amber, you look," Troy pulled her off him, "Professional!" He grinned. "And really happy."

"I am!" She frowned, "Although I don't know how to take the professional comment. Sounds like something dad would say." She gave him a pointed look.

"Move over!" Cole pushed Troy over and wrapped his arms around her. "You forgiven me yet?"

"I told you Cole, months ago, I'm not upset with you," she said into his chest, her voice muffled. "God, have you put on more muscle?"

"Says the girl who looks like she has given up eating," he grunted back. "Seriously Amber, you have always been small, but I don't approve of this new skinny frame."

"I just train a lot. Tae is very into exercise." She pulled back from him, grinning up at him, looking like she was telling the truth. Actually, I looked closer at her expression. She was telling the truth.

Cole let go of her and Tyler was quick to take the opportunity to get a hold of her.

"I've missed you little sis." Tyler lifted her off the ground.

"Yeah. I've missed you too Ty," she said into his shoulder. "I like your neck tattoo by the way," she said as he put her back on the ground.

"Got my other leg done too."

"You will have to show me."

365

"Yeah, Cole got the rest of his back done. In fact, we've all been getting our tattoos finished," Tyler made conversation with her. He was right, we all had been spending more time at our tattooist.

Even me.

And I had one particular one that I had got yesterday that I wanted her to see.

"Must be in our blood or something cause Tae just paid for my back piece," she said, and my eyes widened. She had done what?!

"What?!" Cole snapped at her. "Since when did you do tattoos?"

"Well, first I got that awful mark on my stomach covered, then I got the HellBound tattoo covered, which turned into a theme, which resulted in a back piece."

"I thought you were never going to get that tattoo covered?" Adam picked up on something she had said a long time ago, and moved to hug her.

"I just had to let go of the past. Covering that was well, a needed step." She was hugging him and then frowning. "Why didn't you answer the other day?"

Adam and her relationship I never got. He wasn't overly protective of her. They didn't have the unhealthy relationship she had with Cole. She didn't play with him, like she did with Tyler and she didn't treat him seriously, like she did Troy.

If anything, they just supported each other. Maybe it was because they were closest in age but he was the one that had made the rest of her brothers come around when it came to me. He was the one encouraging me to make up with her.

In fact, he always supported her and I. Like he knew what her heart wanted, and he supported it, but he had told me not to muck up her new chance with a new guy. If she had moved on, I had to let her.

He was the only one of them that knew I hadn't moved on from her.

And right now, they were having a silent conversation with their eyes.

So I was half surprised when he stepped out of my way, letting go of her. Her eyes went from him to me, and that's where they stayed.

After how I treated her, I would understand if she ignored me. The old Amber would have punched me, insulted me, screamed all the reasons I was wrong for doing what I had done.

But the Amber I was looking at right now, well, she wasn't doing any of those things.

Her eyes mirrored mine; pain. It was painful seeing her. After all this time, it still hurt to see her. Hurt more knowing she'd said I'd never get her back.

She took a big gulp of air in, and all her brothers were watching her reaction. Was she going to be childish? Was she going to play a game? Amber knew I loved her. She had all the cards. She could flirt and dance with fire by teasing me with Tae, and I would have to suffer it. Hell, if teasing me was all she was going to do... I deserved a lot worse.

Instead, she took a step closer to me, and then another, until she was standing in front of me.

It was instinct now to reach out for her, so I did, wrapping my arms around her, and she hugged me back. I think I took my first easy breath since she'd left; holding her now. I could breathe easy.

The nerves were gone.

Holding her just felt right.

Everything always became easy when I was with Amber which was why I'd fought so hard, because you don't get handed the perfect woman and then have being with her as easy as breathing more than once.

She was thinner; there was barely anything of her.

"Thank you," she whispered in my ear.

She was thanking me for bringing her back? Did that mean she didn't hate me completely?

"I said I would get you back," I whispered in her ear and kissed her cheek, and then she stepped out of my grasp.

Pulling away from me with a sad smile on her face.

"Amber?"

She turned and my eyes went to Tae.

"We need to change your phone," he glanced at us, but looked like he didn't have any time for us whatsoever.

Which I think shocked the boys.

"Right, sorry Tae," she said and walked to him, taking the phone he was offering her. "Thank you." She smiled. She looked really thankful too. It just proved to me again there was competition here.

His phone started ringing and he cursed. "That will be Lee, making demands as usual."

"He doesn't demand things," Amber was still smiling at him. As if they had had this conversation before. "You just don't want to pick up because you don't know your schedule this week."

He arched his eyebrows at her. "You know me too well."

"Here, give it to me," she said and put her hand out.

"Like always Amber, this is one of the reasons I love you," he said, sending a direct punch to my gut... He just said he loved her. I was mortified. Amber said she would never risk her heart again; had she changed her mind over the course of the week? Less than a week.

She rolled her eyes and answered the phone, her heels clicking as she walked off, riddling off details.

All eyes were on Tae and he didn't seem one bit fazed by that. He looked at all of us, one by one. Summing us up. He was an underworld figure; he knew us, but we weren't meant to know he was the face of an underworld figure.

He wouldn't go into business with us, unless he knew every detail about us.

"So, you must be her brothers," he said, somewhat polite. I think the only reason he was giving them time was because of Amber. "She has told me a lot about you lot. Her stories always seemed to feature one of you."

So they spent time together. Enough time for her to tell him personal stories. Some business relationship.

I glanced at her back. She had some explaining to do.

I wasn't letting her date him. Hell, I wasn't letting her be with anyone apart from me. I was going to get her back. I needed her back. I ripped my eyes off her back, in time to watch the boys introduce themselves and shake hands.

Tae was really making an effort. For a man meant to be as ruthless as me, it looked like we both had it hard for one woman and were willing to do anything to get her.

Amber walked back to us, just as Cole was making conversation with Tae.

"Ok. So your schedule is locked in with Lee." Amber handed him the phone. "And we are locked in for dinner at six."

He grinned at her. I sure as fuck didn't know the man ruthless enough to run TNS to smile or grin, but he did with her.

"Formal or private?" he asked, taking her hand, and pulling her towards him. "I'm hoping for private." He sounded hopeful. It made me sick.

Amber told me she wasn't dating him!

"Private," she smirked.

"At my place or a hotel?"

"Your place."

"Good, just where I want you." He took his eyes off her, and glanced at her brothers. "I just met your brothers. They are everything you said they were".

Her expression changed instantly, she looked defensive. "Are they just?"

He nodded his head. "We can confirm that seven appointment, but you aren't handling it. I want you home."

I knew instantly what he was talking about; he had just confirmed our gun deal. Looks like it wasn't going ahead until he met them. We must have passed, although I made a point not to introduce myself to him. He knew who I was. I knew who he really was.

And the only reason I was doing this deal was so Amber could be here, but it sounded like she wasn't going to be having anything to do with it.

"I'll confirm it, and we can talk about it tonight. You should go, your car is waiting and you have a twelve o'clock." Amber pulled her hand from his, and he was quick to kiss her on the cheek.

"And while I'm gone, I don't want to hear anything on what we discussed on the plane," he looked at her, as if he was telling her off.

She sighed. "I told you I could handle it."

"And I told you I don't want you to."

She pursed her lips. "Fine," she said, but the Amber I knew never backed down.

"I'll see you at my place, tonight. Call me if you change your mind about the seven appointment." He gave her one last glance and said goodbye to her brothers, and left.

So, if the deal was going to go through, it seemed the decision was in her hands. She smiled at her brothers.

"Ok, so I'm tagging along with you lot for the day," she said and went to get her suitcase but Cole was quick to grab the handle and drag it along.

"Good, because we bought a house," Cole said, walking next to her.

"What? You moved out of the clubhouse?" She frowned, like it wasn't possible.

"Yep," they all chimed

"And we are hoping you will be looking to move in." Tyler grinned at her. "Troy said you weren't going back to dad's?"

"I'm staying with Tae."

"Yeah, but he is going to fly out, right? He is visiting?" Troy said, I knew he was dying to know the answer to that question.

Was Amber back for good, or not? I watched her expression, and it wasn't readable.

"Depends on something," she muttered, dodging their intense looks. "And, before you even ask, Tae is a friend; he's not a boyfriend and we aren't dating."

We walked outside.

"So, what's with the private dinner?" Adam smirked at her. "You don't have to lie to us."

"Not lying, and that just means he wants to talk." She came to a stop at the boys' bikes. "He doesn't like having private conversations in public."

"You seem like a couple." Troy only said that because of what we had just witnessed.

I was still staring at her and it was when she glanced at me that I saw the pain in her eyes.

"We aren't," she said firmly, still looking me in the eye. "I've learned my lesson when it comes to relationships."

That was my fault.

"Speaking of which…. I have to see Blake while I'm in town." She wouldn't look me in the eye again.

"Why?" I couldn't stop myself from asking. She said she would never go see him again. She had promised me that. It was on the same night I broke up with her. Was she going back to him?

"He is using my name," she mumbled, frowning. "And it's bothering me."

"How is he using your name?" I took a step closer to her, pushing Adam out of the way, so I could read her expression properly.

She looked up. "He is telling people I'm in charge. I haven't even been in the country and I'm getting heat for it."

"We can handle it," Troy said as he pushed me back towards the car. "No need for you to be brought down by his crap."

She sighed. "Letting my brothers handle him. Tempting."

"Come on Amber, we owe you one," Cole pointed out as he unlocked the car. "I don't know how many times I've been tempted just to be put in holding, just to give him a fight."

"That's exactly what he is after. A fight." Amber ran a hand through her hair. "It mightn't even matter. I might not stay. Then if I fly out, I guess the problem stays here." She was staring at the pavement. "He is making my life hell; God, some days I wish he would just go back to hitting me. At least that would bruise and heal."

My eyes widened. I don't think she realized what she'd said. That she'd admitted to her brothers that he used to hit her. They were all staring at her, and she was still staring with no emotion at the pavement. She appeared to be in her own world.

"Amber, what did you just say?" Cole dumped the suitcase in the back seat and walked towards her, gripping her by the shoulders and breaking her eye lock with the pavement.

She frowned. "What?"

"Did he used to hit you?" Cole was calm, not a hint of anger. It was the very rare side of Cole you would see, before he started shooting or choking someone to death.

She frowned. "Did I really just say that?" She seemed shocked for a second.

Cole nodded his head.

"Um, well." She pushed his hands off her shoulders. "Yeah, he did. It was why we broke up. Wouldn't have broken up if he could control his temper."

"He's dead," Cole said simply, and all her brothers nodded in agreement. "Dead," he repeated. "As of tonight." Cole glanced at me. "You don't really need me tonight, do you?"

He wanted to go and kill Blake. Fine by me. I shook my head. "We can handle it," I said. "But for the record, Blake got a beating for touching her."

Their heads snapped to me. Even Amber was looking at me slightly shocked. I shrugged my shoulders.

"She came back to her house black and blue, and her dad said she had a boyfriend. Turned out to be Blake." I answered their unsaid questions.

"So, that explains his reaction to you when he saw you at my house that morning," Amber said, like she had just put a puzzle together. "And why he was beaten up the day he came and saw me at the house to break up." She smiled at me, and it hit me hard. "You did a good job."

"Well, I didn't love you then so he got off lightly." I'd just said it. I was sick of hiding the fact I still loved her. I didn't fucking care what her brothers thought of me for loving her, but they looked at me like I couldn't possibly have said I still love her. "So, should we go?" I said as they just stared at me.

"Yeah. I have a prison to visit." Cole was the first one to snap out of staring blankly at me.

"You can beat up him Cole, but you can't kill him," Amber said directly. "I don't want you to deal with murder charges and he isn't worth it, but, considering the hell he has been putting me through, I would like it if he beat him to the point of nearly an early death." She smiled knowing Cole would like that.

His expression hardened like he wasn't about to accept that. He would go to prison for murder. Cole wouldn't care.

"Fine, but only because you asked nicely. Now, get in." Cole opened the back seat door for her. "And, are you serious when you say you aren't dating this Tae guy?"

She nodded her head.

"Then you aren't staying with him. No sister of mine is a fling." He closed the door after telling her that.

Good. I liked this even better. Their eyes went back to me.

"Don't even think about making a move Jax," Cole grumbled as he passed me and got in the car.

His request fell on deaf ears. That was exactly what I was going to do. I was going to make a move on her.

I walked around the car. If the boys were banning her from going to Tae's place tonight, it meant she would be staying at their place. I smirked. The boys could handle the gun deal without me. I had more important things to do tonight than hand off millions worth in guns.

***

I pulled up to the boys' new house. They had pulled strings and got the set up on the same day they bought it. When it came to money, they didn't care. They wanted to give Amber a home.

And that's what they did.

I don't think she realized that they bought it for her though.

I killed my engine. The boys were handling the deal and I was going to spend time with the woman I loved.

Yeah. I loved her - incredibly and completely loved her, and I wanted her back.

I leaned my bike to the side and got off. Walking towards the house; I knew she was inside, and that she'd spent the day with her brothers. Her and I didn't get a chance to talk.

In fact, she made it a point not to be by herself with me. The one opportunity we had had, she'd fled.

I rang the doorbell and waited.

The door opened and I grinned immediately on seeing her. She was still wearing her suit skirt and top, but the jacket was gone and so were the heels.

She frowned at me. "The boys aren't her," she said slowly, looking at me. "But you know that."

I nodded my head. "Not here to see them, sweetheart."

Her eyes hardened. "Why aren't you at the deal?"

Because you are more important. I shrugged my shoulders. "Why aren't you?"

She lifted her phone and flashed it to me. "I am."

I saw the camera feed on her phone. "Being the invisible hand?"

She sighed and nodded her head.

"Can I come in?" I took a step closer to her and noticed her clench the door tighter. "Please, sweetheart." I took another step closer to her. I had learned the hard way. I had learned that my life was nothing without her. There was no life without her.

How could I ever think I could live without her?

She was glaring at the porch steps, not answering, not moving, and not letting me in.

"Come on Amber." I reached out for her. My hands landed on her hips, and, dipping my head, I tried to get her to look me in the eye. I lowered my voice. "Please sweetheart."

She looked up and I saw the debate in her eyes. "You should be at the deal. Not here."

The deal was merely the pawn I'd used to get her back. She was the point of the chess game to begin with. I didn't say anything. She had to know I would do anything to get her back, to make up for my mistakes.

She brushed my hands off her, and I thought if she rejected me right now, well I wasn't sure what would be left of me. The only way I had been functioning was because I had known she was coming home but, as of tonight, my purpose to get up tomorrow morning wouldn't be there. I couldn't look forward to her coming home because she was home so I was hoping and praying she didn't reject me.

I'd hoped at the very least it would take her time before she pushed me away, if at all. I'd used everything in me to get her to be close to me. To prove to her I had changed.

But, from the look on her face, she wasn't going to give me a second of her time. I had to think of something. Quick. I had to say something. Stop her ending us altogether. Stopping my chance of getting her back.

"Just give me an hour." I pleaded with her. "I won't stay a second longer."

Surely, she could spend an hour with me? Hell, there was a time in our relationship when she was the one wanting to be with me, when she was pleading to spend time with me.

And I always pushed her away.

And right now as she looked up at me, with hardness in her eyes. I was beginning to feel what she would have felt when I did it.

Please don't do it Amber.

The look in her eyes didn't soften. She was about a second away from slamming the front door in my face.

I panicked. "Half an hour?"

Her phone buzzed in her hand and she looked down at it. "Deal's happening." She looked up. "You did a good job putting that together."

"Does that mean I get half an hour of your time?" I hoped.

She clenched her eyes shut. "No."

Rejection. I wouldn't accept it. "Please, Amber. Just five minutes then. Just let me explain what happened." All my life I had been taught never to be weak, but, in this moment, I was weak. Never let anyone see you as weak. Dad's words repeating in my head.

He was the only role model I had. I admit he was a shitty one and, yeah, I picked up his bad habits. Like the need to be bulletproof. To never let anyone close. To never let anyone see you as weak. Strength was something Johnston's prided themselves on.

But right now, I didn't give a fuck. I was going against every word of advice dad had ever given me.

I reached out for her, cupping her face; God, I needed her to open her eyes. "Please, Amber. Five minutes." She had me begging! God, I couldn't be any more pathetic. "Please." My voice wavered with emotion, just at the mere thought of the emptiness I felt without her. I never let emotion show, so she heard it, her eyes springing open.

Was that what she needed to hear? That I was empty without her?

"Five minutes." I repeated. "Then I'll leave." How the hell was I going to convince her to take me back in five minutes? I didn't care about that right now. Right now the mission was to get inside.

"Ok." She said deflated and stepped back, my hands dropping from her face.

I closed the front door.

"God, I'm an idiot," she muttered to herself and walked into the lounge room. I followed.

She sat down on the couch, tucking her legs under her. Her attention went to her phone. I just stood there staring at her.

"Stop looking at me," she snapped, and looked up. "Seriously Jax, you are acting like you've never seen me before."

"I've missed you." I walked in and sat down on the couch next to her. "Sorry."

"For staring?" she arched an eyebrow at me, as if I would be saying sorry for that.

I shook my head. "For not trusting you the night Mai came. For not believing you." I reached out and tucked her hair behind her ear, needing to see her face. "I'm sorry for breaking up with you. I'm sorry for all the hurtful things I said and I'm really sorry you had to move because of me."

She took a nervous breath in. I could see how nervous she was. She was flipping her phone around in her hand. I placed my hand over her nervous one, and her eyes snapped to mine.

"I'm so sorry Amber."

She finally nodded her head. "Well, you've got it off your chest." Her words hardened. "You can go now."

She was just pushing me away. I sighed. "I still have three minutes."

She scoffed but didn't say anything. I would do anything to hear what she was thinking. Did she still love me? She said she would always love me. What could I do in three minutes to prove to her I had changed?

I had to get her mind off our break-up. The pain in her eyes, on her face… it was killing me.

"You know that history report you didn't do? On that soldier?" I said, recalling something I did want to tell her.

"The one you thought I would do? I did tell you I wouldn't do it."

"Yeah, that one." She knew what I was talking about.

"What about it?"

"Well, you didn't do it, and it scored me an extra month on my parole." That one bad grade. "So, really, you owe me months' worth of your time cause you cost me a month."

"We were partners. You were meant to help!" She shook her head. "Seriously, you did an extra month because of it?"

I nodded my head. "Worst month of my life."

She reached for the coffee table and grabbed her beer; so she still drank. "Well, I'd say I'm sorry but I'm not. I hated school." She shrugged it off, like a month of my life wasted wasn't a big deal.

"Well, I got to stay an extra month because of you."

"Did you graduate?"

"No," I scoffed. "I left as soon as my parole was done."

"I did."

I frowned. "But you said you left school?"

"After I passed by correspondence." She shrugged. "I just was too stubborn to tell dad that I had finished my education. So, instead, I lied and said I dropped out which resulted me being cut off. And.." She sighed. "Me doing everything Tae says."

"You can get rid of him."

"I can't."

"You don't need money." My hand was still on hers and she realized, pulling her hands away.

"Yeah, I do."

I took my hand off her lap and turned to face her more. "Your brothers won't let you go without a thing." I moved slightly closer to her, reaching out and lifting her chin. "I won't let you go without anything," I said firmly.

"You aren't my boyfriend Jax. You broke up with me. I told you if you did, there was no coming back." She looked panicked. Like she was saying that but her body was screaming she was all mine. "Don't look at me like that."

My eyes flashed to her lips. All those times we had had sex played through my mind. All the times she was calling out my name, because that is who she belonged to. Me.

378

Maybe I just had to remind her. I dipped my head.

"Don't you dare kiss me!" She pushed my hand off her face and got up like the couch burnt her. "DON'T SIT THERE AND ACT LIKE NOTHING HAPPENED!"

"I said I was sorry."

"SORRY DOESN'T CUT IT!" She was mad. No. She was furious. The lid on her temper was off, and I was happy to see it come off. I could deal with her rage; I couldn't handle her being distant and accepting.

"What do you need me to do?" I said getting up and walking towards. "Just tell me what you need to hear."

"Time. That's what I need. Time to get over you! Cause I've had over a month and I'm still fucking addicted to you! AND IT'S NOT FAIR!" She screamed. "JUST LEAVE. YOUR FIVE MINUTES ARE UP!"

Tears were threatening to fall from her eyes and she looked at me like she hated me, but, at the same time, loved me unconditionally.

Good. She was pissed off. Now I needed her to get it all out of her system.

"Mai lied," I said firmly.

"I know she did! I told you that! You didn't believe me!" Frustrated, she threw her beer bottle at my head. "I TOLD YOU TO TRUST ME!"

I dodged the bottle and it smashed into the window. Now, this side of Amber I knew well.

"AND I SAID I WAS SORRY I DIDN'T!" I yelled back at her. Ok. Don't yell at her. I took a deep breath in. "I was too late Amber, but I'm here now and I am begging you. Just give me a chance."

"No."

"Amber."

"NO!"

I stood in front of her, taking her clenched fists in my hands. "I love you."

379

Tears dropped from her eyes. "Stop saying that."

"No."

"Just stop it." She unclenched her fists. "Just please let me go. I can't go through this again. I can't handle your mood changes. I can't handle you wanting me one minute and hating me the next." She wiped a tear away. "I'm not strong enough."

"When it comes to you, everything else comes second." I pulled her closer to my chest. "I mean it Amber, everything else doesn't matter."

"What about the club that you love so much?" She scoffed, sounding hurt. "How many times have you pushed me away because of it! You can't just expect me to believe you."

"Have I ever lied to you?" I said firmly. She was glaring into my chest. I cupped her face, forcing her look me in the eye. "Everything, and I mean everything, is second to you. I lost you once and it's never going to happen again."

Her eyes showed debate. "You don't do weaknesses. I'm a weakness."

"No Amber, the only thing you give me is strength." It was what I had been missing since she'd left; the strength to keep going. "I didn't know how important you were in my life Amber, but you have to believe me when I say, you are my purpose."

I was expecting for her to push me away, push my hands off her face, but she didn't; instead her fingers ran down my jaw.

"You'll find a new purpose," she mumbled. "Women go to you easy, Jax."

"I don't want women. I want you!"

"You broke my heart." Tears slid down her cheeks. "And I don't even have one back together to give you." A depressed smile appeared on her face. "Even if I wanted to Jax, there is nothing left. I can't give you something I don't have anymore."

"You have a heart." If there was one thing I was certain about, it was that. The way she loved her brothers. In order to love someone as much as she loved them, she had to have a heart.

She tilted her head; the hollowness that was in her eyes that night we were on the phone was back in her eyes.

"If I had one, I would give it to you again," she said, ever so softly. "Because I never learn from my mistakes."

She was shutting down. I could see it. She was pulling back from me. I wanted her screaming at me again, at least then she felt something towards me. Panicked, I lowered my forehead to hers.

"Let me prove to you that you have one." I was desperate. I knew she had one. I hadn't completely destroyed her heart.

"I don't want to feel what I felt for you again. That all-consuming need to be with you. I don't want that. Can't have that because you will leave me." And she pushed my hands off her and walked away from me. "And then I'll be back here. Hollow again. So what's the point, Jax?" She sighed, turning to look at me.

She still loved me. It was on her face right now.

"I won't ever hurt you again like that Amber."

"Don't promise me that." She ran a hand through her hair. "I can fake a smile. I can fake a conversation with my brothers. I can fake love. My acting skills have got better, but I can't fake what we had."

"Then don't. Just risk it again Amber." I walked to her, feeling all I did was follow her around this room as she attempted to get away from me. "Take a chance on me."

"Which part of the 'I don't have a heart to risk' don't you get!" She looked at me like I was stupid. She let out a frustrated sigh. "You and I were poison."

"We were complicated."

She scoffed, her eyes going wide. "Yeah, that's another word for us."

Us.

I smiled. "You know I love you, right?"

"You keep saying that, but a man that loved me wouldn't have hurt me." She squared her shoulders back, staring me in the eye. "If you really loved me, I would know."

I peeled my vest off and she frowned at me.

381

"What are you doing?" Her voice rose as I unclipped my holsters, dropping my guns on the table and reaching for the hem of my t-shirt and taking it off. "Why the hell are you taking your clothes off?"

I dropped it on the ground. The tattoo I wanted to show her... well, now was time to show her.

Her eyes were still on mine. I reached for her hand and she let me take it.

I placed it over my heart and lowered it, just slightly. "You're right there Amber. In my heart. It's where you will always be." Whether she wanted to love me or not, I would always love her.

She glanced down, her eyes widening when she slowly spread her fingers and then took her hand off, staring at her name tattooed on my chest.

"You'll always be with me. Even if you don't want to be," I said. She could push me away but I would always love her. "I will always do anything for you, and if you can't take a chance on me, I hope I can at least be your friend."

It had come to that point of the evening when I had to admit defeat. I would rather be her friend than nothing. A friend could ask how she was. A friend could spend time with her. I hoped she would let me be her friend.

She was gobsmacked and then she started to do something that shocked me..

"Why are you taking your top off?" I said, my mouth hanging open as she undid the last button, and shrugged it off.

Amber was always beautiful but I wasn't used to seeing it, so it sent me into shock, seeing her perfect skin. My eyes ran across her tattooed stomach and then up her beautiful rib cage and then she turned and lifted her arm.

And then I didn't believe what I was seeing.

"That's my name." I was in shock.

Jackson was tattooed so perfectly on her side.

She put her arm down and turned to look at me. The hollowness that had been in her eyes earlier was gone.

"Like I said. I was marking my body. And you. Well, you left a mark on my heart so I thought it only fitting you had one on my body." She looked down and sighed. "We were good while we lasted."

It had barely fucking started. We spent most of our time fighting or me pushing her away.

"Start fresh with me." I couldn't stop myself from running my hand down her side, my hand following her skin and going to her lower back and pushing her into me. "Make a fresh start with me. One where you come first. One where the club is second and I promise Amber, I won't push you away."

She looked me in the eye. "You won't push me away, even if it is in my best interest?" She was challenging me.

Well, she had me there. If it was in her best interest, I would push her away; it was a habit. It's the only thing I had regularly done to her, push her away.

"If there is another option, no." I couldn't say to her completely I wouldn't put her best interest first. I wanted her, but her safety came first and I would never want to hold her back.

Not now. Not ever. If I wasn't adding to her life, I wouldn't be a part of it.

"My love for you will always come first. Anything I do is because I love you." I pushed her more into me, the fact she was only wearing a bright pink low cut bra hadn't gone unnoticed.

It was basically taking all my willpower to not unclip her bra right now. My other hand reached around her, brushing the clasp of her bra. I could just unclip it. I needed to see her, naked, and completely in front of me.

But I needed her to want me like that.

Her hands went to my chest and I loved her touch. Her hands moved up and stopped on my shoulders. She didn't fight me, as I pushed her completely into me and she dropped her head to my chest.

"How will we work?" she said into my chest. "I can't do hot and cold again."

Her breathing on my chest was welcoming. It was hot and sharp.

"We will take it one day at a time." I ran my hands down her spine. "We can go as fast as you want or as slow as you want."

She pulled her head from my chest and looked up at me. "You really want to do this?"

"Yes."

"You're willing to take shit from my brothers?"

"Yes."

"You will stay away from other women?"

"Yes."

"You will actually show me respect?"

I frowned. "I've always respected you."

"You've always seen me as a weakness." She ran her hand down from my shoulder and I could feel her staring at her name. She sighed. "What does it even matter anymore, I can't give you my heart when I don't have it."

"I'll help you get it back." I held her closer to me, feeling like she was a second from bolting from me. "I promise you Amber, I will help you get your heart back. I broke it. I'll fix it."

She looked up at me, blinking back tears, "How? I've tried. I can't feel anything. I kill without even so much as caring. I don't feel guilt. I just don't feel. So how, Jax? How are you going to fix the hole in my heart?"

"I'll show you." My hands went to the skirt that was at her waist and I slowly undid the zipper. I kissed her shoulder as her skirt fell to the ground. "Starting tonight, I'm claiming back your heart."

"I don't have one."

"Yes you do. I broke it. I'll fix it."

"I'm not your bike, Jax."

I smirked. Now, that sounded more like Amber. My hands went to her hips and I lifted her up, and, as if she knew what I wanted, she wrapped her legs around my waist.

Looking her in the eye, taking all her weight, I took one hand off her and pushed a stray hair that was in front of her face, behind her ear.

"Can I make love to you?" I asked, lowering my forehead to hers.

"You sure you don't just want to fuck me? Less strings in the morning."

I shook my head. "Nah sweetheart, I want to love you." I kissed her cheek. "All night." I kissed her forehead. "Every night."

"You're doing it again." She sighed and dropped her forehead to mine.

"What?"

"Promising me something you can't give."

"Amber, I promise you I'm going to love you every day for the rest of my life." I kissed her lips, at first gentle, but once I got a taste, I was going back for more. I was addicted to the taste of her mouth.

I had forgotten just how sweet she was. How had I forgotten that? It was like being off drugs, stone sober, and then you get your first high. It was sending my body into shock at first, and then I couldn't get enough. The adrenaline rushed through my body as I greedily kissed her.

I didn't even realize I was doing it, but I was moving, needing to get us to a bedroom before I lost control and took her on the couch.

Where her brothers could easily walk in, any minute.

"Wait." She pulled away from my lips. "My clothes. If the boys come home and see them, they will know."

I smirked. "I think they will know when I'm here in the morning." I kissed her cheek. "When I'm kissing you." I kissed along her jaw. "When I'm dragging you off to the bedroom."

She laughed, and I loved the sound of it. It was something I'd missed, hearing her laugh.

"Clothes!" she said, and I walked us back into the lounge room.

"Don't see the point in hiding the evidence."

"You would if your brothers loved to take the piss out of you."
She wanted me to let her go but I wasn't going to. She looked at
me, knowing what I was doing. "You have to let me pick them
up."

"And you promise I can pick you back up as soon as you've got
them?" I arched an eyebrow at her, not wanting her to take this
opportunity to bolt from me.

She nodded her head, but it was the small smile on her face that
had me easing her body down. As soon as her feet hit the ground,
she picked up her clothes and I was taking in the view as she bent
over.

Darn. So fucking perfect, and, just like that, my self-control
snapped.

She had them in her hands and that was enough for me; a squeal
left her lips as I took her legs from under her and carried her, bridal
style.

My eyes ran over her again, drinking her in. I was going slow
tonight. At least the first time.

Then that nagging question was back in my head and I found
myself needing an answer this time.

"So, what's with you and Tae?" I walked her up the stairs.

"Nothing."

"Has he seen you like this?" I couldn't stop the jealousy that
ran through my veins at the thought that someone had had what
was mine.

She tilted her head and then did something I wasn't expecting.
She kissed me. Her hands bringing my face to hers. She kissed me
harder, and I groaned. She'd just got me addicted again.

I stopped at the top of the stairs, not knowing which direction
to take her. As much as I didn't want to pull away, I had to.

"Which room is yours?" I said, my lips barely from hers.

"Ummm..." She frowned. She looked so cute, and it wasn't
helping that her breasts were rising and falling sharply with her
breathing as she thought.

"Sweetheart, you're killing me. We need a room."

"Door at the end, I think." She frowned again, looking more adorable. "Cole put my suitcase in my room and I wasn't paying attention."

"I think your brothers will kill me if they hear I had sex with you in one of their beds." I smirked from just thinking about their reaction, and walked to the door at the end.

"They mightn't come home tonight."

"I hope they don't." With what I was planning on doing to her, it was best no one was in the house.

I twisted the handle to the door, and opened it up. Her suitcase was at the end of the bed.

"Looks like you got the right room," I said, slightly deflated that I wouldn't be doing one of her brother's worst nightmares.

She yawned. "Good. No brothers walking in on my one night stand."

"We aren't having a one night stand."

She gave me a look to say that was all I was capable of.

"We aren't!" I snapped at her. "When are you going to realize I'm seriously in love with you?"

She yawned again.

"You're tired." I stated the obvious. I should be putting her to bed. As much as I wanted to make love to her, she needed sleep. Maybe after a solid night's sleep back in the same country as me, she would wake up in the morning realizing how much I loved her.

"What are you doing?" she said, as I lowered her onto the bed. I then let go of her. Grabbing the blankets which were already pulled back, I pulled them over her.

"Putting you to bed." I kissed her forehead. "I'll come back in the morning."

She locked her arms around my neck. "You aren't really leaving, are you?"

"I'll be back in the morning." As soon as she was awake, I'd be back. "I promise."

I pried her arms from the deadlock around my neck, and lowered her arms to the bed.

387

"I promise when you wake up, I'll be back." I ran a hand through my hair. It was going to nearly kill me to leave her like this. I kissed her forehead again, needing to.

I went to leave her but her hand wrapped around mine, stopping me. I frowned, looking at her hand now locked around mine.

"Then why leave?" She sat up, and yawned again.

"You want me to stay?"

We had never once just slept in the same bed.

She nodded her head, confirming what I thought couldn't be possible. She wanted me to stay. My five minutes had turned into a full night with her.

"Are you going to stay or not?" She sighed. "You don't have to. I know you don't do that. Just sleep with someone." She yawned again. "You can go," she said, deflated, and let go of my hand, like she had made up my mind for me, and laid back down.

I moved across the room and heard her mutter something, but didn't catch it. I turned the light off and closed the door.

I walked back to the bed. The curtains were open, so I could make out her figure and the fact that she had her eyes shut, and had rolled onto her side.

I got into the other side, my arm slipping under her head.

"Jax?" She sounded alarmed.

"Who else do you think it would be?" I kissed her bare shoulder and, with my other arm wrapped around her, I pulled her back to me.

"I thought you left."

"Like I would leave you." Had she not listened to a word I had said tonight?

"It's early, you don't have to go to sleep." Her hand ran down my arm, stopping over the hand I was holding her with.

"I don't care." Having an early night wouldn't kill me. Actually, my body needed one, with the lack of sleep I was running on.

She turned in my arms. "You don't sleep over. Even when we were on the road, we didn't share a room." Her fingers ran across my jaw and I pulled her in, not settling until her head was on my chest.

"I always wanted to, but your brothers were always in the way." My hand ran down her bare back.

"And what, they aren't anymore?"

"I'm never letting anyone get in my way again when it comes to you."

She sighed. "I'll believe that when I see it."

"Just go to sleep."

"If you leave, I'll understand."

I kissed the top of her head. "Not leaving." And I wasn't leaving her now. Not now. Not ever. "Amber?"

"Um?" She was nearly asleep.

"I love you."

"I know."

My eyes went wide. "You know?" She had said earlier she would know if I loved her. She hadn't believed me. What had changed?

"How?"

"I saw it in your eyes." She moved over me, until she was straddling me. "When you said you would be my friend."

"You saying you believed me when I said I'd be your friend?" I couldn't believe that is what made her see it. Her mind was twisted.

"Yep." She lowered her mouth to my ear. "Want to know a secret?"

I rolled my eyes. She was sounding more like her normal self. Her and her games. I gripped her waist and flipped her over, her back sinking into the bed.

My mouth went to her ear and I felt her skin shiver. "When it comes to you, I want to know everything."

She wrapped her arms around my neck and pulled my head down to hers. "I want to revisit those girlfriend rules."

Was she saying? Wait a sec… surely not? Had I got her back? I leaned over to the bedside table and turned the lamp on, needing to read her expression.

She was squinting from the light for a second.

"What do you mean by that?" I asked. "Are you saying…?" My words dried up, not believing my luck.

She smiled. "You're speechless."

I nodded my head. She made me speechless because the thought of getting her back had me speechless. I was going to wait until she was ready. I was going to take her slow but, at the same time, as fast as I could - as fast as she would let me.

I cleared my throat. "So, you want to be…" I needed my brain to work. It had stopped functioning properly as soon as she said the word girlfriend.

"Your girlfriend?" She finished my sentence.

I nodded my head.

She frowned for a second. "I don't know if I have a heart anymore but whatever I have left," she paused and the honesty in her eyes had me "well, you can have it."

"You have a heart." I leaned down and kissed her just over her heart. "I'll prove it to you." I smirked. "I think I want to add a few things to the girlfriend rule list."

"Well, we can't sneak between rooms anymore. It's not like you live here."

"We need to fix that." I couldn't be apart from her. "You should move out."

"I just moved in! It's literally my first night here."

"Fine, I'll just live here."

"You can't just move in!"

"Watch me." I kissed her cheek, and my hand started to wander down that perfect body of hers. "New rule. We don't sleep apart." I had only had a small taste of what it would be like to sleep with her, and it was fair to say, I was not spending a night away from her, unless it was forced.

"I want boyfriend rules." She nibbed my bottom lip.

I smirked. "You setting rules. Now, that's funny."

"I'm serious!"

"Ok, then name one rule." I rolled on to my side, and she turned to face me, that adorable smile I fell in love with on her face.

"One rule. There is only one boyfriend rule," she said matter of factly.

"Ok. I can stick to one rule. What is it?" I was interested in what she had come up with.

"Any woman you touch, dies." She grinned. "By my hand."

"You can't just kill women that touch me!"

"No, I said women YOU touch, and you left out the part about it being at my hand."

I rolled my eyes. "You aren't killing anyone."

"It's what I've been doing. I'm actually very good at it."

"I know." I gave her a pointed look. "And it's stopping."

"You always were protective. More protective than my brothers." She put her hand under her head. "I'll stop when I'm allowed to."

"You aren't working for Tae anymore."

"I don't want to have a fight so back to the rules. My one rule. You touch her, she dies." She ran a hand over my chest "By my hand," she added smugly.

She looked like she wasn't backing down on this. I couldn't simply walk around giving women the mark of death if I touched them!

"We do my one rule, and I'll follow any of yours." She seductively licked along my jaw. "Any rule you set." Suddenly, she didn't seem so tired.

I groaned. "Anything?"

"Anything." She looked at me smugly.

"So, if I wanted a mandatory weekend sex marathon, every weekend, Friday through to Sunday, you would be up for it?"

"I'll be naked and ready," she kissed my lips, "Every weekend."

I groaned. That was even worse, knowing she was up for anything. One rule. I could follow one rule. I never followed rules. Always made sure to break them. Every rule that was given to me, I was hell bent on breaking.

"You're being unreasonable," I blew out as she kissed down my neck.

"One rule Jax, just one rule."

"Yeah, one rule that gives you the right to kill women!"

"Only women you touch." She moved over me, straddling me. "You keep saying you love me. So why would you be touching another woman?"

She had a point. "What is the definition of touch? What if I brushed her arm?"

"I'm not that petty!" She scoffed. "God, if that was the case, I'd be taking people out in the supermarket!"

"Fine then, what is your definition?"

"If your hand so much as lingers on her breast or ass, she's dead…. and I have a question." She sat up, looking rather determined.

"Weren't you tired?" I arched my eyebrows at her.

"I've passed exhaustion. It's a recurring pattern lately. Tae's been having me work at night, and if I don't get to sleep within a small window, I won't sleep for the day."

"How long have you been awake?"

"Don't know." She shrugged and her looked sharpened. "I still have that question."

"Fine sweetheart, hit me with it." I would answer any question she had.

Her face soured and she blew out hotly. "Cole told me something."

I grunted. Well, this was off to a great start. "What shit has Cole been filling you with?"

"He said…" She chewed on her bottom lip. "You and Mai had a special relationship; that I needed to respect that your way of life comes with women who you have special relationships with."

I frowned. Mine and Mai's relationship was not special! I just trusted her.

"How many other women are there that you have a special relationship with Jax?" she asked, sounding slightly anxious to know the answer.

"I didn't have a special relationship with Mai." I wanted to make that fact clear.

She looked me in the eye and that pain that was in her eyes at the airport, well, it was back. "You trusted her more than you did me." Her eyes dropped to my chest like she couldn't look me in the eye for a second longer.

"I fucked up, Amber. I should have trusted you. Not her."

She wouldn't look up.

"It won't happen again." I had learned my lesson. You don't trust women. Well, that wasn't completely true. I could trust one woman and I think she needed to hear that. "From now on Amber, you are the only woman I trust. All women do is give me a fucking headache." And if I had her, I didn't need, nor would I ever would need, another woman.

Realizing that made me see her one rule wouldn't kill me.

I sat up, holding her to me. She still wouldn't look me in the eye. I lifted her head up, her eyes still on my chest.

"That one rule you want," I said, and her eyes sprung up to look at me. "I agree to it."

"Really?"

"Yep." I kissed her cheek. "As far as I'm concerned, if I'm doing that shit, you should be pointing the gun at me."

She grinned and then her grin fell.

"What's wrong?" I said watching her grin of delight going to unsure within a second.

"You didn't answer my question." She chewed on her bottom lip. "How many girls are an exception to that rule?"

"I told you the only woman I trust is you."

"I didn't ask that," she snapped. "I asked how many women you have a connection with; like you did with Mai. You dropped

393

everything for her." She sighed. "Even me." She went and pushed herself off me, and I gripped her, forcing her to stay put.

"I trusted Mai. That was it; and she has paid the price of breaking my trust." I stopped her from getting off me again. The subject of Mai brought back bad memories for me, so I was sure it was bringing up bad memories for her as well. "So, the answer to your question is zero. I don't have a connection, or whatever Cole called it, with any other woman."

Amber looked me back in the eye, "So, there is no exception to the rule?"

"The only woman I want is you." My eyes dropped to her side, seeing my name tattooed right there.

"Can I tell you something?" she sounded sheepish, so I looked back at her. I read her expression; she had done something.

"What did you do?" I sighed.

"I may have made a call," she smiled, "and got Mai's connections cut."

"How could you, when I did that?"

"What? You banned her from the club?" Amber said, slightly alarmed. Like I wouldn't do that.

I nodded my head. "Not to mention what else I did." I had made it my mission to make sure Mai suffered for what she had done. She'd cost me Amber.

"Well, I got Grant to cut his own daughter off," she said smugly. "He didn't have a heart attack by the way."

"Yeah, Mai spat that out after you left."

"Yeah, well I actually was worried about Grant so I called and told him what happened."

"I see you called him, but wouldn't call me." It still bugged me that she hadn't picked up my phone calls that night. If she had, I could have explained what had happened. Could have started begging for her to take me back then, starting that night.

"You didn't want me then."

"I called you an endless number of times that night Amber. You never picked up."

She frowned. "I've learned you can't change the past, but you can change the future." She linked her hands with mine. "So, how about we leave the past where it is. I won't bring Mai up again, if you don't."

I liked the idea of that. I nodded my head. "We'll focus on our future." I loved the idea of having a future with her. I smirked. "New rule. You answer every one of my phone calls."

"That might be hard!"

"Another rule. If you have a problem, you come to me, not your brothers."

"Again, that's going to be hard!" She pulled her eyebrows together. "Why are you making such hard rules?"

"How's not going to your brothers when you need help hard?"

"Well, I don't go to them to begin with," she said, and from the tone of her voice, she thought I was threatening her relationship with them.

"You let them handle your problem with Blake. That should have been a problem you were telling me."

"Well, you weren't my boyfriend this morning and that rule didn't exist," she said smugly, and leaned forward, quickly kissing my lips. "So I get out of that one."

"Fine, but from now on?"

"I come to you." She rolled her eyes.

"Repeat that."

"I come to you!" She did just as she was told. "Happy?" Both her manicured eyebrows arched up.

"Nearly, but I have more rules."

She sighed. "I'm going to regret ever saying I'd follow anything, aren't I?'

"You only answer to me. No-one else."

"I like that one," she smiled.

"I'm in control," I said.

"Well, that one didn't need to be a rule." She rolled her eyes. "You're always in control Jax."

"When it comes to sex, and everything else, my word is law. Understand?"

She nodded her head.

Now to the fun rules. "Every time we have sex, you come a mandatory of twice."

"Is this shower sex, or bedroom sex, or a quickie?"

"Whenever we have sex. I don't stop until you come at least twice."

"You can't have that rule!"

"You said you would follow any rule I set," I smirked. She was really going to regret saying that.

"Yeah, I did say that." She nodded her head. "Fine. You can have me coming twice. IF you can get me there."

"I'll get you there." My hands paused on the back of her bra. "You tired still?"

She shook her head. "Why?"

I unclipped her bra, giving her a clue to what I was thinking.

She threaded her arms out of it and dropped it on the floor. My eyes were glued to her. God, she was perfect. I had never loved a pair of breasts more than hers.

"New rule. You sleep topless." I flipped her over, seeing her smile. "Every night," I added.

"What if you aren't with me?"

"I'll always be with you."

"What if you are on a run or crash at the clubhouse for a night?"

"You'll be coming, and I won't be. Cause one of the rules is we make love every night."

"You really enjoying fucking me that much?" She looked at me like it was impossible.

My hands started to pull her G-string off. "Every night, I want a good dose of you and we don't stop until I say so." I would never get enough of her. Every night I wanted her. "Naked and in my bed, every night."

"Our bed," she corrected me.

I nodded my head. I'd never shared a bed with someone before. "Our bed." I kissed down her neck.

"I don't know how my brothers will feel about you moving in," she mumbled, her eyes closed as I slowly kissed down her body. She was enjoying this, and that is exactly what I wanted. I wanted her to enjoy me touching her.

"Couldn't give a fuck how they feel about it," I said in between kissing over her breast.

"It is their house."

"If it really is a problem, I'll just buy a house and you can move in with me."

Her eyes went wide. "Wait, did you just say move in with you?"

"What's wrong with that?" I frowned, seeing her startled expression.

"We've been back together for a matter of an hour and you want me to move in with you?" She said it slowly, like I was stupid or had said it by mistake.

I nodded my head and stopped kissing her. "So, if your brothers really have a problem, you'll move out?"

She looked at me gobsmacked. "You are serious?"

"Come, Amber, what's the difference between me moving in here and us getting a place?"

"Nothing, I guess." The startled expression slowly eased on her face. "I guess I just didn't expect you to want that. Crashing here is one thing, moving in with you, well, that's a bit more serious."

Actually, when she said it like that... "You're moving out." I wanted serious. Her moving into a house I owned. I wanted that. "I'll give you a few months here while you pick a house, but that's it."

Her mouth dropped open. "Pick a house!"

"I want you happy."

"I'll be happy here."

"Let me re-phrase that. I want you happy in our house. A house you've picked." I went back to kissing her. "Say yes sweetheart."

"I, um, well…"

"Just yes, Amber. You'll pick a house." I wanted her to relax again and close her eyes, but I don't think she was going to do that until we sorted the house issue. "You have a month to pick and a month to move out" I said, making the decision for her.

She opened her mouth to argue, but sighed. "You really want that? Me living in your house?"

"Yes, and it will be our house."

"I guess I don't get an option." She smiled. "Because of the rule that says you are always in control and your word is law." She arched an eyebrow at me.

I smirked. "Good girl." I went back to kissing her, "Now, I want you to relax."

"I don't relax."

"You did before."

"My guard slipped. Won't happen again."

"Amber," I said her name as a warning. If she wanted me to tell her off, I would. "Relax."

For some reason, I had a feeling that was the last thing she had been doing. She hadn't been taking care of herself and I was going to correct that, starting now.

I pulled my boxers off and moved in between her legs. I was going to take her slow, at first. "You still on contraception?" I asked, hovering near her; one push and I'd be in her.

"Injection." She opened her eyes. "You still not fucking randoms not shielded?"

"I haven't been with anyone since you."

She frowned. "That's impossible."

I shook my head. "I told you I love you. Every woman they threw my way, I just pushed away."

"Who threw your way?"

"Your brothers."

Her face melted in understanding. "Well, I'm still on the injection so we are safe."

"Two years."

She frowned. "What?"

"In two years you stop it."

"The injection?"

"Yep. I want you having my kids and in two years, I think we'll be ready."

She looked at me in shock. "Are we seriously talking about kids now? First, we are moving in together and now you are telling me in two years you want to have children with me?"

"I want to have as many children as I can with you." I was about to thrust into her, but first, we had to agree. "Two years, you stop all contraception?"

"You want to have children with me?" She repeated herself like she hadn't heard what I'd just said.

"As many as I can."

"You are serious." Finally, she'd picked up on it.

I kissed her lips quickly "Two years?"

"I'll be twenty."

"Perfect age." I kissed the top of her breast, wanting nothing more than to push into her.

She looked me in the eye; I was serious, she knew that now. She nodded her head. "Ok, two years." She took a staggered breath in. "Next, you'll be proposing."

I smirked. I was going to propose to her, but not tonight. I needed to get her the perfect ring. Something made just for her finger. Yeah, the jeweler was going to love seeing me and the amount of money I was going to throw down to make sure it was one of a kind.

"You ready sweetheart?" I kissed her cheek and she slowly nodded her head. I pushed into her slowly, in no hurry. We had all night.

God, she was warm. I knew every curve of her body as my hand explored her again. Her breasts were made for me. I locked my lips at the base of her neck. Sucking on her, I started to pick up speed.

She was meeting every thrust; even though she was running on no sleep, she was enjoying this, nearly as much as me.

"You ok?" I pulled my mouth off her neck; she had her eyes shut and was doing what she said she didn't do - relaxing.

"With you, I am." The words just coming off her lips. I knew it was the truth as soon as she said it; I could hear it in her tone.

"You happy if I pick up the speed?" I said, not automatically doing it. I was happy to go slow with her. Her body was exhausted, and I had to factor that in. She had traveled nearly twenty hours and, from the looks of it before that, she hadn't exactly been resting.

Her eyes opened and the sweetest smile spread across her face. "You're in control, remember?"

"You aren't too tired?"

Her lips parted just as I thrust into her harder. "No, not now. Fuck me like you are never going to again."

"That's never going to happen." I was never letting her go again. Her days of traveling overseas were over but if she wanted it hard, I'd give it to her hard so I started to thrust into her harder. Watching her face as her lips twitched up, I knew she was getting exactly what she wanted.

"You like that sweetheart?" I went in deeper; the whole going slow thing disappeared now. I wanted her panting. I wanted her coming. I needed to hear her moan my name. I kept going deeper into her; faster. I could feel her clenching around me. She was close, and seeing her face, I decided on a new rule.

"Another rule," I said as I thrust into her, "You come when you're told." I could feel she was so bloody close. "Like now!" I growled.

"I can't." She was out of breath, her back arching. "I can't," she repeated.

"You can!" I thrust harder into her, feeling her slowly clench around me. She was ready to burst. I just had to get her over the edge. "And when you come, you say my name."

I increased our speed, knowing what she needed. I felt her walls clench around me, her face melt in pleasure; I'd got her there. My name coming off her lips as she finished. She was breathing sharply, her arms locked around my neck.

"Good girl sweetheart." I kissed her forehead. "That is exactly what I wanted." Every night. I wanted to see that look on her face, and hear her say my name as she came.

"I don't think I can do that again," she said, out of breath, basically still trembling around me.

"Yes you can sweetheart. You're going to be doing it again in a few minutes." I was going to make her come over and over again. I started picking up my pace, seeing she was recovering. I didn't want her to recover completely. She was sensitive; I knew that as my hand slid off her breast and between her legs.

"No…" her hand shot out, as if she knew what I was going to do. "I can't take any more."

"Do I have to remind you of the rule that says I'm in control?" I growled. I thrust into her deeper for defying me and she moaned, loving everything I was giving her. "You're mine, remember?" I gave it to her harder.

She took her hand off mine. "You're going to kill me."

My fingers explored her sensitive skin, and she arched her back as soon as I touched her. I smirked. She was going to come again, whether she wanted to or not. I could read her body. I knew when to tell her to come. Like right now, as she started to shake.

"Come on sweetheart, open that mouth of yours." I kissed her clamped lips. She was keeping it all built up. "You ready sweetheart?"

She shook her head.

But her body was ready. A few sharp pumps, and she would explode again.

I picked up my pace, "Come Amber."

She shook her head, fighting it.

I thrust into her harder, feeling her walls clenching. "Start moaning, or I'll drag it out." I took her nipple in my mouth and my

401

warning didn't fall on deaf ears; she moaned as soon as my mouth touched her. "You ready sweetheart?"

She nodded her head, breathing sharply. "Just don't make me wait any longer."

She was waiting for me to tell her she could. I smirked. She really did listen. When she wanted to. "Come for me," I whispered in her ear, and I felt her tremble around me again, bringing her forehead to mine, as she panted and my name came off her lips again. "I'm never going to get sick of hearing you come or seeing you come."

"You're going to kill me. Remind me again how many times is mandatory?"

"Twice." I kissed her lips. "But, tonight, we are going for three."

She groaned. "Can't you be happy you got me there twice?"

"I want to set a good record. One I can try and beat every night."

"This! Every night!"

I smirked. "Yeah, sweetheart. Every night." I pulled out of her and flipped her over. She was on her knees when I entered her again. "Now, are we going to set a good record, for our first night back together?"

"One to really mark our relationship starting again?" She kneeled, sitting up, and I placed my hands over her breasts.

"Yeah, one that is memorable."

"I think three would be a benchmark." She turned to look at me, with a smirk on her face. "But I want to know what your personal best is."

"Oh sweetheart you shouldn't have challenged me. You're going to regret that." I picked up my speed, easing her down, my hand running up her back.

"I think I already am," she said through gritted teeth.

I kissed her shoulder. "I'm aiming for six."

She groaned. "God, that isn't possible."

"Now you come when I say, and you say what?" I said, picking up speed again.

402

"Your name," she said, getting breathless.

"Which is?"

"Jax."

"I want to hear it louder this time." I didn't just want her moaning it, I wanted her screaming it.

"What if someone hears?" She said that like it would be a terrible thing. She also said that like that was the reason she had been keeping her mouth clamped shut.

"I don't give a fuck. Now I want to hear it louder."

"You really want everyone to know you are fucking me?"

"Yes." My fingers started to tease her nipples. "I want you screaming Amber."

"You'll have to make me."

"Awe sweetheart, you shouldn't have said that." I laughed; she was going to regret that. She really shouldn't be setting me challenges.

Chapter 48

Amber

I don't know how long I slept for, but it felt like a lifetime. I dragged myself out of bed. I wasn't even mildly surprised to not see Jax here. I think I had slept most of the day away and I couldn't even check the time because my phone was downstairs.

Last night. The memories hit me hard and fast. It was unexplainable. I didn't expect Jax to keep one word he said last night.

I pulled on my sports crop top and shorts. Yep, no way he would be thinking the same today. I walked out of the bedroom with my headphones.

I jogged down the stairs.

"And what do you know, she is awake," Adam greeted me at the bottom of the stairs and then frowned at me. "Are you about to do exercise?"

"Yeah, morning run, it's my routine." I walked around him and headed for the couch.

"It's after four in the afternoon," Adam said, and I shrugged; so much for a morning run. Well, an afternoon run was just as good.

"That thing hasn't shut up," Cole pointed to my phone like it had been annoying him.

"You could have turned it off or woken me."

He scoffed. "Not according to the King."

"What's that meant to mean?" I looked between them.

"Jax wanted to make sure you slept. He also wanted me to tell you he had to leave but will be back." Adam rolled his eyes. "He acted like it was life or death that you knew where he was."

"More like our lives depended on her getting his message," Cole snapped. "Guessing you two are back together?"

"I'm not answering that, but I am going for a run." I backed out of the room.

"It's the middle of the afternoon and it is hot out there."

"I can take the heat." I gave them a firm smile. "Now I'm going for that run."

"You used to be allergic to exercise." Cole crossed his arms. "What changed?"

"Tae got me into it. It's meant to help with my temper," I explained, and lit up my phone; numerous missed calls from Tae. He was the only one that had my new number.

"I'll message you my new number," I said to Cole and Adam, but was more focused on Tae's messages. He needed me. "Maybe that run will have to wait," I mumbled. I was being summoned.

"So, who are you with? Tae or Jax?" Adam asked, sounding hopeful for the latter.

Why had he always supported Jax and I?

"I don't know." After last night, I didn't know if Jax had been serious, or if he had just missed me enough to make all those promises; like repeating he loved me and each time he did, it knocked down one of my walls.

It made something start beating again, that I had thought was dead - my heart, but if he was the one to help me get my heart back, he would also have the power to destroy it again.

Leave me like this again. A barely functioning, autopilot machine, but last night I hadn't been on autopilot; no, he brought out a side to me I thought was dead.

He gave me faith again.

"I thought you were going for a run?" Adam asked as I headed for the stairs.

"Can't. Tae needs me." I walked up the stairs and then paused. "Can you pass on my new number to everyone?" I gave a pointed look to Cole. "Including Jax."

"What is with you, taking him back?" Cole barked at me and walked to the bottom of the stairs. "He isn't faithful. He will never love you and you can do better!"

I knew all these things. I didn't need him reminding me of them.

"I know all those facts." I walked up the stairs and Cole decided he would follow me.

"He will always put the club first." Cole wasn't going to give up. "You will always come second. No sister of mine is a man's second thought! You need to come first Amber." He followed me into the bedroom, his arm wrapping my upper arm. "Don't go back to him."

Didn't he get it? Didn't anyone get it? I didn't get a choice! I don't know why. I couldn't explain it if I wanted to, but Jax pulled me in. Everything about him. He had me. I used to think Blake was the love of my life. Well I learned I was wrong.

Jax was the love of my life. He was the only man that ever made me feel like this. He broke my heart to pieces; to the point I still wasn't sure if I had a beating heart.

But here I was, up and willing to fix what I had left with him.

"I need to get changed. I have to go see Tae," I said, opening my suitcase. I had left most of my things in England because there was one fact I had left out with Jax. Tae wanted me.

He had groomed me to take over here, but I think his feelings of respect and admiration grew into something more.

"Tae seems like a good guy, why not pick him? Or any man apart from Jax?" Cole said, not giving up.

"Tae is a good guy but if you really knew him, you wouldn't be pushing me to him."

Cole crossed his arms. "Is he dangerous?"

"Yes." That was putting it mildly. "I think more dangerous than Jax."

"How can a software designer be more dangerous than the King of the underworld?" Adam asked, walking into the bedroom and then sitting on my bed.

I groaned. Looks like they both weren't going to give up.

"It's a front. Look I have to change." I ran a hand through my hair. "Come on guys. I need to go. Do you have a car I can borrow?"

Cole didn't look like he was giving in. "When you get back, will you explain what you mean about Tae being dangerous?"

"I literally can't."

"Why?"

"Because he could have me killed. That's the type of serious it is Cole. I would get a hit on my head if I shared one detail about him."

"Like we would let that happen." Adam said getting up. "We can protect you from everything."

"This, no-one can protect me from. You can't protect me from the walking dead." The walking dead is what we called silent killers. I was part of the walking dead. Tae had trained me to be part of his silent killers.

I knew what I was a part of so I knew they couldn't protect me from Tae if he wanted me dead.

So I couldn't tell them who Tae really was and I could never tell them what I was involved in.

My phone started ringing and I cursed. "Seriously, he is going to be pissed off." I mumbled and put it to my ear. "Sorry Tae, I took a sleeping pill and was knocked out. I'm up and coming."

"Ten minutes Amber," he said, buying my excuse, and hung up.

"I have ten minutes and if you don't want to be going to my funeral, you will let me change," I said firmly, planting a hand on my hip.

Adam sighed and left. Cole on the other hand, lingered.

"I want your new number," he said firmly.

"I told you I'd give it to you and I need you to pass it on to everyone else." I unlocked my phone and, knowing his number by heart, I sent him a message. "And when I say everyone, I mean Jax as well."

He nodded his head. "Fine."

"Thank you." I waited for him to close my door and then I started to change. Time to face Tae. I knew he would be upset that I didn't go to his house last night and canceled our dinner plans. I had told him my brothers wanted to spend time with me.

I wasn't sure what excuse I could come up with today to leave him.

Then I knew I shouldn't be pulling away from him just because I'd spent one night with Jax. Tae and what he wants should still be coming first and I should be at his house. I shouldn't be living on the high of what Jax had promised last night.

I needed to come back to earth and I had a feeling I would hit earth hard as soon as I saw Jax again and he went back to being cold.

Last night he was just overcome with seeing me again. Yep. That had to be it. It was the only way to explain his behavior. He would have changed his mind by this morning.

***

"I don't like trusting them."

Tae was behind a desk, blowing out a mouthful of smoke. "Bikers can never be trusted."

"Last night went smoothly." I inhaled on my cigarette. It was the only thing Tae and I always did when we had a discussion - we smoked and drank whiskey, although this afternoon it was vodka. He said it was all that was in the house.

He nodded his head. "Smoothly enough for me to consider something."

"That being?"

"You come back to England with me."

My eyes widened. I knew we were going to get to this topic. "You have been grooming me to take over here. Why would you need me in the same country as you? You are more than capable of handling things in England."

"You're strong, Amber," he complimented me, his eyes holding mine. "Strong enough to lead beside me, not under me."

I gulped. Right, we were going to do this. "I don't do relationships."

I had told him that line every time we talked about the lack of men in my life. The fact that I'd never slept with or showed interest in men.

"Lead beside me Amber." He rose and walked around the desk. "I know you say you don't have a heart. I respect that. It makes you great at what you do." He came to a stop in front of me. "I wouldn't just pick anyone to lead with me."

I had to make a logical decision but first, I had to get facts. "So, what are you offering me?"

"A partnership."

"You actually want to share your empire with me?" I didn't believe him. Tae didn't share. He took everything and held it close; with a death grip.

"I want to grow it and you can help me do that." He kneeled down in front of me. His eyes locked with mine. "A partnership." The corners of his lips twitched up. "If we cross the line into sex, I'll be happy, but we can just keep it at business."

Business. No emotion. That was perfect for me. "And you want me in England?"

"I want you with me. Yes, but if we are doing strictly business, we should think about what benefits you would have by staying here." His hand ran up my leg. "Like this deal the bikers are offering, is it worth our time? You being permanently here to oversee it?"

He looked torn, like the last thing he wanted was me in a different country than him.

I smiled. "Tae, you are making me think you enjoyed me annoying you for the past month."

He smiled. "Here I was thinking I could keep that fact to myself."

"You like me being around," I grinned. "You like my annoying questions. You like it when I miss my target practice on purpose."

His eyes narrowed. "I'm not saying I liked you wasting my time."

"You're going to miss our Friday nights, aren't you?" I couldn't stop the grin.

"No."

"Yes you are. You are going to miss me raiding your liquor!"

"I will not miss the empty bottles. Only you would think it was acceptable to empty a bottle and leave it."

"And you will miss me."

He sighed. "Anyway, I know this is a big decision for you." He got back on the topic I had taken us off. "Which is why I'm willing for you to discuss it with your brothers."

My face was in disbelief. "In order for that to happen, I'd have to tell them who you really are."

"I'm giving you permission to do so," he nodded.

"Really?"

"You mean a lot to me, Amber. I trust you, which means I trust your family. So yes, you can tell them who I am and you can tell them what I am offering."

I was stunned. Literally, could not form words; stunned. Tae was secretive. Hell, he kept such a low profile, his main man couldn't even pick Tae in a line up. He did that on purpose and the only reason I knew who he was, was because he broke his silence to recruit me.

He wanted me that bad. He blew his cover and, right now, as he stared at me watching me think, he was willing to blow his cover again - for me.

Tae had never broken my heart because I'd told him I didn't have one for him to break to begin with, but Tae had given me this endless amount of trust.

He trusted me.

"Ok." I said. "I'll umm, talk to Troy about it," I found myself saying.

Troy. He would be the one to go to. Cole wasn't level-headed enough. Tyler was too carefree. Adam would be too concerned.

And Jax wasn't my brother, so he didn't make the cut.

"Good. And I've been thinking of a way to mark our partnership and a way to prove to you I'm serious about you leading beside me."

He wanted me to lead beside me. That still just blew my mind. I was never considered equal. I was always under someone. Never in charge.

"Amber?"

My eyes snapped to him. "Yeah?"

"I have an idea on a way to mark our partnership."

"Ok?" I staggered out, trying to think straight. He was offering me an opportunity anyone in the underworld would kill for. "What?"

"We take out The Pythons."

My mouth dropped open. "But you don't do wars."

"I said we take them out. I have no plan of starting a war; just wiping them out of the country." He stood up. "I've done the numbers. We are more than capable to do this."

"You would let me use your men to take out my enemy?"

"Our men," he corrected me. "And yes."

"Wipe them out," I muttered. I wouldn't just be doing something I've wanted to do since they'd marked me, ruining my body, but I would also be doing my brothers and Jax a favor; they were still at war with them.

I started to think of the facts. This was too good to be true.

"So, if I say yes, I get to take them out?" I asked, trying to see how sweet the deal was. He was tempting me just to say yes now. Wiping out The Pythons was something I really wanted to do.

"I thought we could move on it tomorrow." He shrugged and smiled. "Take marking our partnership early as my good faith in you."

"You're serious?"

"Their Mother Charter is having their family BBQ tomorrow. Most charters are coming in for it. So, we should be able to wipe most of them out quickly."

This was Tae, always thinking ahead. He didn't want a bloody, long, drawn out war. He wanted to do what he always did - set target, and kill and then move on to the next.

"I watched you get that mark tattooed Amber so I know you want this." Tae lit up another cigarette and then handed it to me. "So, even if we wipe them out and you decide to turn me down on my offer, no hard feelings."

I took the cigarette. "No hard feelings," I repeated his words, with emptiness and shock.

"Talk to your brother and then get back to me about whether you want to make a move on The Pythons or not."

I shook my head. "I don't need to talk to Troy for this decision. The answer is yes. You have me completely on board for wiping them out."

He smirked. "Good, cause I was counting on your aim to take those headshots you are famous for."

I smiled, and nodded my head. He had me on board for this. I didn't know about the partnership; I needed advice on that, and not a lawyer's advice, but advice from someone else that had been offered a permanent role in the underworld and taken it.

Troy.

Because I couldn't turn to Jax on this one.

Chapter 49

It was late when I pulled into the driveway. Tae and I planned tomorrow right down to the fine details; researched where we would set up and got the perfect spots from high ground. Their clubhouse was in the middle of rural land, with lots of trees and hills.

So we had plenty of great spots to pick from.

Tae's men were already camping out and setting up. We were wiping them out as soon as their yard was filled with members and their party was in full swing.

I knew there would be children there; and women, but sometimes you have to weigh the odds which was something I needed to do now with Troy's help.

I opened the front door, hearing them from outside.

The boys had set up in the lounge, and were watching football. They glanced at me, but their attention was on the football.

"Jax has been tied up with something at the club," Adam said, his eyes on the television. "He would have called you, but he can't. He said he will be back here tonight."

"Right." My eyes were on Troy as he reached for his beer. "Troy, I need to speak to you." And all eyes snapped to me. They knew I always turned to Troy if I was in serious trouble or needed serious advice.

"What have you done?" Cole's eyes were off the television and on me.

"Nothing. I just need to speak to Troy."

"Well, go on then, he is listening," Cole said smugly, knowing very well I wanted to talk to Troy in private. He was going to make me say it, wasn't he?

"I need to speak to him in private", I said, being forced to. I rarely turned to Troy in my adult life. When they had left, so had my ability to rely on him.

But when I was younger and he was around; when things got serious, when things got hard, when I got in trouble - I turned to Troy.

And that was what I was finding myself doing now.

Troy got up and told the boys to stop bickering. I followed him out of the lounge and up the stairs.

"Guessing you don't want to be overheard?" he said over his shoulder.

"You're right."

He cracked open his bedroom door and then held it open for me.

"They wouldn't dare come up here if they want to keep breathing," Troy said, and gestured for me to head in.

So, how do I go about this? How could I say that one very large underworld figure wanted to go into a partnership with me? That he wanted to share his business with me? His men? His money? Everything? He basically was offering me everything he had.

As if we were entering into marriage.

Troy sat down on the edge of the bed next to me, and I suddenly felt more nervous.

"Ok Amber, you have my attention. Tell me what's wrong," he said calmly, like he had all the answers to my problems.

Ok… time to explain my situation.

***

Troy stayed quiet as I told him everything. Every detail. Starting with who Tae was and then everything else just tumbled out somehow.

I had just finished telling him about the partnership, and I was waiting for his words of wisdom. God, I needed him to say something! Not just prompt me to keep going and explaining.

"So, Jax knows?" Troy finally said something!

"He knew I was working for Tae, yes."

"Explains our gun deal and why he was so firm on it." Troy dragged his hands down his face and sighed. "Well, have you told him about the partnership?"

"Tae said I could tell my brothers. When it comes to Tae, a detail like that is important."

"So, you aren't going to tell him?"

Why was he so focused on whether I told Jax or not? "Why does it matter if he knows?"

"Because he loves you," Troy said matter of factly. "More than I thought he was capable of."

I swallowed hard. Hearing Troy say he thought Jax really loved me, well that had my head spinning for a second. "Still doesn't impact the decision." I tied my hair up.

"Tae is basically offering you marriage, Amber."

"It's a partnership, not marriage."

"You told him you didn't do relationships?" Troy said, arching an eyebrow at me.

"Yes."

"This is Tae's way of getting you to be his wife, without being his wife. This is his way of locking you down on his terms."

I didn't think of it like that. "He said it was just business."

He scoffed. "It isn't business and a man like him doesn't just offer a deal like that. Unless..."

"Unless what?"

Troy looked me in the eye. "Unless he is in love with you." He groaned. "Why do you attract bad men!"

"I really don't know." I was dumbfounded. I had no idea why I seemed to always fall in love with men that had the power to hurt me, but I didn't love Tae, did I?

415

I respected him. I admired everything he had done. I looked up to him, but had our closeness turned into something more? Was Troy right when he said this was Tae's way of locking me down to be his?

"So, what do I do?" Right now I needed to be told what to do. "Tae said I can go back with him and lead, or stay here. I think he knows it nearly killed me, being away from you lot."

"Would he stay if you did?"

"I don't know. I think he would travel back here more if I was here." I spoke the truth of what I thought of the situation. I could see Tae's business trips here increasing if I was here. I don't know why I thought that... I just did.

"Well, he is the first man to put you as equal. You should factor that in before you make a decision."

I nodded my head.

"And tell Jax, Amber."

My eyes snapped up. I couldn't do that. If I looked at mine and Jax's relationship logically, considering our history and how he'd behaved; well, with no emotion, it made sense for me to take this opportunity with Tae and wipe Jax out completely.

"It makes more sense to leave with Tae than it does to stay." I found myself speaking my thoughts out loud. It did make more sense to leave if I put how I felt about Jax aside. If I could think clearly; make a logical decision.

"You never do what makes sense." Troy gave me a pointed look. "Talk to Jax. I think he will help you make a decision."

"I really didn't want to rely on him," I sighed and almost groaned. "He will just yell at me."

"Nah, I don't think he will Amber. If anything, he will be begging."

"Begging?"

"For you to not marry Tae."

I couldn't stop my eyes from rolling. "I'm not marrying him."

"You are. What he is offering is marriage. Maybe even more serious than marriage, considering his position." Troy's hand landed on my knee. "Sorry I couldn't help you."

My lips twitched into a smile. If there was one thing Troy always did, it was help. "You did help."

"If it makes any difference, I never wanted you to have this lifestyle."

"I was dragged into it." I shrugged. "And now it is all I know."

And that was the cold hard truth. I wasn't the girl who flinched at blood. I wasn't the girl that had the captain of the football team following her around. Instead, I had one man who was considered the King of the underworld saying he loved me, and, on the other hand, I had a man whose name struck fear in people, offering me a life with him.

So, who would I pick?

Tae or Jax.

Or should I do the cop out and take Tae's business offer and stay here and keep a relationship with Jax?

But, for some reason, that felt like I was betraying Tae.

God! Why could I never just have a normal problem! Like should I wear my hair curly or straight? Or should I wear makeup today or not?

I groaned and fell back on Troy's bed. "Why does life have to be so hard?"

I heard him laugh but I knew, as much as I wanted Troy to fix the problem, to tell me which choice to make Tae or Jax, he couldn't. It was a decision I was going to have to make on my own.

Jax

All fucking day. All fucking day I was dealing with bickering bikers about money! All complaining that they hadn't got their share as soon as the deal had been settled. Then when I finally sorted that out, a fight broke out about why I wasn't telling them whom we'd sold to.

I didn't have to give them answers.

Still, that caused an almighty argument and fight. Troy got pissed off and left, leaving me to deal with the backlash of the other President's shit.

I think it was his way of paying me back for forcing him to do my work, as well as his, for the last month.

I walked up the hall. All I wanted to do was be with Amber. Cole passed on her new number, but I literally hadn't even had a minute spare to call her.

I frowned, seeing light under her door. It was after five in the morning. Why would she be up?

I opened the door and I had been so quiet, she hadn't even realized. Her eyes were glued to a map in front of her, which, by the looks of it, was covered in maths.

"You're up late?"

Her head snapped up; she looked slightly shocked.

"What has your attention?" I walked towards the bed that she had covered in figures.

"Um, nothing of importance."

"It looks important." Then my eyes hardened as I watched her pick up her work. "Why are you doing maths?"

I knew why she was. I knew why she had taken such a liking to it; because she needed it for making good headshots.

I pointed a finger at her. "I told you, no more killing." It wasn't happening, not on my watch. Her days of taking people out were over. I was going to make sure of it. If she really had a problem with someone, I'd handle it.

"We need to talk," she said seriously, ignoring my question and pushing her notes aside.

Alarm bells were now going off. Something had happened. Something serious, and she was only about to tell me now.

"Why the hell didn't you call me if something serious was happening?" I snapped at her, annoyed. If something was going on that involved her calculating headshots, I should've bloody well known.

418

She picked up her cigarette from the ashtray. "I didn't have your number."

Oh.

"You could have got it off the boys."

"You were busy."

I was positive she was going to make up every excuse possible to justify why she was only now bringing something serious to my attention.

"Well, what's wrong?" I said, walking towards her.

She crossed her legs, looking all sorts of worried. "Nothing's wrong. We just need to talk."

"About last night?" She had to know I'd meant everything I'd said, and I wasn't taking any of it back. I loved her. I wanted to spend the rest of my life with her, but if she had questions or doubts, I'd somehow ease them.

"No," she said firmly. "It's about Tae."

"You're done with him." I didn't see how we could have a conversation about something that was over; then I looked at her closer, reading her expression. "Or so I thought." I crossed my arms, waiting for her to explain.

"Tae is offering me a partnership. He wants me to lead beside him. He is offering me..." she frowned, "a relationship without a relationship. The securities of one, yet no emotion."

I knew immediately I was in trouble. She had to be kidding herself right now? He wasn't just offering her a business partnership, he was offering her... him. To be a part of his life. To be equal. To share his responsibilities. There was only one label for that.

"He wants you to be his wife." The bitterness that spread through me at the thought of her being someone else's wife consumed me quickly, washing through my blood.

She nodded her head. "Yeah, basically."

I just stared at her. I was gone a day. ONE DAY! And this is what happens? How many times did I have to tell her I loved her?

Clearly, my love for her wasn't going to be enough. I shoved my hands in my jeans pockets, feeling all types of sick.

"So what are you going to tell him?"

"He is offering me a life with no emotion."

I scoffed. "You're joking, right? As soon as you agree to that partnership, you will end up fucking him!"

"I didn't say no sex. I said no emotion," she said, clearer. "No worrying if he is going to break my heart in the morning. No worrying if he will change his mind. No emotion Jax. He knows me."

"I know you! He knows the distant, cold, side of you!" I waved my hand at her; it was what she was doing right now - being cold and distant. Like she didn't feel a fucking thing.

She met my worried eyes. "He knows what is left of me."

What do I do? Do I argue with her? Point out all the reasons I am the better man? Why I am right for her. Fuck. I ran my hands through my hair. How many times had she been the one to tell me we were perfect together? I wished I hadn't screwed up my one shot with her.

I looked back at her. I didn't need to even hear it. I could see she had made up her mind. She had come to a decision. Her 'talk' with me, was to tell me she was leaving me for someone else.

I thought I was going to be sick.

"Jax?" Her voice was softer, closer. Fuck, when did she get up? She was standing in front of me.

I didn't need to hear it. I knew I had had one shot with her, I had got one chance, and I'd fucked it up. All day I thought I had got her back, and I couldn't believe my luck but it turned out my luck was the same as it had always been – crap!

"You've already made your mind up." I saw the look on her face. Saw the determination. She wasn't making a decision; she had made it and I knew it wasn't me. I was only offering her my heart, he was offering her the world, with no strings. No chances of being hurt.

After what I had done to her, she never wanted to put herself on the line like that again. She would take the no-emotion option but the really sad part was, there would be emotion. She just didn't realize that yet. Slowly, he would get through her walls. Slowly, she would trust him, and, before she knew it, she would be marrying him, for real.

"Is there anything I can say to change your mind?" I panicked. God, if there was a magic word to say right now to change her mind, I would say it, but I watched her shake her head from side to side.

"No-one can talk me out of it."

There went all my chances. No way of talking her out of it. Well, I was fucked. I'd struggled to live without her temporarily, how the hell was I going to manage the rest of my life?

"I love you Amber."

Her face softened. "I know."

Well, there was nothing more I could say or do. Nothing was going to change her mind. She'd said that herself. I didn't even realize I was doing it until her fingers brushed a tear from my cheek. Fucking crying. God, I was weak.

"Jax." She took a step closer to me and her being closer to me was exactly what I didn't need. She opened her mouth, but I cut her off.

"I don't need to hear it." I didn't need to hear how sorry she was. How she was doing the right thing. For both of us. I didn't need to hear that I broke her heart. Or what other twisted reason she was using for breaking it off with me completely. I didn't need to hear it!

Her fingers brushed my cheek again, wiping more tears away. God, why couldn't I stop crying? "I love you Jax."

"Yeah, I get it, but you want what he is offering." I got it. My one shot with her was over. I'd lost her. Losing her, well I wasn't sure how I was going to live with that.

She shook her head. "I've already said no to Tae." She wiped more tears away.

I frowned immediately. "But you said you'd made up your mind."

She smiled "Yeah, to be with you." She said it like it should have been obvious.

"To be with me?" I didn't believe it. She said she'd made up her mind. I watched her nod her head.

"Is that so hard to believe?"

"He is offering you a hell of a lot more." Was she even thinking clearly? Had she even had a solid night's sleep to be in the state of mind to be making this decision?

She arched her eyebrows at me, standing confidently in front of me. "You trying to change my mind?"

"I just don't understand..." I thought I'd lost her. Now I was just confused.

She smiled and went up on her toes. "I don't love him." There was love in her eyes. I never thought she would be looking at me with love. "But I do love you, so how are we going to break it to my brothers that I'm moving out?"

I was stunned. So stunned I wasn't speaking. So she just stood there smiling. Waiting for it all to sink in. And it did. It took me a minute, and then I grinned and wrapped my arms around her, bringing her to me.

"We need a house first."

"I've already picked one."

"What?" I pulled her back to look at her face; she was grinning and actually looking happy. "You have?"

"Yeah, Cole may have made a remark about my sex life and I snapped." She shrugged. "I don't want anyone, ever, overhearing us, especially not Cole." She suppressed a smirk, "cause he might kill you."

I started to back her towards the bed. "Don't think I can take him?"

"I'm just saying you wouldn't have it in you to kill someone related to me."

"Thinking a lot of yourself again."

422

Her legs hit the end of the bed and I gripped her hips quickly, spinning her around. Sitting on the bed, I pulled her onto my lap.

"I'm just saying I'm very loveable." She grinned at me, sitting on me. Like her old self. I loved watching her like this.

I linked my hand with hers. "Yeah, you are." And I kissed her cheek. "So, you're still mine?" I was slowly coming to grips with the fact she wasn't bolting, even when given the perfect opportunity to.

She leaned her forehead against mine. "Always Jax, even when you don't want me."

"I'll always want you."

Always, for the rest of my life, I would want her. A smirk spread across my lips. I repositioned her on me, so she was straddling me. My hands pushed her skirt up, until it was around her waist.

"Jax, everyone will be getting up soon. We can't do what you are thinking."

The smirk was still on my face. "I don't care if they hear."

"I DO!"

"I have my personal best to beat." My hands pushed her t-shirt up.

"I still can't believe you got to seven."

"We will aim for eight tonight."

"It's morning, and no." She looked at me like she wasn't going to let me.

"Do I have to remind you of the rules?" I took her top off.

"But it's morning, and the rule says every night."

"I missed last night."

"God forbid." She rolled her eyes, and linked her arms around my neck as I fell back on the bed, with her on top of me.

"I know, think I'm hard done by."

"Yeah, you would. Ok we can, but if one of the boys comes looking for me, we stop." She was saying that like I would.

I smirked. "Whatever you say sweetheart."

423

Chapter 50

One Year Later.

Amber

I always knew my past would haunt me. I always knew my mistakes would frame my life. Hell, my dad had told me that on repeat.

He always said, "what you do now will frame your life." And then he would give me that cold, chiseled look of his.

And right now, his words were repeating in my head.

My mistakes. My past. They were haunting my future. Hell, I didn't even have a future now because how could I have a future without Jax?

I walked into the prison. It was my fault he was in here. My stupid charges! I could have faced them; I didn't need him jumping on the grenade life had thrown my way.

All the shit I had done with the TNS had caught up with me. It was my grenade. It was my fault Jax had organized that gun deal with them, and that same gun deal had been watched. TNS got caught with the guns, and who was in charge of the whole thing. Me.

So people talked which led the police to me. I had a lawyer. I was ready to plead guilty and what does my stupid idiotic fiancé do? Hand's himself in for being the supplier, on the condition that my charges were wiped.

What was worse was that he did it behind my back. He organized the whole thing, between lawyers! Even my brothers didn't know he had done it. No-one did.

One night I went to sleep beside him, ready to face my charges in the morning, and the next day I woke up alone, with missed calls from my lawyer.

I had never been, nor will ever be as furious as I was when I'd found out. Nearly as furious as I was now, going to visit him.

Three months. That's how long it had been since I'd woken up in that bed alone with questions - all of which were answered when I picked up one phone call from my lawyer. He was lucky he was already getting moved to a prison because I could have killed him.

I should have known he was up to something; the way he was acting. Taking me going to prison way too calmly. I should have picked up on it, especially the way we had sex that night, I should have picked up on it. I scoffed while waiting at the prison door. I was left with another reminder of that night.

I was pregnant. Three months, and I couldn't hide it much longer. Maybe another month, but then people would know.

I wouldn't have to tell them.

So, right now, as the guard swiped open the door to the private visiting room, where I knew Jax was waiting, I was nervous.

The guard held the door open for me. Right, I was meant to walk in now, and say what? How do you tell someone you love, that they were about to waste six years of their life because of you?

Because that's how long he got. Six years. SIX FUCKING YEARS! And that was them going easy on him.

I was facing three. Three! I could have done the time! I would have done it. Instead, I was going to have to watch him waste six years of his life, all because of me!

How the hell was that fair?

How the hell was I going to live with that? Why would he do that to me? He wasn't saving me. And if he thought that was what he had done, he was wrong.

I walked into the room, and there he was.

I knew what he was going to do, so I was going to do him the favor.

"So, have you come up with hurtful comments?" I said as the door closed, and I looked him in the eyes. "I at least thought you would have Mai here, you know, to really drive the message home to me."

He was surprised at first. Well, he could wipe that surprised look off his face. I knew what he was up to. He was pushing me away. I knew he was going to do it, as soon as I heard how long he got. I also knew he had set up this meeting to break up with me.

I just hoped he got creative. "I'm not going to thank you for what you did for me. They were my charges. I was facing them. Not you!"

He smiled and then his eyes hardened, and I was ready.

"My guns. My problem. Now you know why you are here?" He stood up.

I wished they had cuffed him to the bloody table. If he thought for a second about coming near me, I'd be responsible for another murder.

"I'm guessing to be dumped. I'm just hoping you are creative about it." I crossed my arms, and took a step back towards the wall. If he touched my stomach, he would know I'm pregnant, and if he was about to do what I knew he was going to do, well, I never wanted him near this baby.

He knew I couldn't take the heartbreak of losing him again. Just because he was in prison didn't mean we had to break it off; but I knew Jax. I knew him so well, that I knew he was going to push me away. Hell, he was going to scare me away.

"You always knew the deal, Amber. If I went away, you and I were finished," he said calmly, and walked around the table.

"That was on the condition that you got caught for your own crimes!" My arm shot out. I couldn't have him touch me.

"They were my crimes."

I scoffed. I would not have this argument with him. "Fine. Let's just cut to it. Are you going to push me away? Just because we will be apart for six years doesn't mean we should be for the rest of our lives."

Didn't he see how immature it was to end us? Six years we could face. I would face them beside him, but I knew by his expression I wasn't getting a choice.

"Don't make me hurt you." His expression was still hard, but I saw a split second of pain. "Just do what you're told."

Being told to move on from someone? How the hell do you force your heart to let go? I just glared at him, and when he took a step closer to me, I pushed him as hard as I could.

"How about you do what you're told? You want us finished? Fine, we are finished." I pulled the ring off my finger, angry tears running down my face. How many times had I said to myself I wouldn't cry? "When you get out, don't come looking for me." I pushed him back again as he made an attempt to touch me.

The guards saw it, and I knew I only had half a minute to tell him the rest.

"Hear me Jax, don't come looking for me. We are finished." I threw the ring at him. "I've already cut my brothers off, and when I walk out this door, I will do everything possible so you never find me again." The guards came in, automatically grabbing Jax. "I won't let you ever hurt me again, or him."

Yes, I said him because I was positive I was having a boy. I was so furious and hurt at Jax, it just came out. I would protect my child from him. My child would never experience what it is like for his father to break his heart.

"What do you mean him?" Jax shouted at me, but the guard was already pushing me out. "AMBER!"

The door shut. I saw the panic on Jax's face but I knew he hadn't understood what I'd said. He had no idea he was going to be a father so I hadn't blown my secret. The guard started dragging me down the hall, away from Jax.

I didn't need to be dragged; I would leave willingly so I pulled my arm from his grasp and walked off, more determined.

I knew in order for Jax to never enter my life again, I had to cut my brothers off. I had already relocated. The last load of my stuff was in my car. This was my last stop on the train wreck called my old life.

My hands landed on the door to the exit, and I paused. Was I ready to face a world without him? I swallowed sharply and my hands went to my stomach. It didn't matter anymore. I had to.

I pushed open the door, and took a deep breath in; fresh air. As I walked away from the prison, I made a promise to myself. Never would I let Jackson Johnston near my child. Or my life. Ever again.

Because he had just pushed me and his unborn child away. My child would never experience what it was like to have a Jackson shaped hole in his heart.

I was going to have to live with this hole as it was, but my child wouldn't.